# *Dragadelf*

The Band of Brothers

*Matthew Bunn*

No part of this book may be used of reproduced in any manner whatsoever without written permission, except in the case of brief quotations in critical articles and reviews.

This is a work of fiction. Unless otherwise indicated, all the names, characters, businesses, places, events and incidents in this book are either the product of the author's imagination or used in a fictitious manner. Any resemblance to actual persons, living or dead, or actual events is purely coincidental.

Copyright © <2021> <Matthew Bunn>
All rights reserved.
ISBN: 9798749975031

## About the Author

Matthew first came into the world of fantasy by none other than JRR Tolkien. The Lord of The Rings and other Middle Earth Tales inspired him to one day create a world of his own, in hope to create such wonderful stories as his. Since those days he continued his inspiration into fantasy and fiction by reading the Harry Potter's, The Moontide Quartet, and other fantasy stories.

Growing up aspiring to be an actor, he found comfort in realising his enjoyment in creating and imagination. He landed the role of *Flavio* in The London Coliseum's production of Handel's Rodelinda, which was later commissioned to be performed at The Bolshoi in Moscow. It was here where the luxury of time was presented for him to fully form his trilogy of novels in the Dragadelf series. Combining it with over fifteen years worth of jotting down idea's on paper and the notes on his phone, he found the excitement of his own creation.

Father to a growing and wonderful boy, Teddy, and professional tennis coach, he finds himself with more time of late to continue his other interests in chess, piano, football and the occasional trip to the gym (although very occasional it must be said these days!)

*Special mention of thanks to my sister, Rae, for the editing, and my illustrator Charlotte Strong for the fabulous design.*

*And to all the NHS and key workers, who kept our hearts beating through the Coronavirus pandemic.*

*For Teddy.*
*To make you proud.*

*And for Josie.*
*For the happy times.*

# A Word on Pronunciation

*The re-spelling of names, portrays the correct pronunciation and not the purity and fluidity of speech*

"*Alexandao*" ... Alex-an-dow

"*Ramalon*" ... Ramalon

"*Alicèndil*" ... Ala-senn-dil or Ala-senn for short

"*Rèo*" ... Ray-o

"*Questacère*" ... Questa-sair

"*Lathapràcére*" ... Latha-pray-sair

"*Màgjeur*" ... May-jur or Major for casual speech

"*The Blessèd*" ... The Ble-sid

"*The Durge/Durgeon*" ... The Durge/Dur-jun

"*The Magikai*" ... The Maj-i-kai

"*Jàqueson*" ... Jake-son

"*Joric*" ... Yoric

"*Branmir*" ... Bran-mir

"*Brodian*" ... Bro-dian

"*Gracène*" ... Gray-seen

"*Piroces*" ... Piro-seas

"*Dancès*" ... Dan-seas

*"Caspercartès"* ... Casper-sar-teas

*"Fleurcès"* ... Fleur-seas


*"The Skyurch"* ...The Sky-urch

*"Ildreàn"* ... Ill-dre-anne

*"Xjaques"* ... Xjax

*"Arinane"* ... Arra-nane

*"Rhinoauros"* ... Rine-your-oss


*"Draul"* ... Draul not Drool

*"The Reinhault"* ... The Rine-halt

*"Hiyaro"* ... He-yaro

*"The Boldemere"* ... The Bol-demere

*"Charzeryx"* ... Char-zer-ix

*"Dralen"* ... Dra-lun

*"Drogadera"* ... Drog-a-deera

*"Jòsièra"* ... Joss-iera

*"Clethance"* ... Clethance


*"Felder"* ... Felder

*"Aristuto"* ... Aristuto

*"Max Meigar"* ... Max Mi-ga

*"Ethelba"* ... Ethelba

*"Wemberle"* ... Wem-berley

*"Thorian Mijkal"* ... Thorian Mi-kal

*"Zathos"* ... Zathos

*"Eveleve"* ... Ev-a-leev

*"Mavokai"* ... Mavok-i

*"Davinor"* ... Davinor

*"Lestas Magraw"* ... Lestas Magraw

*"Thakendrax"* ... Thake-un-drax

*"The Ancient Drethai"* ... The Ancient Dreth-i

*"Melcelore"* ... Mell-se-lore

*"Soul Mancing"* ... Soul Man-sing

*"The Understunde"* ... The Under-stund

*"Sarthanzar"* ... Sarthan-zar

*"Medhene"* ... Med-een

*"Ramacès"* ... Rama-seas

*"Ramerick"* ... Rama-rick

Rèo

Terrasendia

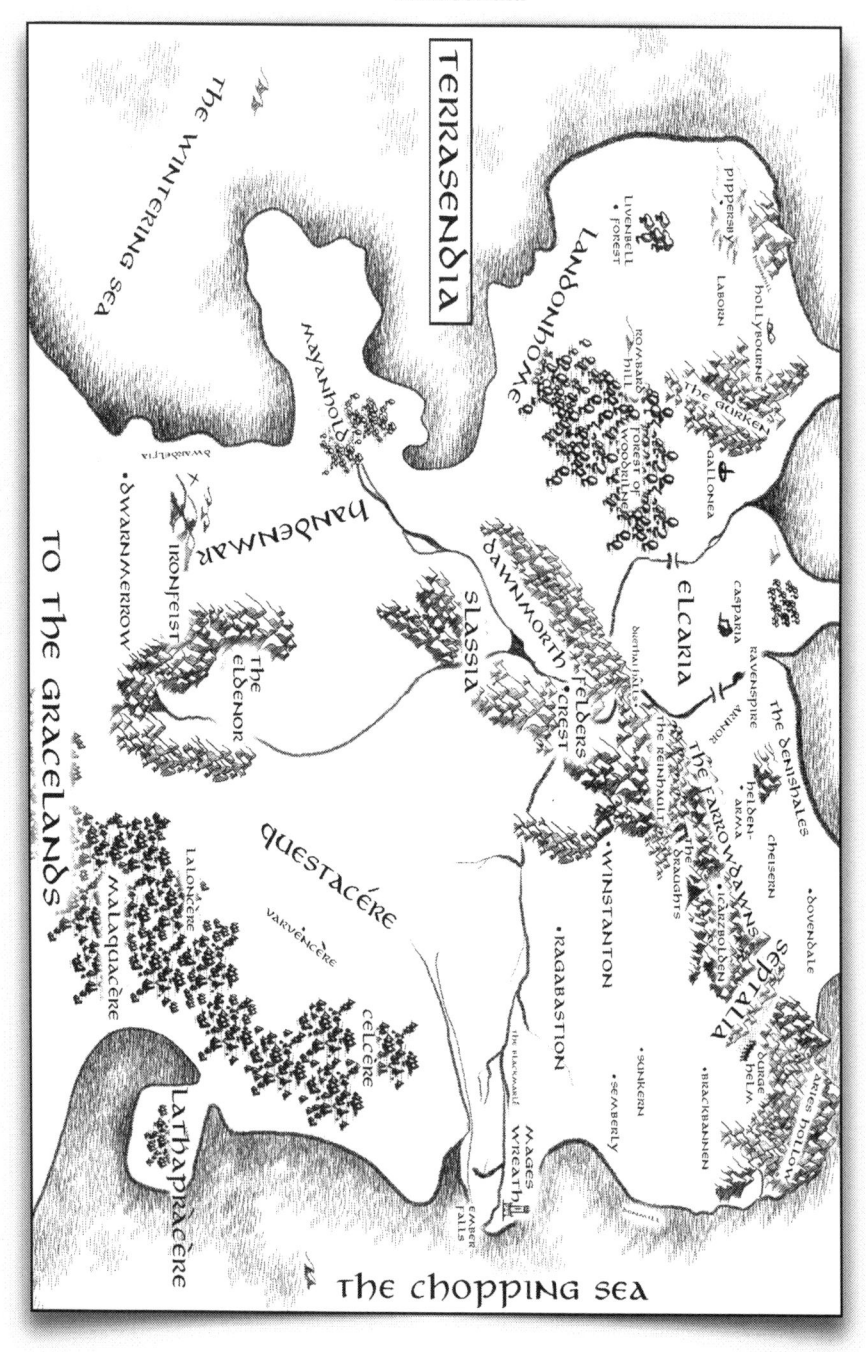

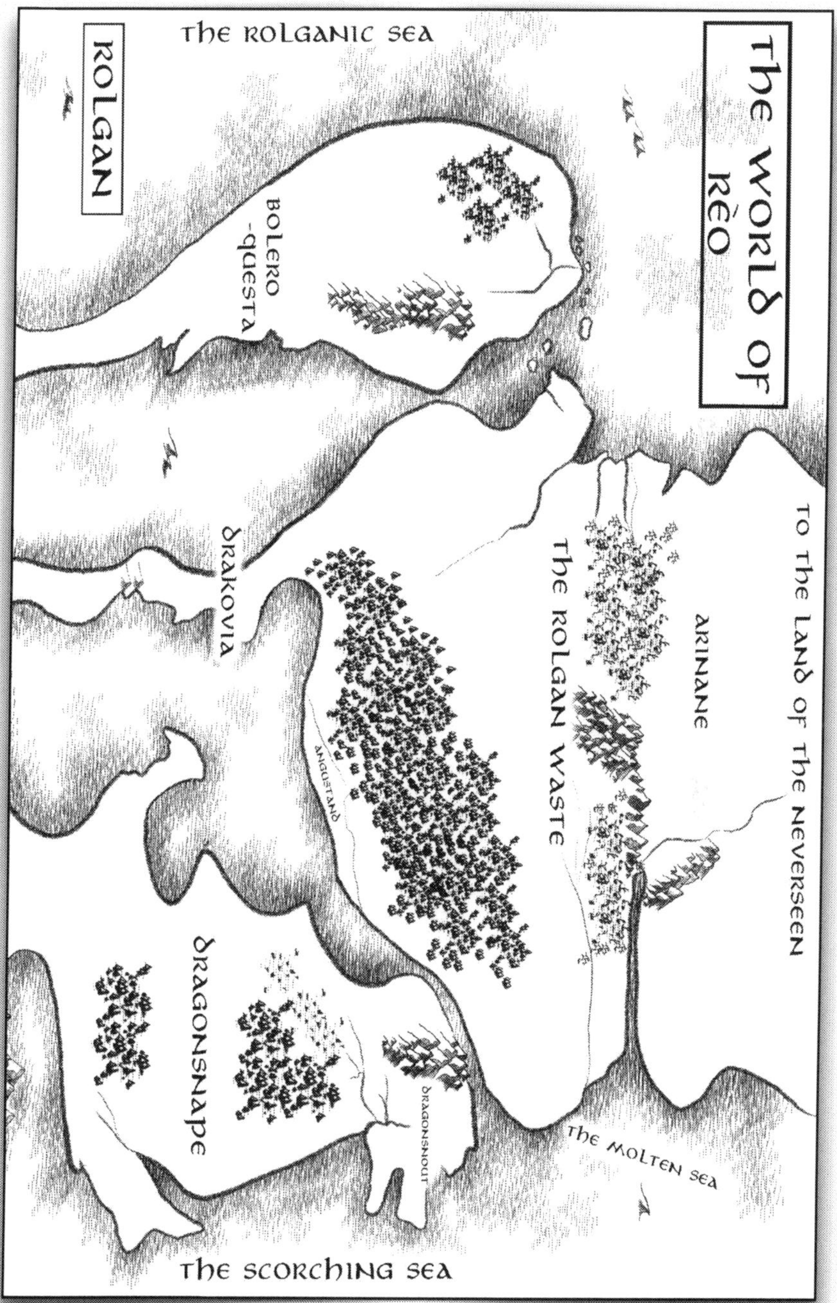
THE WORLD OF RÈO
ROLGAN
THE ROLGANIC SEA
BOLERO-QUESTA
DRAKOVIA
TO THE LAND OF THE NEVERSEEN
ARINANE
THE ROLGAN WASTE
ANGUSTLAND
DRAGONSNAPE
DRAGONSNOUT
THE MOLTEN SEA
THE SCORCHING SEA

Western Terrasendia

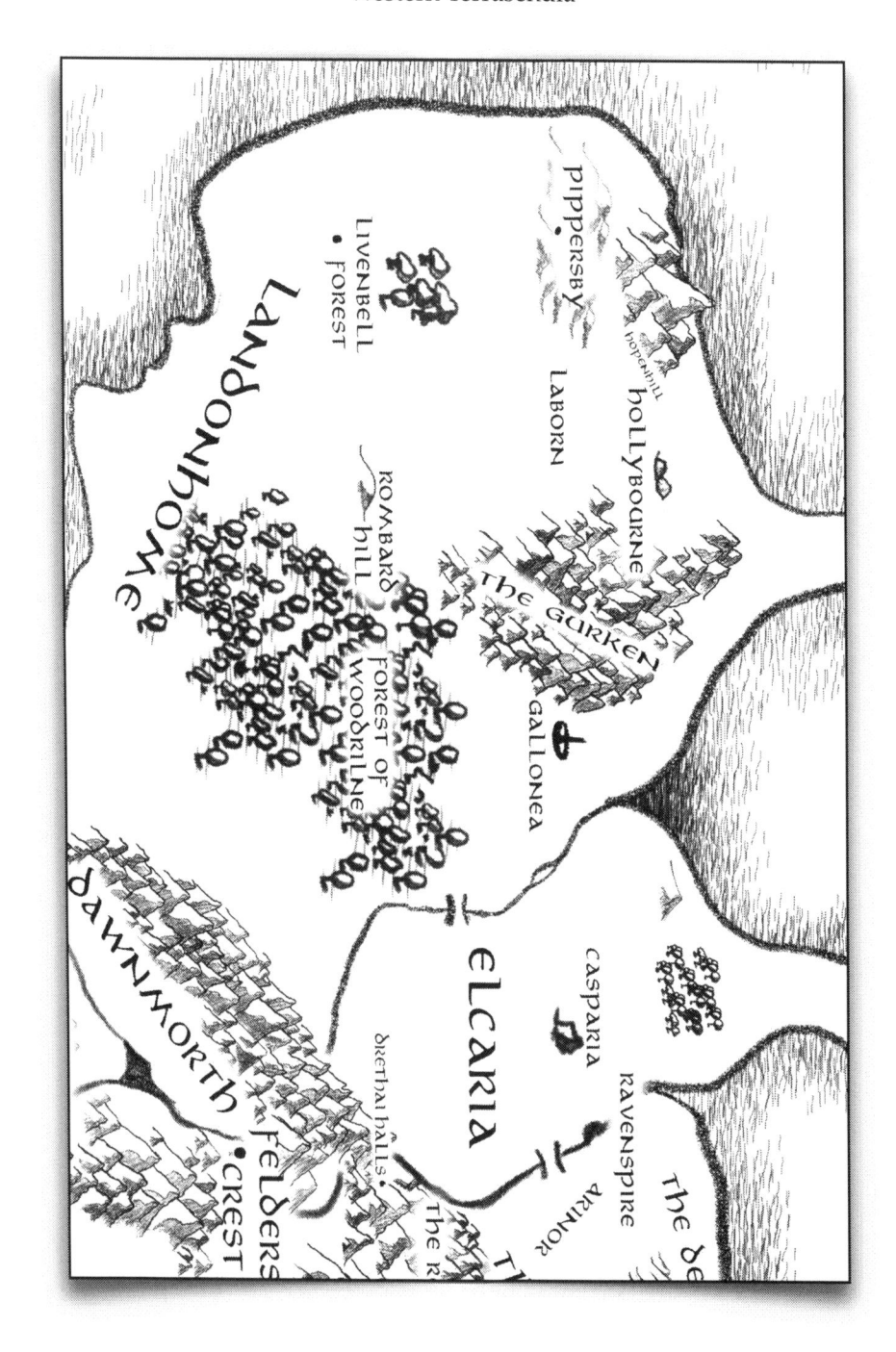

Eastern Terrasendia

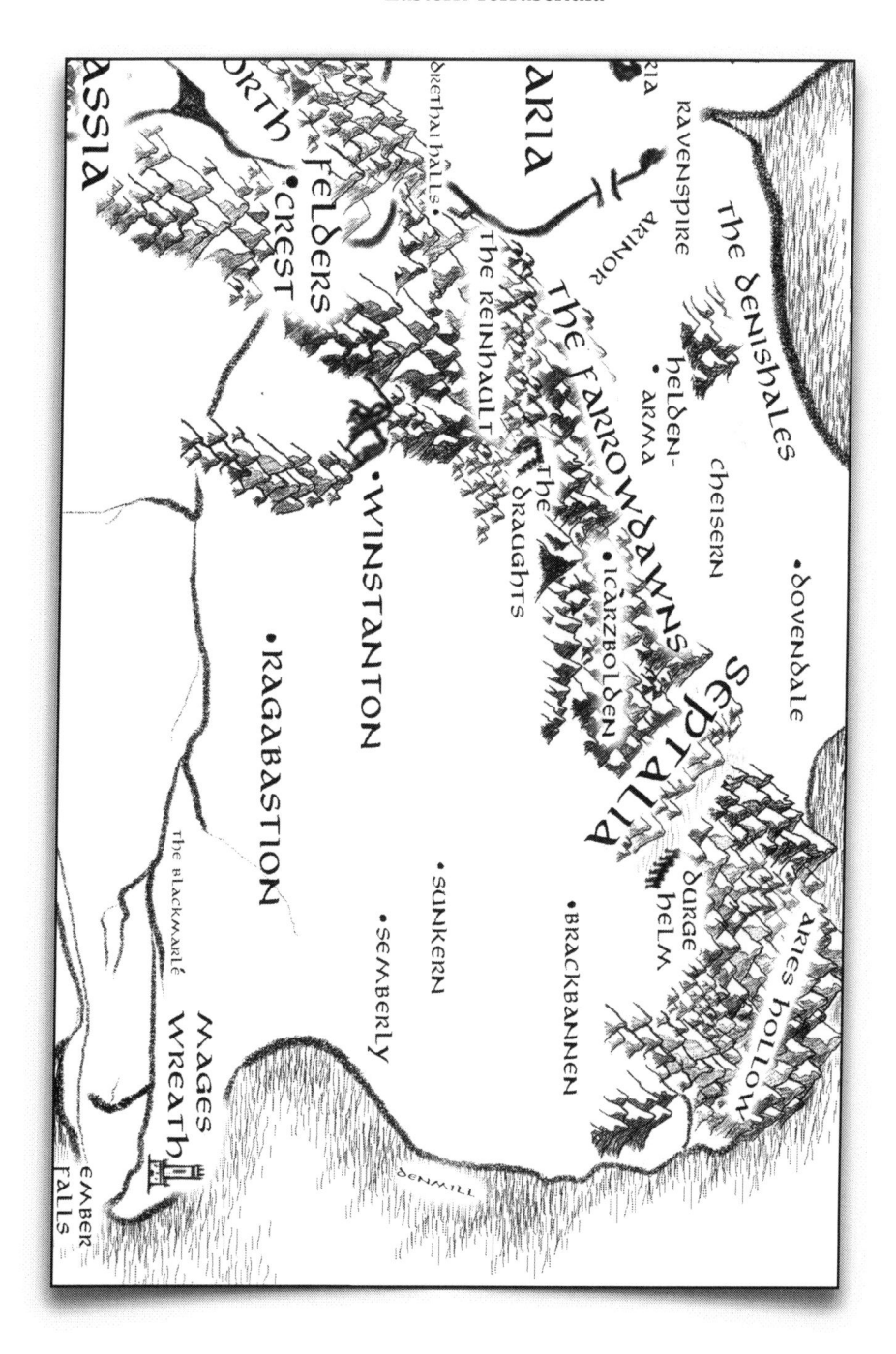

## *A Rivalry in Perpetuity*

The ghostly remains of thirty years ago chilled Ramalon to the marrow. Alas, it was not a feeling of fear but more a sense of destiny as he approached the mountain slope on which Felders Crest sat.

A thrill echoed within every fibre of his relaxing gait, striding toward his birthplace. Each step he took filled him with pride and growing righteousness that he was heading for the next step on his Staircase to Divinity. Whence he reached the top, it was clear what was waiting for him. Immortality. Alas, he was not there yet. He was not totally divine, for he had not yet climbed every step. Only when he had overcome all his challenges would he become the deity he had yearned to be for so long.

## A Rivalry in Perpetuity

The fact that he had achieved so many more things to that point than any before him only fuelled the admiration he had for himself. He had breached the wall of The Dragasphere, something only one other before him managed to do. The one imminently waiting for him.

Felders Crest remained desolate from its encapsulation over thirty years ago. An icy chill distilled the atmosphere. The vast dome of The Dragasphere shone a bleak bronze above and around the city. At first, Ramalon wondered how the remaining five Dragadelf had survived such a cold and unforgiving environment. He quickly surmised the most likely explanation. They had survived so long because of The Dragastone - untouched inside Monarchy Hall - feeding them all the power needed to be reborn all those years ago and now provided them with the essence they needed to exist. Ramalon felt its presence too, as if it was his own.

He had no idea what to expect as he approached the first of many buildings, mostly razed to the ground. Felders Crest was not enclosed in a wall of stone but instead allowed free passage into the city. All was still and spooky. No life presented itself in the grey gloom. He did not fear what potentially lurked and strode forward as if the land itself belonged to him.

He could attempt to call upon the bond of The Dragadelf, which he felt coursing through his veins. Despite not experiencing the bond directly with the remaining five beasts, he was sure it could work. However, in poetic similarity to so many other challenges in his past, he did not feel the need, confident enough in his capabilities. He wanted to enrich himself in knowledge and understand the truth for himself. Though the thrill of the potential power did excite him as it had for so long in that if he controlled one Dragadelf, he could control them all.

Love was not a feeling he knew, but his affection for the Dragadelf he owned, which now lay buried under rock and stone in The Draughts by his brother, Ramacès, turned that mysterious concept of love into anger. He felt the same shadow of affection for the remaining five as if they were his by right. However, claiming The Dragadelf was not the reason he marched toward Monarchy Hall. He sought out the power that governs them all - The Dragastone.

Only one thing stood between him and his desire and he was about to embark on arguably his biggest challenge and steepest step yet. He was going to challenge the most feared Màgjeur Terrasendia had ever seen.

Melcelore.

Ramalon knew that he was waiting for him. His cunning nature had surpassed many landmarks of horror. Because of him, The Dragastone crashed onto Terrasendia thirty years ago, re-birthing The Dragadelf and their horror. All because of a rivalry with his long term nemesis King Felder, who Ramalon had recently learned, was also his father.

Of course, Ramalon had time to figure out the story of them both and how it was Melcelore's ultimate plan to avenge Felder finally. In his mind, he had won - after so long, his long term plan seemed to have come together perfectly. But Ramalon had learned something which he was confident the great dark Màgjeur had not.

As he passed through passageways between the houses and buildings that lined the capital streets, nothing stirred. It was a ghost town, a haunting that distilled the very air itself. There were no signs of the bodies that fell, even as he ventured closer to Monarchy Hall on his ascent of the city's slope.

He didn't believe that this was the same trickery Medhene had practised on him when he first ventured to Dawnmorth. The stillness was very real. He wondered when he might see a Dragadelf or two lurking in the rubble. Alas, he gathered they would gravitate closer to the city's peak as that was where The Dragastone lay waiting.

The streets became more pristine and structurally elaborate the more he passed through the city. It wasn't too long before he approached the foot of a vast set of stoney steps carved perfectly from the foundations of the mountain, which led up toward Monarchy Hall. The steps curved in an immaculate semi-circle fashion with several flatter platforms upon ascending.

He paused briefly before taking the first step. It felt poetically significant somehow - that he was ascending not only physically, but metaphorically also in his Staircase to Divinity. He purposefully took a righteous step and began to climb.

He kept his eyes transfixed on the hall for some time before breaking his gaze away to view the city below. He could see for several miles right up to where the walls of The Dragasphere sat. Still, nothing moved, though he could sense he was being watched.

He came to the first flat platform of the steps, where he took a few moments to admire the view and ease the lactic acid building in his thighs. He was about halfway up when he noticed the air growing cooler and crisper. Not cold enough to ice the surroundings but fresh enough to see his breath steaming from his mouth. A sense of

## A Rivalry in Perpetuity

foreboding was in the air and it wasn't too long before he continued his ascend.

Monarchy Hall wasn't just a lone building; it was surrounded by other halls and palace-like structures that housed members of royalty. Ramalon had no doubt he was born in one of these buildings, replaying the memory he had when he saw his mother back on Dawnmorth.

The peak grew ever closer and suddenly that icy chill breathed through him, like a ghost trying to latch onto his warm muscles. He could not yet see the tall doors of Monarchy Hall but the reason for the freeze became apparent.

A plethora of white orbs floated from the direction of Monarchy Hall, gliding gently above him and casting onto various points of the city below. It was like a constellation of stars above, through the thick bronze haze which coated the sky, passing through its cloud beautifully as they all drifted to their destinations below. There was beauty in the way they danced through the air, but the reality was far more sinister. Ramalon knew what this meant and what they were. The city lights freckled below before the stillness slowly eased, gravitating toward Ramalon. The Boldemere had awoken.

The orbs began to frantically collect below him as it was clear they were under instruction to head for Ramalon. The deathly shrieks came to him before the white spheres that powered their dead bodies began to race up the steps toward their target. They were finally close enough for Ramalon to assess his enemy in detail. The charred corpses darted towards him in unnatural, frenzied, puppet-like movements. His attention focussed on the more noticeable characteristic of The Boldemere - their eyes. The wide-eyed glare of a living soul being controlled by its mancer, begging for their suffering in purgatory to end. Ramalon turned to what was left of his once pure heart and conjured a wickedly satisfied smile as he embraced yet another challenge in his path. He would oblige their wishes.

The bulk of The Boldemere below was a mere hundred metres below him when the sound of splattering bodies falling from the mountainside surrounded Ramalon's position on the steps. About twenty corpses landed with a grotesque thud, breaking bones and mangling limbs on their landing. With the unnatural power that drove them they all managed to reanimate themselves, getting to their feet and charging at the Ròagar.

Ramalon had anticipated the attack and came well prepared. As the rapidly enclosing militants flew in his direction, he relaxed the flow of his unrelenting connection to his protecy and unleashed a whirling tornado of fire around himself, instantly incinerating the immediate corpses that surrounded.

The sound of glass smashing confirmed their souls were escaping, fuelling Ramalon's poetic notion that he was freeing them at last. Before he had time to marvel in the release of their souls, the main bulk of The Boldemere was upon him. The look in their eyes was a desperate cry for help but the nature of their charge was not a friendly one.

Ramalon dug deeper, tensing with the effort and released a more devastating hurl of fire to the frontline of The Boldemere. Though his attack proved successful in halting their approach, thousands of corpses continued to pour from the city in a seemingly endless flow. He had not the time to eliminate them all, which he felt confident in his unrivalled strength he could do. However he did not want to end the potential possibility of losing their use for himself.

He was in a little conundrum in how to halt their advance. He made his way to the top of the steps, fending off the charging corpses from below. His idea was that the closer he got to Monarchy Hall, the less chance they would have of gravitating toward where The Dragadelf potentially lurked. He did not know if it would work but he didn't see any other way.

He finally got to the last step and hurtled a devastating wave of fire below, taking out many militants and allowing him a moment to gather his thoughts. He noticed the freed souls floating up toward the clouds above, before fading out of sight.

The solemn reprieve gave him a single moment to turn to his destination at last. He had arrived at Monarchy Hall.

Through all the premonitions and visions he had seen in parallel dimensions, he could not quite believe he was staring and the momentous and famous building with his own eyes. The now gaunt cathedral-like structure presented an essence of gloom sat upon another platform. The doors were closed and Melcelore was nowhere to be seen.

The reprieve was short as more of The Boldemere rushed up. Ramalon had no other choice but to head for Monarchy Hall in the hope to fortify his position and block their advance.

As he raced closer to the final steps which led to the platform before the great building, a sudden slice of luck presented itself.

## A Rivalry in Perpetuity

Several corpses sprinted toward him before suddenly collapsing in a heap, the bright orbs of souls rising out of them in the process. It was as if they had passed through a particular point they could not cross intact. Ramalon was surprised to see that some sort of spell was stopping them but did not understand why. Perhaps it was the work of Melcelore deliberately toying with him on his arrival. Or maybe there were magics within the foundations of Felders Crest that were to that day, still in place - he did not know which was more likely. Regardless, his instincts once again proved helpful as The Boldemere no longer hurried toward him. It was clear they were aware of the spell in place and gathered in a curving position on the platform where they sensed they were safe. They did nothing but stare at Ramalon with those pleading eyes.

With the immediate danger pacified, he set his focus back to why he was there in the first place, turning to Monarchy Hall and approaching the famous tall doors. On edge every step of the way, ready to defend himself against Melcelore whom he was confident was on the other side. Alas, he was not the reason a course of adrenaline rippled through him - thrilling him. He knew that the heart of all his power was mere moments away and he had come home to claim it back.

With his protecy charged and willing, he thrust the doors open. The weight alone took additional strength to slowly prise and reveal the very thing he had come to bear - The Dragastone.

It laid upon the broken throne where his father once sat some distance down the long hall. The luminous colours of lime greens, oranges and whites shone marvellously. Ramalon felt the power it presented instantly - tingling on his skin like the warmth of the sun. It filled him as he felt whole for the first time in his life. A special bond of possession ran through him, justifying that it was his to own. He was home. Alas, Melcelore could not be seen.

Ramalon knew the deceptive and clever nature of the dark Màgjeur and knew he was probably watching him closely. He did not care. Nor did he fear what would happen next.

He slowly entered the long stretch inside Monarchy Hall, approaching The Dragastone ahead and felt that familiar freeze that chilled the air. Ice had grown in many parts of the hall which Ramalon was unclear as to why. He did not believe that simply walking up and taking the heart of all power would work by any stretch of the imagination, but he wanted to force the issue. It seemed like a game of who speaks first, bleeds first. Ramalon had no intention of speaking first. He was the one he felt Melcelore had to answer to. He felt that divine right elevate his confidence to play God and make Melcelore kneel before him, despite his fearsome reputation.

He was moments away from The Dragastone being in his hands and stopped short of grabbing it. He wanted to remember the first time he touched The Dragastone as being a moment of pure ownership which was unchallenged and undeniably his. Touching it at that point, knowing what was imminently going to happen, did not feel right.

The icy chill increased dramatically, spiking the hairs from the back of his neck and at that moment, Ramalon understood why. He forced the issue once more and slowly drew his hand toward the anomaly of power which he felt growing the closer he got, enriching him with strength, before suddenly the moment he had been waiting for arrived halting his physical touch.

*"And so, we meet at last,"* came the deep, powerful voice of Melcelore behind.

With his back turned, Ramalon did not question that it was really him. That surge of power ran through his veins that he had arrived at the most critical moment of his life. In no hurry, he slowly turned around with confidence to view the demonic figure of Melcelore, in his legendary entirety, some distance down the stretch of Monarchy Hall.

The ten-foot-tall figure looked like neither man nor demon. He was a hybrid of the two with his skin bearing a mirky dark green colour; his light green eyes struck a poisonous look as they gazed into Ramalon's soul. His impressively crafted gauntlets and steel-plated shin coverings bore a wicked touch. Straps of silver-plated armour covered various limbs and torso but did not protect his entire body, exposing his ripped obliques and muscular thighs.

Melcelore's godly stance was the most imposing figure Ramalon had ever seen in his life. Uncharacteristic of what he presumed he would look like being a Màgjeur. He assumed he would be wearing a dark cloak of some sort.

One thing did please Ramalon in his fearless process. He noticed that the ice that coated much of the surroundings came directly from Melcelore. It delighted him because it confirmed that Melcelore's primary affinity was ice - a component that he had not yet acquired but was on his Staircase to Divinity to claim all six. Having already acquired: fire, volts and earth, he felt compelled to take ice from Melcelore now. The man who orchestrated his father's death and who also challenged his right to The Dragastone. It felt destiny was on his

# A Rivalry in Perpetuity

side.

"Màgjeur Ramalon," Melcelore addressed him coolly.

"You've been expecting me?" Ramalon replied casually.

"For many years. I've been watching you for some time."

Ramalon did not want to engage in conversation. Instead, he felt comfortable just listening to what Melcelore had to say.

"It seems your father made yet another mistake. For all his bravado and Kingship, I'm sure he didn't foresee his own spawn becoming an evil worthy of Sarthanzar's bidding… But I did."

Melcelore gradually walked toward him, though some distance remained. His heavy boots thudded and echoed a gentle crunch of ice around the hall. Melcelore smirked, laughing deeply with his mouth closed.

"I've been waiting for this moment for many years. You carry your father's naivety perfectly. It was the very thing that killed him. And it will be the same thing that kills you."

"I sense there is some confusion of allegiance."

"Indeed," Melcelore confirmed.

Melcelore stopped his advance to allow the static tension to crackle between them. Despite both sides confident in their demeanours, it blinded them to how tense the atmosphere became. Were they to have an audience, there would be many uncomfortable shuffles and physical stillness to prepare someone to strike first. However, Melcelore was equally patient and decided that moment was not yet upon them. Instead, he embraced the stand-off, treating the situation as if they were two old friends who had not seen each other in some time.

"I suppose you have come here for that," Melcelore indicated to The Dragastone gleaming on the broken throne. Ramalon did not look away from his target for a second. "You have come to claim that which you have been led to believe is yours. The heart of all power. Fingertips away. How foolish you are to believe that such a thing could ever be yours, Ramalon. The Dragastone is mine!" Still, Ramalon did not react. "Of course, you are smart enough to know this. So I assume you have truly come here to *join* me in my endeavours? Why else would you so easily concede your life to me?"

Ramalon pondered for several moments, looking at The Dragastone. Behind his eyes, his philosophy was processing. That draw of power fuelled his confidence. Never in a millennia would he consider joining with Melcelore. He was born to lead, not follow.

He looked back toward the dark Màgjeur and moved aside, encouraging Melcelore to take it freely. However, the dark Màgjeur was not so easily fooled and saw right through him. He knew Ramalon would not give up what he had desired for so long so willingly. The corners of Melcelore's mouth lifted, almost in admiration of his confidence.

"Perhaps, I have underestimated you," Melcelore confessed. "I sense a great deal of similarities between us. That feeling you felt when your brother killed two of my Dragadelf, when he found out our perfect plans, thwarting them at our expense. And how you sought out the weakest of us. Alas, Ramerick is still alive. May I ask how you could allow that?"

"I could ask you the thing," Ramalon retorted plainly.

"All in good time. Would you like to know just how I deceived your father?"

Ramalon entertained the idea and remained silent. He thought it might be in his best interest to let Melcelore continue and impose in his own way. He was sure answers would naturally flow and more importantly unveil things for which, in Ramalon's mind, Melcelore had missed.

"You must know by now Terrasendia has been blind for too long! They did not foresee my plan for many years in the making. Yes, Ramalon. It was I who brought The Dragastone crashing onto that throne. It was I who defied the strongest containment spell ever to exist. I entrusted Draul with my armies to wreak havoc on my enemies. All because a selfish Màgjeur took what he wanted when he wanted! It was I who was responsible for the death of your father!"

Ramalon remained silent and still as ice. He would not be provoked into responding with emotion as he genuinely did not feel it inside.

"I suppose I should be thanking you for avenging my Dragadelf," Melcelore continued. "You were responsible for Ramacès' death at The Draughts. I was watching, very carefully, the moment he destroyed my portal. I heard your heart wretch when the Dragadelf had its neck snapped in half. I cannot deny his unearthing of my secret became a little problematic. You could not begin to understand just what it takes to have done what I have. I stood there Ramalon, in front of the Dragadelf." Melcelore closed his eyes, lost in the memory replaying the moment he transported one of the Dragadelf into The Draughts. "The privilege to have the legend as mine to own. It's loyalty unquestionably mine! I placed my hands on its head, for which it was

## A Rivalry in Perpetuity

thankful its master had given it the respect it deserved. Just like that I felt its soul, more mysterious and wonderful than anything on this world and sent it along with its body into The Draughts!... I could not move for days. The power nearly killed me." Melcelore returned back to reality and faced Ramalon who was still and listening. "Are you impressed?"

"... I am happy for you."

Melcelore deeply laughed with a wicked tone.

"*Happy*, you say? You do not fool me, Ramalon. *Happy* is not something you feel. But I am glad you admit that it is something which you could never achieve yourself."

"Of course," Ramalon replied honestly. "But you lost the battle for The Draughts."

"As did you. Were it not for your brother's discovery my retribution would have been swift. But no matter. Things have changed. There are many moving parts to this story Ramalon. The most important of which is the connection you have with that stone!"

Ramalon aired a hint of smugness.

"And yet, for these many things to happen, many other things have to fall in place," Ramalon thoughtfully said.

"Things that only the wisest of us could ever foresee. Every answer to every question you've had of late, lies on that throne."

Ramalon asked himself the reason why Melcelore was telling him all his plans so openly? Was it a mark of respect to someone who had achieved such a scale of evil just like him? Or maybe he was trying to intimidate Ramalon by boasting his achievements, which drew one logical reason as to why.

"The Dragastone," Melcelore continued, "has given you that invincible power. And I know this because it runs through my veins too! Isn't it extraordinary!? How your father gave you the rights to that stone! Of course, he was not aware that I would have taken it for myself!"

"You fletched from my father."

"I did. And in doing so, The Dragastone is mine. And so too are The Dragadelf. Yes. When your father's blood ran through my veins, they saw me as their true master. So I'm afraid to say, you've journeyed a rather long way to be disappointed."

"Perhaps," Ramalon thoughtfully replied.

"I saw many years before my capture just how powerful you would become. I've orchestrated your life hence to the point where you have so willingly come to me at this moment, right here, right now. Because for all the strength that you have built, it was always destined for me. And you've made it so easy for me by coming here. For once I have harvested your powers, none will defy me of my right to rule this world!"

Melcelore declared his intentions as simply as he could. Ramalon's stance did not change. He looked at the dark Màgjeur with those deadpan eyes, almost not appearing to register a single word. Alas, he listened and understood every syllable.

"I have a question for you," Ramalon finally weighed in. "For all your power and skill in foresight, you have not asked the most important question... How myself and my brother could have controlled The Dragadelf?"

Melcelore remained still as if he was expecting a continuation of the question, for which did not come. Ramalon was happy to wait for Melcelore's reaction. After a tense pause, the dark Màgjeur finally chuffed and smirked in admiration.

"You think your divination exceeds mine Màgjeur Ramalon? You think a simple question undoes the mastery of my plan?"

"And yet, this simple question has."

"I think not. But I will give you credit, that's for sure. You're certainly an upgrade to your father. And yet, as my power grows, so does my curiosity. So tell me then. Impress me. How did my first Dragadelf, end up obeying the son of my sworn enemy?"

"I imagine it is difficult for you," Ramalon teased. "To accept them worshipping another."

"Worship you say?" Melcelore snorted, unimpressed. "You may have a claim to their loyalty, but know this. You will never surpass what I have surpassed. You will never accomplish that which I have. You are not The Dragadelf's true master. If you were, I would not be alive today..."

So many things were falling into place for Ramalon. He could not fathom how much he knew, and Melcelore did not. Was the dark Màgjeur really so blind and naive to all that has happened? How could he have missed things so apparent to him?

"Have you seen how you will die?" Ramalon chillingly asked. Melcelore's expression was less impressed, yet still upbeat. "Because I have," he calmly confirmed.

"And what may I ask gives you this gift of foresight?"

"... A rivalry in perpetuity," Ramalon declared.

## A Rivalry in Perpetuity

Melcelore's face dropped suddenly. He knew what that meant but still defied his old nemesis to the end.

"Your father is dead!" Melcelore harshly declared.

"Yes, he is dead. For that, I congratulate you. When you imprisoned yourself, my father believed he had won. Against the man he had long wanted to defeat and show the world how Kingly he was. Therefore, he stopped looking into the future because, in his reality, there was no need… Or so he made you believe," he delightfully pondered at the revelation, but very quickly toned his words more deliberate. "The reality is that his war with you is not yet over. Tell me, when you forged your masterful plan, how long after you escaped and fletched his blood did you yourself stop looking ahead?"

Melcelore's face turned a little more satisfied. "I didn't need to. I had claimed the ultimate victory there was. Your father's blood runs through my veins. You cannot get more defeated than that. Like a cowering dog that knows he is beat! I defeated your father once and for all! To claim that I, Melcelore, am the most powerful Màgjeur ever to exist!"

And just like that, the penny had dropped in Ramalon's mind, confirming the vital piece of information Melcelore had missed. The dark Màgjeur's stance rose higher and higher, the more he believed his unrivalled strength. Ramalon, however, remained calm and measured through Melcelore's declaration. He was satisfied that what he knew still gave him the upper hand.

"You seem like you do not fear the greatness before you," Melcelore probed, noticing Ramalon's calmness. A sense of growing desperation began to fester in Melcelore's demeanour.

"Why should I fear that which is flawed?"

"You question my triumph!?"

"Oh, yes. I question that. And also, I provide the answer."

Melcelore's stunned demeanour turned offensive and angry at the denial of his victory.

"You see," Ramalon went on, "your rivalry with my father was only the beginning of a chain of events, all leading to this moment. Right here, right now. My father's endgame. His one wish for this land was to acquire peace - all he has ever wanted for us all. After he defeated you, that would have happened. Of course, while your rivalry with him created quite the opposite, his plan is still in motion. And how poetic is it that I, Ramalon, have to be the one to tell you that you have yet to defeat him still."

"You're blind, Màgjeur Ramalon. How on this world can your father still oppose me while he is dead?" Melcelore asked, expecting there to be no logical answer.

Ramalon's eyes turned a little more intense and sinister toward the dark Màgjeur. After a long, intense pause, Ramalon declared the answer.

"... Through me," he confirmed.

And with that, Melcelore's face turned to disbelief. Instead of point-blank refusing Ramalon's theory, he actually embraced it. Wisdom told him that it was entirely possible for Felder to have planned this beyond his death. After all, that was what Melcelore did to Felder all those years ago.

"You see," Ramalon continued to educate his rival, albeit with a little more youthful arrogance, "my father saw one step ahead of you, one final time. When you believed that he had stopped looking into the future after your imprisonment, he saw right through that. He saw your masterful plan and knew he could not stop it himself. You were too good for him. And so, he put motions in place for you to believe that you would claim victory over him. But what you failed to see is the claim of ownership over The Dragastone. In his final moments thirty years ago, I have learned that he gave that power to his three newly-born children. Knowing that one of them would, as you say, become a mighty power. I stake my life that when you came to claim that stone you were furious when you realised you couldn't claim it yourself." he pressed, practically giddy with how well it was all coming together. Melcelore's face was that of anger-fuelled embarrassment as the truth stung. "When you fletched from him, The Dragadelf recognised my father's blood in yours and therefore gave you the impression they worship you. And you fell so perfectly into his trap. I bet there wasn't enough prophecy in the world to have helped you see that."

Monarchy Hall became once again a space of great tension. It seemed the gravity of Rèo surrounded the nucleus of both opponents, hinging on a moment that would deter the course of the future.

"Your father did not foresee this!" Melcelore denied forcefully.

"My father foresaw his own son become more powerful than either of you put together. And so led you to believe for so long that your plan was the final nail in the coffin... Only, that nail has slowly been eased out of the wood. He saw that you would stop looking into the future once you believed you had won. *That* was your mistake. And I am here, in this moment, to deliver my father's destiny..."

The intensity inside Monarchy Hall rose considerably, embracing the inevitable event. The stars aligned for Ramalon, not just off the back of his father's plan, but also to claim what he had come for.

Melcelore's shock shifted to anger, realising that his masterful plan he had built for so many years, would remain unaccomplished.

Suddenly, amid the tension came an impressive ball of growing ice from Melcelore's right hand. In response, Ramalon had a choice of affinities but settled to conjure a flame with his left, honouring his father.

"You can try..." Melcelore challenged as both Màgjeurs braced for the sudden contest.

They released their energies with full thrust and intent on one another, clashing in the middle of Monarchy Hall. Fire met ice in a violent combustion between the two juggernauts.

Initially, they both struggled to comprehend just how powerful the other was, experiencing the full force of each other's wrath. Ramalon's face did not contort and grimace like his opponents whose teeth clenched together, occasionally vocalising his suppressive tension. Instead, his intensity lay behind his eyes as they pierced into Melcelore's.

The contest remained relatively even, but perhaps for the first time in Ramalon's recent memory, he began to feel a little overpowered by the legend of Melcelore's strength. He grasped just how masterful the dark Màgjeur's understanding of The Protecy was. The nuances and intricacies combined with the sheer velocity of ice he expelled was near perfect. A slight admission to Ramalon was that his own understanding was inferior, though the colossal duel's projective outcome was far from straightforward. Ramalon held on to the one resounding advantage that Melcelore did not have. The true ownership of The Dragastone - which he believed whole-heartedly would not fail him.

It was more powerful than any force known on Rèo, that much was clear, but the mystery of just how deep the dark Màgjeur's strength really was created uncertainty as to who had the absolute advantage. Ramalon began to feel the pressure as he struggled to find a way to press his power into the combustion between them, often spewing out scorching flames and glacial spikes onto the foundations of Monarchy Hall, rupturing structural parts of the stone interior with ease.

The longer the duel went on, the more Ramalon felt the decline of his power. Melcelore's beam of ice gradually began to creep toward Ramalon's position. He tried as best as he could to relax his protecy and though successful at allowing additional fire to flow through, slowing the advance, the sphere of ice and fire still gravitated toward him. Ramalon was in trouble and even though he understood this, that undying confidence and foresight only increased his stance and belief that he would prevail.

Melcelore's face turned more satisfactory in his successful advance. Ramalon fought back by thrusting the ball of ice and fire into Monarchy Hall's roof, obliterating it instantly and breaking the chain. The legendary building's foundations still had earth magic running through its structure, giving it additional support. However, the combined velocity of the two Màgjeurs shattered the ceiling with ease, causing the rubble to fall onto them.

They both dealt with it in different ways. Melcelore entombed himself with the affinity of earth he possessed, turning himself to stone. The falling brickwork and slabs crumbled as they landed on his defensive form.

Ramalon meanwhile conjured a network of lightning bolts to zap the falling rubble into tiny particles of sand, softening the impact. The slight reprieve gave him a chance to go on the offensive to Melcelore, who occupied centre stage.

He relaxed the flow of the connection with The Protecy and unleashed a thunderous bolt of lightning into the solar plexus of Melcelore, who initially seemed affected as his body of stone slid back due to the force. However, his earth magic's additional defence squibbed down the shocks, halting the attack and allowing Melcelore to smile sadistically, heavily grinding his cheeks made of stone.

Fire did not work, nor did volts. The other remaining affinity he had yet to try was earth itself, but going toe to toe with the same path felt a feeble choice. Alas, that continued trust in the power of The Dragastone assured him he would not fail.

He impulsively channelled the bond of earth, uprooting large fragments of the marble ground of Monarchy Hall, lifting them high into the air, past the broken ceiling and sent them crashing down onto Melcelore. In response, the dark Màgjeur prepped two fists of stone enlarged to twice the size, meeting the falling marble with incredible left and right hooks, breaking the debris and causing minimal impact. Though many similar fragments were conjured up and dealt with in the same manner, Melcelore did not seem affected by any stretch of the imagination, and it was Ramalon who was running out of ideas. The variety of affinities was a successful weapon in his fight against Davinor, but this was entirely different. This was Melcelore, whose own strength was so great, it defied the conventions. The power of The Dragastone so far counted for nothing.

He switched back to fire and forced a continuous flame onto the tombed body, which surprisingly, Melcelore chose to defend with a wall of earth in front rather than allowing the fire to hit him and absorb the heat. Ramalon did briefly wonder why this was but concentrated on his attack more intensely. It was not too long before it was apparent what was happening. The flames he was conjuring were the very thing that was building Melcelore's shield and making it stronger. Luckily for him, he read what was happening just in time because the moment he stopped his flume of fire, Melcelore hurled the shield across the stretch of the building, heading straight for him. Judging by the weight and force of the large fragment rapidly flying toward him, he did not feel confident he could stop nor shatter with anything he possessed. The only option he had, forced him to mimic Melcelore, turning himself to stone and accept the blow.

It hit his statued body with the force of a meteor, propelling him through one of the last remaining pillars still standing of the decimated Monarchy Hall and into the side of the ruins.

Ramalon was broke. Despite his defence, he had never experienced that much pain in his life. Much more so than when Lestas Magraw invaded his mind with a searing knife. He did not have the strength to continue his defence of earth, as his body transformed back to its original flesh, lying defeated on the ground.

His eyes were closed, his breath shallow. Though alive, he could not believe how the power of The Dragastone had allowed him to fail so impressively. Was he so wrong in that its power was unrivalled? Or was Melcelore just too strong a Màgjeur than he could have possibly imagined? He was so confident that Melcelore had missed his father's masterful move in foreseeing and entrusting Ramalon to end their rivalry that he could not understand how he was not triumphing. Instead, defeat was staring him in the face as Melcelore approached. For a brief moment, Ramalon considered the possibility that he was wrong.

The lull in the fight gave Melcelore the chance to speak to his defeated opponent on the ground.

"Just like your father! Foolish in life... And foolish in death," he declared, standing tall and victorious.

Melcelore wasted no time preparing his protecy of ice once more, not an ounce of sentimentality as the final hurdle in his rivalry with Felder was within one blow.

However, the feeling of defeat for Ramalon all of a sudden turned a sharp corner. A feeling that this was not the end for him. Quite the opposite. He mysteriously began to feel a familiar sense of strength, which fuelled a more active sense of fight that was far from over despite his fallen body. At that moment, Ramalon's concerns over The Dragastone silently diminished. The route of destiny had opened and he understood their fate. He kept the knowledge to himself.

In the process of their epic fight, they had both briefly forgotten about one major component in this story. Perhaps the last question of so many moving parts and Ramalon could not have wished for the timing of such importance to be more opportune. Melcelore felt the sudden shift in presence too.

He slowly turned around and looked up toward the skies to view one of the legends, crunching its claws onto the remains of the broken roof. It's beautiful wings, the size of boat sails, spread wide covering the span of the hall from above. Its unrelenting gaze bore down onto the two powerhouses below, silently judging the situation. An air of uncertainty consumed its demeanour.

A Dragadelf had emerged.

Both Melcelore and Ramalon remained in awe of the stunning phenomenon. A possession which, under their own realities, they believed they owned. Melcelore turned to Felder's son, feeling even more triumphant than ever, proudly sneering at his marvel.

Ramalon remained silent and still, bearing a rare, delicate gaze toward the beast above.

"The final piece of the puzzle," Melcelore announced. "Now, you will truly learn the mistakes of your father. I am The Dragadelf's one true master!" he defiantly concluded.

The dark Màgjeur walked backwards to allow space between them, while Ramalon gradually stumbled to his feet. Melcelore had instructed the Dragadelf to engage Ramalon, fluttering its enormous wings to gently land inside Monarchy Hall. The powerful gusts blew soot and debris into the sides of the demolished building as it landed with ease. The Dragadelf slowly crawled toward Felder's son, who recognised this as a very familiar picture to thirty years ago. A physically battered Ramalon stared down into the Dragadelf's gaze

## A Rivalry in Perpetuity

without an ounce of fear or anxiety.

Melcelore stood at the entrance of Monarchy Hall as he gave his final command.

"Kill him…"

The Dragadelf responded to his order immediately, wriggling in frightening preparation to see it through. Ramalon's stance did not change as the beast suddenly thrashed toward him across the hall, roaring with terrifying might and purpose. Its cry could be heard from miles away as it bellowed straight toward Ramalon. It had obeyed every command that was given to him by Melcelore… All but one.

The fires it was instructed to burn did not erupt from the Dragadelf's unhinged jaw as commanded. Instead, it arrived within just metres of Ramalon and breathed its deathly roar harshly onto him, rippling his hair and robes with a foul stench.

It was only when commanded that it halted its putrid cry. Alas, it was not Melcelore's command which stopped it but Ramalon's.

A somewhat confused Melcelore looked on at the brief moment of stillness, trying to work out why his order was not being fulfilled.

"I said, kill him!" he repeated with more intensity, a faint undercurrent of vulnerability tainted his words.

The Dragadelf did not respond, which filled Ramalon's heart with more hope than he ever thought possible as he knew what it meant. The beast merely looked into the eyes of Ramalon with a sense of recognition and respect. The moment Ramalon had foreseen and waited for had at last arrived.

Melcelore's chest began to rise and fall more noticeably the more he lost grip over the situation.

"KILL HIM NOW!" Melcelore desperately bellowed.

Nothing happened. No movement, nor suggestion that the Dragadelf heeded to the dark Màgjeur's command any longer. At that moment, it was proof to Ramalon of where it's loyalty truly lay.

"With its true master," Ramalon thought aloud.

The Dragadelf seemed to pick up on the same notion and gave a cheeky blink of the eyes to agree with him. And now was the time for Ramalon to impose the truth of the tale. The answer to why the beast obeyed Ramalon was simple to him. Though Melcelore had Felder's blood running through his veins, giving him the impression that he was their true master, Ramalon was right all along. The Dragastone, which belonged to him, gave him the more vital claim over The Dragadelf than anything on this world. It was after all, Felder's endgame and he was right to trust his inherited ownership of it.

A dumbfounded Melcelore had also quickly unravelled this and the penny was dropping faster than The Dragastone he sent down thirty years ago.

Ramalon commanded the Dragadelf to snake round to face the dark Màgjeur again, protecting its rightful master with its massive frame. It's tyrannosaurial head intimidated Melcelore as it snared down into the green eyes of the dark Màgjeur. The allegiance was total.

After a long silent pause, filled with betrayed anger, Melcelore quickly understood and once again adapted. The rules had changed and the most fearful Màgjeur ever to walk Rèo took matters into his own hands.

"So be it!" he quietly declared through gritted teeth.

The dark Màgjeur conjured an astonishing glacial spike and aimed it straight at the heart of the Dragadelf. Its carriage was too big to meander out of the way in such an enclosed space by proportion to its size, nor was it quick enough to melt the spike before landing. The only course of defence came from its now-confirmed true master.

Ramalon quickly turned himself to stone and with unnatural speed, ran straight past the defenceless Dragadelf and leapt with tremendous thrust into the direct line of the ice spike. The embodiment of stone did not pierce but he was still sent flying back and smashed effectively into the Dragadelf's colossal head before landing in his father's throne, crumbling its foundations further.

Ramalon froze in ice and stone, burying The Dragastone behind him. He could now only look on, helplessly from the High Throne on Terrasendia.

The Dragadelf meanwhile, spasmed on its way to the ground. The crushing blow was not fatal, though the effectiveness of Melcelore's attack did dazzle the great beast. A merciless Melcelore threw more spikes of ice at the Dragadelf but this time it was ready.

It breathed a tremendous flume of fire, melting the ice instantly. Not only that but the fires continued across Monarchy Hall onto Melcelore himself, which did not stop.

The dark Màgjeur once more had to be on the defensive and quickly created the same wall of stone as before. The shield grew ever more rapidly as the fires fuelled Melcelore's defence.

Ramalon could only watch on from his father's throne and worked out that despite the Dragadelf's insane power, the one thing it did not have which Melcelore did, was that touch of genius and cunning, which made him gravely prepare for the inevitable.

The Dragadelf could not sustain its dragonbreath any longer as it needed to inhale. Melcelore timed the brief moment where the fires relaxed to impressively yell with all his might, causing the stone to shatter into a thousand sharp pieces, suspended mid-air from the ground to the broken roof, reminiscent of a swarm of wasps.

The moment Ramalon foresaw and yet was powerless to stop.

Melcelore hurled every shard and fragment into the beast, who also struggled to defend. Fires erupted from its mouth once more to disintegrate a portion of particles; alas, the sheer number heading towards it meant that most soared passed the fiery defence and pierced directly into the legendary beast.

Its wail broke Ramalon's heart, confirming the fatal pain. The sails in its wings ripped with ease. The blow nicking the wings thinner bones. Its carriage had also been grotesquely pierced open as holes prominently emerged from its throbbing belly. Molten blood red as a scarlet rose poured out, steam hazing off. The sound of a dragon whose lungs were pierced was perhaps the first time in history such a wound occurred. The intense wheezing of the beast clutching, gasping for simple air added to the incredible sadness. Its injuries were fatal, and for the second time, Ramalon witnessed just how mortal these perfect beasts were. He couldn't help but be reminded of the agony when Ramacès killed his Dragadelf, giving another sense of grave inevitability.

The mythical creature continued to writhe in agony, desperately trying to scramble free unsuccessfully due to its wings no longer of any use. Melcelore marched toward it with purpose, looking as strong and victorious as ever to which the Dragadelf, frightened and defenceless, cowered into the corner of Monarchy Hall like a beaten dog. It often looked toward its true master expecting him to come to his aid again, which Ramalon painfully could not.

It attempted to defend itself by unleashing its dragonbreath toward the oncoming juggernaut, but that too proved to be toothless as the inferno instead wisped out of the multiple holes that decorated its carriage and neck. Its only hope rested in the compassion of Melcelore... Alas, compassion and Melcelore were two things that just did not register together.

To add to the distasteful misery, Melcelore stooped before the writhing helpless beast, took one deliberate look toward the trapped Ramalon and once again demonstrated his ruthless nature.

He extended his hand and produced an earthy stone-like substance down the Dragadelf's throat, instantly cutting off the reduced air supply. The wheezing gasps turned to intense strains; its struggle intensified significantly. Not even through the holes in its neck and body were its lungs receiving oxygen as Melcelore had cruelly covered those parts with earth too. The Dragadelf squirmed like an eel underwater, desperately searching for hope as the growing weight of suffocation became too much, slowly draining its life.

Ramalon could not comprehend how much hatred he had for someone than at that moment, helplessly looking at the smirking proud-of-himself Melcelore who was now feeding off of his gloat. It was perhaps the only thing that could provoke an emotional response from Ramalon and make him experience sadness. He could not comprehend just how sorry he was for failing the Dragadelf and how he felt responsible for failing to protect his possession.

The attempts to wriggle free gradually died down as the beasts insides filled with stone, pinning it down until at last the remaining movements came with one last effort to turn its beautiful head toward its master on the throne. Their eyes met with that cruel sadness before the Dragadelf's eyes slowly turned grey, lifeless and into stone themselves. It was dead.

Ramalon's insides had never been so distraught with anger and hatred. Even more so than his feud with Davinor, this was no comparison. It felt personal. The Dragadelf were his to own, like the children he knew he would never have, and someone had taken away that irreplaceable happiness. He stared upon the lifeless perfection and how he wished he could turn back time and bring it back to life, along with the other two Dragadelf that had fallen. The paternal instinct inspired him to passionately attempt his next move as he intensely looked at his rival in despair. There was one card left to play.

Melcelore's attention now turned back to Ramalon who remained helpless on the throne. For the first time, the dark Màgjeur appeared to tire.

Despite the pain Ramalon was experiencing, it did anger him that he experienced a subtle admiration for Melcelore in that he just would not be beaten. A defiance that he subtly learned from.

"It did not have to be this way," an exhausted and hurt Melcelore suggested. "Its death is on your hands. But no matter. The Understunde awaits you. As does your father. Màgjeur Ramalon…"

Melcelore once more tried to bring down the curtain on this fight

## A Rivalry in Perpetuity

before Ramalon had called upon his last remaining defence. Just before the final blow, Melcelore readied his protecy of ice and heard that deathly growl that he was all too familiar... Only this time, it was not singular.

The dark Màgjeur turned around to view the last remaining four Dragadelf that Ramalon had silently summoned surrounding the broken roof above. They had answered their master's call.

It did not take long for them to gather what had happened, with Melcelore directly in the middle. There was no way he would be able to attack the helpless Ramalon as they had space and position to aim their fires to protect their true master.

The balance in this uncertain duel had tipped in Ramalon's favour, to which Melcelore also acknowledged. Despite his legendary strength being enough to kill one Dragadelf, the question over whether he had enough in reserve to destroy them all was evident on his defeated face. He couldn't.

Despite Ramalon's frozen expression, the satisfaction behind his eyes was total.

The four Dragadelf embers were already fuelling having understood what had taken place and targeting Melcelore as the enemy who had violated their loyalty just like Ramacès.

Melcelore and Ramalon's eyes met with more of a personal touch than at any point in their duel, their intentions clear.

"*Avenge...*" Ramalon commanded through the bond he shared.

The Dragadelf instantly obeyed and unleashed their devastating dragonbreath onto the lonely Melcelore below. Unable to run, fight back or counter, he defended himself once more under the embodiment of rock and stone only this time the fires proved too great for him.

The insane heat made Melcelore scream in agony as his defence was not strong enough. The rock coating his body began to grow, almost trapping him in the same way as Ramalon. He knew he had no chance of escaping that time. The heat began to slowly thaw out Ramalon's binds, enabling him to gradually move once more and resume his body back to the original flesh. His body was free and took a brief moment of rest to contemplate on the momentous triumph that was moments away.

The fires continued to surround and trap Melcelore, buried inside what looked like a boulder. Ramalon knew he had to be very careful with what he chose to do at that pivotal moment.

He remembered the promise he gave to The Ancient Drethai in that he vowed to provide them with Melcelore's soul. He now had the means to do that and honour his word. However, he was ultimately conflicted. Melcelore's primary affinity was with ice, a vital component of his Staircase to Divinity. Acquiring it from Melcelore would be perfectly justified as it would mean something profound to him in his poetic reality. In addition, if he manced from Melcelore and gave The Drethai his soul, it would be them that would own the right and possession over The Boldemere. Something which irked him greatly the more he thought about it. However, despite the weighing up of consequences, the benefit of what he truly wanted made him come to only one conclusion.

"… This is my world!" Ramalon whispered to himself.

It seemed like the script was written for him as he commanded The Dragadelf to cease their fires. Melcelore was buried inside a tomb of thick rock. Ramalon instantly obliterated the enclosure to reveal the brow-beaten legend. His body flumped to the ground despite being still alive. The suffocation he had suffered was sweet justice to Ramalon, in revenge for what he did to the Dragadelf moments earlier as he clasped desperately for air. He didn't even feel the need to disable Melcelore's use of The Protecy as his victory neared.

The dark Màgjeur laid helplessly before Ramalon as he magically lifted his body to kneel, like a puppeteer pulling strings to a rag-doll, almost in mockery. Melcelore's once striking green eyes turned dull and faint as he stared into oblivion. Felder's legacy had reigned supreme.

Ramalon concluded there was only one way to end this. He withdrew his gaze and stepped aside to allow Melcelore a clear view of the Dragadelf he had suffocated. To the side of its magnificent carcass gleamed The Dragastone on Felder's throne. The two main concepts that had consumed Melcelore in his long fight served as a mark of ultimate defeat.

Ramalon calmly waded over to his father's throne and in full view of Melcelore and The Dragadelf above, he slowly drew his hand toward The Dragastone. Before his fingertips touched the mysterious anomaly, he felt the presence of its power which was undeniably more potent than anything he had ever experienced and finally laid his palm onto the stone.

His eyes closed to feel the ecstasy run through his veins, engulfing the power it held. It did not overwhelm him. The ultimate strength it gave him filtered into his body perfectly. He took a moment to feel the relief of such a journey to get to that point had paid off. The challenges and hurdles he had to overcome were nothing short of exceptional. Alas, he did succeed them.

The remaining Dragadelf all roared toward the sky in recognition once more of their true master's greatness. Melcelore could barely look on in his suspended state. Once Ramalon had revelled in his happiness, he conjured a rare smile and turned to his fallen opponent in the middle of Monarchy Hall. He made sure he left Melcelore with enough strength to have a good look at his mistakes. Once Ramalon was satisfied that he had unquestionably defeated him, he finally brought down the curtain on the fight, instructing the remaining four Dragadelf to rain their molten breaths down onto Melcelore once and for all.

There were no mature screams of agony. Just an air of victory as the flames burned. It was right for Ramalon to allow The Dragadelf to be the ones to finish it. After all, it was Melcelore who created the event which inevitably re-birthed them onto this world for his selfish gain.

A white ball of light lifted from the ball of heat and disappeared into the haze of The Dragasphere above, making its way presumably to the gates of The Understunde and confirming Melcelore's death.

A satisfied Ramalon brought an end to the inferno and there laid Melcelore's torched corpse on the ground. Black smoke wisped from the charcoaled remains of the ten-foot-tall legend, who was no more.

Ramalon had only just realised what he had done. He had defeated the most feared Màgjeur ever to walk Rèo. And what that ultimately made him astonished him to the core. He looked up toward The Dragadelf and it seemed that moment was long-awaited for both parties. A sense of home and togetherness was restored. He genuinely could not remember happiness on this scale, looking upon the legendary beasts which were his to own.

The euphoric feeling of The Dragastone became more vivid in his palm. He held it in front of his eyes to see the purity and flawless nature of its existence. It was perfect. And it was his. At least for now. In his mind, there was perhaps one more thing which interrupted that total assurance of his claim… The image of Ramerick's face, which he never forgot, slapped him across the eyes. If he was correct in his assumption that his father gave him the ownership over The Dragastone, there was nothing to suggest that he didn't give it to Ramacès and Ramerick too. Of course, he had already dealt with one of those problems, but at that moment, he firmly established Ramerick as his final step. Only then would he be considered immortal and unquestionably divine.

The touching moment was interrupted by thousands of white orbs gently floating towards the haze above. The fractured ruins of Monarchy Hall allowed him a clear view as to what was happening. It looked like a beautiful storm, only in reverse. The death of Melcelore ultimately meant that The Boldemere, which he had stored on Felder's Crest, had now escaped their hosts and were free at last.

Despite the repercussions of betraying The Ancient Drethai's promise, he would rather the consequence of their loyalty if it meant he could take this perfect opportunity of acquiring the affinity of ice. He ruthlessly valued that was more important than their allegiance.

He was in no rush. He slowly and triumphantly walked over and rested on one of the decimated pillars just admiring the graceful view of ascending stars. A moment of peace ensued. It took some time until the souls breaking free from their hosts on the city below began to slow down.

He would watch every single one float up like bubbles from the bed of an ocean and into the haze above. Until at last, a solitary soul bubbled its way behind the rest. He wondered who it belonged to. Was it a man or a woman, or even a child, he thought? Did they have a good life or bad? Were they even going to The Gracelands, or did they deserve the fate of The Understunde? The philosophical nature in Ramalon gave him more understanding of life itself, in that it was precious. Alas, it only made him want to protect the only thing he cared for. The Dragadelf that were left.

The last remaining soul escaped into the cloud above and then a stillness that lasted a lifetime.

After his moment of gathering his thoughts, he turned back toward the middle of Monarchy Hall and approached Melcelore's corpse. The Dragadelf looked on from above, willing him to do what had to be done.

Ramalon happily obliged.

He extended his hand to the remains of the dark Màgjeur and scythed his burnt flesh in the same manner as Melcelore did to his father thirty years ago. Sweet justice consumed him as he avenged his father once and for all.

Hot knives aggressively carved into his chest, accumulating blobs of blood above him, reminiscent of a claret globe. Ice particles

## A Rivalry in Perpetuity

prominently infused through it along with the elements of earth and other substances. There was enough there for Ramalon to finally extend his hand and absorb the fletched affinity. It magically filtered into his palm, ascertaining its power, until at last Ramalon felt the strange sensation of crisp ice running through his veins. The hairs hackled down his spine and arms; his body shivered in the frost.

The confirmation of his growing strength was mirrored by a collective roar from The Dragadelf above once more, recognising their masters growing divinity.

After a long pause realising his arm of power, his breath was shallow and he mercilessly thought about his next move.

"Two more to go," he satisfyingly said to himself.

Suddenly his gaze was drawn out of Monarchy Hall once again as an unexpected event was unfolding outside. He made his way to the entrance to stand in full view of Felder's Crest below. However, it was not the foundations below which drew his eye… It was the anomaly developing from above.

He noticed in the clouds a strange form of light bleeding through. Though it was faint, he wondered what it could have been. To his knowledge, nothing could enter The Dragasphere except for himself and Davinor via his secret. Could Melcelore's portal allow travel both ways, he thought?

Feeling intrigued he sent a soft ball of fire upward in an attempt to dispel the haze. The fire disappeared and slowly ignited the clouds across the span of The Dragasphere.

The more the haze slowly started to dissipate, the more transparent the viewing became. It suddenly dawned to Ramalon what it could potentially be as the light began to move frantically. He couldn't believe what was happening. His heart began to thump a little faster as he gathered just how exceptional this was.

The haze dispelled and to his utter surprise, the light was not singular. Instead, it was thousands upon thousands of tiny white orbs that had only just escaped their hosts from below. They desperately bounced against the walls of The Dragasphere, trying to escape to their freedom at last. It looked like that same constellation of stars that aggressively bumped into each other, spanning for many miles.

The conditions of The Dragasphere had remained. Nothing went in, and nothing went out. Ramalon did not at any point fathom that it applied to the captured souls as they could not escape the enclosure set by The Blessèd thirty years ago. It just seemed a natural conclusion that once they were free, it would be impossible to stop them from sailing to the end of their roads. It seemed as if it was written for Ramalon as he could achieve something that had never been done once more. This landmark of history provided him with the platform to once again display his merciless intent. It cruelly rose to the surface as he took the opportunity to extend his greatness.

He indulged in the exceptional circumstance and extended his hand toward the souls above. Without hesitation, he opened up his own soul to begin the process of claiming theirs for himself. To his delight, one by one, the network of thousands of encapsulated lives were sucked back down toward Monarchy Hall and funnelled their way toward his palm.

They filtered seamlessly into his hand, gently flashing once confirmed into his possession. The strobes of light lit up the madness on his face and in his eyes. He heard their plethoric cries and voices in his mind on their way through, to the point where they became so many that he could no longer distinguish any one person. Instead, it was now a crowd of desperate begging to allow their souls to be free at last, which only grew louder. Ramalon did not oblige.

As they continued to gravitate into his hand, he knew somewhere was Melcelore's soul, who was perhaps the only one who would not give Ramalon the satisfaction of pleading for his existence.

Never before had any Màgjeur completed the process of both fletching and Soul Mancing from the same person - to fletch from a Màgjeur requires the host to be already dead, and in turn, their souls would have already escaped. However, in this truly exceptional scenario, it was perhaps the only condition in which both could happen. Not only has he now acquired the affinity of ice, but he is also in possession of hundreds of thousands of souls to use at his expense.

As the flashes of light bounced against his body, he realised fullheartedly that his arm of power had grown longer than any Màgjeur to have walked Rèo. And it would not stop there. In his self-written challenge, there were still holes to be unquestionably divine and he began to process the next hurdle in his ambition. However, at this marvellous moment, he took the opportunity to indulge in the sense of undeniable pride in what he had just achieved.

Ramalon had climbed the next step on his Staircase to Divinity.

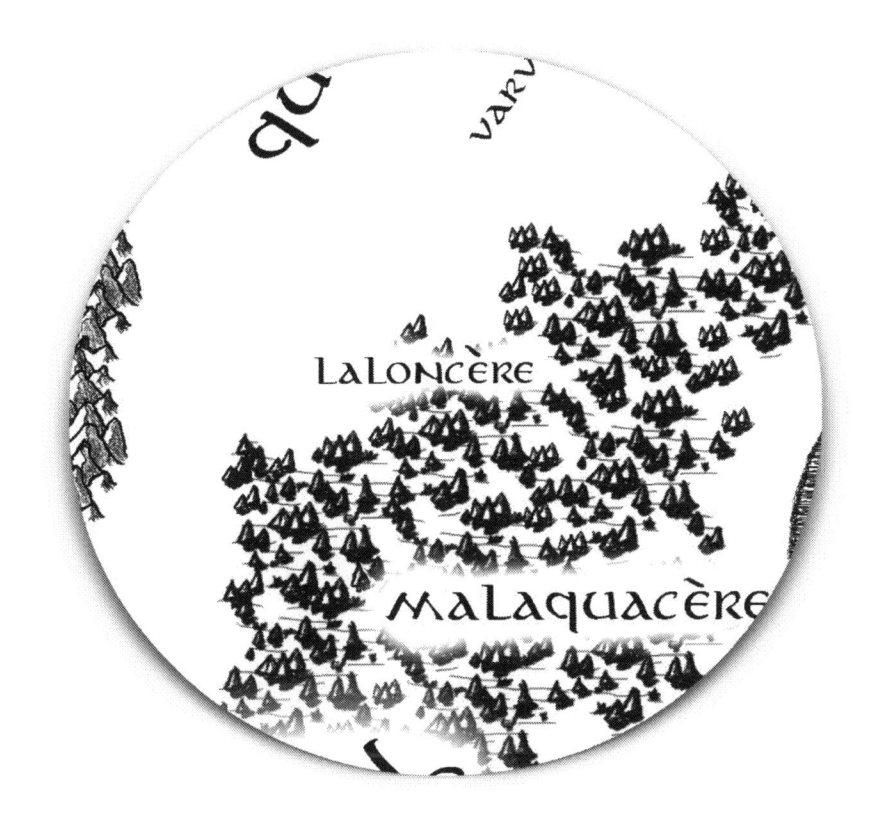

## The Last Endeavour

 The gentle flame above Jàqueson's tomb flickered against Ramerick's face. He would sit alone on a bench made of stone every day upon the peak of Laloncère, staring at the ball of light that hovered above his son's resting place.
 The white swash of falling rivers coated much of the enclosed valley below. Autumnal golds and browns decorated the place with such warmth that it presented a sense of peace and tranquillity that Ramerick absorbed. The dusk from the setting sun shone through the surrounding trees that did not sway as the air was so still.
 Not an ounce of sadness touched his heart as he reminisced over the memories he had with not just his son but Amba as well. It represented the only materialistic thing he had to draw upon, the memories of

what was once his perfect life. Alas, it was not yet over for him. His demeanour had not changed since laying his son to rest as, in his reality, he fully believed even weeks after his funeral, that he would see him again. After all, that was his promise to them both and a nobleman would always be true to his word.

He often glared across the green grass to Joric's flame, whose body remained in Drethai Halls. Only the memory of his life was commemorated. The image of his heroic last moment, which turned out to be in vain, did evoke a sadness within him which he could distinctly separate from his son.

He was, however vaguely aware that he was feeling strange. It was not an emotional attachment but more a peculiar sense that had latched on to his consciousness. It had governed him way before his son's death, going right the way back to when Amba died. He questioned whether her death sparked certain impulses that he had experienced so many times since, but somehow that didn't match up. That invincible feeling that drove some of his choices of madness was unexplainable even to that day.

As the days rolled on, he barely slept nor ate, choosing to take comfort in his self-isolation. It gave him the time to contemplate how different things could have been. So many things had to fall in place for other things to happen and Ramerick couldn't help but think there must have been something he could have done. Alas, he struggled to come up with an answer. Fate consumed him and the more he struggled to piece together the answers, the more he accepted that he was never meant to have that happy ending.

Every event that happened came as a consequence of something out of his control. How unjust and unfair, he thought. He came to learn that his father King Felder, had set in motion plans that needed to be made to restore the good in Terrasendia and eradicate the inevitable evil. Despite being the victim of his father's choices, he did not resent what had to be done, even to his detriment. He sensed that similarity in himself and had he been in his father's position, he would have done the same.

"Ramerick?" came his mother's voice from behind.

Eveleve's beautiful white dress sparkled against the other flames that peppered the resting ground. Her beautifully kept light hair draped passed her shoulders, looking upon her son with concern.

Ramerick did not respond. He was still entranced staring into the flame, as if Jàque and Amba's faces were smiling back at him, willing him to go on.

"They would be very proud," she continued with a hint of happiness as she approached.

"They are. I can see," he directed his response mainly to the flame.

"Tell me about him. My grandson."

Ramerick conjured a smile.

"He would have made you laugh that's for sure." Eveleve shared her beautiful smile too. "Such a bright young boy. He never stopped, always looking for the next adventure. We took him to the horse master every morning to ride the mildens. We couldn't afford all too much, so we loaned one for him. He called him Arrow as he was quick and flew through the air. Gave Amba a heart attack every time it bolted," he gently laughed. "But I was always confident he'd never fall off. It seemed natural to him. As did so much."

"He sounds like he was his father's son," she perched on the same bench to his side.

"He was. Though he had this fascination with The Protecy. Something we did not share. For some reason, he was attracted to the air more than the others. Aristuto was his favourite. He wanted this ability to fly, which I could never understand. We didn't like heights so where he got that from, I have no idea. I promised I'd take him one -" he stopped short as he remembered his promise to take him Gallonea one day. Somehow, that struck him a little harder, as if he had momentarily forgotten that wasn't going to happen.

"Son?" she asked as his attention drew into himself.

"And one day, it all seemed to change. At the time, we never knew how he caught Malerma. Such a rare disease and we never thought anything else of it apart from just bad luck. But then we learned it was all part of a far wider evil."

He couldn't help but remember his hatred for Brody and how it was right for him to have died for the mistake he made. The only redeeming feature he could think of was that he did give him the means to escape with The Time Stone back on Ravenspire and would have worked were it not for the events that unfolded beyond his actions.

"When he created his Blessèd Wheel, never would I have imagined he would be studying his own grandparents."

"He sounds like he had a very astute mind."

"Oh, he did. He was very bright, the bugger," Ramerick conjured another subtle bounce of laughter. Eveleve found it warming to hear her son talk about Jàque so comfortably. "He created this Blessèd Wheel, every twelve members, each placed on every hour of the clock. I learned more from that than my own findings. He would sometimes randomly check if I was concentrating, snapping his fingers to get my attention, like he was the professor."

"He sounds cheeky."

"He was. I wouldn't want him any other way."

"Sad to say that I can't say the same. I do wish there was another way I could have experienced time with him. And with you."

"That wasn't your fault."

"No. No, it wasn't. But like you, I'll always ask myself if there was anything I could have done to protect you. To protect him."

Ramerick certainly couldn't deny that had she been around; things might have been entirely different. Her powers of life may have helped preserve Jàque's. However, he understood that her presence ultimately would have endangered their true identity and put them at risk.

"Tell me about his mother," she diverted. "I understand she was your wife-to-be?"

"Blessèd no! I could only wish for that." He paused a few moments to replay the image in his mind of her beautiful face, stunning red hair and a smile that warmed the heart. "I don't think I would have been that lucky. I'm not even sure she would have said yes had I asked."

"You're too modest, son."

"It's true."

"It seems like you both were made for each other. Both strong. Kind. Gentle at heart. Were more people like you both, it would make the world a happier place."

"One day, I will pluck up the courage to ask her."

Eveleve tried to hide her concern at what appeared to be a delusional state of mind. She knew there was no way that could happen, but what concerned her most was that at no point did her son seem to be noticeably grieving.

"Son. I have to ask you," she lowered her tone. "What makes you feel this way? That you will see them again."

Ramerick continued to stare at the flame blankly.

"I don't expect you to understand."

"Then help me. I'm afraid for you. I deserve that right being your mother."

Ramerick gently smiled.

"Yes, you do. As I said, I don't expect you to understand. It's not a

# The Last Endeavour

hope. It's not even a feeling. Ever since that day Amba died, I've been connected to something which I can't explain. It's what has driven every decision I've made since. It's stronger and clearer than a premonition. It's more an inevitability."

"When did you see this?"

"... Every moment since."

"Since?"

"Since he died. I keep seeing his face. I keep seeing her face... I see them now," he said, staring at the flame representing his family.

"They are dead son," she tried to be a little blunter in the hope that the message will land. She was after all the Blessèd Mage of Life, and if anyone were to be more sure of what could and couldn't be done with life, it was her. "Clinging onto hope leads to madness. I cannot allow you to fall down that path. You are my son. And you have been through so much that has been unfair to you. You're a good person, who does not deserve to fall into the pit of insanity. Not while you have strength left. Not while you have something to give to this world."

Ramerick's face turned darker and his eyes narrowed, as if he remembered something which he had briefly put to one side during his time of reflection. Filling more with brewing anger and hate as he latched onto his last defining intention.

"I have only one more thing to give to this world," he said, more defiant and detached.

"You wish to kill your brother..."

He did not respond. Instead, he turned his head to her and bore his gaze veiled with poison intently into hers. Not an ounce of shame, nor regret of wanting to do so.

"You wish to kill Ramalon," she stared once more for clarification.

"It's the last thing I'll do before I see them again," he responded with more immediacy.

Eveleve's face turned more worried than before as if she was genuinely scared of the prospect of both her sons going toe to toe. More worrying to her was that she was perhaps more informed about what Ramalon had become - the epitome of evil.

"That is my fear, son. I share no love for what Ramalon has done. But I do fear I will lose you in this, your last endeavour."

He shook his head in denial. "This is my last purpose; the only one left to give to this world. And I will not fail!"

"At what cost?"

"At any cost!"

"I don't think you understand the power your brother possesses. He is more a threat to everything we hold dear than anything we have ever experienced. He is too strong for you, my son. And I will not allow you to give your life away so easily."

"You think I will fail?" Eveleve was forced to stop short at replying before gently nodding her head. "Do you not think that I, being his brother maybe the only one to stop him?"

"Ramerick! There is a reason your father did not tell me about Ramalon. He saw entirely what he would become and knew I would have done something to stop him becoming what he is now. The shame I bear is already too much."

"But it was not your fault! You said it yourself, my father's plan is still in motion!"

"Yes it is. And although I am struggling to work out our roles in the fight that is to come, what we do know is that there is something mysterious that connects all three of you, other than just your bloodline."

"How so?"

"Both your brothers have had a claim to the control of The Dragadelf. Now that would not happen if it wasn't for something they adhere to."

"You're telling me they both can control a live Dragadelf?"

"More than that. They worship them, for a reason unknown to us all. It's the reason we must protect you at all costs because if they had this claim over them, then there is nothing to suggest you do not have that claim too! Ramalon did not try to kill you because he wants some unquestionable right to the bloodline. He tried to kill you because he wants the loyalty of The Dragadelf to be his, and his alone! Ramacès is dead, which means he will be coming for you. We need to find out precisely how you all are connected in this way."

"So I can control a Dragadelf?"

"Theoretically. Yes."

"Even though I have not enchanted The Protecy."

"That remains to be seen."

The stakes rose a little higher for them both. The notion that Ramerick's last purpose was to kill his brother conflicted entirely with what Ramalon needed. It would seem a simple case of winner takes all.

"And this I assume is all part of my father's plan?"

"Again, that remains to be seen."

"And what of Melcelore? How does he fit into all this?" His eyes tailed away, remembering something that was said a while back.

"Son?"

"Dancès."

"Dancès? The Elcarian?"

"You know him?"

She nodded her head. "He is said to have an insight into true clairvoyance. One of the rare few who can. What about him?"

"He told me about his premonition. One that he said was more real than anything he ever understood in his delving of time. He told me that he saw The Dragasphere collapse. He said that once that happened, Terrasendia would be in peril. And that I will have a role to play."

Eveleve did not take premonitions as concrete evidence that something would happen; however, she did not rebuke the idea. It would match what Felder said about Ramerick being the one to restore balance to the world of Rèo. Nor did she refute the notion that The Dragasphere was impossible to destroy. Despite the strength and legend of the most successful containment spell ever to be created, she came to learn that the conventions of what they were always led to believe would somehow be unearthed by the exceptional circumstances Ramalon presented.

"He did not say how," he continued, "but I think it would only be a matter of time before Melcelore finds a way to dismantle it from the inside. The Time Stone was his plan all along. Once he had it, he could reverse the spell and let The Dragadelf wreak havoc and destroy all that's good and green. But I'm sure he would have another plan in case that didn't work."

"And maybe when that moment comes, the only one strong enough to stop him would be Ramalon?" Eveleve suggested. "Maybe that's what he saw. Perhaps that was your fathers plan?"

Ramerick disgustedly shook his head at the thought of Ramalon becoming a symbol of heroism, knowing he was responsible for his son's death. Alas, that did not add up to him at that moment. They both could not put their finger on the specifics of Felder's plan.

"I have a feeling that if you are the one to restore this balance, we may not know what role you have to play until events unfold."

Putting the events that could be perilous into the hands of the unknown certainly worried them both. It inspired them to understand just what was happening, for they knew they still had much to discover.

"Your brother will pay for what he has done, my son. He killed Ramacès," she tried to hide her pang of guilt for being unable to stop that. "He also killed a member of The Blessèd Order. Twin that with the mystery of being your father's son and the ability to control The Dragadelf, he has become the gravest danger we have seen since the days of Sarthanzar. Which is why we must do this together. All of us."

Eveleve rose from the bench and looked down upon her son. An air of uncertainty tainted her face.

"It will happen tomorrow. The summoning of The Blessèd Order. You will attend, as you are just as important to this than me… Perhaps even more so."

Ramerick nodded to accept the invitation before staring back at the flame. Eveleve gathered he wanted some more privacy and so respectfully left him to ponder alone.

As he stared at the flame, it no longer represented the face of his family but instead a hooded figure of what he presumed Ramalon to look like.

The conversation with his mother did inject a little life into him, giving him more determination to snap out of the bubble he had been inside since Jàqueson's death.

It was the first time for many days he recognised how hungry he was. A little more recognition that his body had been under some form of considerable stress.

He wondered if his mother had secretly given him some essences of life to perk him up before establishing all it was, was simple love. It provided that touch more than magic ever could, and realised his mother had given him that just by a simple conversation. A reminder to himself that he wasn't alone after all.

## *Initiating Vendetta*

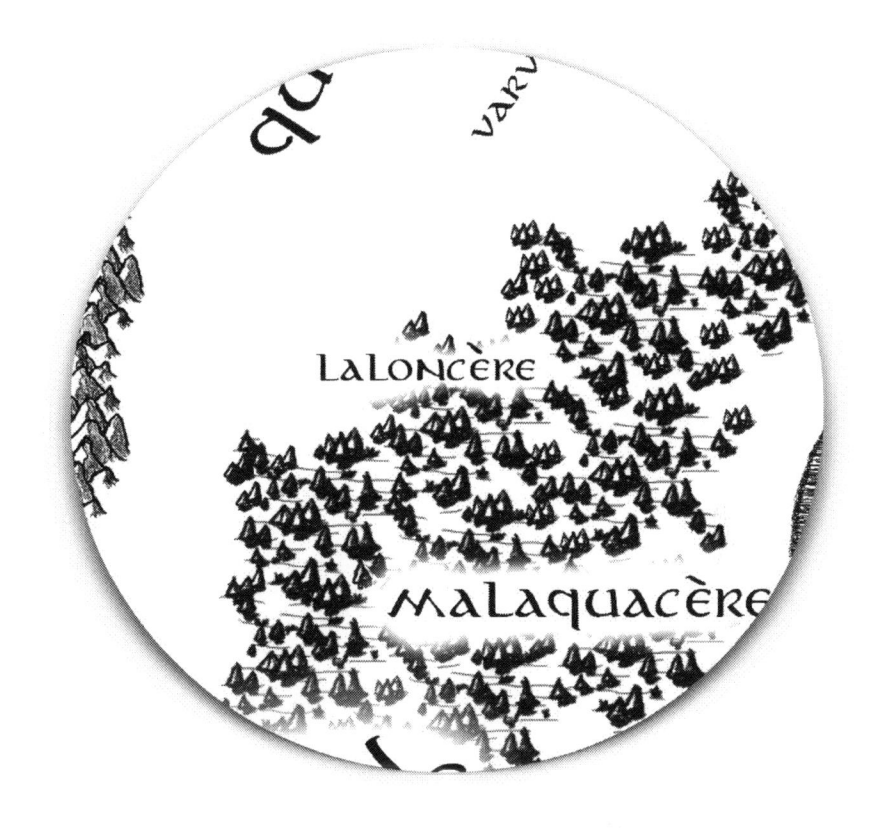

Several hours had gone by, and after grabbing some hearty food that laid aplenty in his chambers by the Questacèrean maids, he felt the need to breathe some fresh air.

For the first time since arriving on Laloncère, he started to appreciate the full beauty the valley had to offer. The dull greyness of his vision of late began to piece together the combination of autumnal colours. The golds, browns and yellows reflected off of the vast lake below. The tranquil sight of falling leaves dusted the skies as they landed on the pagoda-like roofs that topped many of the houses and structures of Laloncère. As Ramerick wandered the hallways, he would often hear the native Cèrean language as it bounced off the ear like sweet nectar. A mixture of elongated vowels twinned with a delicate sharpness to the consonants birthed a particular rhythm that sounded like their words were dancing on the licks of fire.

Laloncère was not populated by many but did strike him as a place of safety and restoration. Something he knew he deeply needed. Alas, he had no desire to rest, knowing the historical importance of the next day.

As he continued to amble around, he noticed the diverse nature that surrounded. He had read about the famous Mions that existed, half man-half lion, but had never seen one. He peered below toward some of the trees to view a family of four, playing on an improvised swing made from the branches. Two cublings and two adults, bearing ginger, long-haired scarves from their manes, happy as can be. A daughter and a son, younger than what Jàque had been, smiling beautifully and exposing their sharper canines, constantly craving their parent's attention to play with them. To which they happily did. Laloncère would not be their typical habitat as they prefer warmer climates in the north but he gathered they were here for protection. They were no different in terms of their relationship to one another than any family of nobleman. Strangely, it reminded him of his own that existed somewhere deep in his consciousness and the ghosts that replayed his memories of them.

Despite the fact he had never used The Protecy, his understanding of such a practice wasn't entirely useless. He noticed several Màgjeurs dressed in typical dangling robes hold tiny pieces of long wood that he wasn't all too familiar with. They'd conjure various magics and energies that he knew was not the standard form of protecy. He worked these people out to be Wandlers. Very rare as such a practice was out shadowed by the power of The Protecy. A part of him admired how some remained faithful to what they loved deep down.

He perched himself on a stoney bannister overlooking the lake below, several buildings and what appeared to be the main entrance to the left, which slalomed like a vein on its way into the mountainside.

Suddenly a twang of pain hit his leg.

"Ow!" he gasped, rather peeved.

He turned round to inspect the cause of the mild pain to see his aunt Gracène stumbling on her walking stick to join him by the bannister.

"Oops, sorry! Didn't see you," she ironically said, her blind eyes transfixed in an upward stare.

Ramerick instantly forgave her, despite his initial annoyance, though he did not know what to say. She had been a significant reason why he was still standing there at all, and were it not for her; he might never have survived. They both stared out onto the beauty of the valley, not entirely sure of what to say.

"Oh, do shut up will you!?" Gracène jested.

"I didn't say anything."

"It's about time you did." After a short pause, she took a deep breath. "I was born here you know. Many a year passed. As did your mother."

"You never told me you were my real aunt."

"What a stupid thing to say! We all grow up believing the perceived world around us. Your mother entrusted me to protect you, and so I gave you the ultimate form of protection I could. Not giving you that sense there was something in your life that was missing, gave you no reason to ever doubt the life you led... You were a bloody pain in the arse to raise, I tell you that!"

"Thanks," he mildly replied, not quite ready to engage in humour, alas Gracène did smile.

"It was a pleasure, my boy," she said with a hint of difficulty. "I will always consider you a son."

"Thank you... Thank you for giving me that life." He wholeheartedly meant that. "I will never forget it. My mother said you gave up so much to protect me. Is that how you lost your eyes? You never told me."

"Indeed. I sacrificed my sight so that I could see more than most. And who needs eyes anyway, overrated if you ask me!"

"But why did you have to?"

"Because every day, evil tried to uncover the real truths about your identity. Darker powers like Melcelore and The Ancient Drethai for instance ever sought out to find The Lost Blood Monarchs."

The simple mention of The Drethai provoked an angry trigger at the thought of their involvement in Jàqueson's death.

"Were your blood ever to reach those evils, it could be harvested for terrible things. The power it holds could strengthen them and was just something too unbearable to imagine. So in order to shield you, I had to repel their vision with the sacrifice of my own. Only by giving up my pure sight, could I see the unnatural more clear than day and hide you from that which sought your existence. And only once did it fail."

"... Because of me," he revealed with that similar pang of guilt.

"It wasn't your fault my lad. You did what any good father would have done to save their boy. Anything!"

"But it wasn't enough was it?"

Gracène reluctantly drew another large breath. "It was only a matter of time before the evil would force it's hand and expose your existence. The move that Melcelore played was beyond my skill to see. I could not detect the malice in Brody as the dark Màgjeur concealed his involvement. He must have sensed through my defences there was something to hide, which led him to Brody's involvement… I failed you."

Ramerick instantly turned his head to her, snapping him out of self-pity.

"You have failed no one! I promise you, what you have done for me, for Jàque, for Amba, I can never forget. You gave me a life! A life I was never really meant to have. And I will do everything I can to make you proud."

A tear began to trickle from the whites of Gracène's eyes.

"Now there's my lad!" she returned with a smile sensing there was indeed life in him still.

Ramerick also felt the same impulse of life filter into him. The love of his aunt had given him that little more inspiration to continue and live for everything he could.

"You have made me proud already. Don't give up. Fight every day as if it's your last. And don't stop till you have given this world everything you can possibly give."

"There is only one more thing I can give to this world."

"So do it!" she encouraged. "But do not do it alone, for he is too strong for you."

Ramerick looked back toward the lake with growing acceptance that Ramalon was indeed something that he knew to himself would be his biggest challenge. Despite the sense of destiny compelling him to believe that he was the only one that could stop his brother, he knew The Blessèd Order would be the one to forge the plan. He only hoped that it did involve him and that he can fulfil his vendetta.

His gaze was drawn to the stoney forecourt below where two riders on the most beautiful mildens had cantered through the entrance. One albino white with silver flecks, the other golden brown, their hooves clopping gently on the stone. Ramerick did not know how but he instinctively recognised the first rider before hazarding a guess as to the identity of his companion.

"The Blessèd Mage of Water," he said as he noticed the pale blue-skinned Màgjeur. Her fins morphed from her elbows and shins, her head shaped slightly odd but more streamlined, adding to the

## Initiating Vendetta

suggestion that it would help her in her natural habitat. "Lady Wemberlè."

"Indeed. It has already begun. They are on their way."

"And that must be Zathos! The Blessèd Mage of Electricity," he directed to the bald dark-skinned man, bearing a vibrant purple cloak with subtle stitchings of lightening woven into the fabric. "I remember Jàque mentioned they were married on his Blessèd Wheel."

"A fiesty combination!"

Shortly followed another two Màgjeurs on grey mildens, echoing their hooves on the forecourt. The Questacèreans gathered the reins of all four mounts as their masters dismounted. Wemberlè and Zathos greeted the two Màgjeurs with hearty enthusiasm. They clearly had not seen each other in such time and seemed genuinely overjoyed to be once again reunited.

"Ah yes! There he is. Aristuto," Gracène confirmed.

Ramerick instantly perked up, knowing that he was The Blessèd Mage of Air. He was the one Jàque admired and aspired to be. It was often debated whether he was stronger than Ethelba. Among experts however, it was almost unanimous that he was the most destructive Màgjeur left.

A sudden sadness occurred as he remembered his promise to his son to take him to Gallonea to follow in his footsteps one day. Somehow, despite his total belief in seeing his son again, he felt taking him to Gallonea would never be.

"I thought he went missing some years ago?" he inquired.

"Not missing... Captured."

"Captured!? By who? He must have been very strong to have captured a Blessèd."

"Not he. She. His own daughter Medhene. Also known as The Crimson Lady."

"I've heard of her. But why were we told that he went missing?"

"To protect the land from the horrors that really existed. Were they to know a Blessèd Mage was held against their will, the name of The Blessèd Order would be weakened. Medhene didn't want the world to know either, in fear they would find him, and so kept him in secret. Until only recently she was killed."

"Who by?"

Gracène looked in his direction as if it didn't take much to work out who did it.

"Ramalon?" he asked half-knowing.

"Yet another reason why this meeting has been called. You see that man down there? Accompanying him?"

"Yes."

"His name is Mylanus," she indicated to the rather dashing looking Màgjeur with slighter longer hair. "He wasn't known to us until after his escape, but for many years he played the role of Medhene's most trusted, while in secret was in fact sworn to Aristuto and orchestrated his escape. We came to learn it was not possible to inform the outside world of Aristuto's whereabouts in fear of his cover. So he mastered his escape almost single-handedly. Bloody brave boy!"

"Indeed."

"More will come!" Gracène informed. "We will also be joined by a few more guests. Myself, Bella, a man named Ramavell who birthed you all those years ago, who I'm sure will be interested to see you again. He was the one who figured out that you and your brothers hold this mysterious bond over The Dragadelf. And also one of the finest enchanters to have ever existed will be there too. A descendent of one of the founding members of The Protecy and his insight could prove to be the difference between success or failure in stopping your brother."

"What's his name?"

"Clethance. Peculiar things are being discovered about The Protecy, unearthed by The Blessèd Mage of Protecy himself."

"Davinor."

"Yes. Despite his own mastery in the enchantment, there were things he did not understand, bringing his own questions and theories of the practice. Alas, he will not be in attendance tomorrow."

"Why not?"

Gracène looked in his direction in the same fashion as before, indicating the answer.

"Ramalon killed The Blessèd Mage of Protecy!?" he asked eyes wide in disbelief.

"Just another one to his growing list. This one was personal to him. Word has it that it was Davinor that sent Ramalon down the path of darkness and started this catastrophe."

Ramerick felt a little smaller by hearing of his brother's achievements. He began to wonder just what he could do when his brother was undoubtedly smarter and more powerful than himself.

"And this, Clethance, he can help us how?"

"There is one question that we need answering. And he may be the only one alive who can fathom such answer. What really happened thirty years ago when your father died? In particular, what did he do to The Dragastone? Why can both your brothers and presumably yourself create this impression of mastership over The Dragadelf when nothing else could? Confirmation of such a question can help us understand this connection and perhaps just how to defeat your brother! Clethance will tell us all what he believes happened which may just help us stop him."

Ramerick pondered. So many avenues led him to believe that his father's plan was still in motion. It wasn't entirely inconceivable that he may yet play a pivotal role in the story of moving parts.

"And what of Melcelore?" he asked.

"He is locked away inside The Dragasphere. Unknown to us he created a portal which I must say being my field, was the greatest defiance to The Dragasphere imaginable. Alas he continued his plan in secret to one day unleash onto Rèo. But your brother Ramacès put a stop to that," she said with a smile.

He had not thought about Ramacès all too much but learned he was a proud man and similar to himself.

"We may come to learn tomorrow just how he discovered such plan... But for now, The Dragasphere is between him and all he wishes to burn. And so, we let Melcelore rot!"

Suddenly Ramerick's mind went into a spin, warping and twisting in a fashion similar to when Dancès took him on his journey through clairvoyance on Casparia. Although this time, despite his mind being elsewhere, he knew his physical presence remained where he stood on Laloncère.

*His mind's eye was cast to a location he knew all too well. Felders Crest. It instinctively brought back memories of the visions he had experienced many moons ago during clairvoyance with Dancès. The Dragadelf's burning embers onto his father's body came back to memory, the magical moment he said his name, to Melcelore's icy glare, which he could never forget.*

*More potently, the particular image he saw felt more from someone's point of view. It was as if he was directly standing in the middle of Monarchy Hall, clear as day. A combination of icy stabs pinched his face while at the same time feeling a surrounding warmth. It was such an odd yet vivid sensation as he viewed the carnage of Monarchy Hall. It looked battered from pillar to post. The ceiling had been obliterated, seeing the top of The Dragasphere above.*

*However, what drew his gaze and attention most was that similar feeling of invincibility that ran through him in the same way as he had experienced of* late. And it was a lot more immediate than he thought.

For some reason, he could see himself holding The Dragastone, which was as flawless and striking as ever, right before his eyes. Strangely, in addition to the ice and fire he felt, so did two other sensations that he noticed. Gentle sparks tingled his fingertips along with a weightier, more substantial feeling of gravitas in his physique. Such a contrast of affinities confused him and he did not know what it meant. He felt as the stone was his to own in part, sharing its claim with another.

The moving image began to flicker and all of a sudden, he was no longer staring at The Dragastone. Instead, he was now the other side of it, staring directly through its glaring shine and into the eyes of a Màgjeur he now recognised.

"Hello brother," Ramalon confirmed with a hint of amazement.

The first real moment they had come face to face and they bore no love for each other. Mutual hatred and disdain for the other ensued. For Ramalon, it was the feeling that his divinity was challenged and Ramerick for the blame he put on him for Jàque's death.

He could not tell Ramalon's intentions at that moment but did not fear his evil brother as he stared into his cold eyes.

His gaze turned around to inspect the surrounding horror. Lying motionless and butchered on the ground, the body of Melcelore. He recognised the demonic figure immediately through his clairvoyance with Dancès. His chest and abdomen artificially ripped open, the green poison in his eyes was black and dead. The legend of his father's nemesis laid carved, charcoaled and defeated by presumably his brother before him.

Ramerick worked it out. His eyes widened with more realisation of what this all meant. The literal notion that he was standing in Monarchy Hall was proof to him of one thing. Ramalon had gained passage inside The Dragasphere.

Everything began to add up. This was no fabrication and Ramerick understood by all accounts that he had indeed killed the most feared Màgjeur of all time. The realisation sickened him to the core, understanding that he had reached yet another landmark.

The troubling question was why he saw this? Was this a message to send to the world that he was the one to be feared? Or a symbol of gloat? He remained sceptical that it could be some visionary ploy or trap.

Though it did become apparent to him that Ramalon saw him as a threat to whatever it was he wanted to achieve. Otherwise, he would not have seen that at all. Nor for that matter would Ramalon have made a deal with The Ancient Drethai, scorning him and causing the death of Jàqueson. He believed that he *might be the only one to stop Ramalon from achieving his malice with each growing thought.*

He turned back to his sinister-looking brother past the glare of The Dragastone. Ramalon's face did not look like that of someone who had a desire to impress or show off.

Ramerick decided to declare his intent.

"You will pay for what you have done. And it will be me to deliver your end!"

Ramalon's icy stare met with Ramerick's white-hot rage.

*Their vendetta had begun.*

It wasn't too long after their stare into each other's soul that Ramalon looked up toward the sky and unleashed a cataclysmic bolt of fire, connecting with the roof of The Dragasphere with tremendous impact. The ground shook and quaked before Ramerick saw The Dragasphere rapidly crumble under the flames, obliterating to white blinding light.

The connection broke off and Ramerick was staring once more at the feet of his aunt Gracène, lightly panting as he understood what had happened.

"Ramerick?" Gracène asked with concern.

"I saw him…" he replied with eyes darting.

"Saw who?"

"… Ramalon."

Gracène grasped the realisation quickly within her foresight expertise, that he had been connected in some way to a foreign event. She was not worried about his mental state as the bond he just experienced was purely emotional and not physical. Alas, she did not have the skill to view what he saw.

"He spoke to you," she said assuredly.

"And I spoke back," he replied, nodding his head.

"What did you say?"

"I told him what he already knows… That I will be the one to bring his end!"

Gracène sighed with heaviness. She knew this was grave.

"Where did you see him?"

"… Inside. He did it," his mind trailed off in awe of recognising his brother's achievements. "He made it inside The Dragasphere."

Gracène's face was far graver than he'd ever remembered.

"Did you see how?"

He shook his head. "No. But Melcelore is dead! Ramalon killed him!"

After a short pause, the weight in Gracène's demeanour became apparent as she did not believe that was entirely impossible considering the mystery and power of Ramalon.

"How sure can you be?"

"It makes sense now!" he said, more assured of what happened with each growing thought. He turned to the blind eyes of his aunt and spoke with total confidence. "That was my father's plan all along! We've been wrong about this from the start. It was my father who saw his own son become more powerful than them both. I saw Melcelore's body, ripped open by Ramalon. He ended my father's rivalry once and for all!"

"My lad, do not allow yourself to be embellished by prophecy, he is too strong for you. He would not have invaded your mind were it not to reveal exactly what he wanted you to see. Showing you this leads only to peril. If what you saw was true, why would your father destroy a monster, knowing another would take it's place?"

Ramerick pondered. He had not the answer as that truly did not add up.

"I don't know. But this happened. It was more real than anything. There was a moment where I actually was him."

"And what did you feel at that moment?"

He tried to recall his feelings. "Powerful… Invincible in fact. That similar feeling I have felt for so long. But when I was him I felt a whole range of things. Hot and cold, heavy but energised. It was amazing! But what's more, I saw what he plans to do next…"

"My lad?"

His eyes darted with more acceleration, processing how much it made sense. He stumbled upon a recent memory that could help him prove what he instinctively unearthed.

"I need you to find someone for me. I need to speak to the one who has already seen it. I can prove this all Gracène."

"Who is it that you need me to find?"

"Dancès. The Elcarian."

Gracène smiled as if she has heard of him. "I shall find him."

"No need," came the voice of Dancès himself.

In typical fashion, he approached from out of nowhere behind Ramerick. He appeared whole in his standard loose-fitted robes which dangled at the wrists and ankles. His medium-length grey hair dangled by the sides of his temples.

"You have a habit of doing that," Ramerick claimed.

## Initiating Vendetta

"When one's name is requested, I have the skill to be present," his crisp voice spoke. "One of the advantages of being nearly dead."

Ramerick remembered he was no longer something of the material world and more of a version of preservation his soul allowed him to exist. He gave a sly nod toward Gracène, but Ramerick had no awareness for introductions.

"I need you to confirm something for me," he impulsively asked, getting to the heart of his summons.

"I see The Time Stone is no longer in your possession," Dancès figured.

"I suspect you know what happened?"

"I do," he replied, nodding his head. "And for that, you must accept my deepest apologies for not having trust you whence you ventured to Ravenspire… I was a fool. And in fear. You were right to trust your heart."

Ramerick knew it did not matter what happened to The Time Stone in the larger picture. He did not hate him nor despise him. At the time, he helped him escape from Ravenspire with the stone, which at the very least gave him the chance to have those final moments with his son.

"I need to ask you. When you saw this premonition, what exactly did you see?"

"With my limited skill, I saw the collapse of The Dragasphere."

"That's impossible!" Gracène implied. "Nothing could break down the wall!"

"Forgive me but even with my limited skill, I can say in no uncertain terms this will happen! After that I saw The Dragadelf rain fire onto the land by the one they can pledged their allegiance to."

Ramerick's heart thudded in anticipation for the answer to the vital question.

"And who, did you see was the one they answered to?"

"I am sorry to say, but that part alluded my skill, my friend."

And just like that, it appeared to confirm Ramerick's suspicion.

"It's Ramalon!" he confidently clarified. "It was always going to be him!"

"Your brother?" Dancès replied with equal concern, remembering his name when clairvoyanting back on Casparia.

"You saw the collapse of The Dragasphere once Melcelore had The Time Stone."

"That would assume to be correct. Upon reflection, once he had the stone in his possession he could have caused it's destruction and dismantle it!"

"But Melcelore never got The Time Stone as you now know. And yet, you have seen this happen anyway. Which means there is only one other explanation as to who could have destroyed it."

Dancès looked toward Gracène, who already knew what was to be said and gently nodded to confirm with growing assurance.

"The one The Dragadelf answered to, the collapse of The Dragasphere, all of it, was never going to be Melcelore," his eyes trailed off again. "We're in more danger than we realise! We must stop him. Otherwise what you saw will be upon us!"

"And how do you propose we do that, my lad?" Gracène worryingly weighed in, half expecting any plan to be futile now that it has been confirmed in Dancès' premonition.

"The only thing we can… The Dragasphere must not fall."

Ramerick raced down the hallways of Laloncère, skudding around corners to inform his mother of what he had learned. He was so sure of it. That connection he felt with his brother was undeniably genuine and he saw first hand Ramalon's intention. It would match entirely the ambition of an evil that has plagued to such heights.

Gracène had let Ramerick know where his mother's chambers were, and despite not knowing exactly, it was not difficult to navigate around the structures. He ascended a few flights of stairs and approached a magnificently crafted archway carved from stone. As he passed through it, he came to a circular garden surrounded by the an elaborate stoney architecture. In the centre was a raised platform in the where he presumed his mother could be found in her chambers. There were no windows just like many other chambers within Laloncère, as the valley provided a particular warmth and shelter from the wind. The woven pillars met at the top to create a wonderfully entwined dome. Below it sat Eveleve, releasing gentle energy into various plants and flowers that flourished at her touch. A hint of white symbolic of purity and life seemed to blossom from her hand, landing on the plethora of flora.

"He's inside!" he shouted to his mother as he hurried up the steps of the raised platform.

"Ramerick?" She looked up to find her son skidding to a halt before her, hands on his knees as he tried to catch his breath.

"Ramalon. He's inside The Dragasphere!" he panted.

"That's impossible," she said with a dismissive shake of her head.
"No. It's not. I've just seen it."
"Seen it how?"
"Something connected me to him. I don't know if he meant the connection or not but he also showed me what he plans to do. He's going to destroy The Dragasphere! We have to stop him!"
"Tell me what you saw."
Ramerick gazed downwards as he replayed the images. "I stood there. Right where father died. And I saw him!"
"You saw your father?"
Ramerick shook his head. "No! I saw Ramalon! And I spoke to him."
Eveleve waved her hand in front to stop him from speaking before dashing over to one of the nearby trees that looked hundreds of years old. She placed her hand on the crisp, dry bark and although nothing appeared to happen physically, Ramerick suddenly felt a wave of energy breathe through him. It was the strangest sensation he had ever experienced and he wondered why his mother would have done that. She released her hand and turned back up toward her son.
"What was that about?"
"We need to be so careful now. The simple fact that he has made contact with you concerns me. We cannot allow him to see our plans. I have instilled additional essences of life into everything that is good and green on Laloncère. If he can infiltrate your mind, he can see our intentions. This will stop him from doing so, for he is the symbol of evil that life will always repel!"
Suddenly the tree she had instilled gradually and delicately began to smoothen out, suddenly more revitalised in its appearance. As too did the rest of the garden which started to grow exponentially. Blossoms of flowers began to flourish, mixing with the dazzling autumnal colours. The forestry spread not just around Eveleve's chambers but also beyond, slowly up the slope of Laloncère and around, almost jungle-like but with more elegance. She had demonstrated her powers of life, giving it extra protection to all that would harm what's good and green.
"The power of royal blood," she said. "He knows who you are, and now where you are. You have the blood that he needs to claim full right over The Dragadelf."
"Mother, I think I've found the truth as to what connects us all and truly why he wants me dead."
"Why?"

"It's The Dragastone."

"What makes you think this?"

"I saw it. I saw it through his eyes, and then through mine, more real than anything. It was right in front of us both and it felt undeniably ours. I don't know how it connects us to The Dragadelf but it must be that."

"The Dragastone…" Eveleve pondered as if it was something she had previously considered. "That would explain a number of things. Exactly how, will hopefully be explained tomorrow. What else did you see?"

"I saw The Dragasphere collapse."

"That will not happen."

"Mother, I've just confirmed it with Dancès. The premonition he told me about matches this entirely. He said The Dragasphere will be destroyed and once that happens all on Terrasendia will perish. He originally presumed it would have been Melcelore to do it, but mother, Melcelore is dead."

"Gracelands!" she murmured, her mouth slightly agape, trying to fathom whether this was all possible.

"Ramalon showed me that it was by his hand. And I don't find that so hard to believe. I think that's what father's plan was all along. He saw Ramalon would become what he has and perhaps felt he was a necessary evil. Perhaps the only way to stop Melcelore from undoing the spell himself."

"That makes no sense son. Why would your father foresee this plan in allowing the demise of one monster, only to create another far more powerful and more of a threat to us all?" Ramerick pondered. He had not the answer as that would not make sense in his mind either. "On top of that," she continued, "how would he have gained passage? The Draughts, we have come to learn, were the only way inside or out and that took Melcelore decades to construct."

"I don't know. But let's imagine this is true and that he did find a way in. With everything that Ramalon has achieved to this point, could we really doubt he would be strong enough to defeat him?"

Eveleve began to admit a sense of truth. Alas, she did not feel entirely confident and was ultimately conflicted. Premonitions were not exactly preludes and were looked upon with great skepticism, but the establishment her son made with The Dragastone was indeed substantial.

"Why would Ramalon show you this if it were true?"

"I honestly don't know."

"It is not that I doubt what you saw. I am anxious because, why would you see this if it wasn't for Ramalon's gain? That's what worries me."

"Can we really ignore this? What if it really does happen? What if The Dragasphere really does collapse? What then? Will we just try and fight him when he comes?"

Eveleve sighed. She knew the risk was too significant to do nothing.

"That is something the Order must decide. But even I have to admit, this is beginning to make more sense. If your father really did foresee this, then I believe we are further away from the truth than we thought."

Ramerick clocked a small change in his mother's eyes to suggest that she had just realised something important.

"Mother?"

"Yes son?" she replied, trying to hide her realisation.

"What is it?"

"Nothing… Just a lot to take in thats all."

Ramerick chose not to probe but couldn't forget that moment.

"The link you have with The Dragastone could also explain your feelings of late. Of how impulsive and reckless you say you've felt. Maybe the connection has just grown progressively stronger."

Ramerick hummed in acknowledgement as that could well be true.

"But I haven't enchanted The Protecy yet."

"Another question we will have for the summoning. You may not need to have to experience its presence. Clethance may shed light on The Dragastone which may lead to more answers."

Ramerick noticed the white, entwining necklace that draped over her neckline, resting on her chest. A tiny orb in the middle gave the gentlest sparkle which did not come from a reflection, more a creation of light itself.

"Is that yours," he asked, indicating to the necklace? "Your protecy stone?"

Eveleve smiled. "How did you work that out?"

"I didn't. I don't know much about magic and all that energy stuff."

"We should never really let on to anybody where our stones lie. It's the unwritten rule."

"You don't trust me?" he asked with irony.

"With my life." She unclipped the necklace and held it delicately in her hands. "This is the smallest protecy stone ever known. It has been in the family since the beginning of The Protecy many years ago. Naturally, it will pass on to you."

"Not for many years I hope!"

Eveleve forced a smile, but her eyes did not follow suit. It was the same type of cover-up that he saw moments ago and he knew she was not telling him something.

"But all in time," she quickly said. "The most important thing right now, is that we need to work out *your* role in restoring balance to Terrasendia. Something tells me if we are to trust your father's purpose, we must believe in you."

Before Ramerick could find the appropriate question to ask, a Questacèrean maid approached. Her gown immaculately fitted with woven stitchings providing an elegant finish.

"All your guests have arrived Lady Eveleve. Shall I inform them to convene tomorrow noon as planned?"

"No. It must happen now."

Eveleve looked toward Ramerick. Both their hearts started to beat a little faster, slightly fearful of what challenge truly lay ahead as they were about to embark on the first step to stop Ramalon.

# The Summoning of The Blessèd Order

"Seldom is such a momentous moment," Eveleve began. "Alas, this is not a usual time. We are living a truly unprecedented attack on all that is good and green. This rare occasion, where the spawn of Sarthanzar has never been so real, is upon us, and it falls on each and every one of us to answer the peril of Ramalon. Make no assumption that what I am about to reveal is not true, because what we thought was impossible, has now become a genuine threat… Ramalon has entered The Dragasphere. And we believe he intends to use his unimaginable power to bring it down. I call upon us all to understand the threat we face and protect that which we were placed on this world to defend in this truly exceptional time."

Intense silence met her opening statement as the remaining

members of The Blessèd Order sat frozen on their seats of stone, absorbing the gravitas of such peril. They realised what was at stake and how grave the situation had become.

The summoning took place where Ramerick first saw his mother on the circular platform atop of Laloncère. The diminishing sun flickered off the vast lake, setting the tone of an ever-darker situation. The moon was not yet in full view, still more of a crescent silhouette in the fading sky.

Rarely did The Blessèd Order come together as some of their differences often collided. The very fact that they had all answered the call ultimately proved how serious they took the threat. The common ground they shared in the protection of Terrasendia eventually overcame all differences: uniting them with that one purpose.

Because of what Ramerick saw, Eveleve was stringent in bringing the timing of the meeting forward. The Blessèd had only just arrived. She spearheaded the gathering while Ramerick sat next to both Gracène and Mirabella to one side. The chairs made of stone were all placed in a circle, so everyone was in full view of each other.

In attendance were the remaining members of The Blessèd Order: Aristuto, Ethelba, Wemberlè, and Zathos were more recognisable to Ramerick. However, it did not take him long to work out the others, who were lesser-known.

Going around the circle, a rather large man dressed in cool, ice-blue robes was undoubtedly The Blessèd Mage of Ice and King of Questacère - King Thorian Mijkal.

Next to him sat a sturdy and robust dwarf whose physical appearance was short and stout. Ramerick knew him as The Blessèd Mage of Gravitas, who also was the King of the dwarves in Handenmar - King Thakendrax. He knew where the capital of Dwardelfia was and knew he had journeyed an awful long way to get to Laloncère.

Though not entirely necessary, Eveleve asked two more chairs made of stone to be placed directly opposite her. They both sat empty as they separated Thakendrax and the next Màgjeur, who was much older and undoubtedly The Blessèd Mage of The Mind - Lestas Magraw. Ramerick wondered briefly why his mother thought that necessary before continuing his perusal of the council members.

Next to him was a man in more tatty black robes, matted black hair, whose appearance was ragged and gave the impression almost that he was homeless. That had to be Mavokai, The Blessèd Mage of Death, he

## The Summoning of The Blessèd Order

thought.

The other next to him was slightly more normal, bearing light beige robes and a stern looking face caused by high cheekbones and an intense stare. He worked out that this was Max Meigar, who often glanced toward Ramerick with a subtle indication that he was of interest to him before breaking eye-contact to soften the tension.

He experienced a wave of subtle sadness, as he realised he would not necessarily have known the names of some of them were it not for his son's Blessèd Wheel he constructed many moons ago.

Completing the others in attendance was another elderly man in fine black robes with a claret underlining on the inside who Gracène mentioned briefly was Ramavell, the man who birthed him thirty years ago. And lastly a man who he did not recognise.

*"That must be Clethance,"* he thought.

A smaller man who seemed to be easily in his seventies. His eyes were a little slanted and almond-shaped, droopy wrinkled skin sagged under his eyes and cheekbones. Along with everyone in attendance, he was eager to explain his expertise.

"You may be asking yourself how can we be sure that The Dragasphere is at risk of collapsing?" Eveleve continued. "We have received word of a premonition by a man whose insight into true clairvoyance is reliable, and he has seen its destruction. Usually, premonitions are not foundations to act upon, but twin that with the connections and events that have unfolded, we cannot ignore the possibility. I'm sure you're all aware by now of the power Ramalon has acquired."

Some of The Blessèd Order noticed the empty chairs in the circle where Felder and Davinor would have sat. They were considered the head and deputy head of the Order.

"As some of you know, I have been in hiding for thirty years. This was not by choice of my own. I have learned it was all a vital role, in a far wider part to play in my husband's plan. A plan to acquire peace which, to my knowledge, is still in motion. To defeat the darkest Màgjeur Terrasendia has ever suffered, he had to construct a plan that was far more complex than we could ever have imagined. Our duty is to ensure its completion - despite what we have just learned. Melcelore is dead," she confirmed with additional weight to her words.

Everyone in attendance was already listening sharply and seemed to take the news of the death of Felder's killer with skepticism rather than relief. "His death was only part of his plan and we now need to discuss the next step."

"Dead? How?" Magraw asked.

"By the hand of Ramalon himself. Who I may add now for those who do not know is my son."

Magraw looked sideways to some of the other members to see if they shared similar intrigue, to which they did.

"Thirty years ago I gave birth. Successfully may I add thanks to Ramavell here," she indicated the older Màgjeur who returned the gratification with a gentle smile and nod of the head. "Alas, I gave birth to triplets who I had to say goodbye to the moment they were born."

Ramerick immediately looked into his mother's eyes to gauge how she would emotionally react to having declared that. Her brave face and confident tone was an exceptional mask to the pain he saw through her eyes.

"And to say I am lucky they all survived would not be entirely accurate." The sharpness in the conversation rose upon hearing that. Some clearly knew of the truth surrounding her sons. "One of them I can proudly say is sitting among us today," she declared looking sideways to Ramerick, who in return looked a little embarrassed. Not a bashfulness like a kid surrounded by his friends and his mother telling him how much she loves him, but it was instead the notion that he didn't want to draw too much attention.

"Good Gracelands," Mavokai happily claimed with a smile, exposing his ginger teeth. "He looks like a bloody Blood Monarch for sure!"

"He has his father's ferocity!" Ramavell praised.

"Hear hear!" Max Meigar also said with an approving nod of the head toward him. That profound eye contact was there again before turning back to Eveleve.

"Yes, he is alive thanks to my sister and Mirabella. He would not be here today were it not part of my husband's plan to keep him and my other two boys safe. But as you may have worked out, he is Ramalon's brother, as is another. Ramacès died trying to stop his evil upon us. Struck down by that very same evil. If there is any measurable doubt in your minds as to the lengths Ramalon will go to have his desires are fulfilled, just look to how he is responsible for the death of his own brother. Let that fact serve as proof that he will stop at nothing!" Eveleve grew quiet at that to collect her emotion at mentioning her son's fate.

# The Summoning of The Blessèd Order

Again, some like Meigar already fathomed this with his experience with Ramacès. However, for others it was new information.

"There is something that binds my three sons with a connection far more potent than just their monarchy blood. This bond has given both Ramalon and Ramacès the experience of controlling The Dragadelf. With the help of Clethance, he will explain how."

"Forgive me, my lady," Thakendrax interrupted in his stern, deep, gravelled voice. "You say your husband artificially and deliberately created a monster in your son, only to defeat another? Why on Rèo would he do that only to give us a far graver problem?"

Ramerick had thought that was particularly concerning, given the same question was asked several times already.

"Because it was the only solution strong enough to defeat Melcelore. He became too strong, even for my husband. For many years he intended to bring down The Dragasphere and must have believed during his deliberate imprisonment that he would triumph. But it seems my husband saw right through that," she triumphed with a small smile, "and allowed his own son to conclude their rivalry."

"That still does not answer the question. Why would Felder see all of this, giving Ramalon this power, rising to destroy the most feared Màgjeur of all time while ultimately becoming more of a threat? It is far more perilous and does not make sense!"

"Though I do not have the answer, Master Dwarf, everything points to one concept."

"Which is?"

"That his plan is still in motion... through him." Eveleve slowly looked to Ramerick again, followed by the rest of the Order, until they all stared at him. "The balance of good and evil lays within him. The only way to stop Melcelore was indeed by Ramalon, and now it seems the only way to stop Ramalon is through Ramerick. I am compelled to believe that was my husband's plan."

"And I suppose your husband left you a note telling us exactly how he is to restore this balance?"

Eveleve ignored the disrespectful slight to her late husband before continuing.

"No, he did not. There were many things he did not tell me, for I would have likely stopped much of his plan were I to have known of my children's fates."

Thakendrax shook his head. Dwarves were not known for their openness. "Prophecies and visions are suspicious even in trusted hands. I am also struggling to understand the immediate threat that is alleged for one simple reason. Ramalon would not have been able to enter The Dragasphere in the first place," he sternly claimed. Lestas Magraw and Thorian Mijkal nodded their head in agreement.

"I understand your doubts," Eveleve calmly said.

"He has entered it." Meigar confirmed forcefully, with all eyes now turned to The Blessèd Mage of Earth. "It was his intention all along. Ramacès died trying to stop him. If we have information that he is inside, we cannot ignore it like The Lady of Life has said."

"Superstitious are we, Meigar?" Thakendrax rhetorically asked.

"That's not helpful, King Dwarf."

"I think you forget that when we constructed The Dragasphere, nothing went in, and nothing went out. Only in the land of fantasy can impossibilities occur, a land you have always been living in, eh Max?" he snarled stubbornly.

"Master Dwarf!" Eveleve interrupted. "I implore you to be sensitive."

"How can we be so sure he is inside?" Thorian Mijkal asked, pressing the issue.

"I've seen it…" Ramerick announced.

The meeting turned very cold indeed. Not in a temperature sense, but more a bone chilling tone that Ramerick's first spoken words were of concern.

"You've *seen* it?" Mijkal slowly asked, unconvinced.

"Yes. I was connected to him moments before this meeting. And I saw him inside Monarchy Hall. I saw Melcelore's body carved like a piece of meat. He spoke to me and showed me precisely what he wanted to do -"

"- You were connected to Ramalon?" Magraw said incredulously. "And we're having this conversation as openly as we are? He could be watching right now!"

"Do not be alarmed, Lestas," Eveleve assured. "Despite Ramalon's arm of power, he can not reach us here. I have made assurances of that."

"So we're basing the level of this threat on the vision of a simple nobleman?" Mijkal asked.

"It's not just that," Meigar defended. "It's the sense that everything Ramalon has demonstrated so far leads us to believe this is upon us."

"Ah, come now, Master Meigar. I believed we were here on credible information, not dreams and wishes."

## The Summoning of The Blessèd Order

"Would it be easier for you to understand if I used the term *nightmares?*"

"Max!" the Questacèrean King attempted to reason.

"Wake up from your stubbornness!" Meigar beseeched. "For those that do not believe the seriousness of this, it is a far graver threat than we have ever seen. I appreciate the icy temperatures in Lathapràcère have numbed your mind, but do not underestimate Ramalon!"

"I'm not even going to attempt to reason with such stubborn belief in a fantasy!"

"My friends!" Eveleve tried to neutralise the tension. "We do not always see eye to eye -"

"- Couldn't be more truthful!" Magraw claimed.

"But we all each have a responsibility, and I urge you to not to turn away from yours. We all must remain open, even though at times the threat may seem unlikely and even impossible. But that is our duty!" Eveleve reminded with more impetus.

Tensions simmered down gently, though the sharpness in the atmosphere was still rife.

"I also find it very difficult to believe," Thakendrax picked up albeit in a more sensible tone, "that Ramalon could become more powerful than the darkest Màgjeur ever to set foot on Rèo."

"This is where I would like Clethance to explain," she indicated that it was time for him to shed light on the concern. He gave a gratified nod back to her before clearing his throat.

"Thank you, and good evening," he confidently said, his words sharply pronounced. "I am Clethance, and as some of you may know, I am the last living descendant of Zoldathorn…"

The summoning became somewhat bemused. Furrowed eyebrows and sideways glances ensued.

"Zoldathorn?" Mijkal inquired dubiously.

"Yes. The founder of The Protecy."

"It is common knowledge that The Protecy was invented by a small band of enchanters and not just one," Magraw ponced.

"That is correct to common knowledge, but in truth, Zoldathorn was the pioneer. He was a superstitious man. He did not want his name tarnished was it to be used for such evil. He worked closely with the others and they all decided to announce the practice as a collective responsibility."

"So what do you bring to the table?"

"Through simple bloodline, his extraordinary understanding hath passed to me. There are nuances and intricacies I have inherited that are - how do I put this delicately? Beyond you."

Magraw instantly choked at the insult, striking a reminiscent scowl of somebody who just swallowed a wasp. Meigar tried to hide an entertaining smirk at his expense and took an instant liking to Clethance.

"Less insightful, maybe a better term?" an offended Magraw suggested, biting his tongue.

"I am under no illusion the knowledge you all hold is utterly divine in your own paths, but forgive me for saying there is much about The Protecy that you do not understand. Davinor was perhaps the only one who delved into the practice's understanding to such length and detail, which I have to say was impressive. Alas, he is not here."

"And we shall get to him in due course. Clethance, can you explain to us what you think happened thirty years ago? There is clearly some connection with what my husband did when we created The Dragasphere and the power Ramalon possesses."

"For that, I bring your attention to The Dragastone and what Felder appeared to have done to it. It wasn't until Ramavell here had suggested there may have been an irregularity when it crashed down on that day."

Ramavell and Clethance were good friends. They had known each other for many years, and it was because of Ramavell's suspicion, which sought the advice from Clethance to determine that there was more to be understood regarding The Dragastone.

"Cast your mind back to that day..." Clethance continued. "As we now know, The Dragastone did not crash into Monarchy Hall by sheer chance. It was orchestrated by Melcelore. From what Lady Eveleve has learned to me, it is without question something Felder foresaw but was unable to stop. Because of this notion, he had no choice but to let it crash into the capital and forge his plan in secret. The plan to defeat Melcelore even in his death."

"Speak clearly, enchanter," Thakendrax suggested, looking rather frustrated at what appeared to be overwhelming information.

"As Felder already enchanted his protecy he could never use the stone for himself, not unless performing such acts of evil which Melcelore would have done. Instead, with what was presumed to be in his last moments, he implanted a rune of ownership onto The Dragastone. But instead of keeping it to himself, he gave that ownership to someone else..."

# The Summoning of The Blessèd Order

"To Ramalon," Eveleve worked out.

"Yes. To Ramalon, but also his other two newly born sons," he intriguingly revealed, looking at Ramerick.

Everyone's heads turned back toward Ramerick, who was surprised to hear almost confirmation with what he half new in that he has some establishment with The Dragastone. It would explain why he had felt so impulsive and invincible of late.

"And in the process," Clethance continued, "activated a so-called three-way protecy, which has never been seen before. As The Dragastone did not come from Rèo the convention is different, and therefore does not interrupt the natural concept of The Protecy. This would allow all three of his sons to enchant their own protecy as normal, whilst unknown to them, have their energies flow through The Dragastone and receive a magnification, a boost of it's power if you will, to devastating effect. That is as simply as I can possibly explain, the reason why Ramalon has become the power he has..."

"Gracelands..." Ramavell uttered, taking a moment to digest.

"Forgive me Clethance," Wemberlè said, "but I thought you could never pass your powers onto another?"

"That is a misconception. It is seldom known, but to give your protecy to someone else, the owner's life must be sacrificed, which it was in Felders last moments."

"It would make complete sense," Eveleve speculated. "The only way to stop Melcelore was to make his son even more powerful than him."

"Correct."

"But again we come back to the baffling notion as to why he would do that, knowing an even bigger threat would consume us," Thakendrax argued, landing on a truth that no one had the answer to.

"I can only share with you my expertise," Clethance continued. "I also fear that in addition to understanding this before us, Ramalon has put us at a disadvantage. He would naturally have had time to develop the bond he has with The Dragastone and enhance his power further. May I ask if anyone here knew of him in his early stages?"

The meeting fell silent, looking at one another.

"I first came across Ramalon during the first round of The Màgjeurs Open," Magraw announced.

"And considering the alleged power he has now shown, I am assuming he was not as strong as today?"

"Correct," Magraw admitted with reluctance. "That was the first real moment Davinor became obsessed with his power."

"How is this relevant?" Eveleve asked.

"Learning about the activity and behaviour of his early experience with The Protecy could help understand his trajectory," Clethance said. "The insurmountable energy would not have been apparent to him in his early stages of The Protecy, purely because his understanding of how to relax the connection was not as advanced. Improving the connection is crucial for him to ascertain more power. It now seems like it is only a matter of time before he understands just how to do that. And what is more, I fear he has yet to discover its full potential. Twin that with the darker path he has gone down, fletching from others giving him this terrible ability to inflict multiple affinities."

Ramerick had a thought. He remembered the feelings he experienced earlier that day when he was connected to Ramalon.

"Forgive me, enchanter," Mavokai said, "but in your opinion, is it possible for any Màgjeur to fletch more than two affinities?"

"What makes you ask?"

"Being my field, when one fletches it involves ripping a part of someone's existence. Unlike Soul Mancing where it rips a part of another's soul, fletching secretly rips a part of you as it is a service to death. Not many people to exist have enough evil inside them to withstand the intense threshold the practice entails, let alone to achieve it more than once. Even Melcelore did not have enough malice to withstand its self-barbarity on multiple occasions. I guess the question I am asking is if there is a way The Dragastone could give Ramalon that higher threshold to fletch multiple affinities?"

"Oh yes, I believe it can. And not just twice. I fear he will realise that for him, there is no threshold…"

"He's already done it…" Ramerick announced, bringing a chilling tone to the summoning. "I felt them. When I connected with him. It's like I felt everything he could. Hot, cold. Heavy but energised. I'm guessing those are affinities of fire and maybe ice? And perhaps earth and air? Or maybe electricity, I can't be sure."

"If what you felt was true, Ramerick," Clethance continued, "it would confirm that the potential Ramalon could achieve surpasses the imagination of many sitting here. Melcelore's main affinity was indeed with ice, and so it only adds to the suggestion that he did truly kill him. What's more, The Dragastone would give him that additional defence to darker paths and go into a territory that no Màgjeur has gone to since the days of Sarthanzar…"

# The Summoning of The Blessèd Order

Clethance paused to allow the information to sink in before gently continuing his lesson. By that point, the sun had set and the crescent moon was shining its blue onto Laloncère, which was well lit by candle fire and torches. Reminiscent of how dark their realisation of what was growing inside Ramalon.

"Just what is his limit? What is Ramalon really capable of? Could he truly bring down The Dragasphere? After what we are uncovering, is it impossible for Ramalon to achieve such an unprecedented landmark?"

"Yes," Magraw barked arrogantly.

"Impossible," Thorian Mijkal also stated. "Despite what we are learning, the combined power of The Blessèd Order outweighs the current strength of Ramalon, I am sure of it."

"Have you seen him first hand?" Meigar challenged. "Have you seen his power demonstrated before you?"

"No, I haven't, but that's irrelevant."

"We have," Zathos contributed in his bouncing voice. "And I felt it first hand. My volts connected with his, and I tell you all… It was the strongest thing I have ever felt in my life!"

Zathos' concerns were greatly noted. He rarely spoke, and so when he did, people listened. It did partially simmer down the fears of Mijkal and Magraw, who still were not utterly convinced.

"What did it feel like, Master of Volts? To engage with Ramalon?" Clethance asked.

"Honestly?… I felt I was going to die," Zathos admitted. "Like fighting something unnatural. The supernatural. No matter how hard I tried, he not only matched my efforts but surpassed them. And what worries me is that it did not seem difficult for him. He felt almost thrilled by the challenge. He understood very clearly at that moment, that he was far stronger than myself. And perhaps all of us combined…"

Despite Zathos' rare admittance, it did not sway the perception of Magraw, Thakendrax and Mijkal, who still had huge doubts.

"This is all assuming of course, that Ramalon has entered The Dragasphere, which I still maintain is a totally outrageous claim!" Magraw declared. "If Ramalon has acquired this certain power, he would never have been able to use it to gain passage!"

"I too agree," Thakendrax offered his support. "We cast it ourselves. The combined power of The Blessèd Order could never be breached, let alone by one man."

"But it has been breached King Dwarf!" Meigar argued.

"Melcelore's construction of The Draughts defied it outright."

"That is a true exception! The dark Màgjeur's concealment was too masterful, taking many years to construct. Ramalon could never have done such a thing with the time he has had on his darker path!"

"I strongly disagree. Suppose there was one way in and out of The Dragasphere, which leaves the potential for another. After all, each and every one of us agreed to blind our own eyes to what is inside to make absolutely sure nothing else could see in or out."

"Choose your next words carefully, Meigar," Magraw warned.

"Whom may I ask suggested that in the first place?" Clethance asked.

"Davinor," Meigar answered with slight reluctance, in fear to inflame Magraw's undying loyalty.

Clethance's eyes drew downward in thought as he hummed inquisitively. He became increasingly alarmed at a certain hypothesis.

"Why would that be relevant?" Eveleve asked.

"When you created The Dragasphere you created it with the intention that nothing could pass through its walls. Can I ask you all to search the very bizarre extremities of possibility here? Is there any chance whatsoever that a passageway could *secretly* have been created? By one of you?"

The members of the Order actively looked around at one another.

"Are you suggesting that we have a traitor on this council?" Magraw questioned incredulously.

"Traitor? No. Davinor is not here and yet, he did suggest that the eyes of The Blessèd Order be blind to all that was inside. What if he suggested such a thing for his own gain?"

"Preposterous!" Magraw spluttered, coughing as he exclaimed. "Davinor was a tremendous servant to all that is good and green!"

"I admire your loyalty to defend him, but it seems a perfect fit. A more simple answer to the question of how Ramalon entered The Dragasphere."

"He hasn't entered The Dragasphere! I cannot listen to such nonsense being repeated over and over again." Magraw came to stand, seemingly at the end of his patience.

"Lestas!" Eveleve forcefully said. "We must not rule anything out."

"I agree," Mavokai stated quickly along with several other members.

"I appreciate that Davinor had his flaws," Magraw admitted. "He started this all, twisting the knife into Ramalon's mind for his own

# The Summoning of The Blessèd Order

selfish greed, but he did pay for it with his life! And I urge the Order to remember all he has contributed to our understanding of The Protecy. We cannot tarnish his name because of some theory!"

"Lestas," Mavokai interrupted. "This does make sense. After all, we know that Davinor is not dead in his entirety. His body yes, killed by Ramalon. But not his soul. It was heinously butchered only for Ramalon to take for his own."

"And if Davinor did create somewhere, somehow a gate into The Dragasphere," Meigar contributed. "Then Ramalon would be able to access the same right as the passage would recognise Davinor's presence within him."

Magraw huffed and shook his head.

"You cannot deny that suspicions over how Davinor could use more than one form of protecy were rife."

"That's absurd! He was divine by right!"

"Only in his knowledge of protecy stones," Clethance confirmed. His confidence did not seem to wilt in the presence of such prestigious individuals. "Not in his right to use more than one affinity of the same path. His understanding of The Protecy and his divinity was classed because he understood protecy stones like no other, myself not included in that bracket. I truly believe that Davinor blinded the eyes of The Blessèd Order for him to practice the darker platform of fletching."

"A very serious and damaging accusation! What proof do you have?" Magraw asked

"None," Clethance admitted, which was met with an arrogant bounce of laughter from Magraw. "But it is irrefutable that he broke your trust. Only in the last twenty or so years has he been able to demonstrate more lines of affinity. Once The Dragasphere was constructed, he could have used the first ten years to practice his darker deeds. Enriching himself in this divine attribute to use more than one affinity. It would give the impression of his natural divinity rather than the falsehood he demonstrated all these years. An artificial empowerment, if you will. And who could see what he was up to as your eyes were blinded upon his suggestion!" The seed of doubt he had planted was beginning to take root in the council's minds, but Magraw rejected it, unable to accept the truth.

"Now that is just slandering the name and sovereignty of everyone here!" Magraw impulsively claimed.

However, the reaction from the rest of the Order did suggest that

Magraw was on his own. Not even Thakendrax and Mijkal could muster any support. His isolation gave more proof that Clethance's accusation was beginning to land on several truths, making perfect sense, which the Order started to believe.

"Lestas," Eveleve calmly said. "Please sit."

After recognising that he was by himself, he huffed once more and gave a gentle nod of the head out of respect.

"My lady," he reluctantly said, returning to his chair and turning silent.

A familiar pause distilled the meeting once more to process the betrayal of Davinor. It seemed ever more likely and logical that what he was being accused of had credibility. Magraw however, remained stubbornly loyal to him.

"Whilst we are on the subject of multiple affinities, I do have another question master enchanter," Wemberlè delicately asked. "You said earlier it was against the law of protecy for a Màgjeur to legally enchant more than one affinity. I'm curious. It has never made sense to me how Felder could enchant The Protecy of fire and time both."

"An essential question Lady Wemberlè. And the answer to which only strengthens the case for Davinor's illegality. Affinities are actually divided into two main categories. You have your destructive affinities, fire, water, air, earth, ice and volts, which are more common. And you also have what I call manipulative affinities, which protecy stones can enhance the use of. For instance, time, gravity, so on and so forth. There are darker routes of affinities also, clairvoyance, conjuration, fletching and Soul Mancing, to name a few. What Màgjeurs are not so aware of is that you can enchant one affinity of both paths. The structure of magic that binds The Protecy can allow only the very adept of Màgjeurs to ascertain both paths. Alas, one must be destructive and one manipulative; you cannot have two of the same unless you fletch. Felder was known for his mastery of time and fire because his strength and understanding legally allowed both."

The fascinating discovery was new to almost every Blessèd Màgjeur on the council.

"But we already have a Blessèd Mage of Fire," Wemberlè indicated to the silent Ethelba next to her. Her petite body was so small; her feet did not touch the ground. Her cute tail however, did, remaining calm and collected.

"Correct, but Felder's affinity was not with fire and I very much doubt he would have won a firefight with yourself," he indicated to

# The Summonìng of The Blessèd Order

Ethelba.

"So you're saying that potentially I could enchant a destructive affinity, enchanter?" Mavokai asked.

"Potentially yes. But the question and ultimate risk is, would your body withstand the intensity of both paths? It is a heavy burden which Felder was strong enough to carry."

"So if I attempted to enchant, ice for example, what would happen?"

"The Protecy will either reject you before the process commences or accept if your constitution matches. If that happens and your body really cannot take its intensity, you will be forever trapped by the weight of having two paths."

"So it's not a clear case of, if it works it works, and if it doesn't, it doesn't?"

"Absolutely not, no! This is why it is not common knowledge. Imagine the allure of Màgjeurs trying to enchant both paths and ultimately not knowing the risk if their bodies are not strong enough? Paralysation, suffocation, extreme vulnerability are all some of the symptoms that could ensue."

"Would my husband have known this?" Eveleve asked.

"It's unclear. Forgive me for saying this, but I believe that Felder alone could be the only one strong enough to have withstood the use of both lines."

Magraw rolled his eyes at the notion he would not be strong enough.

"How could this help us understand what we know of Ramalon?" Meigar asked.

"It could confirm several things. My understanding is that Ramalon killed and fletched from Master Aristuto's daughter, Medhene? Is this correct?" he asked of The Blessèd Mage of Air.

Aristuto's face was calm, but he listened to every word. His release from his capture for many years had come as a timely boost for the Order. He gently nodded his head in reply.

"It is good to have you back, my friend." Mavokai smiled to him, remembering the sacrifice he was willing to give in exchange for his release, which never happened due to the dishonour and deception of The Crimson Lady.

"Thank you. Out of the frying pan and into the fire, it would seem."

"Under usual circumstance," Clethance continued, "when one fletches they would simply take the same level of strength from that victims protecy. However I fear it matters not how strong a Màgjeur

Ramalon would fletch from, as whatever affinity he would chose to conjure would in effect receive the same magnification of power from The Dragastone. Your daughter had the darker affinity of clairvoyance. Ramalon would have certainly fletched that from her as well as her affinity of volts. This proves two things. One, like fletching, he can withstand the threshold of both routes of destructive and manipulative affinities because of The Dragastone's power. And two, he now has the skill through clairvoyance to connect with Ramerick. This exposes us."

"I am concerned with this connection," Mijkal said. "Even more so now that we have learned the connection happens on Ramalon's terms."

"That is a concern of mine too," Mavokai admitted. "You say you connected with him as if you were him, and then you weren't? It seems specific, deliberate in fact."

"Correct!" Mijkal acknowledged. "This is not encouraging, I must say."

"And also this premonition, I cannot seem to find the will to agree with it." Thakendrax chipped in. "Together, it seems like the work of manipulation. We cannot act on what Ramalon wants us to see."

"But can we do nothing, Master Dwarf?" Zathos asked.

"If that's what it takes to let the evil of Sarthanzar rot, then so be it!"

"What's to say he can't escape The Dragasphere?" Wemberlè asked. "Surely, if he has found a way in, he can find a way out too!"

"I'm not sure he'd want to escape," Ramerick said. "It seems like he has everything where he wants. He seems very methodical and the only way he's coming out is if he really does destroy The Dragasphere."

"Which he will not be able to achieve under any circumstances." Thakendrax states confidently. "So let him rot in the pile of filth he has created for himself."

"So you would have us do nothing?" Wemberlè asked Thakendrax.

"It's worked for the past thirty years!"

"Typical mindset!" she tutted.

"Slandering my people, are we?"

"Not your people. Just you!"

"My Lady!" Mijkal attempted to mediate.

"How dare you!" Thakendrax fought back as he came to stand abruptly.

"The threat of Ramalon is real!" she claimed, coming to stand also. "And we must act if we are to stop him! We have seen him perform his

# The Summonïng of The Blessèd Order

mastery in The Draughts and only won because of an event beyond our understanding!"

As the argument boiled over, Meigar cast his mind back to Ramacès' sacrifice and remembered something very significant. He almost shared his thought with Ramerick once more, glancing into his eyes to suggest he wanted to tell only him what he was thinking.

By that point, several members of the Order were throwing insults back and forth, mainly from the trio of Thakendrax, Magraw and Mijkal to Wemberlè and Zathos, claiming what was real and what was not. Some were getting rather personal, to which point Eveleve had to interrupt.

"Enough!" she ordered.

It was only out of respect for The Blessèd Mage of Life that they stopped. The rage and feistiness left a spicy zing to the mood before Eveleve insisted on a pause to calm tensions.

"Well that went well," Gracène jested.

"My lords and ladies. If what Clethance suggests is true in Davinor's betrayal, and for all that we have unearthed in this very meeting, we must all be on side. We cannot allow our differences to cloud our judgement to the most significant threat we have and will likely ever face."

If looks could kill, half of The Blessèd Order would have already killed one another. Eveleve had to find a way to unite them all, despite their historical differences.

"I must ask the question to you all that determines what we do next. Do you believe the threat is real?..."

After a long pause, Ramerick was hoping that they would all say yes. It would confirm the connection he had with Ramalon to be accurate and for Dancès' premonition to have more credibility.

"Without question," Meigar confirmed rather quickly, met with several nods of the head by Zathos, Wemberlè and even Ethelba.

Mavokai and Aristuto nodded their heads too. All eyes were on the trio whom so far had resisted. However, the weight of reality was pressing them hard, and although no confirmations were acknowledged, they did not indicate that they would continue to refute the idea.

"What we have learned from Clethance answers another vital question regarding the Dragadelf."

"I have read your book on The Arcadelfs Master Meigar," Clethance praised. "I know Hiyaro well. I'm not sure he told you of me, but he lent me your pages which I hope you don't mind."

"Too late to stop now, I guess," Meigar mused. "My studies of the Dragadelf have been thorough for many years, as you all know. They answer to nothing but power and the only way to control them is if they recognised a power greater than themselves, this all makes complete sense. The only concept they could ever adhere to is the presence of The Dragastone. If Felder gave that ownership to his three sons, they all would claim their allegiance and the perception that they are all The Dragadelf's true masters."

Meigar's conversation about The Dragadelf appeared to have successfully distracted tensions in the meeting.

"I agree with your theorem," Clethance nodded. "I hear that you knew Ramacès well."

"I was, by mere chance may I add, I did not know who he truly was until events unfolded. Albeit I knew him by the name of Alicèndil. Hearing confirmation that he inherited the same power as Ramalon is telling. I saw the scale of his power first hand. No one sitting here could have had the strength to snap the neck of a Dragadelf. The same power from his protecy was also used to help him withstand and stop the beam at the battle for The Draughts, which could never have happened without the sheer magnitude The Dragastone provides. They both have proved beyond any doubt that they have inherited The Dragastone's ownership. And in turn, the fealty of The Dragadelf - it is the only conclusion. And what's more… Is that there is one yet to reveal their own destiny of such claim," he indicated to Ramerick, who everyone looked upon with intrigue.

"Now that may come to some useful advantage," Mavokai encouragingly suggested.

"Let us focus on one thing at a time," Eveleve quickly said.

Ramerick detected that she was keen to avoid that conversation. He knew somehow that the fact he had not enchanted The Protecy could perhaps become the only thing that could challenge his brother - a notion that, upon confirming his connection with The Dragastone, galvanised him. If he had a share in the destructive power the stone provided, he welcomed every possibility he could to gain his own revenge.

Could that be the vital piece of information that Dancès mentioned in that Ramerick would be the one to restore balance, he thought? By ascertaining this tremendous power, could that be enough to stop him? Could he control The Dragadelf too, and perhaps use it to his

## The Summonïng of The Blessèd Order

advantage? Ramerick didn't refute the idea and caught the blind eye of his aunt Gracène to his side, looking at him with an encouraging smile.

"My Lady," Mavokai continued, "you mentioned we all must be open to possibilities."

"Yes, I did," she reluctantly admitted.

"And if this is all true, which by the sounds of it, it is all very likely, then your son may be our only chance to defeat Ramalon. If he enchants The Protecy, he would have the same right to use that power."

"No! It is the entire opposite," she defended. "This only confirms why we must never let Ramalon near him. Not for my sake but for us all. If Ramerick enchants The Protecy, I fear Ramalon could get to him much easier."

"That would be correct," Clethance contributed. "The fact that Felder gave all three of his sons equal right would mean that Ramerick would forever be exposed."

"But it appears Ramalon is already forcing our hand, my lady." Mavokai informed. "If Ramalon brings down The Dragasphere, how on Rèo can we stop him? How do we stop The Dragadelf, which appear under his command? Not to mention the horrific notion that we have yet to discuss the number of souls he has manced! The corpses at his disposal are frightening. If he opens the gates of The Understunde onto us, Ramerick's claim and fealty over The Dragadelf could be the only thing to stop him."

"I appreciate the temptation is attractive," Clethance continued, "but his lack of experience in The Protecy would not be enough alone to challenge Ramalon. On top of that, were Ramerick to die, it would open the path that Ramalon needs for total ownership over both subjects. Should that happen, none of you and indeed, all of you combined would not be able to stop him. Ramerick, under all costs, must live."

The weight of reality began to sink in as they collectively began to understand just how at risk they all were. Even the trio of Blessèd Màgjeurs, who caused much resistance, did not strike looks of refusal.

Ramerick on the other hand felt a little disappointed, as the idea of giving him access to this unrelenting power was not considered a good idea. He wanted to be the one to avenge his son's death and struggled to fathom how to do that without enchanting The Protecy.

"Okay, let's assume," Mijkal continued, "that Ramalon is inside and somehow can bring The Dragasphere down. How do you propose we stop him? Prevention should be preferable than cure."

Another grave pause existed in the summoning until Ramerick propped up a more straightforward solution to many moving parts.

"The Dragastone," he whispered, half in thought.

"My lad?" Gracène quietly asked.

"Everything we have spoken here all points to one thing..." he hinted.

"Ramerick?" Eveleve asked.

"The Dragastone must be destroyed."

The stillness and lack of initial reaction from every member of the Order appeared to land a simpler intention.

"And how do you propose we do that?" a more reserved and reluctant Thakendrax asked. "Are you forgetting that The Dragastone lies inside the most dangerous place on Rèo? Where your brother *apparently* resides, protected by The Dragadelf and all sorts of horrors Melcelore appears to have left behind. Not to mention the possible idea," he said, swallowing a portion of his pride, "of entering The Dragasphere which in itself is beyond my understanding of how to achieve!"

"But it could be possible," Mijkal pressed on. "We would just need to be sure that destroying it would work."

"It would." Meigar confirmed with growing confidence. "The last thirty years of encapsulation, twinned with the artificial nutrition The Dragastone has supplied them has made them dependent on its energy. If destroyed, their unnatural constitutions would not be able to survive without the power that fuels them."

"And in addition to that," Clethance took over. "All affiliation with Ramalon and Ramerick's ownership to The Dragastone would end. He would not be supported by the power of the stone and would no longer be a threat."

"So, just to be clear," Mijkal said. "With all that we have learned tonight, is the threat of Ramalon solved by simply destroying The Dragastone?"

"Yes," Clethance confirmed. "*Simply* would be a term I would refrain from using. It would need one of the brothers to terminate its connection to destroy the stone outright. They would need to have it in their hands for that to happen and could take some time. However, Ramerick would need to enchant The Protecy to initiate the termination. How you get the stone, is in your hands..."

It was clear upon hearing Clethance's expertise that destroying The

## The Summoning of The Blessèd Order

Dragastone would end the threat of Ramalon. However, that familiar silence existed once more as no one in the summoning could fathom how to do so. Ramerick felt proud to offer what he knew and had experienced to The Blessèd Order but was quickly shunned as he looked over to his mother. She displayed that similar look of dismay in her eyes which were drawn to the ground. It was a subtle look that Ramerick clocked, just like earlier. What could she be thinking right now? he asked himself. It was clear she was hiding something and almost confirmed it by bringing the meeting to an abrupt halt.

"I think this would be an appropriate time to retire for the night," she quickly said with a gentle quiver to her words. She rose from her chair. "Thank you all. Let us rest our minds and convene tomorrow. Hopefully, we will have more insight as to how to destroy the stone."

Eveleve wasted no time wading through the middle of the circle and past Ramerick, whom she did not even acknowledge as she swiftly exited back to her chambers. It did not take long before the rest of the members followed suit, some refraining from contacting one another.

"That was a little strange," Gracène said.

"That was," Ramerick agreed. "Is she okay?"

"She'll be fine, my lad. Now here, help me back to my bed. You younglings have more patience than me, but my buttocks are so numb I can't feel my feet!"

"I'll take you," Mirabella said as she came to stand too.

"Thank you," Ramerick said.

"Goodnight, laddie," Gracène said.

"Goodnight," he replied, giving a gentle nod to them both.

As they both stumbled away, he noticed Meigar being one of the last ones to leave. He gave a gentle nod of farewell before returning to his chambers. The only ones left were Ramerick and Ramavell, who looked across to one another.

"Ramerick," he said profoundly, his accent: mature, crisp and well-spoken. "Can't tell you what a pleasure it is to meet you again after all these years."

"It is good to meet you too, Ramavell."

Ramavell bounced a subtle laugh. "You've grown into the man you were born to be."

"I'm not sure what kind of man that is."

"You're just like him, you know. Like your father. Mighty and fierce!"

Every time Ramerick heard that it sparked a little happiness inside.

"Everyone says that about him."

"He'd be very proud of you. And of Ramacès."

"You met my brother?"

"I did. You both share your father's character quite remarkably. Both full of courage and heart. That's what made him the finest man there ever can be. At least that's what they all said anyhow. I didn't know him too well on a personal level."

"I would like to have met him."

"You don't look alike, by the way."

"I gathered. I don't look like Ramalon."

Ramavell raised his head gently, remembering it was a cause for concern that they both connected on Ramalon's terms.

"No. I don't know what Ramalon appears to look like either. Had I known all those years ago when I pulled you all into this world that Ramalon would become what he did, I would have stopped it for sure!"

Ramerick was exhausted from today and couldn't fathom delving into another conversation by answering with, *but then Melcelore would have found a way to escape.*

"So what part of my father did Ramalon inherit?"

"His mind, I guess. Metaphorically speaking, of course... I'm sorry to hear about your son," he hesitantly said.

Ramerick did not respond. He temporarily put the image of Jàqueson to one side during the summoning.

"Don't be. There's nothing to be sorry about. If you see sadness, I apologise for giving off the wrong impression."

"You're not sad?" Ramavell queried.

"Should I be?"

"After the loss of your son?"

"He's not gone. He's in here," he directed to his heart with his fingertips. "I'll see them again soon."

"I see," Ramavell fathomed he was still in the early stages of grief and chose not to probe.

"Is my mother okay?"

"I believe so. She is struggling to understand her role in all this."

"I'm proud to have her as my mother."

"She is proud of you too. I've stayed with her all these long years. I've looked after her in her darkest places. I've done my best to keep her believing that one day she would be vindicated of her choice to let you go. That choice is paying off now, having seen you again."

# The Summoning of The Blessèd Order

"Dark places? What do you mean?"

Ramavell hesitated briefly before reluctantly sighing.

"Your father was a good man. Honourable and true to all that is good and green on this world. But he did leave your mother in a very dark place. Sacrificing himself with all these questions left unanswered confused her somewhat. She didn't feel entirely trusted, which you can understand."

"What did she do? In her darkest moments?"

Again Ramavell hesitated.

"Ramavell?"

"... The grief and pain she bore made her attempt to destroy her protecy stone on several occasions."

"But she's The Blessèd Mage of Life. Why would she have done that if..." The penny suddenly dropped. "She tried to end her life?"

"On several occasions," Ramavell quietly confessed. "Losing a child as you have experienced takes away a part of you. Your children are everything. Your life no longer is the most important thing when they are born. Instead, that importance passes onto them. You're suddenly someone's hero. Someone to look up to. Someone whom without, they simply would not become a life. Take that all away from someone, leaves you falling. Falling into a pit that is difficult to stop. Your mother fell into that pit. It was only at the moment of seeing you that she began to climb out of it..."

The weight of guilt Ramerick felt for his mother grew more substantial than before. The sacrifice wasn't even her choice and brought to the surface an emotion that he seldom felt these days. Love.

"Do you believe what my father did was right? Not telling my mother all this?"

Ramavell hesitated.

"It's difficult to say. Maybe your father only entrusted his own vision and mastery into true clairvoyance to see this through. Perhaps if he told someone of what would really happen, others could understand that too, like The Ancient Drethai, for example."

Ramerick drew his gaze away briefly, remembering the arrow shaft inside Jàquesons heart, dealt by Orbow. His establishment with the ghosts of Terrasendia rendered him hateful and vengeful towards them too.

"Are you okay?" Ramavell asked.

"Fine," he responded quickly, eyes ablaze.

Ramavell nodded as he didn't want to intrude on what appeared to be a private moment.

"You are not alone in this. Remember that. We are here and after tonight's summoning, you will never have to go through what you have ever again."

Ramerick nodded his head. "Thank you."

"Now get some rest. You will need it."

Ramerick did not take the advice to get sleep all too often, but in a way, he found it comforting for a more senior figure to guide him once in a while, even in such a small moment.

"Goodnight."

"Goodnight," they bade each other farewell.

Ramerick left and headed back to his chambers. His mind was full of intent and determination to prepare for what was to come. However, the one thing that galvanised him moments before his mind drifted off into a light sleep was that they now had some direction in this hurdle, to defy his brother. And in particular, he had one thing that became his obsession, the image of it gleaming in his mind. To destroy The Dragastone.

# A Last Resort

"Where are you?" Ramerick asked in his mind's eye. His head lay soft on his pillow in his chambers. A dangerous choice he knew to connect with Ramalon; alas, he felt no fear.

His eyes opened after several hours of trying to establish the spontaneous bond, and there it was... The Dragastone gleaming right in front of him as clear as day. Like before, this was no dream. He felt its energy, its power, his ownership over the anomaly as it sat upon the ruins of his father's throne.

The ease as which he managed to walk into this connection did not distract him, despite knowing it was an impulsive choice to yank the lion's tail once more. Ramalon had heeded his request and obliged.

He approached the steps leading up to the platform the throne sat upon and stopped to look at the heart of power nestled in the rubble. He looked upon it with such assurance that if destroyed, his vengeance would be complete. Though that was the aim, he knew the reality was much crueller to accept.

Suddenly he felt the presence of his brother glide up to the side of him, side by side. They did not need to look upon one another to confirm who the other was. They both stared upon their father's inheritance, silently challenging the other to claim it.

He felt Ramalon turn toward him, feeling his cold, emotionless stare gaze right through him. He slowly turned back to return the stare, finding the youthful face of his brother. No words were needed to declare their intent. Ramerick was trying to fathom why Ramalon would allow him to make contact. So far, it seemed only to benefit Ramerick to see all of this. To understand his enemy, showing his weakness and the arm of his power.

Silently, Ramalon turned his head toward The Dragastone once more, not a single blink of his eye as he approached it. Ramerick did not interrupt what Ramalon was showing him, staring now at his silhouette from the stone's shine, which was no longer in the line of sight.

He could make out Ramalon's hands as they reached for the stone and felt his own fingertips tingle, suggesting that Ramalon now had it in his grasp. A hint of jealousy pricked his conscience as it seemed to glow at the hands of another.

When Ramalon turned back to face his brother with his typical intense stare, a sense of foreboding was born when their eyes met. It was as if not even Ramalon knew what would happen next until his eyes closed, concentrating on channelling his focus onto the stone in his hands, which shone brightly into his face.

It looked as if an exchange was taking place. Just what was he doing to it? he thought. He began to lose breath quite quickly, sharply inhaling and exhaling at the discomfort - A discomfort that Ramerick began to actively feel too. It was a delayed reaction, but the pain Ramalon was experiencing was being reflected onto Ramerick also.

His chest began to ache and pang with sharp stabs as it rendered him to the ground, clutching at his ribs. He looked at his brother, who also was kneeling in pain, his hands glued to The Dragastone, melting almost into its casing as if he couldn't let go even if he wanted to. Violent shocks reverberated into Ramalon's body until the threshold of pain began to simmer down for them both.

Ramerick felt a little more empty inside. Dead. As if a part of his soul left him. However, it was overshadowed by its replacement of more power and strength than he had ever felt. And it terrified him. What has Ramalon done? he asked himself.

# A Last Resort

*Before he could fathom the answer, Ramalon looked flush into his brother's eyes, his stare more cold and intense than ever, before the connection began to dissolve around him.*

Ramerick woke sharply from his bed, shaking from the cold as his body was drenched in night-sweats. His eyes darted across the room, realising what this could have meant.

It was the third hour of day when he raced to the summoning once more as already everyone was in attendance. He was hoping that somehow everything that Ramalon showed him was a fabrication. Alas, he couldn't bring himself to believe it.

"Ah, there you are, laddie -" Gracène greeted him as if they were only waiting on him.

"- We need to destroy the stone now!" he pleaded to The Blessèd Order, totally out of breath.

"Ramerick?" Eveleve asked. "What happened?"

"I - I just saw him again."

"How is that possible? Did you attempt to make contact with him?"

"I did," he hesitantly replied.

"You cannot allow him in. It will make us vulnerable!"

"I know, but I just... Something tells me everything he is showing me is true!"

"What happened?" Clethance asked.

"He held his hands on the stone again and did something to it. I don't know what. But we felt the same thing. Like something was being ripped away from us, but then it latched onto the stone. What's more, we both experienced a surge of power. He's stronger. Much - Much stronger than before!"

Clethance and Meigar both showed the weight of concern on their faces.

"Stronger how?" Wemberlè queried.

"I don't know. I was hoping you could tell me." All at the summoning looked directly at Clethance, whose face was far graver than it had been before. "Clethance?"

"... It sounds like Ramalon has implanted his soul onto The Dragastone," he announced dryly. The room almost vibrated under the new level of tension.

"He's preserved his soul?"

"No. Soul Preservation is different; he would need to sacrifice his life for that to happen. He has simply improved the connection twofold, giving The Protecy a purer access to its power. This must be how he intends to destroy The Dragasphere."

"Are you telling us Ramalon's power has doubled?" Mijkal gravely asked, his panic beginning to set in.

"In effect, yes."

"Is it enough!? To destroy it?" Thakendrax asked, the concern beginning to fester more potently.

"Only you would be able to calculate that…"

The summoning fell silent once more.

"This is all becoming very real," Zathos loomed as the reality began to dawn upon them.

Ramerick looked toward his mother and noticed that reluctant look in her eye once more. She couldn't bear to look at him.

"I cannot trust this," Magraw said. "I cannot trust what you saw. It is entirely in your brother's hands. I implore every one of us not to give in to its temptation. It is purely an illusion!"

"My lady," Mavokai said, entirely ignoring Magraw, "if this is true and he brings it down, Terrasendia will not survive. Surely the risk to do nothing is too great?"

"We must not allow this order to be manipulated!"

"Lestas!" Mijkal weighed in, "The Master of Death is right. At first, I was not alarmed, but now, I am fearful. Suspicious and utterly afraid of what he can do. I say we act!"

"And what of Ramerick here," Magraw continued to lecture impressively. "You say you felt your soul leave you. Has your soul left you? Is it implanted onto the stone you do not have in your possession?"

"No," Ramerick replied.

"Not to make matters more confusing, but that would be impossible," Clethance learned. "The fact that he experienced the same pain is of concern. Despite your connection, it makes no sense how you felt what he felt."

"Are you suggesting that perhaps Ramalon deliberately made me feel that way?" Ramerick asked.

"Yes. Without question. Your soul is not implanted onto it; I can assure you."

"All the more reason for us not to trust what he is seeing!" Magraw strongly rebuffed.

"And what if Ramalon really does have enough to force his way out of The Dragasphere?" Mavokai said.

Magraw huffed once more as he didn't have the answer.

"Ramalon may have improved his arm of power," Clethance continued, "but he has also exposed his weakness."

"How?" Ramerick asked.

"His soul now rests entirely within that stone. It confirms the theory that should The Dragastone be destroyed, as would the one who's soul resides within it. Along with everything connected to him."

"What do you think, my lady?" Meigar asked of Eveleve.

Her silence spoke volumes, regularly in deep thought. On occasion, it looked as if she wasn't taking part at all in the discussions, her mind floating elsewhere nonchalantly.

"I do not know what to think," she confessed. "I am torn. Torn because I do not necessarily trust what my son has seen. But ultimately, if it is true and we do nothing, we will not survive the malice from within."

"My lady," Magraw tried to reason, lowering his tone to be more understanding. "Even with excelled power, the walls of that spell are impregnable! He cannot get out by force. And I fear he is playing on your fears. On our fears! I would know being my field. This is a desperate hope that we will fall into his trap!"

"Even if what you say is true, Master Magraw," Ramerick confronted, "the risk of you being wrong is simply too great…"

Though Magraw did not agree with it, he struggled to disagree on the other hand.

Suddenly a rather deep rumble began to drone from afar. It did not seem as if it was airborne, but more coming from deep beneath their feet.

"Do you feel that?" Meigar asked to the summoning.

They all felt it too, wondering what it could be. It was more than a sound now as the ground began to shake more intensely. The reverberations became so intense, some of the older Màgjeurs began to rest on the seats of stone. The noise started to drown out also as Ramerick's mind once again mellowed out into his familiar trance, bringing him to his knees. Luckily this time, Gracène was close enough to him so that she could latch her hand onto his arm amid the quake they all were experiencing.

*His mind's eye flew directly inside Monarchy Hall once again to see Ramalon charging up his protecy. It quaked the foundations of Felders Crest's, and with one primal yell, he released a catastrophic flame into the roof of The Dragasphere.*

*It hit with the force of a volcanic eruption, shaking the walls of the* containment spell so violently that The Dragasphere actively moved to heal the damage. So much energy was released that it made Ramalon crumble to the ground in a heap. It was clear he had given it everything he had with his new-found power, and although the devastation did not bring down The Dragasphere in that one blast, Ramerick's mind flew skywards and up toward the point where the blast landed.

Ramerick could only watch on helplessly, scared of what may be shown to him. It was then that Ramerick understood the horror in its entirety and saw that Ramalon's attack had indeed created a split in the roof of The Dragasphere. The fissure was so small, yet so significant; he could hear the air squeezing out of it, like a balloon which had ever so slightly been pierced. His heart fluttered at the realisation that The Dragasphere could not heal that part of the roof...

Ramerick's worst fears were confirmed as he saw the black silhouettes of wings and jaws fly toward the fissure and offload their molten filled bellies, accelerating its demise.

His mind flew back, dissolving and warping to reality once more.

One final impulse shook so viscously, it brought down some of the structures and crumbled parts of the valley rocks that enclosed them, splashing hard into the lake. And just like that, the quake simmered down and ended to calm again.

Ramerick's mind returned to him as he stared into the blind eyes of his aunt to confirm what he saw.

"It's started." Ramerick breathed. "The Dragasphere is dying!"

Gracène looked at him, her glossed eyes reflecting the same panic he felt. She nodded her head also to confirm her fears.

"I saw it too..." she replied equally startled.

It was clear to him that using her powers of foresight, she was able to latch on at that moment and see exactly what he saw.

"That was unquestionably him!" Meigar claimed.

"Never before have we suffered such an attack." Mavokai warned.

"Do you doubt it now? The Dragasphere is under attack!"

"Yes... It is -" Ramerick breathlessly confirmed. "It's already begun! And we are out of time!"

"Impossible," Magraw grumbled, "we would have been able to detect if it were destroyed."

"It's not destroyed, at least not yet. It's damaged. The advanced power he's got wasn't quite enough to take it down outright, but it was enough to form a crack on the ceiling itself..."

"Gracelands!" Mijkal said. "And with that weak point he could instruct The Dragadelf to accelerate its destruction!" Mijkal panicked.

"That is also happening as we speak," Gracène slowly confirmed.

"You saw what he saw?"

Gracène gravely nodded.

"With respect, that doesn't make it true," Magraw pointed out. "It only confirms that you too saw what Ramalon wanted you to see."

"Which brings us back to where we were before," Thakendrax said.

"I, for one," Mijkal imposed, "believe the risk is too great to do nothing! Especially given what we have just experienced."

Several of The Blessèd began to express once more their own opinions, but rather than quarrelling this time, the consensus with exception to Magraw, was relatively amicable and on the same wavelength. They were leaning toward the idea that something imminently must be done.

"It is clear," Mavokai said, "That we must act, now!"

Everyone appeared to agree, some enthusiastically, some reluctant… Eveleve more so for the latter.

"The question is, how?" Mijkal asked. "How do we stop it from falling?"

After a thoughtful pause, Eveleve finally broke her silence.

"There is only one thing we can do."

All heads and attention now entirely focussed on her. She looked across to Mavokai who gave an equally reluctant nod back toward her. She inhaled a steady breath before explaining what had been on her mind for some time…

"My lady?" Meigar queried with raised eyebrows.

"The only way to stop him is if The Dragastone is destroyed. For that, Ramerick must enchant The Protecy and destroy it before it's too late," she reluctantly resigns.

Ramerick was happy, despite his mother's reluctance, that finally he would get a chance to claim his power and stand a chance in destroying The Dragastone.

"But my lady," Meigar calmly asks, "even if that does happen, we could never get him to the stone for him to do so. Let alone simply walk into the heart of Felders Crest unchallenged with no experience of how to use the practice. It is a suicide mission!"

"Or perhaps not," she reluctantly continued. "For many years, I think I have known this moment would come, and I can put off the pain I will have to inflict, no longer," she directed that last part toward Ramerick.

He began to wonder what she was talking about; his beating heart came to his attention a little more. His enthusiasm began to dwindle at the prospect of what she was about to say.

"What do you mean?" Ramerick asked pointedly.

"There is only one way we stand any chance of retrieving that stone. The only way Ramerick can gain passage to Felders Crest without being killed himself…"

"Mother?" Ramerick asked with growing concern.

Eveleve turned to her son in the view of the whole Blessèd Order.

"You must become, The Blessèd Mage of Life," she revealed.

"Eveleve!?" Ramavell gasped, echoed by several others at the shock of what she had suggested.

No one was more shocked than Ramerick, who remained stupefied upon hearing her idea. Everyone instantly realised what her suggestion entailed. For Ramerick to become The Blessèd Mage of Life, Eveleve would have to sacrifice her own so that he could ascertain her power of life preservation. His rising encouragement rapidly sunk and escaped from beneath his feet.

"… Absolutely not!" Ramerick weightily said, immediately dismissing the insanity.

"This is the only way. Twin the powers you will inherit from me with the power of The Dragastone and you would be very difficult for him to stop."

"Invincible?" Mijkal asked.

"No one is that righteous," Mavokai explained. His expertise as The Blessèd Mage of Death provided invaluable insight. "But the threshold of death he could endure would surpass anyone that has ever lived, Ramalon included."

"If you are asking me to take your life to save others, I'm going to selfishly decline!" Ramerick refuted.

"Eveleve," Mirabella approached. "You cannot ask this of your own son!"

"The evil that is upon us forces our hand… Forces me to respond in the only way that could save us. No matter the cost. No matter the sacrifice."

Ramerick began to understand when he noticed those moments of covering up her sadness. He gathered she must have had some notion about her required sacrifice much before that moment and hoped to exhaust every possibility to avoid coming to that end. The Blessèd Order also seemed to collectively reject the idea. They all responded initially in the same manner of shock. However on reflection, they searched the very darkest parts of their hearts and souls to understand that despite the unforgivable sacrifice, it would present them all with a chance to stop The Dragasphere from falling and save Terrasendia.

"I am not sad for my own life, let me make that clear," Eveleve heroically continued. "I am sad because I have to say goodbye to my son once more. I have to fail you again in order for you to succeed."

"Mother no..." he began to break down, shaking his head, the moisture gathered in his tear ducts reflecting more light off of his eyes. "Please don't do this!"

"This is the only way, my son."

"You cannot possibly ask me to do this. I can't do it - I won't do it! After all I have lost, how can you ask me to lose you again? I just can't..."

"Son," she attempted to console him, encroaching on his space which made him recoil instantly to the platform edge, shaking his head in denial.

"There has to be another way. There just has to be!"

"We are out of time. And you are the only one who can stop him now. You are the only one who can provide peace to the land once more..."

Ramerick turned his back and looked down onto the valley of Laloncère below, burying his face in his hands as he tried as desperately as he could to be brave and not to sob his heart away... Alas, he failed and could not stop his heart from breaking once more, convulsing his cry into his sweaty palms, his chest and diaphragm bouncing intensely as he rode the wave of emotional tide.

The Blessèd Order began to feel the burden of responsibility, some unable to hide their own sadness to what they were witnessing. Alas, they began to realise that this had to happen. The only way to repel the extreme inevitability they now faced was by upping the stakes and making that sacrifice that could provide the ultimate difference.

Suddenly, enchanting The Protecy no longer became a thing of allure for Ramerick, instead it was now just a necessary means to all be part of some plan. He felt used. Abandoned once more. He could not work out why life had treated him this way. The brief moments where the colours of golds and browns came back, began to fade away once more into greys and shadows, the more he understood what was required of him.

"Eveleve," Ramavell reasoned. "There is no guarantee your sacrifice would work."

"It will. I have already discussed with Clethance and The Master of Death over such a possibility."

"What possibility?"

"Of Ramerick stealing that stone from underneath his feet!"

"Why did you not speak of this plan before?" Mijkal gravely asked.

"Because this is the last resort. I was hoping, foolishly may I add, that there would be another way, hence why I had summoned you all. Alas, there is not."

"What are you suggesting?" Meigar asked, keeping one eye on an inconsolable Ramerick, whose back was turned on the summoning.

"There is a way inside The Dragasphere… Through my sister," she directed to Gracène. "Her skill into portal magic is unique and has vowed a secret oath of silence, never to use that skill on The Dragasphere. However I think considering the circumstance, it would be entirely reasonable to break that vow, for the greater good."

The Blessèd Order fathomed as much. They comprehended that her skill was so great it was entirely possible for that to happen. They understood despite the spell's unparalleled strength, there was always going to be an exception.

"She will open a portal into Felders Crest and as The Blessèd Mage of Life, Ramerick can enter and repel much of the evil that resides there."

"Much of?" Ramavell asked dubiously, his hurt at what needed to be done becoming more apparent.

"Despite being a manipulative affinity," Clethance learned to them, "he could still use it to protect himself against Ramalon. However, in addition to that, we would need to enchant a destructive affinity to aid his defence further. Though it would be inferior to Ramalon's due to his understanding of the connection being stronger, it would give Ramerick additional fight."

"It will also stop Ramalon from invading his mind and seeing his plans. The powers of life will also give him the ultimate form of protection and repel his evil," Eveleve explained.

"So you're sending your son through the gates of The Understunde!? Only to what? Hope Ramalon doesn't notice?" Ramavell suppressed his outrage.

"The plan *is* for Ramalon to notice," Clethance said as he revealed something from inside his robes of outstanding beauty and magnificent colours.

Everyone who saw the protecy stone he had just revealed looked upon it with awe and mesmerisation. Ramerick however, was not interested, remaining on the edge of the platform.

"Good Gracelands, look at that!" Mijkal said.

"The protecy stone of Zoldathorn itself! The first-ever to be enchanted," Clethance said, pride laced in his words. "And we are uniquely fortunate. With a few tweaks, it is almost an exact copy of The Dragastone. It is the foundation of all protecy."

"Why are you showing us this?" Thakendrax asked.

"Because, as mentioned before, Ramerick would physically need the stone in his hands to terminate it and would take time. It would only take one of the brothers to initiate its termination, but he would not achieve it in Ramalon's presence."

"And so the plan is for Ramalon to fall into our trap." Mavokai explained. "They must engage and Ramerick must somehow switch the stones!"

"And when that happens," Thakendrax countered. "How does Ramerick escape with the real Dragastone? Surely Gracène would not leave the portal open?"

"No, she cannot," Eveleve contributed, "the amount of strength she will need to open it in the first place will exhaust much of her energies."

Gracène slowly raised her arm gestured with a clenched fist, almost in mockery for her physical strength.

"So how does he get out of there?" Thakendrax asked again.

"As you will recall, an ancient spell surrounds Monarchy Hall to protect the High Throne," Mavokai continued. "Anything which is inherently dead simply cannot pass. I will implant a death rune onto Ramerick, which will only activate once Ramalon strikes him. By that point, Ramerick would need to have completed the switch and have the real Dragastone in his hands. The spell would recognise that Ramerick is dead, but because of his powers as The Blessèd Mage of Life, he would not die and simply cast him back out onto Laloncère with the stone."

"And if Ramerick is struck before that moment? Before that switch happens? What then?"

"That is the risk we are taking," Mavokai confirmed.

The concern once again snowballed. Even Eveleve, who came up with this plan and discussed it at length with The Blessèd Mage of Death, Clethance and Gracène, knew of the risk. However, they were simply out of time to assemble another plan.

"We are hoping the additional source of life Ramerick inherits would help defend him long enough to orchestrate the switch successfully."

"I will go with him," Meigar offered heartily. "He cannot do this alone."

"No, Master of Earth," Eveleve commanded. "If Ramerick does fall, we need The Blessèd Order to be at full strength. He must do this alone. This is the only real chance we have of saving this world... Are we all in agreement?"

Such a harsh question to ask of them all, yet necessary. Some did not want to agree in fear they would hurt Eveleve by supporting her death.

"Eveleve," Ramavell argued, "what if Ramerick fails? What if Ramalon proves too strong for him. We would lose you. We would lose him... We would lose hope."

Eveleve smiled.

"That will not happen, my friend. He is the one to restore balance to this world. And we must believe in that if we are to stand a chance. My husband would not have foreseen this and allowed everything to happen if he saw our ultimate demise."

The Blessèd Order collectively began to lose faith in what was Felder's apparent foresight. Such complexities and moving parts did not make finding the answer to such peril straightforward.

"The odds are not in our favour," Magraw counselled. "We must put Terrasendia on full alert. If Ramerick falls, we must be ready for war!"

Magraw's apparent blessing to this quest spoke volumes, despite his disagreement in its entirety.

"Then I ask this order if anyone objects?"

The stillness in the room was unilateral confirmation that this was perhaps the only plan they had to destroy The Dragastone and that they were in agreement. They had only one more to convince.

"Ramerick?" Eveleve delicately asked.

He did not answer and remained motionless with his back turned on everyone. He was so close to the edge of the platform as he looked down some hundreds of metres below. It dawned on Eveleve what he could potentially do.

"You say you want to see them again? You say you want to take your son to the mildens every morning? You say that your wish is for her to say yes?... Not yet, my son. Not yet. Your journey has not yet finished. Some day it will, and when that day arrives, the world will be a safer place, because of you and what you choose to do. You cannot give up! Not while you have the strength left to avenge them!"

Ramerick remained still, despite hearing every word. Eveleve's voice turned a little less sympathetic, which was not her character. It was the easiest way to make him understand what was needed of him to fulfil his role.

"Son? We are out of time. And we need to know you can do what must be done. I have always struggled to understand my part to play in your father's plan. But now I have. And I think I've known all along. Now it is time that you did too…"

He slowly turned around, his eyes: dead, gormless, bloodshot and utterly emotionless. He had no more grief left to give. Just how much more he could endure plunged him into the abyss of uncertainty once more.

"What must I do?" he whispered.

## A Mother's Love

"First things first," Clethance explained to an utterly defeated Ramerick. "We need to enchant The Protecy. However, if we enchant and you do not have the powers you inherit from your mother, you could be exposed to Ramalon. We must initiate both enchanting and the passing of ownership at the same time, which I can help with."

Eveleve and Ramerick both stood opposite one another in the centre of the gathering; The Blessèd Order surrounded them, compassion etched into each of their faces. Ramerick could not fathom just how betrayed he felt by his life. After everything he had endured, all that suffering, this was the final straw - the thing that would shatter the remaining fragments of his heart to dust. There would be nothing left of him after this. He looked skywards to any god there ever was, as if

## A Mother's Love

questioning the cruel nature of the higher power that saw all the terrible events that had unfolded come to pass, all for him to be the one to charge through the gauntlet of impossibility once again.

Eveleve continued to stare into his vacant expression. His mind was elsewhere, forgetting his purpose, forgetting why he was there, briefly forgetting who he was. It was more bearable for him to try not to care as it provided him with that emotional shield and coping mechanism which hung by a perilous thread.

"We need you to choose an affinity to enchant," Clethance explained. "What would be your choice?"

Ramerick's slight shake of the head suggested that he had heard Clethance's question but chose not to respond.

"How about fire?" Eveleve suggested. "After your father?"

"That has a nice continuity, don't you think?"

Ramerick honestly couldn't care at that point and subtly nodded his head to agree after giving some apparent thought.

"Fire it is," Clethance said as he produced another protecy stone from within his robes and placed it into Ramerick's hands.

Ramerick didn't even look at the stone which was placed in his hands. Clethance gathered Eveleve wanted to say a few final words and gracefully backed away.

"Son? Are you there?" Still no response. "I know you're in pain. All you have suffered, the burden of it all was never meant to be placed upon your shoulders. But it is," she delicately confessed.

"Please, don't," he weakly replied, squeezing his eyes shut hoping he would wake up from this nightmare.

"Sometimes, the world needs a hero. They need someone who will do what must be done to protect the good this world has to offer, whatever the personal cost. Because there is good. Plenty of it. I can't tell you how proud I am to have you as my son." She spoke her words so softly yet they nearly tipped him over. "This was meant to happen, just as your father foresaw. I guess it's symbolic that your father and I pass into The Gracelands, both leaving you with something that might be the difference to save this world. I was meant to give you my powers of life to help you fight that which would replace it with death. I understand this was my role all along. I was always meant to give you life twice…"

Eveleve concluded with a sad smile as a tear rolled down her cheek and sprinkled onto her dazzling white dress. Tears began to fall from several other members as well, most notably Ethelba, Ramavell and

Mirabella. Even some of the men whose front was tough and at some times emotionally despondent began to feel the guilt of sadness.

Clethance sensitively approached once more.

"We can no longer delay," he quietly said. "We must begin."

Ramerick gritted his teeth, breathing more intensely through his flared nostrils as the time had come. He reluctantly looked upon the protecy stone in his hand. Its mirky green casing mixed with spots of transparency.

"Place the stone in your right hand," he indicated to Ramerick, which he did. "Place your hand over his," Eveleve did so with her left hand, cupping over the roof of the stone. "Place the necklace in your right hand," he indicated to Eveleve. "Place your hand over hers," to which he did, connecting both the stone and necklace with their hands. "My lady, you know what to do from here?" he asked, which sounded more like a statement as he already knew the answer.

"I do," she nodded.

"Very well. Ramerick, repeat after me… *Bolero, cestanya, bothera.*"

Ramerick swallowed the gathering saliva in his glands.

"*B-Bolero, cesta-nyab-nyab othera,*" he struggled.

"Concentrate! Breathe… And again. *Bolero, cestanya, bothera.*"

"*Bolero. Cest. Anya. Both… Bothero.*"

"*Bothera!*"

"*Bothera!*"

"And again! *Bolero, cestanya, bothera.*"

Ramerick's breathing became more challenging as he seemed to choke on every intake of breath, his heart unable to take much more.

"*Bolero, cestanya, bothera!*"

"Good, and again, close your eyes."

Ramerick's eyes squeezed shut as he concentrated on the incantation.

"*Bolero, cestanya, brothera!*"

"*Bothera!*"

"*Bothera -* I can't!"

"Yes, you can, focus your mind -"

"- Stop! Stop… Please," he pleaded, backing away from his mother and breaking the enchantment. He dropped the stone in the process, struggling to find the strength and will to follow this through. His blank state had rapidly turned to panic. He could not do this.

The Blessèd Order were understandably torn. They did not interrupt and complicate matters further. Instead, they showed compassion for

## A Mother's Love

how sensitive the situation was and allowed Ramerick the time to gather himself.

It was only when Ramerick's breathing began to slow down that Magraw surprisingly offered his hand.

"Perhaps I can be of some assistance," he rose from his chair.

Ramerick did not take the offer too comfortably. It was strange how The Blessèd Mage of the Mind offered his help, despite expressing multiple concerns about the plan. Alas, he gathered his overall support laid with the democracy and integrity of The Blessèd Order's decision.

Magraw looked over to Eveleve almost to ask permission to enter his mind. She gave a gentle nod of the head. Magraw inhaled a large breath to compose himself.

"Will you look at me?" he asked of Ramerick, to which he slowly complied. Magraw's voice became trance-like, almost like a hypnotherapist casting his spell. "Close your eyes... Focus on my voice." Ramerick reluctantly obliged. "Place in the forefront of your mind, your brother. See his face. See his eyes... See his intention. Can you see it?"

"... Yes," he quietly responded.

"Open your eyes... What do you see?" Ramerick slowly opened them to see only Magraw standing alone. The Blessèd Order were no longer there. "Look around you..."

Nothing apparent was being shown to him apart from the disappearance of everybody else.

"Where did they go?" he asked, knowing this was an illusion.

"Look beyond, Ramerick."

He took a little wander to the edge of the platform again to view Laloncère below with its exponential greenery created by his mother not long ago. The colours of greys and shadows did not appear to him in his mind. Instead, it was full of life. Golden autumnal colours filtered back, the swashing of rivers falling into the vast lake flowed and the birds chirped their tunes.

All of a sudden, he could smell the thick, intense aroma of smoke invading deep into his lungs. He coughed deeply to unclog the airways, hucking up phlegm in the process. The forestry below had begun to burn. He could hear the crackling of dry wood as the radiating heat from the fires warmed his face. Laloncère looked as if it had turned into a forest fire. Molten lava spewed from where the rivers ran white. The birds and their songs above sank and drifted into their molten graves below. There was no life there that could live. The gates of The Understunde were apparent to him in the metaphorical sense.

The last thing he saw was a speck in the distance, flying toward him. It grew more prominent the closer it got, leaving a devastating trail of fire and gusts that obliterated anything in its path. Ramerick watched on as he saw a single Dragadelf soar towards him before it flew right overhead and destroyed everything in its wake like a devastating hurricane...

Ramerick's eyes squeezed shut, despite understanding it was an illusion. When his eyes opened once more, he viewed the entirety of the valley below. It was grey, but this time it was not his perception but more reality. Ash and soot blanketed the slope, reminiscent of poisonous snowfall decorating the pagoda-like structures. It was symbolic of everything, black and dead.

"*Welcome home, friend of the shadows!*" he heard the voice of Dreanor behind him.

He turned around to view the chairs of stone and saw each member of The Ancient Drethai sitting where The Blessèd Order once sat. He fearlessly walked into the middle of the circle of chairs, confronting another piece of unfinished business. He stared up at Dreanor where Magraw had been, his mind quickly shifted, showing him the arrow shaft wedged into Jàqueson's heart, a brutal reminder of his last endeavour. He understood what this all meant.

"*It is what shall come to pass, if Ramalon succeeds,*" Magraw claimed as Dreanor.

The more he understood he had a vendetta to settle, the more it galvanised him to achieve his final pledge. He knew to himself; he could never see his family again while Ramalon lived. He also knew this was the last thing he had to do, the final pain he must endure before eternal happiness awaited him at the end of it.

"Okay," he resigned, turning back to Dreanor with a little more determination. "I can do this."

Ramerick closed his eyes and prepared himself with a large inhale and exhale of breath. He opened his eyes, and suddenly he noticed The Blessèd Order present once more as if they were always there.

Magraw nodded his head which Ramerick returned with a reluctant nod of appreciation.

"Son?" Eveleve whispered.

"I'm ready," he declared.

Clethance set up the ritual once more in the same manner with the stone in one hand and the necklace in the other as their palms

## A Mother's Love

connected. Ramerick now had that little more strength to look into his mother's eyes that time. Her character did not waver nor shake in the face of her end, to which Ramerick took courage. The ultimate form of bravery to give your life for another was admirable beyond anything Ramerick could fathom.

"It is time," Clethance restarted. "Repeat after me. *Bolero, cestanya, bothera.*"

"*Bolero. Cestanya. Bothera.*"

"Good. And again."

"*Bolero. Cestanya. Bothera.*"

"Close your eyes. Keep repeating the incantation."

Ramerick obliged. "*Bolero, cestanya, bothera. Bolero, cestanya bothera. Bolero… Cestanya… Bothera… Bolero… Cestanya… Bothera…*"

He began to feel the warmth in his protecy stone as it began to accept him. At the same time of growing heat in his right hand, he experienced a sensation he had never felt before in his left. It was likened to that of adrenaline absorbing into his arm, fuelling him with courage and strength. It became euphoric as the life from his mother's necklace began to spread into his whole body, landing lastly on his heart. The ecstasy became so intense his eyes were forced open and all he could see was a beautiful combination of whirling flames and swirling streaks of light around both him and his mother, encompassing them both in a bubble of light and fire. Both energies infused together to create the spectacular sphere which no one else could see past its walls. In a world of their own, the delicate moment signified that the enchantment was taking place.

As they stared into each other's eyes, there was not an ounce of sadness in Eveleve's face, which couldn't have contradicted more with her son's, as her time was near.

"Close your eyes son," she instructed him quietly and gently.

Ramerick was so reluctant, scared that if he did, he might never see her again. He cherished what he believed would be his final moments with her and couldn't help but drop a tear from the side of his eye. The droplet itself contained miniature streaks of light to confirm the exchange of her life was successfully taking place.

"It's okay," she soothed, bringing their hands together, cupping both objects in her hands with Ramerick's now on top. "Close your eyes… Think of them…"

Inhaling one more breath, he obliged and squeezed his eyelids shut. Eveleve took one last look upon her son before she too closed her eyes forever, giving him one last gift...

He became distracted from the enchantment's final stages and imagined himself back in his home in Pippersby. He saw both his son and Amba playing in the lounge, as if ghosts; playing happily, laughing, tickling one another. He wanted to join in but knew it wasn't real. It made him happy to see them live again - to exist, albeit just in his mind and was enough to give him the strength needed to strive for that moment. To keep living. To keep fighting. They both stopped to look at him and smiled, just like they did every time he came back from work. He smiled back and his heart thumped much stronger than before.

It gave him that focus and determination to face his demon. He was alive in himself again, seeing the colours gradually bleed back to their original state. He knew the time to go to them was not now and felt the enchantment finally coming to a close as the image slowly faded away and back to the darkness of the back of his eyelids once more...

His eyes slowly opened and the enchantment was complete.

Standing before him was his mother, whose eyes were frozen shut, her body motionless and still. Alas, she had turned to cold stone itself. Her final pose now sculpted of hard rock, like a beautiful angel that bore her gentle smile that would soar for eternity.

Her final gesture was that of her outstretched hands to her son that cupped both her necklace and Ramerick's new protecy stone. A subtle whirl of fire swirled inside while the necklace glowed a fluorescent white. It expressed her blessings, but to him, she gave so much more than that. She gave him the reminder that he was loved and that love was eternal for as long as you had something to live for. It reminded him more potently than ever that he did have something to live for and that he was one step closer to making it to that moment he yearned for. The magical moment that he would see them all again...

It strengthened his cause. His mind was calm. He was ready.

"Ramerick?" Clethance asked.

He noticed the sadness in the atmosphere as The Blessèd Order viewed the statuette of Eveleve in the middle. He chose to leave the necklace and the protecy stone in his mother's hands for safekeeping which he felt right and symbolic.

He looked around The Blessèd Order, who clearly expected him to buckle to his knees from the sacrifice they had just witnessed. Alas, they did not see someone stricken with grief any longer. They saw a man whose determination and strength rose to the surface. His eyes no

## A Mother's Love

longer dead but full of life and drive to fulfil his destiny.

One by one, they began to bow their heads in recognition that Ramerick was now, The Blessèd Mage of Life.

It wasn't too long before Clethance and Mavokai began to bring him up to speed with the plan. Ramerick, all the time, listened carefully to the details of what must happen. The risks and what he was likely to face.

Clethance gave Ramerick the stone of Zoldathorn, which he'd added a few colour changes to look like a complete copy of The Dragastone.

"So remember, you must initiate the switch of stones *before* he strikes."

"Understood," he answered. "How far away from Monarchy Hall will I be?"

The whole Order looked toward Gracène.

"I will only be able to get you to the other side of the wall," she answered. "The rest will be down to you."

"I have a bad feeling about this," Aristuto whispered to Zathos.

"The death rune I have implanted onto you will only activate upon a lethal strike but it's presence within you should hopefully give you the skill to pass by undetected."

"That's helpful to know," Ramerick mused.

"However, should you need it, your powers as The Blessèd Mage of Life, enforced by the power of The Dragastone, should repel much of what's inside until you reach Monarchy Hall."

"Including a Dragadelf?" Thakendrax asked.

Mavokai hesitated and looked toward Meigar for confirmation.

"If all we have learned is true, Ramerick has a claim to them. It's uncertain what would happen if they all coincided together."

The tension rose back to its familiar point, knowing that sending Ramerick into the belly of the monster again seemed suicidal. Ramerick however, did not appear dissuaded.

"I do not fear what is to come!" Ramerick declared. "Open it…"

Gracène slowly rose from her chair and stumbled forward a few steps on her walking stick to gather some space.

Mavokai spoke some final words to Ramerick. "You are about to step foot into the realm of the unknown. The gates of the Understunde await, my lord."

It felt weird to him to be called *my lord*, but what didn't feel weird was a sense of goodbye. He knew to himself that somehow this was not goodbye. He would make it back regardless of the mystery of horrors that laid directly ahead of him. He felt powerful. Strong. More assured than he had ever been to fulfil his task.

"Do it..." he insisted to the last remaining member of family he had left.

Gracène nodded her head. "Good luck, laddie," she bade with no jest attached. It almost felt like a heartfelt plea to make it back. He had never heard such a grave undertone in her voice. "Try not to bring back a Dragadelf with you."

Or so he thought.

Hearts began to beat. Pits began to sweat. Fingertips began to shake as Gracène turned to the edge of the platform. She steadied herself and closed her eyes.

No one knew what to expect. Except for Davinor's presumed entrance and Melcelore's portal in The Draughts, it was unclear what they would see once the portal opened. They readied themselves just in case what they would see threatened them.

The thud of Gracène's walking stick landed on the ground. She held out her right hand and aimed it into thin air toward the platform's edge. With her head bowed to concentrate, she found a way to open the gates of The Understunde.

They sensed a little struggle in her ability to achieve such a feat; after all, she was defying the magic of the strongest containment spell ever to exist.

She opened up a small, circular entrance to the other side with her skill, which was pitch black. The circle grew outwards, increasing the size of the portal to presumably inside The Dragasphere. A wave of offensive stench breathed out onto the platform, instantly killing some of the greenery and flowers that surrounded, suggesting that nothing but evil and death resided inside.

The Blessèd Order looked to Ramerick, feeling ultimately guilty they could not go with him, but they took confidence in looking at a man who looked determined not to fail. He burrowed the stone of Zoldathorn deep into his tunic and breathed in the rancid smell, confronting it head-on.

He fearlessly stared into the darkness and like a lone star in the dead of the night sky, he marched straight into the abyss of The Dragasphere.

## *Felder's Legacy*

The bronze haze of The Dragasphere became more apparent the further Ramerick ventured in. Waves of stagnant stench stung his nostrils. His eyes did not trick him - he was inside the most dangerous place on Rèo.

He stumbled over rocky terrain on his journey before eventually coming to a clearing where he could see the capital of Terrasendia in its entirety.

There laid the famous slope the city was nestled in. The place in which he was born and had seen so many times in parallel dimensions, it seemed strange to finally see it with his own eyes as authentic and real as anything. With that same steady flow of confidence flowing through him, he continued his march across the plain leading to it.

After his initial recognition of where he was, his gaze flew toward the ceiling of The Dragasphere, expecting the legendary beasts to be offloading their molten filled bellies onto the fissure, accelerating The Dragasphere's demise. But they were nowhere to be seen.

He thought that was strange and his suspicions immediately bled to the surface, every sense heightened as he prepared for whatever came next. He continued across the barren plain leading toward the city.

He could see some distance away that the whole place was decimated by dragonbreath. Thirty years of charcoaled ruins left everything black and dead. No life could have lived there. All was quiet. Still, spooky. The eerie ghosts of the hundreds of thousands of people that never made it out haunted the remains.

The concept of becoming The Blessèd Mage of Life made him ask himself whether Ramalon could indeed kill him. However, it was still vital that he avoided any fatal attacks before his task was complete or Mavokai's death rune would activate and cast him out.

He sifted through the desolate city and noticed its gradual incline. He imagined what it must have been like thirty years ago when The Dragadelf came. What happened when The Dragasphere was being completed? Did the people know they couldn't escape once it had? He thought about the tremendous loss of life that day and how impossible it must have been for the families to explain the horrific truth to their young. Did they tell them, or did they tell them it would be okay to quell their fears? What would he have done were he in that position and had to tell Jàque that he was about to die? It was difficult even contemplating as it would have been impossible, despite everything he had endured.

At some point, he wondered when he would confront a Dragadelf and what would happen at that point should one or all of them come. It sickened him even to be associated with such inherent evil, which they were. The thousands of lives lost at their wrath and fury that day proved it and only kept his poisonous affiliation because, without it, Rèo would be in graver danger. Alas, they were not the reason he had come. He had come for one purpose - to steal The Dragastone and destroy it, crippling his brother's plans and seeing the means to his end.

He continued wading through the foundations before a long set of stairs carved from the mountain led up to his destination. Still, nothing had presented itself. No wind nor sound except the gentle crunch of his footsteps. He briefly wondered why he didn't see any corpses rotting on the ground, or why he was walking through unchallenged. He knew Ramalon would have something cunning prepared for him but kept his wits about him as he continued his brave ascent to the final steps.

And there it was, coming into view as he reached the top - Monarchy Hall. He sensed The Dragastone's presence was near and walked toward the final set of steps leading up to the platform before the famous tall doors.

The walk went on forever, or so it felt to him. He was approaching, without a doubt, the most pivotal moment of his life. The balance of the world hinged on what happened next. A pure battle of light versus dark. Of good versus evil. Of life versus death.

He was only metres away now from the doors. He knew his brother was on the other side. He could sense him. Feel him. That connection was rife once more, growing ever stronger the closer he got. The answer to every riddle, every problem laid beyond the tall stone doors. Ramerick waited patiently and inhaled a large breath of death, knowing his brother on the other side would initiate the opening of the doors… And how right he was.

The crucks and grinding of steel were heard as the doors slowly opened and he saw some distance down the stretch of Monarchy Hall, sat on the broken throne of his father, his brother Ramalon calmly waiting for him. The spectacular glow of The Dragastone gleamed from his hand.

They both looked upon one another from afar, not quite believing it was real. Alas, it was. No tricks. No parallel dimensions to connect them. The circumstances that led them both to that very moment were momentous and how humble they both felt to be a part of something so vital in Terrasendia's history. However, their opposite opinion over that association could not be further away. One could not want the attention and the importance more, while the other couldn't think of anything worse.

Ramerick did not fear his brother. After the initial amazement, the importance of his task took over, fearlessly walking into Monarchy Hall. Ramalon allowed him to approach unchallenged, not quite sure exactly of what to say to the brother he had never physically met.

The carnage of Monarchy Hall looked the same as when they connected not so long ago. The ceiling was obliterated. The structural beams remained intact because of the earth magic instilled into the foundations many years ago. The lifeless corpse of Melcelore lay desecrated on the ground.

The internal turmoil he felt back then in the vision was not present in him now upon viewing the same scene, however there was one big difference between the vision and the reality. The massive carcass of a Dragadelf laying silently in the corner was definitely not there before - Ramerick would definitely have remembered that. He took a moment to marvel at the sheer size of the beast. Its signature tyrannosaurial head just as he had pictured in his mind - formidable and ferocious even in death. As abhorrent as he found them in their nature, he couldn't deny seeing it in the flesh was a sight to behold. He wondered briefly whether it had perished by Ramalon's hand, left slaughtered on display to demonstrate just how powerful he had become. But upon reflection, that did not make logical sense. The death of another Dragadelf loyal to him was certainly something he would not want. He knew about the two that had escaped The Dragasphere and had been destroyed and counting the one dead in the Hall left just four more. Still, four Dragadelf were more than enough to cripple all that was good and green.

Ramerick stopped his advance some twenty metres away, giving them some much-needed distance to look upon one another. Ramalon remained calm while a hatred boiled under Ramerick's skin. The urge to strike the other first was so intense; it was like opposite ends of a magnet trying to pull one another together. It was Ramalon who made the first move.

"Hello brother," he said, mimicking the same way he addressed him in their connection. Ramerick did not respond, nor have any intention of doing so just yet. He concentrated entirely on his task of trying to orchestrate stealing the stone. "I must admit, I'm surprised you made it past the wall. I guess our father would be proud. You know, the one we never met. The one who valued our lives so little that all three of us were just pawns in a plan. Nothing more than jigsaw pieces in a puzzle. And now you and I are the last of our father's legacy. How does that make you feel, brother?"

Ramerick tried not to respond by rising or falling to his manipulation. Instead, he remained calm and collected. Ramalon bounced a peal of subtle laughter in his brother's attempt to stonewall him.

"It feels like we've known each other all our lives, doesn't it? How I know your insecurities, your weaknesses, your desires. And how you know mine. Yes, brother, you've seen what it is that I will achieve. I'm

## Felder's Legacy

just surprised you came so willingly, for I cannot do it without you."

Ramerick fathomed as much, although he admitted to himself he was confused. He wondered why he had shown him the split in The Dragasphere, only to find out that it never actually happened. He was so sure it was real, he'd have staked his life on it. After all, that was Ramalon's intention and so naturally made sense. He gathered from that moment that all Ramalon needed was to kill him to make that happen, which didn't change anything as Ramerick knew he must not die at his brother's hand.

"I guess you're here for this." He lifted The Dragastone with one hand, presenting the anomaly in all its glory. The beautiful swirling colours sparkled from the stone's casing. Ramerick's eyes did not waver. They were transfixed into his brother's eyes. "The final piece of the puzzle! Isn't it just amazing? The answer to all our questions lies in my hands," he continued in his manipulative tone.

Ramerick could not hide the truth from his eyes. They both knew and understood the other so well; it did not need confirmation. Yet, he chose to remain silent and measured.

"It's certainly a little conundrum our father left us, but no matter. Its power is undoubtedly mine to claim, as is so much more! Take a look over there," he indicated with his hand to the Dragadelf's lifeless body. Ramerick obliged and looked toward the phenomenal specimen to their left. "How do you feel about that? What was once such a beautiful life, now nothing more than a sad relic of memory."

It was indeed a magnificent creature whose eyes were that of stone. He admittedly felt a sudden sadness that its life was no longer until he remembered that such a life was evil and had taken many lives itself. He finally landed on relief more than anything else. He looked back toward Ramalon with no apparent remorse or emotion, just a continuance of his intention.

"You do not deserve their loyalty," Ramalon shook his head in disgust. "How dare you lay such a claim to something so beautiful! So rare! So perfect! Our older brother couldn't see them for what they are and neither can you. The light has blinded you both!"

Ramerick's lack of response started to frustrate Ramalon, like an itch on the brain he couldn't scratch. Surely he would have had to say something in this momentous moment? he thought. He rose from their father's throne, The Dragastone still in hand, and looked a little more intently into Ramerick's harrowing eyes.

"They said you would come... The Ancient Drethai," Ramalon

probed, changing tactic.

The simple mentioning of their name irked Ramerick and brought back those chilling memories that had haunted him forever since. Ramalon sensed that he had hit a particular nerve.

"Come now, brother, do not despise me for what happened to your son. You should thank me for what happened. Melcelore over there had very different plans for him; I assure you that. Wasn't it fairer, kinder even, that he experienced a quick death and not the one that was destined for him? What I did?… It was mercy…" he whispered.

Ramerick's defence began to crumble. His body remained still and motionless, but his eyes could not hide the internal suffering at being reminded of Jàqueson's death. He couldn't hold on to his composure any longer, feeling his brother's evil would flourish were he not to stand up to it.

"I told you what I was going to do," Ramerick finally replied, his tone a dangerous whisper. "And I will not rest until it happens."

"There you are," Ramalon replied, a little more satisfied. "The brother I've never known."

"Where are the rest of them? The Dragadelf?"

"They're close by… Resting," Ramalon informed with a hint of intrigue. "It takes much more than you think to bring down such a spell as this." He gestured widely to the dome enclosure.

Ramerick was concerned about why he hadn't seen them yet and frankly didn't know what he would do if one confronted him right now.

"You will not win Ramalon! Whatever it is you want, you will not destroy all that is good and green."

"Brother, it is not a question of *if* I will destroy it. It's simply a matter of *when*."

"Not while I stand. For as long as I live, you will never fulfil your destiny."

"That is where your wrong, brother. I have only three steps left to climb before I reach the top."

"The top of what?"

"The Staircase to Divinity…" he began to gloat and marvel in his growing strength. "Each step I climb represents my growing powers, and no one can stop me from achieving those last three."

Ramerick furrowed his eyebrows; he had no idea what that meant despite feeling like somehow he should. And then it dawned on him so clearly. He had already acquired four of the six destructive affinities, which would leave the remaining last two in water and air. As for the last one, he knew with certainty what that was.

"And what is the top?" he asked, knowing full well the answer.

"... You," Ramalon declared. "You are the final step to divinity. And once you are dead, no one will contest the deity I was born to be! No one will question my right to make the world see what I see, through the eyes of a god!"

It was clear now Ramalon's intentions to make Ramerick's death the last step in his self-conjured metaphor, claiming the full right over The Dragastone, The Dragadelf and all destructive affinities.

"It might work if people believed they needed one," Ramerick argued, not that he cared much for Ramalon's warped ideology.

"Oh, but they do, brother, they do! Don't you see? It's what this world needs! For too long, we've imagined a world without one. No aspiration of hope, of believing that there's anything or anyone higher than the life you comprehend. Too many of us fall into the pit of weakness, hoping that the strong offer their hands to stop us from falling... Those hands never reach out!" he delivered, a little more angrily as if it had affected him personally. "Instead, the weak fall and they carry on falling. Loneliness is a dark place. And so that is my purpose. To provide them with that hand. A faith, a hope that they are worth this world's time."

"The hand of Sarthanzar."

"Please! I am no spawn of such mythology. I despise the notion that everything I do is in his name. My duty is my own, to unshackle the possibility that someone greater than themselves is there for them in their times of need. All the while, Sarthanzar sits on his molten throne and does nothing! Just like this world, they both are too blind to see just how similar they are. The false impression-hood that it gives, a drive, a flourish of self-esteem! But fear not. For I *will* be that god, when I climb that last step! And when I do, this world will be free from falsities, oppression, unjust inequality. A fair world. A perfect world..."

No matter how much deceit lay in someone's demeanour, not even Ramalon could deny the previous statement and Ramerick took everything he just said as true.

"So why have you not done it already? Taken your last affinities? Surely you have enough evil inside you to do it."

"I don't take pride in feeding on the weak. A dragon's pride flourishes only when the prize is worth its time."

With that, Ramerick gathered he would only fletch and take that which is symbolic and sentimental to him, which gave him a very good idea of who Ramalon might go for next. However, something that did not add up to him was that if he was his final destination, why would Ramalon kill him now while he still had two affinities left to acquire? It didn't make sense to him.

"And yet, here I stand…" Ramerick said, almost encouraging his brother to engage.

"There you stand," he responded in equal intention.

"There is just one flaw in your perception," Ramerick informed. "Something you have missed."

"No. There is not," Ramalon denied, shaking his head in the process. "I have seen all I need to see."

"Then, you are blind. Brother. You want power more than anything on this world, and yet you fail to recognise the most powerful thing there is. Something that will eclipse you, making you nothing more than a memory."

"And what might that be?"

"… Love."

Ramalon did not appear to react, but Ramerick could sense he was tapping into a sensitive area that Ramalon did not know was there, surprising him with how much it affected him. He began to blink a little more frenetically. It began to fuel his anger a little more.

"Nothing compares to it," Ramerick continued. "It's not materialistic, it's not conjured in any form apart from the effects it creates. And I feel sorry for you that you can't ever access its true power."

"And what *love* do I get from this world!?" he spat the term with spite, finding it comical that it was even a real thing. "Nothing… It turned its back on me and it will burn for doing so! Our older brother died, the apparent rightful King on Terrasendia. And who may that fall to, I wonder? Yes, brother, to me! But do you think this world will honour me as their King? Am I not worth the name!? No! I think not!"

"This world will never accept the symbol of evil you bring."

"Evil is just a perception, a subjectiveness as is power. This stone? Gives me all the power and so-called love, I will ever need."

"Our mother loved you when we were born."

"And then our father took that away!" Ramalon responded, a little shook. "Don't you see brother? He stopped me from feeling what you feel, because it only makes you weak, and weak would never have defeated the greatest dark Màgjeur of all time! Allowing simple emotion such as love is a poison! A pathway to weakness!"

"Then you are more lost than I ever thought. And I do, I feel sorry for you that you can't feel what I feel," a tear began to roll down the side of his cheek as he remembered the face of his son and Amba throughout. "Your only perception of love comes from the poison of power that stone presents! I am sorry that there is so much evil and hate inside you that you can't understand. Love is eternal... Unlike you!"

Ramalon was charged. He did not like his philosophy to be brought into question and displayed a rare pathway into his anger, bringing his rage to the surface.

"Say your last words," Ramalon urged, "for I will stop them echoing into eternity!"

"... For Jàque!" Ramerick declared defiantly, charging his own affinity of fire for the first time.

"Our father's son indeed," Ramalon also charged himself.

That inevitable moment to strike was born as both brothers prepared to unleash their intent onto one another. Ramerick felt The Protecy pulse through his whole body with scorching heat which he then erupted from his palm, conjuring a magnificent fire of bright white onto his brother.

Ramalon responded by yelling with all his might and conjured a flume of black fire with equal impressiveness which connected to Ramerick's in a cataclysmic climax. The colours of their attacks symbolised the fight of life versus death, ferociously ripping the air of any present oxygen.

Ramalon held The Dragastone in one hand while the other threw his attack. Ramerick, on the opposite side, was ultimately surprised by the amount of force he was conjuring. Despite never using The Protecy, he felt it was unnatural to have this amount of power surging through him. Backed up by the support of The Dragastone in his brother's hands, he unleashed his intent towards him so confidently; he felt that familiar invincibility running through him once more.

The duel appeared equal to that point, which astonished Ramerick. He thought surely Ramalon would be able to conjure more energy as his soul was implanted onto the stone and create an advantage? However, he gathered that he had never faced his powers of life, which gave him the platform to shine magnificently. Though, it did not distract him from what he needed to do. He needed to find a way of stealing The Dragastone from his brother's hands.

Ramerick knew that Ramalon was aware of what was at stake for him too. He knew that if his hands managed to touch the stone, technically, he could destroy it there and then, all but ending his life and everything associated with it. Hence it made him fearful that he had something grave to lose.

Ramerick changed tactics and tried to manipulate their fires' connection, manoeuvring it in different directions, spitting out flames in the process. It did not work, as their connected fire remained strong.

The Blessèd Mage of Life was beginning to run out of ideas already and had the stupendous thought of trying to tap into a foreign area. He had no idea why, but he thought about trying to open up his presence to The Dragadelf, not that he knew how or what would even happen if he managed to achieve it. Alas, he gathered that would not be a smart decision and made him wonder why they had not been present thus far.

Ramalon began to increase his foothold within the duel, forcing Ramerick back, sliding the balls of his feet along the ground as he tried to withstand the pressure. The black fire began to consume the area above and around Ramerick's smaller white fire. Like an orb, his defence of life and fire proved effective and Ramalon struggled to break through. However, he knew it would not last and he had to try something new.

He remembered the value in relaxing that internal energy causing the flow of The Protecy to be stronger and so wasted no time in making that happen. As he did, the heat within him grew exponentially, fuelling his attack with more power that halted Ramalon's and even forced the white wave to push back the black wall of fire.

In the process, he noticed a particular realisation in Ramalon. It was as if he, himself, had never experienced that amount of force in his own protecy before and was confirmed by The Dragastone lighting up brighter than before. It shone like a solar flare as both their protecy's relaxed through it at the same time.

Suddenly a slice of luck was presented to him. He saw through the rippling waves of heat Ramalon was wailing in intense pain and had dropped The Dragastone to the ground. What was that? Ramerick thought. Ramalon's agony was continuous and it seemed as if he couldn't maintain his fires for much longer, choosing to overcharge the combustion to create a rapid explosion.

The explosion forced Ramalon into the wall behind their father's throne while Ramerick was sent flying back along the stretch of Monarchy Hall. Somehow in the chaotic melee, The Dragastone had rebounded off several walls and landed on the ground between them both.

Ramerick could not fathom what happened but took the opportunity to quickly gather himself and make a run for the stone. Ramalon meanwhile, regained the strength to stumble back to his feet, clutching at his severely burnt hand, which cruelly blistered. He looked toward Ramerick, who had stopped immediately upon recognising he'd made it back to his feet. They both realised what had happened at that moment. Somehow opening both of their protecy's at the same time created so much heat that it affected the casing of The Dragastone, hence burning Ramalon's hands.

It took them both by surprise but Ramerick had no time to sit and contemplate. He was closer than Ramalon to the stone and despite their temporary standoff, he made another run for it.

Ramalon unleashed a lightning bolt, changing up his choice of affinity to see what his brother would do. He did not know how he did it, but Ramerick managed to defend himself with white swirls of light that instantly squibbed down his brother's volts. It was as if life was on his side, protecting him like a living entity, though Ramerick knew he had to be so careful not to be struck too soon. One slip or one hit by Ramalon's bolt would activate the death rune and cast him back to Laloncère. He still had to switch the stones.

Like a gauntlet, Ramerick continued to slalom through, deflecting Ramalon's continuous attacks as he remained stationed by their father's throne. Why was Ramalon not actively attempting to retrieve the stone? he thought. He knew Ramalon could not afford The Dragastone to be destroyed but had no time to ponder why.

He was moments away from picking up the stone when Ramalon seemed to act desperately, offloading several ice spikes that Ramerick defended with a tremendous wall of white fire. Ramalon's attacks were insufficient as the defence held successfully. Ramerick grabbed the stone of Zoldathorn from within his robes and was just moments away from achieving the switch, but was diverted by a colossal surge of black fire once more from a desperate Ramalon, doing everything he seemingly could to stop Ramerick from touching that stone.

The distraction proved effective and caused Ramerick to defend. The force met Ramerick's defensive wall with a mystifying light that forced both their eyes to squeeze shut. For a moment both brothers were blinded in pure light.

Ramalon yelled, impulsively and recklessly thrashing his earth magic onto the building, desperately preventing his brother from touching the stone. The ugly chaos resulted in fragments of the ground being uprooted, walls crumbled and spewed into the air, while the ground quaked and shook vigorously.

Ramerick, whose sight was still recovering too, stumbled back and away from the gleaming stone which was bouncing all over the place. He made several attempts to go after it, outstretching his arms for balance and scanning for the light the stone presented.

However, it seemed Ramalon had acquired his sight first. He brought the rumbling to a very rapid halt and unleashed a lightning bolt at the feet of Ramerick, who froze immediately.

The atmosphere had simmered down to complete stillness. The only sound came from their intense breaths which came in waves, drained from their efforts onto one another. The realisation and horror in Ramerick's eyes narrowed as he caught sight of the magnificent gleam the stone presented slap bang in the middle of them. Ramalon saw it too, though it was unclear who would get to it first.

Ramerick fell to one knee out of utter exhaustion from their duel. He doubted whether Ramalon had experienced that much fight in his life, which was clear from his weary face. He continued to think about how he could grab the stone, making random plans to get it.

However, it was Ramalon who regained stamina first and took full control. He began to encroach on the stone slowly. Ramerick struggled to his feet, but his knees gave way, buckling and landing in a tired heap on the ground.

"Such a shame…" Ramalon panted as he continued his slow advance onto the stone. "So close, and yet, so far!" he mocked triumphantly, though still breathing heavily.

He cracked a very rare smile, displaying his relief at stopping his brother from claiming and ultimately destroying the stone. It was as if at that moment, he wanted Ramerick to see that he would go on to become the deity he was born to be. And that there was nothing anyone could do to stop him.

"Goodbye, brother," Ramalon concluded.

Suddenly, Ramerick made one last gallant attempt to race toward the stone with as much stamina he could muster. He conjured that similar wall of fire, twinned with life's essence to aid his advance but this time Ramalon was ready for him.

Agonisingly close, Ramerick made a lunging thrust and outstretched his hand, mere fingertips away from landing his palm onto the stone. However before contact, Ramalon sent a devastating lightning bolt rippling through the air which pierced through Ramerick's defensive wall and landed flush into his heart. Alas, his hand did not make contact with the stone between them. Ramalon had landed the blow in the nick of time.

The pain reverberated intensely through Ramerick's body. The blow was fatal. The life that was once rife within him was being replaced with grappling death. Mavokai's death rune was activated, causing the ancient spell upon Felders Crest to cast him from Monarchy Hall and back to the source of the rune.

Never before could he have imagined such a contrast of feelings and emotions within his body as it swirled inside and out, churning every surface imaginable before the pain began to mellow out into nothingness once more.

Before he did, he saved one last remaining thought. It was not of his son and Amba as it would likely have been if he were to pass into The Gracelands. It was of The Dragastone. His defining intention.

## *The Key to Inevitability*

Ramerick's heartbeat was the first thing to come to his awareness, thumping out of his ribcage like a trapped manic monkey. The feelings and sensations began to flood back also, hearing voices vaguely on the surface of his consciousness.

He understood the bizarre notion that he just experienced death. Albeit, because of the powers endowed on him from being The Blessèd Mage of Life, he withstood death's claim.

"*Ramerick... Ramerick*! Ramerick!" he heard the voice of Ramavell attempting to revive him.

At first, his vision blurred as he came around, but he very quickly established that he was back on Laloncère by the feet of stone that belonged to his mother.

Ramerick came to a sitting position, breathing heavily from his efforts. The Blessèd Order stood in anticipation for what Ramerick was about to reveal.

"Thank Blessèd you survived!" Ramavell celebrated, most relieved.

"What happened?" Mavokai urged. "Did you get it?"

Ramerick looked up toward him with that similar fatigued and resigned look, still slightly dazed from his weariness. He reached into his robe to produce the similar swirling of lights the stone of Zoldathorn presented. The Blessèd Order was somewhat confused as they did not have the skill to tell which one was which.

"Well? What are we looking at?" Mijkal asked.

"That, is not the stone of Zoldathorn," Clethance confirmed with a growing smile.

Everyone in attendance stared at the magical relic of The Dragastone that sat in Ramerick's hands. The relief that the plan had worked sank in. It joined them all to see that now, they had the upper hand. What could Ramalon do, moments away from having the stone destroyed and ending it all?

Though to some, more noticeably Magraw and even Meigar were surprised, suspicious even, that he had pulled it off.

"Well done, laddie!" Gracène congratulated. "Well done!"

"What happened?" Mavokai asked.

"Yes! What happened indeed?" Magraw interrogated.

"We fought," Ramerick explained breathlessly. He came to stand, helped up by Ramavell as he addressed his audience. "There was a moment when we both were blinded. Luckily I was close enough to it to make the switch before he noticed. I had to make it seem as if I didn't have it so that he would strike me when he had the chance. I did everything I could to retrieve Zoldathorn's stone. Otherwise, he might have suspected something."

"You brave boy!" Thakendrax praised with a smile.

"So that's it?" Mijkal pressed. "That's the real Dragastone!?"

"It is," Clethance confirmed once more.

"It was strange, though," Ramerick continued to recount the experience.

"Strange how?"

"How I managed to stand up to him. I didn't expect to match him and I don't think he did either. Was it my powers of life?" he asked to Mavokai.

"It's hard to tell. He would not have come across a challenge such as yourself, that's for sure."

"There was a moment when I produced so much power that the stone lit up. It burned his hand when it did, giving me the chance to steal it. I don't know what happened."

"The stone experienced both your protecy's open at the same time," Clethance explained. "It would have given you both clearer access to its purity and henceforth give you both greater power."

"What about it burning his hand?" Meigar queried.

"The stone's casing must not have been able to handle the intensity of both users at one time."

Meigar continued to ponder silently.

"There is also another thing. The Dragadelf were not accelerating the split when I arrived. In fact, I didn't see any of them. Well, one I did, but it was already dead."

"How did it die?" Mavokai asked.

"Ramalon told me Melcelore had killed it during their fight."

"So now there are four left," Thakendrax clarified.

"Still four too many," Meigar warned.

"Does any of this matter?" Mijkal asked. "We have the real Dragastone! Right there! What are we waiting for? Let's destroy it now before The Dragasphere falls!"

"Wait!" Magraw urged. "I am gravely concerned once more. You tell us you did not see The Dragadelf accelerate this apparent split. I am of the conclusion that what you saw in your brother connected to you did not happen at all."

"Nonsense Lestas, come now! We all felt it."

"None of this adds up," Magraw shook his head.

"When I asked where they were, Ramalon told me they were resting," Ramerick informed.

"*Resting?*" Magraw examined. "A very peculiar time to rest, don't you think? The most pivotal moment of both your lives and they just happened to be *resting*?"

Suddenly, the prestige of achieving such a plan had its triumph squibbed down exponentially. The ease at which Ramerick seemed to achieve his goal seemed to click in the minds of the Order, heavy suspicion sinking deeper in their resolve.

"We have The Dragastone!" Mijkal continued to argue. "We can end this all. Right now! I don't see what we are waiting for. Does it matter if Ramalon did attack The Dragasphere? Does it matter what Ramerick saw anymore? What can Ramalon now do to stop the stone's termination!?"

"I do not like this," Zathos weighed in.

"This was a mistake," Aristuto too voiced his concern as he concluded that this was all too easy.

The Blessèd Order continued to argue their points once more with the familiar stance of Mijkal and Thakendrax on the side for destroying the stone.

Meanwhile, the voices began to mellow out and fade in Ramerick's mind as it began to wander, as it so often did. He began to imagine everything that had happened to him as a result of The Dragastone's existence. He blamed it for every moment of hurt and emotional pain he had ever suffered. The images were more vivid than ever before, undoubtedly down to the fact that he had the very reason for all it sat nestled in his hands. His mesmerisation continued to intensify.

His eyes closed, heightening the sensations the stone presented in his fingertips. For some foreign reason unknown to him, it was as if the stone was willing him to destroy it. It was not Ramalon invading his mind like before, as he knew that couldn't happen any longer due to his mother's inheritance. It came from the stone itself. He did not feel he was strong enough to withstand the manifest that began to poison his mind. The impulsive nature that was all too familiar began to grapple his desire once more. It urged him to follow through with the temptation, which was now too strong to dissuade.

With each growing thought, his intention grew stronger. All it would take was one simple opening of the connection to the stone and it would all be over. Forever. The pain would no longer be there, he thought...

Suddenly in the process of thought, the penny dropped in Meigar's mind. He understood so clearly what was happening and his fright rose to the surface.

"Ramerick?" he nervously asked as he steadily rose from his chair. He slowly approached him, keeping his footsteps so light; it was like he was trying not to wake a sleeping lion.

The debates very quickly came to a silence, noticing the severity of Meigar's petrification. No one had ever seen the level of concern on The Blessèd Mage of Earth's face before. He understood at that moment just how exposed they all were and what Ramalon's plan was all along...

The Blessèd Mage of Life did not respond in the middle of the circular platform. His eyes trance-like, motionless and in deep thought,

The Dragastone still in his hands.

"Ramerick, you must listen to me," Meigar very calmly continued, afraid that one misplaced movement might trigger an explosion. "You must drop that stone. Now…" Ramerick did not respond. In fact, it wasn't clear to anyone if he'd heard a single word. "Ramerick?" he repeated with a little more urgency. "You must, drop that stone, now!"

Still, no response. The tension was made worse by Ramerick's lack of response. There was no telling what was going through his mind.

"Come back to us," Meigar continued. "Whatever it is telling you, it's not real. You hear me? It's not real. You must fight back! You are strong! Just like your mother! Just like your father! You hear me!? You, are, strong!" he implied with greater purpose.

Still, Ramerick did not respond, remaining motionless.

Meigar was several metres away and calculated that the risk of doing nothing was far from safe and so rapidly attempted to swipe The Dragastone from his hands.

"NO!" Ramerick screamed at him. Demented and out of control he opened his eyes wide like a possessed maniac and instantly opened up the connection to The Dragastone in an attempt to destroy it.

Suddenly, upon doing so, his hands gripped the stone uncontrollably as it began violently electrocuting The Blessèd Mage of Life.

"NOOOOOO!" Meigar wailed.

He attempted to swipe of the stone once again, however when his hand landed, the volts shocked him sharply, propelling him back to his chair of stone.

The Blessèd Order rallied their unilateral panic but did not know what to do, feeling quite the fools for not foreseeing this trap. Ramerick wailed in severe pain as the violent shocks continued to inflict sheer agony onto The Blessèd Mage of Life.

"WHAT'S HAPPENING!!??" Ramerick cried out, instantly coming back to reality.

"IT'S A HEX!!!" Mavokai informed.

"WHAT DO WE DO!?" Clethance hurriedly asked.

Mavokai shook his head. "… There's nothing we can do," he gravely whispered.

Ramerick continued to wail in pain, trying at every moment to let go of The Dragastone, but he could not. Almost as if it had a grip on his very soul and had no intention of letting it go. Trapped inside the connection of barbarity, it butchered portions of his flesh and ripped it from his limbs. His skin rapidly regenerated due to his powers of life preservation but it sadistically prolonged his torture. Though without it, he would not withstand the threshold of pain.

Members of The Blessèd Order attempted to prize his hands away by releasing spells but they did not work, rebounding off of him and, in some cases, inflicting more trauma. There was nothing they could do except watch on helplessly.

Ramavell attempted to break Ramerick free from its lethal bind but was stopped by Clethance.

"NO, MY FRIEND! NO!" he pleaded as he struggled to restrain Ramavell.

"RAMERICK!" the Medimage cried.

Suddenly, Clethance realised the real horror of what was happening. In the midst of Ramerick's painful trap, he knew that the stone was not being destroyed but that the connection of Ramerick's protecy was fully open, which left only one conclusion.

"Oh no…" he gravely whispered. He did not know where to look, flicking his head to The Blessèd Order and back to Ramerick frantically. "What have we done…?"

Meanwhile, amid the painful event, Ramerick used what strength he could to connect to his brother on his terms to find out what was happening. He could see entirely what Ramalon was doing inside The Dragasphere. He had planned it all.

"IT'S RAMALON!!!" he desperately wailed.

Without wasting any time, he saw Ramalon in his mind, charge up his affinity of fire and with one mighty conjuration, he unleashed, with all his might, the execution of his plan.

"AHHHHHHHHHHHHHHHH!" Ramalon yelled.

His biblical flame rapidly scorched out of his right hand and seared vertically toward the roof of The Dragasphere. The catastrophic attack was backed up not only by his own connection to The Dragastone but now also Ramerick's opening of The Protecy, which gave The Dragastone a two-fold magnification of power.

The cataclysmic heat burned so hot that it ripped straight through the concealment and beyond the skies of Rèo. The Dragasphere did not crumble in its entirety; however, the fissure that it now created could not be repaired.

Ramalon could not hold the devastating attack, which had just achieved something no one had ever thought possible…

The Dragasphere had been breached.

He fell to the ground drained, as too did Ramerick on Laloncère as the hex had finally ceased its bind. Presumably, Ramalon no longer had the stamina to keep the curse alive due to his efforts.

Ramerick had dropped The Dragastone onto the ground, which no one dared to touch. The aftershocks in his body still caused immeasurable pain. He could only process the spent, heavy feeling he and his brother were sharing in their minds. They both laid on the ground, utterly exhausted. With what remained of Ramalon's strength, he commanded the last four Dragadelf to soar toward the split and unleash their molten filled bellies onto it, accelerating its demise. A carbon copy of that which he saw before he went into The Dragasphere.

Ramerick had not the strength to keep the connection between him and his brother open and with the same effect as going to sleep, he let the connection fade away, admitting defeat to his brother. Ramalon's deceitful plan all hinged on that one moment, for which he had triumphed.

Ramavell was first to come to his aid when it was safe to do so. He gently placed his hands on his temples in an attempt to calm him and restore strength. His trauma was severe, his eyes widely opened in horrific realisation for what had just happened and what was upon them all.

"… It's happening," Ramerick whispered in shock. "It's really happening…"

The Blessèd Order understood that Ramalon's plan had worked and that the impossible was now a reality.

"Gracelands save us," Clethance prayed. "Please tell me this is not true…"

Magraw wanted visual confirmation. "Gracène?" he delicately asked. "Do you have the strength to allow us to see?"

A weary Gracène looked utterly shattered still from her efforts of opening the portal for Ramerick's earlier venture inside.

"I can try," she said weakly. "But I cannot hold it for long." Mirabella put her hands around her shoulders, deeply concerned. "It's okay," Gracène assured. "I have enough strength, one more time."

She remained sat on her chair of stone and extended her hand to the edge of the platform. She struggled to initiate her skill and grappled even more to maintain it. However, the circular portal she was renowned for did open once more to view The Dragasphere from many miles outside. As the opening became more extensive, the picture of what they were seeing became clearer. Their horror for what they were looking at could not be understated.

Portions of The Dragasphere had now cracked, exposing many more fissures within the containment spell. It looked like shattered glass, filled with veins of fire, which spread miles around the orb that had protected Terrasendia for thirty years. Nobody knew just how long it would take for the completion of it's destruction. But one thing was clear to them all. The Dragasphere was dying.

"Gracelands," Mijkal uttered.

What became clear was that when Ramalon showed the visions of his fire splitting The Dragasphere and The Dragadelf accelerating its fracture, it was merely a glimpse into one version of the future, of what could happen should they fall into his trap… And fell for it, so perfectly they did, for The Dragasphere would never have been breached if Ramerick had failed to get the Dragastone.

Even in Ramalon's unrivalled strength and implantation of his soul into the stone, it still would not have been enough to pierce through the walls. The opening of both their protecy's simultaneously was the only possibility Ramalon had to produce that much power and initiate its destruction. Ramerick was the key to inevitability.

A deafening silence was born with nothing but the gentle swaying of the wind in the trees to remind them that time still passed in their catatonic state. Magraw was right after all and Dancès' premonition had come true. There was a unanimous feeling among them all as they helplessly watched on that Terrasendia's worst fear was now upon them. The fight for their lives laid ahead.

Clethance creased his brow at the wellbeing of Ramerick, who was still in shock, but also toward The Dragastone. His inspection intensified as he noticed something rather peculiar had happened to it. It meant many things but he deemed it was not the appropriate time to reveal such information at that moment.

The Blessèd Mage of Life was waning; The Blessèd Order had stalled, unable to process the reality happening before their very eyes but equally unable to deny it and the tremendous mistake they had made.

"Close it…" Zathos quietly whispered to Gracène. They had all seen enough.

The circular portal diminished smaller and smaller, bringing their view to a close before that stillness was born again and the terrifying realisation continued to sink in.

Ramalon had opened the gates of The Understunde.

## *A Possible Resolution*

Laloncère went into a frenzy. The Questacèreans hurried to send as many bluewings as possible to alert Terrasendia of the imminent threat they faced. They rippled out of the towers to inform every corner of the land that The Dragasphere was collapsing. What came with that knowledge was the real horror that haunted them all.

The Blessèd Order looked dumbfounded, utterly shook that they were deceived on such a level. The unprecedented situation however, had forced their hand.

Ramerick had been placed back on his seat of stone, his energy and restoration rapidly recovering from his devastating experience.

The Dragastone remained on the ground, shining harmlessly in its ethereal colours, but it's ghostly curse haunted the atmosphere.

Clethance continued to examine the stone's current state from afar.

"How long do we have? Before it falls?" Mirabella gravely asked, afraid to know the answer.

"Days," Meigar confirmed. "Maybe less."

"And then what?"

"... Then the end of everything we know," Mavokai stated as he took centre stage. "Terrasendia will not be strong enough to repel The Dragadelf and all the souls Ramalon has at his disposal. Every soul that Melcelore acquired now belongs to Ramalon..."

"How is that possible?" Mijkal asked. "He fletched from Melcelore, he could not have taken the souls he had manced."

"In fact, he could. Those poor souls could not pass the walls of The Dragasphere when Melcelore died. Ramalon simply took them for himself," he lowered his tone for the latter part.

"How many?" Mirabella questioned.

"At least a hundred thousand."

The summoning fell silent to learn that was the main bulk of his army. The sheer number frightened them to the core. Because the walls of The Dragasphere had been breached, The Blessèd Mage of Death could sense manced souls with his divine power and so the accuracy of his assessment was in no doubt.

"So what do we do?"

"The only thing we can. We defend all that is good and green with every fibre of our core. Every man and woman with the strength to bear arms will be called upon to defend their way of life! This is simply a matter of survival."

"You sound like you're giving up Master of Death?" Thakendrax accused.

"On the contrary. I'm bracing us for the reality -"

"- Off to The Understunde with that!" the dwarven King spat. "He's not yet confronted the stubbornness of the dwarves of Handenmar! I say let them come and taste our steel!"

"Do not compare your admiration and passion for your people's spirit with the wrath of The Dragadelf!"

"Bah!" Thakendrax shook his head in denial.

"I too fear for my people," Mijkal admitted. "But I am with The Master of Gravitas here. If this is to be our end, we will make our stand echo into The Gracelands and beyond! The legacy of Terrasendia is something he can never erase!"

"I do not hear a solution to our survival..." Magraw interjected. "I,

## A Possible Resolution

for one, do not intend to throw in the towel! *We* have made the gravest mistake," he struggled to keep the blame from his tone, knowing he was against the initial plan to steal The Dragastone in the first place, but controlled his tongue to avoid pointless arguments. Placing blame would not help them win this fight. "And now, *we* must correct it. It is our divine duty, for if we fail, we will all die."

"His perfect world…" Ramerick whispered, being supported by Ramavell who continued to care for him by his side.

"Ramerick?" the Medimage asked gently.

The Blessèd Order turned and listened to him.

"That's what he wants. He thinks the world should be a certain way. His way. In his mind, the world turned it's back on him. And now this is his way of turning his back on the world. He yearns to become the god that this world has never seen. I should have seen it…" he confessed in self-pity.

"It was deception of the highest skill. He deceived us all," Mavokai said.

"I walked straight into his trap. Everything he did was so deliberate. So calculated. Making me believe that I stood a chance. He knew at any moment he could have killed me, but led me on. He wanted to claim his last two affinities before he got to me, and I should have worked that out!"

"This is not helping Master of Life," Magraw admonished as if he were a child. "We have a world to defend!"

"Last two affinities?" Mavokai queried with interest.

"He told me about this, Staircase to Divinity?" he recalled. "I don't know what that is but it sounds like his own map to achieving his endeavours. Each step represents an achievement no one else could surpass. He already has the affinities of fire, earth, volts and ice. And he mentioned acquiring them only from people that *meant* something to him. Entirely purposeful - sentimental even. And now he has two more left before he gets to me. His final step."

"Why are we wasting valuable time philosophising over this?" Magraw barked, unable to hide his annoyance. "The Dragasphere is dying!"

"This might help determine what his next move is!" Mavokai defended with a little more urgency. "Ramerick, what's his intention now?"

"He's weak," he replied in deep thought, trying to pin-point precisely what he planned to do next. "But when his strength returns, I don't think he'll wait to destroy everything there is and create his perfect world. While still climbing those steps."

"What's his next step?"

Ramerick looked over to The Blessèd Mages of Water and Air.

"He will come for you both," he nodded to Wemberlè and Aristuto, who did not react. It was as if they were half expecting it.

"Why the two? What is sentimental to him about them?" Mijkal asked.

"Lady Wemberlè harmed his Dragadelf during The Draughts," Meigar offered, making sense of it. "I'm sure he has not forgotten the emotional pain that must have dealt him. It gave Ramacès the time to close that portal and kill the beast."

"And as for me," Aristuto explained, "I was the first one of us that he had officially challenged. His first insight as to how much potential he could fulfil. I'm sure for him, it was a marvellous moment to remember."

"Then that will be his next move," Ramerick informed.

"And how sure are we that the Master of Life will be last?" Magraw asked.

"It sounds a certainty." Mavokai declared confidently, death being his field. "It's a mechanism he's devised for himself. If he has created this so-called Staircase to Divinity, he will see achieving it only his way! His mind is so bludgeoned with the infatuation of death that he only would see killing as a way of reaching that next step. He has a signature way of taking a life. He's not just some reckless, senseless murderer. He's measured. Poetic. Everything he does is for a reason. Every target he acquires, he's thought about a thousand ways of killing them already and chooses the one which will fulfil his romantic licence more. The mind of a self righteous killer. If Ramerick was told he was at the top of that list, I would stake my death on that being true!"

"Then we must make protecting you three our top priority!" Mijkal suggested.

The Blessèd Order all agreed, except Magraw.

"I do not see how this is a long term solution. Once Terrasendia burns, it is only a matter of time before he finds them all and kills them. By which point, this land could already have perished!"

An annoying sense of fact ran true in Magraw's words. However, Clethance stumbled silently on a potential solution while the battle plan was being hashed out by the Order.

"Then we must stop him, before he stops us!" Mijkal cautioned.

## A Possible Resolution

"The question is, how?" Thakendrax asks. "We have already tried once. We failed."

"It is clear we cannot fail again!" Mavokai implored. "This is our last chance. And time is not on our side…"

"*Time,*" Clethance quietly said, examining The Dragastone with more intrigue. "There may be a slight glimmer of hope…" Clethance breathed, as if speaking his thoughts aloud would shatter any hope they carried..

"Speak clearly, enchanter!" Magraw impels.

"We have been strangely fortunate."

"Fortunate?" he snorted, a little offended. "In case you do not realise, The Dragasphere is collapsing which means, The Dragadelf will escape along with all the malice that Ramalon holds!"

"It is clear we will not be able to defeat him on the fields of battle, which is why we must take a different approach. Look…" He guided everyone to look at The Dragastone.

"What?" Magraw asked as he looked at the stone and did not see why he was being asked to look at it.

"Look a little closer," Clethance suggested.

As their pupils began to absorb the swirling lights within its casing, they began to notice a small crack that had appeared. The fissure was not necessarily substantial, but it was cause for optimism.

"Gracelands…" Meigar whispered, his encouragement rising.

"You see it, yes? The twofold opening of protecy created so much intensity that it could not withstand the sheer force that flowed through it. It is damaged," he optimistically said. "And presents us all with a possible resolution. If it is damaged, it *can* be destroyed!"

"But Clethance, the only way we can destroy the stone is if Ramerick initiates its termination," Wemberle said. "How can he do that if every time he attempts it, Ramalon activates the hex?"

"That is the conundrum, my lady. We need to find a way. And we need time to find the answer."

"Time that we simply do not have!" Magraw strongly said.

"Then find time! Make time, slow him down, halt his forces, do whatever it takes to preserve life! This changes everything! It shows us that the stone is vulnerable when more than one of its protecy's are open at the same time. Our survival depends on finding the answer to its destruction before Ramalon's armies destroy Terrasendia!" Clethance concluded.

Ramerick looked over toward Meigar who seemed yet again, in

deep thought. He had stayed relatively silent since he returned and gave the impression that he knew something compelling.

"What if Ramerick tried again?" Thakendrax suggested. "The hex will surely be painful, but it may destroy it?"

"No!" Ramerick vehemently rejected. The horror in his eyes could not be hidden. "I could never do that again! It was the most painful thing I've ever experienced in my life. For that matter, I could never use The Protecy!" he concluded, utterly frightened at its prospect.

"With respect Master of Life, you may have to."

"Not if I can help it."

"There's no telling how much resistance the stone has anyway," Clethance explained. "It may take days of attempting its termination."

"With every second we stand here, debating about the what *if's* and the what *could's*, we are wasting precious time we could be using to rally the defence of this land!" Magraw impatiently claimed.

"If it's clear we cannot stop Ramalon's invasion," Mijkal said, "then I think finding time to destroy this stone is imperative!"

"Then we must decide quickly what it is we are to do," Mavokai directed, a sense of urgency becoming second nature. "How can we make time against the inevitable?"

Lost for ideas, Magraw once again continued his presence like a thorn that would not be forgotten.

"Very well. If time is what we need, then perhaps, I could suggest a way," he directed to Wemberlè and Aristuto, dangling the idea in the air like a piece of meat that was too high to reach.

"What are you suggesting!?" Zathos asked, a little concerned.

"The fact they are now a target provides us with a solution. With all three of you in one place, it will make it very easy for him. But - I must be delicate in my words here, I'm wondering whether it would give us more time if they were as far away as possible...?"

"You mean away from here? From the protection of the Order?"

"That is precisely what I am saying."

"You may be Master of the Mind, but it is filled with illusions of dust if you believe sending my wife to fight Ramalon is the answer!"

"Lestas, no one here except Ramerick would be able to stand up to him," Mavokai explained.

"I am aware of that," he said with an increasing level of difficulty to his words. "But you cannot deny that if Ramalon comes for them first, it will bide us the time we so desperately need."

"I do not want to hear another word on this!" Zathos demanded.

## A Possible Resolution

"Besides, that doesn't matter," Zathos argued. "When he unleashes his armies onto us all, he will come for them regardless. We need to defend them, not abandon them to provide some *time*!"

"It would matter most! The longer The Master of Life is alive, the more chance we have of destroying the stone!"

"And the more lives will be lost!"

"Lives will be lost regardless, Master of Volts! The matter of how many lives can be spared will depend on how quickly we can destroy it!"

As they continued to argue with one another, Wemberlè and Aristuto fondly looked toward each other with a sense of inevitability. It was as if they both knew what the other was thinking and were both in agreement. They shared a gentle smile.

"This is my wife! Not a pawn to sacrifice en-prix!" Zathos defended.

"The question of how to create more time was asked, and I have offered a solution. Do not take this personally," Magraw continued his ruthlessness.

"Personally? Why are we even discussing this?"

"My love..." Wemberlè interrupted her husband.

The expression she gave toward her defensive husband gave him all the clarity he needed to understand her intentions. He was quite taken aback by his wife going against him.

"No... I cannot allow you to do this! It is not right!"

"We *can* provide that time," she struggled to go against his wishes. "It seems no one else can."

"Wemberlè?" Zathos cautiously confronted his wife, worried she might not understand the weight of what she was getting into.

"It's alright," she soothed. "If time is what The Master of Life needs, then time is what we can give. We will not have much of it left if we do nothing. If we just... Defend. If Ramalon comes for me, he will have a hard time doing so where I will go..."

"Please don't -" Zathos pleaded.

"- This is bigger than us, my love! I am so sorry but The Master of Mind is right. It's okay. I will take refuge in the oceans to the east where the waters will protect me more than any of us here."

"And what if he does come?" Zathos pleaded with her desperately. "The people defending you will die!"

"Precisely. Which is why no one must be there when he does."

"No," he shook his head. "That's not what this has to be! We must find another way. A way where we can protect you. Protect you both!"

"Our destinies have always been protecting that which is good and green. If I do this, it could make all the difference."

"For what? We have no precise plan here. It's not a reasonable thing to ask someone to give up their life for some *time*."

"It could be the only thing reasonable enough -" Magraw said.

"- Could you please hold your tongue!"

"And if I sit idly," Wemberlè continued. "Waiting for him to come to me? How many people will die trying to defend me? That's the opposite of my purpose. Our divinity defends others, not the other way round."

"And what about me?" he asked, a little upset and embarrassed that she hadn't seemed to consider him in her decision. "You expect me to just allow you to fall at his hand?"

"You think I will fall?" Wemberlè feigned offence, knowing it was not his intention to doubt her, but needing to reassure him of her clear mind, "This is not a suicide. I very much intend to surpass him."

Not that anybody noticed, but Magraw's eyes reluctantly drew to the ground as he believed the contrary.

"He will have a hard time killing me in my playground," she continued. "If he wants me, he will have to come and get me!"

"It matters not how strong you are! You could send every drop of every ocean onto him but it will not douse the inferno that is Sarthanzar's hand! Please, my love," he begged again in desperation.

"Master of Volts?" Ramerick wearily asked. "Think of what I have lost." He pleaded with the little energy he had left. "Think of what I have sacrificed…"

Zathos immediately dropped his head in recognition that no one had lost more than Ramerick. He did not want to appear insensitive.

"You cannot blame a man for trying to defend the love of his life…"

"No, I cannot. I know what that feels like too," Ramerick admitted. "But if Lady Wemberlè is willing to do this, I'm not going to lie, it will give me more time. And it will take my brother far away from me. That in itself is important enough!"

Zathos took a huge inward breath. He looked to his wife and did not know what to say. She cupped his hands and looked into his eyes. She smiled.

"This was meant to be," she delicately said. "And it's okay. I have to do this. And you know I do… The oceans are mine!" she addressed the Order. "Ramalon's mind will certainly have turned to delusion if he thinks he will reach me there!"

## A Possible Resolution

"Thank you," Ramerick said.

A teary Zathos looked over toward Magraw who avoided eye contact. It was not a malicious look but more a painful admittance that Magraw's ruthless idea had affected him directly. It was not a nice place to be at the end of.

"I will fly to The Rolgan Waste," Aristuto informed them with a strong undercurrent of confidence.

Several of The Blessèd Order members took to that with growing encouragement, knowing that he was perhaps the strongest destructive Màgjeur in the entire Order.

The Rolgan Waste was a consistent hurricane created thousands of years ago by its natural geographical location. The structure of such a geological system produced a cycle of warm air, twinned with the flat landscape creating a devastating hurricane that had not stopped for many years. It was said that it was so destructive that no one had ever gone beyond it to Arinane and The Lands of the Neverseen. It was greatly welcomed as The Blessèd Mage of Air would be in his own element too.

"He will have a hard time getting to me as well. Though, with all my heart, I hope it will not have to come to that," Aristuto continued.

"So do I," Ramerick said.

"And what of The Master of Life? Where will you be residing when Ramalon is off completing his remaining steps?"

"I don't know yet," he shook his head. "I'm completely in the dark."

"As are we all," Magraw huffed, followed by a short icy silence.

"Then it's settled," Mavokai confirmed. "Master's of Water and Air will begin their journeys immediately. As for the rest of us, we must find our places when the curtain comes down. For that, I urge us all to follow our hearts," The Blessèd Mage of Death poetically said, for his did not beat.

Aristuto however, knew that not to be accurate, for he had seen it many years ago when he chose to sacrifice himself to keep him alive from Medhene. It would never be forgotten.

"Go. And with the valour and grace of our divinity, defend all that is good and green!"

## *Master of Survival*

    The Blessèd Order wasted no time preparing their mildens and Windermares to their relevant destinations. Their accompanying bands too, saddled up for the voyage.
    The chances of survival were slim. They had no other purpose than to survive what was to come and preserve as much time and life as possible. Though they did not take comfort in that a specific plan was not formed, they had no other choice but to trust that Ramerick would find a way to destroy The Dragastone. The weight of the world grew heavy on his tired shoulders but he stood tall in his demeanour, ready to do what was necessary. Seldom did he admit that he needed help but knew it was required to stand any chance of success.
    The four main realms on Terrasendia that were to be defended laid

mostly on Landonhome, Septalia, Handenmar and Questacère.

As for the forgotten realm of Elcaria, they would leave King Caspercartès and his people to fend for themselves. The Blessèd had learned the truths and illegality of The Elcarians and deemed they were not considered a part of all that was good and green. Their abandonment was punishment for their crimes.

The remaining realm of Slassia was also no considered worthy of any protection as nothing resided there due to Medhene's witchcraft and sorcery.

The Farrowdawns remained strictly forbidden, for its danger was now more potent than ever. Now that The Ancient Drethai were resurrected and at large once more, they would haunt the mountainscape and make it even more perilous. As they saw Ramalon as their deity, The Blessèd wondered just what role they had left to play in fulfilling his deeds.

King Thakendrax and some of his dwarven advisors would ride for Handenmar on their stout Rhinoauros's - small, cantankerous looking mammals that were part of the family of Grozlers, albeit much kinder and obedient in nature to their masters. Their heroic horns that stuck out from their foreheads were an indication of their masculinity. The bigger the horn, the more they would be recognised as the alpha-male. Thakendrax's of course had the biggest horn. Their destination was for Dwardelfia, the capital of the realm to which they instructed their people to make way with haste.

King Thorian Mijkal and his band did not have far to travel on their humble mildens but still wasted no time in drawing his forces and as many of his Questacèreans back to Lathapràcère.

Mavokai, Gràcene, Mirabella and Ramavell would all remain on Laloncère as it was an essential strategical location. Twin that with the fact that many of the lives there would not be able to move in time to a safer place, they chose to stay and defend what would be considered one of the relics of Terrasendia in which Laloncère was.

They all made their way to the vast forecourt to see the bands off in their endeavours. The only ones not in attendance were Ramerick and Clethance.

Magraw would usually have resided on Mages Wreath were it not razed to ruin, thanks to Ramalon. His choice to make way to Durge Helm was more because he had nowhere else to go.

Ethelba and The Knights of Rolgan that accompanied her made their way back to Rolgan to acquire reinforcements. It seemed through her silence that Ramerick's journey had deeply touched her and wanted to do everything she could for him and Joric. There was only one destination that led her heart.

Aristuto, accompanied by his great friend Mylanus would not be returning to his home on Gallonea as his chosen path led him further north to The Rolgan Waste.

As too did Wemberlè, as she prepared her voyage alone to The Chopping Sea, east of Mages Wreath. She consoled her heroic husband as Zathos tried to hide his sadness at the gates of Laloncère. He did not want to believe that would be the last time he ever saw her but couldn't help but feel plunged into fear that it may well be. They were interrupted by Thakendrax, which came as a slight surprise.

"My lady," the dwarven King solemnly approached. "Though our differences have been known, it would have been an honour to protect you at this grave hour. For that, you must accept my sincere apologies that I cannot be there for you when the time comes."

Wemberlè smiled, grateful the dwarven King found the time to think of her.

"Thank you," she replied. "Protect your people. It is what we all must do."

"My lady, Master of Volts," Thakendrax bowed his head with grace.

"Blessèd be with you."

Thakendrax saddled up onto his Rhinoauros, highly decorated in a Kingly manor, before being joined by several other of his dwarven companions ready to depart.

"May the power of The Blessèd be with us all," he firmly concluded before their Rhinoauros clopped their hooves onto the cobblestone and rapidly cantered out of the gates. The dwarven band rode into the slither of the surrounding mountain that sounded like an applause, and disappeared out of sight.

The Questacèrean King, accompanied by no less than twenty Knights all riding their mildens expertly, was next to depart.

"Gracelands be with us," The Blessèd Mage of Ice fearfully addressed the forecourt. "Let us turn not to hope, but to trust."

He concluded, bowed his head, and led his band swiftly into the mountain and for Lathapràcère.

"And so our little band grows smaller," Mavokai said as Laloncère diminished in energy and sound.

"But stronger," Meigar said by his side before making his way back up to the platform where the summoning took place.

As he did, Mavokai saw Aristuto about to mount one of the Windermares, whose wing had dipped, allowing its master to climb on.

"Thought you'd leave without saying goodbye?" he said to The Blessèd Mage of Air as he turned. "My old friend."

They placed their right hands on each other's shoulders and smiled for the first time since that dreadful situation with Medhene. Aristuto would never forget about the sacrifice he had been willing to make for him.

"Why should I say goodbye? Afraid I will not return?" he replied lightly.

"It is good to see you again."

"Thank you for what you did," Aristuto quietly said.

"Tried to do."

"You did what you felt you had to. Despite my urging against giving my daughter what she wanted."

"She asked nicely!"

"She was a brat!" Aristuto claimed of his late daughter.

"All our lives, you said I never listen to you. I thought I might as well stay consistent," Mavokai ironically jibed.

"Even in the darkest of times, you still find a way to find to prove yourself, Master of Death."

"It's my role, I guess. And I suppose this is the man we owe our thanks to?" he indicated to Mylanus, who arrived on his Windermare. To the side of him was Ethelba, who would accompany them both to Rolgan along with several members of her band.

"It was a close call," Mylanus smoothly said.

"What are you talking about? I had him!" Aristuto claimed, recalling the moment he duelled with Ramalon.

"Of course you did!"

"Amateurs, he's still learning the trade," he claimed to his apparent apprentice. "I've taught him everything he knows."

"Just not everything you know," Mylanus sarcastically replied, rolling his eyes.

"Come. We must not delay."

"Can't take the humour," Aristuto whispered to Mavokai.

He vaulted on to the bare back of his white Windermare gracefully. The forecourt was clear and long enough to provide a runway for them all to fly into the dusk.

They were almost ready when Zathos and Wemberlè said their

goodbyes. A moment of privacy was respected for them both. Their foreheads gently leaned into each other, eyes closed, praying with everything they had, they would find their way back to one another. They did not know entirely what to say and kept their emotions silent, knowing that expressing them would only make the inevitable more difficult to accept.

They looked into each other's eyes, despite smiling being the last sentiment to rise to the surface, they bravely mirrored the expression. They did not need words to tell the other they loved each other, for they knew. Wemberlè galvanised herself with an encouraging breath and climbed up on a different Windermare to the one she gave to Ramacès at The Draughts. She left that one to her husband in the hope that it would provide an omen of luck.

She joined Ethelba, The Knights of Rolgan, Aristuto and Mylanus.

"Blessèd be with you all," Mavokai said, unable to completely disguise his fear.

"And with you, my old friend," Aristuto said, his deep sadness was difficult to hide.

With that, the Windermare flexed their muscles and rapidly blended into a gallop across the forecourt. As they went by, Wemberlè had eyes only for Zathos as she sped away and did not look away until the wings of her milden spread, just like the others and elegantly propelled them from the ground to their ascent.

Zathos, Mavokai and some of the Questacèreans who'd helped their swift exits watched on to see the image that was reminiscent of a flock of birds flying into skies, grow smaller and smaller. Zathos remained brave as the main bulk turned one way, while a smaller speck he knew to be his wife broke off from the pack, gliding alone to her destiny.

The rallying frenzy had calmed, leaving a ghost of tranquillity on Laloncère once more. The gentle breeze could once again be heard bristling against the trees, the chirping of birds echoing in their nests.

Alas, the peaceful nature was not the same for Ramerick as he only had eyes for The Dragastone, which he had not touched since the hex's barbarity. Clethance was sure that it was safe to touch but Ramerick remained fearful. It was an experience he would do anything to avoid going through again. Were it not for the essences of his powers of life; he would undoubtedly have died. And that made him fearful as his promise to Amba and Jàque had not yet been fulfilled.

"What possessed me to do that?" Ramerick asked. "It's like I was someone else entirely."

"The physical touch must have generated a particular temptation."

"Understatement."

"His soul is implanted onto this stone. Though he is vulnerable to its destruction, you must resist its temptation. Can you handle that?"

"… I don't have a choice," Ramerick reluctantly said. Clethance indicated for him to pick it up. "Is it safe?"

Clethance nodded. "As long as you resist the urge to terminate it again."

That did not fill Ramerick with total confidence. He admitted to himself he was somewhat vulnerable. Regardless, he embraced his fear, more prepared that time and willed himself to approach the stone.

He bent down and slowly drew his hand to it, getting flashes of its electrocution. He successfully ploughed through that barrier and finally wrapped his palm around the stone… To his relief, nothing happened.

He allayed his expression with a deep sigh. He came to stand and felt its poisonous nature burn within, attempting similar temptations. But this time he was aware of it and was able to resist its mysterious allure which had rendered him helpless. He felt more in control. His desire to gain revenge on Ramalon inspired him further the more it tried to seduce him, filling him with additional hatred and determination to find a way.

"I will destroy this stone, Clethance. One way or another."

"He will know the stone is damaged. I think he will be fearful if we found a way to open the connection without you getting hexed."

"There may be another way to do that," Meigar said as he entered the platform.

"How?" Clethance asked.

"I feared revealing this sooner in front of many would weaken our chances."

"Chances of opening the connection?"

"Yes."

"Please, enlighten us."

Meigar recalled some of the forgotten parts in the whole story and was convinced they still had a role to play.

"Do you believe your father's plan is still in motion?" he asked of Ramerick.

He looked upon him, relatively surprised as that was not at the forefront of his mind. However, upon reflection, he gathered that it still was and nodded his head.

"I believe he would not have seen all this, knowing there was no path to eventual peace."

"Precisely."

"My mother…" Ramerick began before sparing her a thought. "She also believed his work was not finished when Melcelore died."

"I firmly believe we are still in the realms of what your father foresaw. When he claimed The Dragastone that day, he could only do it by sacrificing himself to complete the ownership, similar to what your mother did for you… But I have come to the conclusion that there is another who has embraced that same idea, to preserve survival."

"Who?"

"Ramacès."

Ramerick was surprised, he had not the faintest thought about the brother he had never met but his intrigue had been piqued.

"But Ramacès is dead," he replied, a little confused. Meigar did not respond. He remained intense in his demeanour, almost as if the revelations inside were being ignited once more. "Max?"

"Dead in body, but not in soul," he said, more optimistic.

Ramerick looked to Clethance, who also returned a confused look. However, a shade of encouragement began to develop.

"What does that mean? That my brother is still alive?"

"I am saying very strongly that I do not believe his soul has passed into The Gracelands yet. I believe he still has a vital role to play. He may have seen all along, just like your father, that he would never have been able to escape his fate, and so implanted his soul onto something before he turned to stone, preserving the very thing that could help Terrasendia survive this. Though precisely what that something is, I am not sure."

"How do you know this?"

"Because I gave him the means to do it. To survive."

"Preserve his soul?" Clethance asked, his confidence grew.

"Yes. He took a very fond obsession to it once I learned to him the benefits, for reasons I am only beginning to understand. He was the smartest man I'd ever known in my short time with him. His eye for someone's intentions was near perfect and when the time came for your brothers to collide, he would have left Terrasendia with perhaps the ultimate weapon to defeat Ramalon. But more, I think he did so with the intention of leaving *you* with that weapon."

"What weapon?"

"His access to The Dragastone!"

"I'm confused," Ramerick confessed. "Access? Access how? To its power?"

"Yes and to his share of its ownership."

"That does not make sense, Master of Earth," Clethance explained. "Even in this unprecedented scenario, we have already seen that Ramalon's power is far superior."

"That is correct, but that is because you have yet to claim it…" he said.

"Claim The Dragastone?"

"Or at least, Ramacès' share of it."

Ramerick looked to Clethance. He neither confirmed nor denied that it was possible for that to happen and was happy to let Meigar explain further. There was no letter of the law to resort to. Instead, Clethance had to determine the practicalities themselves based on his expertise and what seemed possible. Meigar indulged in a little thought for himself before smiling and letting out a very masculine laugh, as if he had realised he'd been tricked.

"Max?" Ramerick asked. "What is it?"

"Gracelands. What a man…" he proudly whispered to himself as it sounded like he had just discovered precisely what Ramacès had done.

"What is it?"

"How did I not work that one out sooner?" he asked himself. "He learned that for Soul Preservation to take place, a sacrifice of life must be exchanged. That is exactly what happened at The Draughts! He sacrificed his life and when his body turned to stone, no one at the time knew what was truly happening. He was exchanging his life to preserve his soul and placed it onto something not even Ramalon saw. Right under his very nose," he whispered, unable to hide his beaming smile. "Ramerick, Ramacès' soul lays inside his Meigarthian sword!"

"What does this mean?" Ramerick pressed, his excitement running away with him.

"It means that there is a way to kill Ramalon…" Clethance confirmed after learning of the details. His speech became slower as a result of landing on a possible answer. "Should this have truly happened, there is a way to destroy The Dragastone. The Dragadelf. All of it! We've already seen the stone unable to take both of your protecy's at the same time. Were a scenario to happen where all three would be open, it's a practical certainty the stone would not withstand the power surge!"

"That's how we kill Ramalon!" Meigar concluded. "And end this once and for all!"

Ramerick became charged with enthusiasm and believed that he now had something tangible to aim for. They had a purpose and an intention that no longer rendered them blind.

"Hold on, so you're saying that my brother's soul lies in his sword? How do I access it?"

"Simply touch it," Meigar advised, "and his soul will be activated for as long as your hand is connected to it."

"And more importantly, you will be able to terminate its connection!" Clethance revealed.

"Using the sword?" Ramerick asked.

"Yes. If the sword in your hand should make contact even with the slightest of touches onto the stone, it could activate Ramacès protecy of termination. Twin that with your own and it would matter not if Ramalon activates his hex. One way or another, the stone will not be able to withstand the intense threshold!"

A moment of stillness was born. They had found a way. They looked upon one another with a general agreement that this all tallied up and that everything they had learned and discovered gave them a direction of what to do next.

"If the sword is in his hands, will he be able to use Ramacès' share of The Dragastone's power?" Meigar asked Clethance.

"That would appear correct yes, the hex is activated only when he attempts to terminate it. Not for when you open it for your general use of protecy -"

"- No!" Ramerick vehemently defied, driven by utter fear. "I meant what I said. I will never use The Protecy again! I cannot risk going through that pain. It will kill me."

"It won't, Ramerick," Clethance assured him. "If anything, it is to your advantage as Ramalon knows it would risk its destruction -"

"- I will not use it!" Ramerick insisted. "It has already been the cause of so much evil! I cannot think of anything I would rather do than use it for its destruction!"

Meigar looked to Clethance a little concerned about his reluctance to use The Protecy, knowing it seemed nearly impossible for him to achieve his endeavour without it.

"Fine," Max conceded, "but you must accept, embracing your fear could prove the difference."

"I need to get to that sword!" Ramerick confirmed. "That is what will prove the difference!"

"So, how do we get it?" Clethance asked.

"That there is another conundrum," Meigar reluctantly said. "His sword lays in his hands. And his hands are suspended high in The Draughts."

The positive energy suddenly slipped away like water in a sponge. So overawed by finally uncovering a plan, the reality of making it work was now another hurdle in itself.

"So, we must get to the sword before Terrasendia perishes?" Ramerick asked for confirmation.

"Take The Dragastone with you," Clethance instructed. "It matters not where it is anyway for Ramalon could use its power regardless. You will not have time to bring the sword back to Laloncère."

"A race against time!" Meigar said. "Time, that Terrasendia will give you as much as it possibly can."

"What do I do? How can I get there unopposed?"

Meigar stopped short. It was true; Ramerick would struggle to get to The Draughts on his own and suggested the only thing he could.

"Though the powers you have inherited will deflect Ramalon's attempts to trace you, I admit you will need help. The quest to the belly of the monster will prove perilous. We sent you through the gates of The Understunde alone once. We shan't do it again! I will send a Bluewing to Hiyaro at The Reinhault and instruct him to assemble a small band to aid you."

"Aid us, you mean?" Ramerick corrected.

Meigar's face was that of a man who was discouraged from letting on the truth. He realised he had not revealed where his place laid when Ramalon comes for them all.

"Max? You're coming with me, right?"

"I cannot," he sadly revealed.

"Why? You've been there before, you can help me."

"It would matter not if your brother came. Getting you there is the task I could help with, but from there, the rest really is down to you. And you alone. Mavokai was right. We all need to find our places when the curtain comes down. I ride for Durge Helm to be with my brother."

Not that Ramerick was best pleased to hear that The Blessèd Mage of Earth was not going to be his travelling companion, he did understand the decision. He so wished he was in a similar position and would also choose to be with his family at the darkest of times.

"I hope one day I have that choice…" he said, holding back a slight tear.

"Hope is what is keeping us going. And I place all my hope, in you. In the son of Felder, to finish his work. To honour the reason he and all of us were placed on this world. To protect that which is good and green. If I am to believe in that, I must believe that you will do what is set before you."

Ramerick reluctantly bowed his head to acknowledge the responsibility.

"I will!"

"Ride for Winstanton. I will instruct Hiyaro to meet you there."

"Thank you," Ramerick said.

"So this is it…" Clethance announced. "The road to survival."

"A dangerous and uncertain road at that," Meigar said. "Once again, the weight of this world rests upon your shoulders, Master of Life. But if anyone can restore balance to this world, then it is you. Everything you have gone through, the hardship, the sacrifice, the impossibilities you have had to endure, against your fight to it all is a remarkable symbol for everything we hold dear! A symbol we must all take courage from if we are to survive this. And Blessèd be with you boy, that you will prevail! Get that sword and destroy that stone!" he finished proudly, giving Ramerick hope and confidence to see his quest through.

"Thank you," he replied, allowing every word to build his confidence.

"Though I must admit, your journey will see far more joy than mine," Meigar mused.

"How so?"

"You don't have to listen to Lestas Magraw ponce all the way to Durge Helm!"

Ramerick recognised the humour and despite the graveness of the situation, managed a subtle laugh.

## The Promise of a Deity

The purity of air that The Dragasphere let in, began to diffuse the foul stench that had consumed the encapsulation. It was only a matter of time before the dismantling was complete.

Against the night sky, the light from the orange veins burned across the magical dome. The cracks and fissures were now so vast; they could easily allow space for a Dragadelf to soar through. Alas, then was not the time.

Felders Crest remained still, surrounded by The Dragasphere's slowly crumbling demise. Even The Dragadelf, who crunched their claws into what remained of Monarchy Hall's ceiling, admired the spectacle.

Ramalon however, did not. His eyes were shut, restoring the energy he had spent in his devastating duel with his brother. He sat on what was left of his father's throne, lost in thought. The Dragastone was no longer in his possession, but he cared not for he could use its power at any time and knew it was safe from termination. The stone of Zoldathorn that gleamed on the ground meant nothing to him and ignored its existence.

In his restoration, he marvelled once more at his achievement. Power fuelled him and he felt almost disappointed that he may never experience the thrill of that much power again.

He became aware of The Dragastone's vulnerability, sensing it was damaged somewhat. However, he took confidence in the fact his brother would never use The Protecy again, petrified that either he would be hexed or it would allow him that similar magnification of power. It was something that he could not ignore. After all, a part of his soul lived literally in the stone, which was now in his brother's possession.

The time for his strength to fully recover was near. He knew what step he had to climb next.

Suddenly, through the molten cracks of The Dragasphere, black wisps of cloud swirled down from the skies before landing smoothly at the doors of Monarchy Hall. The shadows thickened and morphed into something more substantial as the thirteen black ghosts made their way inside. Their King, Dreanor, spearheaded their V-shape formation. The Ancient Drethai had come to pay homage to their deity.

The doors to Monarchy Hall were wide open where they saw Ramalon resting on the throne some way down the stretch of the building. The Dragadelf stalked them from the roof above, bearing their gaze down onto the oncoming ghosts of Terrasendia who did not shudder on their approach. Now that their curse was lifted, they could walk freely into Monarchy Hall.

Their walk toward Ramalon, whose eyes remained shut and head remained bowed, was less than victorious - marching toward him with intent which was quite clear. Dreanor's face was that of conflict which he struggled to hide.

They had ascertained the knowledge that Ramalon had broken his promise to give them Melcelore alive. They had seen that Ramalon had acquired the affinity of ice, which implied that he must have killed and fletched from Melcelore. It ultimately meant he could not give them his soul to serve justice, which was his promise.

## The Promise of a Deity

Confirmation of Ramalon's betrayal laid mangled on the ground as they passed Melcelore's mutilated corpse to the side of them. It left them all trying to suppress the reeling emotions inside.

They arrived at the few steps that led up to the platform where Ramalon was resting. They bowed their heads courteously. Dreanor's eyes flicked back up quickly, betrayal lit the fire behind his cold dead expression.

"Master..." his tone chilled and purposeful. Ramalon did not respond. "I can't say how pleased I am to see you alive," Dreanor's praise was shallow and didn't go unnoticed. "Master?"

Ramalon's eyes opened, but his head remained bowed. He did not raise it to regard Dreanor, instead he kept his intense gaze directed to the ground.

"Why have you come?" Ramalon questioned.

"We have come to honour our pledge of allegiance. And to see you honour your word," Dreanor carefully said, his eyes flicking momentarily to the body of Melcelore. He knew he must tread carefully and was risking the wrath of Ramalon but he was unable to simply forget what was promised.

"My word?" He raised his head toward The Ancient Drethai below.

"Yes, Master. Your promise to us."

"Remind me... What promise was that?"

Ramalon's eyes narrowed, his tone became more menacing with every word. Dreanor's anxiety rose, as too did the rest of his Order.

"The promise of giving us what we have wanted from the start... The promise of Melcelore *alive!*" he angrily clarified. Despite his internal fear, his stubbornness to defend his prize of justice was worth more than his life, which he was putting on the line as he challenged his deity.

The intensity in Ramalon's eyes pierced through the Shadow King as he slowly rose from his throne, causing him to take a small step back.

"You gave us your word!" Dreanor chafed, desperately trying to put more volume behind his words. Ramalon's broken promise hung heavy in the air as the Drethai's grievances were confronted head on. Ramalon's harrowing stare and unpredictable nature created a dangerous dimension.

"And what of your word? Master of Shadows?"

"My word?"

"You promised to give me my brother. You failed. And yet, you demand reciprocation? Because of your failure, the path to my final step grows more challenging."

"A challenge you will overcome, Master!"

"Do not screen your shortcomings with compliments," he warned. His jaw tightened through his words as his temper flared. "And yet, there you stand, challenging what I have failed to give *you*? This is my world! And you will bow to me!"

They traded an unbearable moment of eye contact, searing through one another before Dreanor finally succumbed, squeezing his eyes shut and bowing his head once more followed by the rest of The Ancient Drethai.

"Forgive me, Master."

They felt honouring their pledge of allegiance was more out of utter fear rather than a choice of their own. Dissatisfied by not receiving what they had always wanted in claiming vengeance over the dark Màgjeur who had made them suffer for so many years created more of a reluctance to submit. However, of that fact, Ramalon was fully aware and decided a demonstration of his true undeniable divinity was in order to seal their loyalty.

After indulging in a long pause, Ramalon turned his right palm up, keeping his gaze on them all, and conjured a small white orb that shone brightly from his palm.

All eyes of The Ancient Drethai became transfixed on the shining light and could not hide their confusion. The realisation quickly began to sink in over the possibility of what their deity was demonstrating.

"It cannot be," Dreanor whispered.

"See for yourself…" Ramalon uttered before extending his palm, sending the orb gliding toward Dreanor.

The orb stopped in front of the Shadow King whose reaction was that of total shock. He understood whose soul it was that was being presented before him.

"Impossible!" he breathed.

"Even more evidence of how my divinity is just and true. Only a god can achieve the impossible…"

All members of The Ancient Drethai enclosed on what they knew was the soul of Melcelore, suspended before them. They stood in a semi-circle, closing their eyes to listen to their life-long nemesis' echoing cries to them all. It filled them all with a small piece of gratification and fulfilment. Its light bounced against their black and burnt complexions, creating many shadows which were distinctive of their natures. Dreanor smiled, listening to Melcelore in his mind. He gloated as he understood he now had the platform to torment him, forever. As did they all.

All thirteen extended their palms toward Melcelore's soul before ripping the white globe into twenty-six pieces. The white streaks streamed into both their hands, listening to his cries of defiance as he passed into their possession. They rejoiced, knowing that there was nothing he could do until the orb had finally disappeared.

The Ancient Drethai's retribution was complete.

Their satisfied dark demeanours shone. They had received what they had always wanted since forming their Order so many years ago and felt empowered, knowing they had a piece of Melcelore's soul to torment for eternity. They had one person to thank for it and were more than determined to show their gratification.

Ramalon, however, did not smile in recognition of any thanks. Instead, he remained focused on his own ambitions.

"Thank you, Master," Dreanor humbly thanked. "We remain entirely loyal to your cause and remain completely at your disposal."

"Were you not already?" he asked menacingly.

"Our faith in you is total and unwavering. That is our promise, in which we will never break!"

"No. You will not. For if you do, I will do what I promised. Should you fail or betray me, I will leave your souls at the feet of Sarthanzar himself!"

"We understand," Dreanor assured him. However, he could not help but let his intrigue get the better of him. "May I ask how? How have you achieved the process of fletching *and* Soul Mancing? I cannot understand," he hesitantly queried.

Ramalon did not respond. He merely stared at Dreanor, knowing full well he chose to betray The Ancient Drethai for his own gain and that it was only because of a truly exceptional event that allowed him, in the end, to honour his word.

The cunning Dreanor had quietly gathered that too. He figured in some capacity that Ramalon was deceitful in that he did not intend to give them his soul and had gotten lucky. Regardless, Dreanor understood that in the balance of eventuality, weighed up against Ramalon's apparent dishonesty, that it was enough reason for them to continue their pledge of undying allegiance.

Without confirmation of the details of such a miracle, Dreanor acknowledged once more his respect for Ramalon and chose to leave it alone.

The moment of marvel had simmered down which allowed Ramalon to take centre stage once more.

"I am, however, faced with a complication," he said as he walked down the steps to be on the same level as The Drethai. He meandered around in thought.

"Complication, Master?"

"It seems my brother has become The Blessèd Mage of Life. Something I did not foresee. So much for the *love* of our mother," he muttered furiously to himself.

"How does this stop you from achieving your endeavours?"

"Because, those powers of life have granted him a defence from me. A repellant in my attempts to connect with him. I cannot see him, nor influence him any longer and know not of what he plans to do."

"We all have pledged ourselves to you. What do you ask of us?"

"He will attempt to destroy The Dragastone. Though he will never achieve it, the hope of doing so will provide much resistance on my final stretch."

Ramalon pondered. He didn't want to admit it to anybody apart from himself, but the notion that he did not know what his brother was planning made him vulnerable.

"Master?"

"This is where you have the chance to redeem yourselves," Ramalon continued. "You will find my brother and you will bring him to me, alive…"

"You understand, your brother's powers will also affect our attempts to find him as well?"

"You're The Ancient Drethai. Find a way!"

"It will be done. Master," Dreanor confirmed, reiterating his promise. "And what of The Dragastone?"

"… Find my brother and you will find the stone. Bring them both to me."

"We will not fail you!"

"I'm sure you wont," Ramalon threatened. He sensed his strength growing once more and came to declare his intent. "One more thing. Just how many people were on Felders Crest that day thirty years ago?"

"At least a hundred thousand Master," Dreanor informed. "Why do you ask?"

Ramalon did not answer. He knew that it was more than the four

The Promise of a Deity

realms combined but wanted its extermination to be without question. He fathomed an idea to acquire even more.

He looked back to the Shadow King and continued. "May the lungs of Terrasendia tarnish. Let the veins of this land flow molten rivers. Let the skies suffer in dragonbreath, while I claim what is mine by right."

Ramalon waded through the line of The Ancient Drethai and made his way toward the doors of Monarchy Hall. Following him atop of the building were the four Dragadelf who wormed their way across after him. The Drethai quickly followed suit.

They viewed Felders Crest below and all was still. The last remaining portions of the containment spell that had enclosed the city had crumbled to nothing at last.

The Dragasphere was no more.

"It is time…" Ramalon declared with a whisper.

He extended his right hand and aimed it high up into the sky. Ramalon's palm ejected a blinding ball of white light which soared through the air and like a firework, gracefully exploded above the capital. The debris of thousands of white orbs, representing his acquired souls, spread across Felders Crest and like a blanket of snow, slowly fell and nestled into their destinations.

The light The Manced created was still for many moments before collectively, they began to move. The rotting corpses that hosted each soul were suddenly animated and came to stand.

Their harrowing eyes blazed full of life, desperately begging to be free of their purgatory. Alas, Ramalon had other ideas and used their existence for his own retribution.

He wasted no time instructing his empire to split up to their destinations and destroy all that was good and green. The remaining four Dragadelf roared, firing their crackling furnaces into the sky, which was so loud, it deafened much within a mile radius. On cue, The Manced began to file out of Felders Crest to inflict their master's retribution.

A host of some hundred thousand began to disperse into three different directions. The sheer numbers each accompanied by a Dragadelf, would be sufficient to overpower each destination. One to Handenmar, one to Questacère and one to Durge Helm. Ramalon had other plans for Landonhome.

The Dragadelf continued their rallying cry. The Ancient Drethai stood triumphantly behind their deity. With Ramalon the nucleus of it all, fulfilling his destiny.

## Standing Alone Together

All over Terrasendia, the word had spread. The life of everything they knew was now under threat and The Blessèd Order had instructed every corner of every realm to defend themselves. The underlying purpose was to provide as much time as they could. Though for what reason, they were not entirely sure as Ramerick's quest was to remain secret.

Each capital city rallied and pulled the civilians into their strongholds for greater protection. Some remained stubborn in their livelihoods and chose to stay where they had lived all their lives, which created much personal conflict within populations. The majority accepted it was a matter of life and death, but others who were naive enough to dismiss it refused to cooperative, while others seemed merely unafraid of death.

## Standing Alone Together

On Landonhome, every corner of the nobleman realm had been summoned to Gallonea. Though Rombard Hill was the capital, the legendary fortress had never failed them.

King Romany was reluctant to issue the order, wanting to remain on the capital, but Queen Cathany had changed his mind. Romany still pretended he was the strongest man on Rèo, standing heroically and utterly useless, hands on his hips while the wind gently swayed his furry beard.

The population of Landonhome was not too many, far fewer than that of the oncoming host that trudged toward them. They needed help and they knew it.

South of Landonhome, the dwarves of Handenmar, wasted little time in riding their Rhinoauros' to Dwardelfia, the capital that resided on the shores of The Wintering Sea. Bands from all cities and populations did not hesitate to heed to their King's call. Even the famously stubborn dwarves of Ironfeist accepted Thakendrax's summons.

The more gentle and wiser dwarves of Mayanhold and Dwarnmerrow stacked every explosive they had and rode with care as swiftly as they could to the dwarven capital.

Thakendrax used his powers of manipulating gravity to increase it around Dwardelfia. The dwarves were naturally accustomed to his power, which contributed to their shortness in height. The additional gravity over time squashed their spines but they grew stronger and stouter as a result. That could not be said for those not used to the gravitational pull and would slow The Manced down. As for its effect on a flying Dragadelf, Thakendrax remained anxious as it had never been tested before.

East of Handenmar were the Questacèrean elves who also were pulled to the capital of Lathapràcère. The capital's strategical location high up on a mound would make any advancement very difficult indeed. Twin that with the fact that there was only one path of land toward it would make surrounding them rather challenging, even for The Manced, who boasted plethoric numbers.

King Thorian Mijkal was wise enough to understand that the odds were stacked against them and that once all his people had filtered into the city, he began its fortification using his powers of ice to enshroud the capital and beyond. Lathapràcère, like Mages Wreath, was not protected by walls. Instead, they used their skills in the art of magic and equine mastery.

North of Questacère was the realm of Septalia. Every stronghold was instructed to make way to Durge Helm once more. The War for Septalia was still rife in their minds, having recently achieving a glorious victory, by however small a margin. This would be known as The War for Terrasendia.

Luanmanu had resumed his role as The Durgeon of Septalia, letting every band and stronghold know that they would almost certainly die should they stay where they are. The Durgeons did not waste any time in rallying their populations toward the capital.

The strongholds of choice for each realm also had their own unique defences.

Gallonea was designed in such a way that the circular walls that defended it could spin, making advances very difficult to scale successfully.

The land before Dwardelfia was perfectly situated to plant networks of explosives, spikes and sludge to slow the enemy down. Along with Thakendrax's gravity, it would be difficult to penetrate.

Lathapràcère's defence lay in Mijkal's skill of a sub-freezing climate that the Questacèreans were more than used to. Some five hundred Màgjeurs complimented their King's powers and would be used to repel the ground invasion. However, their defence's main bulk would come from their impressive mounted lancers, who were saddled and ready.

Durge Helm was not defended by magics or affinities, keeping to their sovereignty even in the darkest times. Instead, they took the time to reinforce structures and keep The Manced at bay by covering the plains that laid between them and the nose of The Farrowdawns with barbed spikes and oils which would be set alight at the opportune moment. Trebuchets and longbow archers would halt them from afar.

Every corner of Terrasendia braced itself for the inevitable war that was to come. And how soon it would be upon them was even more frightening. Yet for all their planning and mustering, they could do little to defend themselves against a Dragadelf. Though each stronghold had plans for such eventuality, the confidence in their best defence against such a formidable and immeasurable force remained dubious at best.

In terms of killing a militant of The Manced, it was common knowledge that if an orb was destroyed, it would be killed. However, should the body be fatally wounded and the soul was to survive, its unnatural animation would enable the host to continue its evil intention.

Each realm stood alone, but bonded together with a common purpose. How long they had depended entirely on the hearts and courage of all those that chose to defend that which was good and green.

Meanwhile, on Laloncère, Ramerick was in the final stages of preparing his quest. He went to the one place which reminded him of his purpose. He indulged in what was now considered a luxury in time itself and went to kneel by the small ball of fire that represented his son's resting place.

It was as if the longer he stared at Jàqueson's warmth, the more it burned within him, igniting the new fire in his heart. A lasting reminder of what he needed to do before he saw him again. He felt empowered. Spurred with determination. Getting his hand on his brother's sword was the only thing that he wanted. The key to his one purpose, to destroy The Dragastone and kill Ramalon once and for all.

He took one last look at Jàque's resting place, absorbing every portion of motivation he could squeeze into him before turning and making his way back to the platform on which his mother rested.

Unknown to him as he walked away, Jàqueson's flame delicately flickered against a gentle breeze as if acknowledging his father's promise.

Ramerick stood before Eveleve's outstretched hands of stone, cupping both his protecy stone of fire and her necklace of life. He took the chain and clipped it around his neck, which dangled by his heart. He dressed it up with his clothing, which also contained The Dragastone that he enclosed in his tunic. He chose to leave his protecy stone of fire in the hands of his mother for safekeeping.

He was set. Ready to accept the responsibility that had fallen on his shoulders and protect that which was placed upon him. He could only hope that through everything, his father was right all along and that he would be the one to restore balance. That was a far cry to that current moment, where actually achieving his quest felt near-impossible. Alas, it was the only path to survival.

"You carry your bloodline with perfect continuity," Meigar appeared behind him. "She would be proud of you."

"Let's hope it counts for something."

"You ready?"

"I am," Ramerick nodded with determination. "Are you?"

"… Not even remotely."

"It shows you're human, I guess."

"Yes. Yes, I suppose it does. We often forget we are mere mortals in our divinity. Just like you."

"I sense you're not here just to say goodbye?" Ramerick probed.

"There is one more thing that I ask you to consider," Meigar hesitantly said.

"Knew it."

"And I'm afraid it may be asking too much of you."

"I'm used to it."

"I do fear for our survival," he admitted. "We will lose this fight, Ramerick. You really are our last hope, and though that does not hinder my belief in you, I fear we are vulnerable in another way."

"Why doesn't that surprise me?"

"His glorified notion to mance souls has poisoned his desire. If he does come for us directly and we are not protected, I don't want to imagine a life in purgatory. A life in his possession."

"What are you getting at?"

"There is something that can protect us all from that. Something that I have done myself during my time in The Draughts. You are The Blessèd Mage of Life. There may come a time when we need courage and strength. You can give us that. Use the powers you have and the essences of that stone! Instil every portion of life you can muster onto this land and it will protect all that is good and green from that malice. It could be the difference between life and death -"

"- You mean using The Protecy?" Ramerick asked, rather underwhelmed.

"Yes," Meigar admitted.

"I told you before, I would never use it again."

"Even if it inspired the hearts of all to endure? Even if it saved the life of Terrasendia?"

Ramerick hesitated. He was reluctant to agree.

"The life of Terrasendia will be saved if I get my hands on that sword."

"And what of your conscience? You have been blessed by your mother. Given to you are the divine powers of life, there is no greater gift! You have a responsibility. Remember that when the hour is darkest…"

Meigar bowed his head and resigned himself to the idea that he had done what he could to convince him to use his powers of life to spread hope at the time it was needed most. As he attempted to leave,

## Standing Alone Together

Ramerick couldn't help but feel a pang of guilt for his stubbornness.

"Max?" Meigar stopped and turned to look at him. "I'm afraid..." he whispered.

"As are we all, Master of life. But you are not alone. And you never will be."

Meigar concluded and left Ramerick to stew in the possibility of using The Protecy again. At that moment, his fear of using it tipped his decision very heavily towards never using it. However, the notion that it could be used for some good did annoyingly stick with him somewhat and if it could make the difference, he admitted he may have no other choice.

He hadn't had much time to indulge in the limits and workings of his new gifts, but he remembered what his mother did when he learned that Ramalon could invade his mind, using her essences of life to exponentially grow around Laloncère. It was a poignant moment that was difficult to shake. If the moment ever did come, he felt he'd know what to do.

As he walked away from the platform, he turned a corner to a sharp pang that suddenly whacked the back of his legs.

"Ow!" he exclaimed, knowing instantly that it was his aunt Gracène again. "I'm not going to have any legs left!"

"Do shut up boy!" she jested, smiling cheekily. "You were going to leave without saying goodbye weren't you?"

That was true. The overwhelming events made him regrettably forget about his aunt. He felt guilty as she was the last of what he could call family.

"I'm sorry, I thought it would be easier that way," he lied.

She shook her head not believing a word of it. "You forget I can see more than most. It's okay," she sympathised, stumbling to him and with her free hand placed it on Ramerick's side. "You have enough on your plate laddie."

"Aunt Gracène I just want to say -"

"- Ah!" she interrupted before he could say thank you for everything she had done for him. "You don't need to say it. I know... I believe you by the way."

"Believe me?"

She hummed in agreement. "That you will see them again..."

Her words warmed his heart, to know that he wasn't delusional after all.

"How do you know?"

"Just because they're dead, does not mean they're gone," she concluded with a warm smile.

Though he wasn't sure if this was just some motivational ploy, it inspired him more than anything before. He could not find the words to express how much that meant to him, vindicating him of his grief.

He stared into her blind eyes once more, knowing she could see back somehow and smiled before walking away with great difficulty, knowing it could be the last time he ever saw her.

When he was gone, she closed her eyes and smiled to herself.

Ramerick made his way down to the forecourt, his milden was saddled up and ready to depart for Winstanton. He wasted no time mounting the white horse, gathering the reins and turning to view Laloncère for what would be a final time in his mind. Its beauty radiated within him and left him with all the reminders he needed to fulfil his quest.

To his surprise, another milden arrived next to Ramerick. This one however was a white Windermare, whose impressive wings brushed its sides, partially covering the rider's legs.

"Fancy a companion?" asked The Blessèd Mage of Electricity.

Ramerick couldn't help but smile. He looked up to one of the balconies and saw Meigar looking down at him fondly. A reminder that he wasn't alone.

He gathered that Zathos had nowhere to go. His wife had embarked on a heroic voyage to give him that time and he figured that Zathos' only other place on this world, aside from at his wife's side, laid with him and his endeavour and the wishful idea that he could perhaps save his wife should Ramerick get that sword before Ramalon got to her. Though he confessed to himself, that was ambitious.

"I'd love one," he said, a little stoked.

"Then let us not waste a moment more," Zathos said.

Ramerick looked up one last time to Meigar, who was joined side by side with Clethance, both raised their hand to bid him farewell. He did the same along with Zathos. After, they cantered into the slither of the mountain and headed north to Winstanton.

## The Forgotten Realm

The pale faces of The Elcarians drooped toward the ground. Their robes quivered. Their harrowing fear was rife. The enormous circular hallway of Casparia was peppered heavily with the congregated civilians that stood on the many levels. They waited silently and frightened in the presence of such greatness.

Ramalon had come.

He had soared to Casparia on one of his Dragadelf, which he instructed to remain outside its walls. He did not need its presence to impose his mark.

Like a Durgeon, he examined each face as he quietly walked along the lines. They did not return the eye contact. No one dared move in case it risked his wrath. It was likened to that of having walked to the gallows, awaiting their execution.

They all had learned the terrible fate of Melcelore, their lord and master and that it was by Ramalon's hand.

Elcaria understood that The Blessèd Order had cast them out, leaving them to fend for themselves for their crimes. They would be considered a lone state without the help and support of Terrasendia, making them an easy target.

Their King had summoned every civilian in the land to Elcaria upon learning of The Dragasphere's demise. The total population of Elcarians was in excess of twenty thousand which had attracted Ramalon initially.

Ramalon continued the painfully slow descent of the capital until he reached the bottom. He was met by The Elcarian Order behind King Caspercartès and Queen Fleurcès, who had paid him the honourable decency of greeting him in the main hallway and not the throne room that sat beyond the long stretch.

Even The Elcarian King did not dare approach Ramalon as he continued his slow, measured walk toward them. It was evident in Caspercartès' demeanour that he too shared the fright of his people.

"My Lord and Master," Caspercartès greeted with enthusiasm and open arms, not entirely sure of how to address him. "What an honour it is to be blessed with your presence." He spoke as if Ramalon had not just flown in unannounced on the largest and most deadliest creature known to the world. As if the news of his most recent deeds had not yet reached them. Ramalon did not respond. He merely looked at Caspercartès with those sharp, intense eyes. His face remained calm and menacing, as was increasingly becoming characteristic for him. "Your legend is famous," Caspercartès continued to flatter. "I dare say there is not a soul alive that has not heard of your greatness. How can The Elcarians be of service to you?"

Ramalon still did not respond. The awkward silence made Caspercartès' fake smile even harder to maintain.

"This is my wife," he impulsively diverted to Queen Fleurcès, who also struggled to hide her fear.

"An honour it is," she splurged out as she joined her husband's side. She gave a gentle bow of the head. Ramalon furrowed his brow; confused at the gesture.

"Were you to summon us to Felders Crest, we would have answered the call," the Elcarian King uttered. "Though we are gracious of your presence, you need not have come to us. We will follow you in your endeavour. Without question. And as strange as it may sound, I know what it is you desire… He walked these halls not so long ago, you know. Ramerick. And he did not take too kindly to his punishment."

"And what punishment would that be…?" Ramalon finally responded, his eyes burning a hole through Caspercartès. It did nothing to ease the mounting pressure, only adding more oil to the fire.

"The, punishment, of treachery. My lord," he stuttered.

"Treachery?"

"Yes. He attempted with several accomplices to halt our cause. A cause which benefits you, my lord."

"Benefits me?"

"Yes! Everything we have here can aid you in your desires. We pledge ourselves to you. In totality!" he swallowed a build of saliva.

"But it wasn't until just recently that you were sworn to somebody else…"

The smiles of both Elcarian Monarchs slowly faded away. They knew Ramalon was aware that Melcelore was the one they answered to and that their useless attempts to entertain him had fallen on its backside.

"Yes…" Caspercartès sheepishly said. "Forgive us…"

Ramalon began to slowly circle not just them but The Elcarian Order behind them. No-one dared to turn and view him. Instead, they remained rooted to the spot. Their humiliation was in the audience of the thousands of Elcarians who watched on from the levels above.

"Do you know what I hate?" Ramalon quietly perfumed. "I hate being in the minority because I choose to do the right thing…"

"My lord?" Caspercartès said.

Ramalon began to speak almost as if no one else were present and more to himself.

"Something this world seems to forget so conveniently, is the value of continuity. When Ramacès died, the rightful King on Terrasendia should have fallen to the next one in line. Which so happens to be me. Terrasendia would pay homage to the pure line of the throne in Monarchy Hall. Not that it matters to me, it only justifies my path. But if only they saw that everything I do, was to strike the balance of equality. The promotion of fairness. And yet they chose to fight everything I am fighting for…"

"We will fight for you!" Fleurcès quickly spoke in a desperate attempt to demonstrate their loyalty, descending to her knees. "Without question!"

Ramalon quietly hummed.

"Fear? Or respect?" he mused.

"I'm not sure I understand."

"It's a simple question."

"I, guess, fear?"

"Interesting..." Ramalon whispered as he continued to circle the fearful Elcarians, a predator stalking his prey. "And what of you?" he directed to Caspercartès.

"Fear," he admitted after a beat of hesitation, unsure which answer would placate him more. "It's necessary to obtain order. Though respect is also a powerful tool, people will follow you if they respect you. My lord."

"... And do you not respect me, Elcarian King?"

Again, Caspercartès did not know precisely the answer Ramalon was looking for and began to wilt under the growing tension in the room.

"Of course I do," he nervously replied. Ramalon appeared to take subtle offence to his answer, which Caspercartès recognised instantly. "My lord?"

"... I am not your lord," Ramalon interrupted a little more sinisterly. "I am your deity. And you, you are a pawn. Just another piece of the perfect puzzle. My perfect puzzle. Alas, the Elcarian piece is not necessary, but rather a luxury..."

The fear inside Caspercartès cranked up another level to the point where he could no longer hold it behind his eyes.

"Please..." he begged, joining his wife on both knees, understanding Ramalon's thinly veiled intention. "I beg you. Do not kill us! We will be faithful to you! Our lives will be devoted to your cause, that I swear!... Please! Master! Deity! Be merciful..." he concluded with a frightful whisper.

Ramalon's expression did not change. He was not fuelled by emotion but mere intention. He aired the possibility of sparing their lives, which filled the silence with a piercing knife, before landing on his answer.

"Your bodies will be spared," he announced.

Caspercartès slapped a huge, relieved smile across his face as he nervously continued.

"Merciful! Our merciful deity!... Thank you, you have my respect, and the respect of all -"

"- But I cannot say the same for your souls..."

Instantly Caspercartès knew what that distinction meant as the Elcarians started to feel strange, gradually morphing into the familiar, sadistic feeling of their insides being churned, outside in.

"Master!? Master, please!" Caspercartès gasped.

Ramalon did not answer him. He merely watched on as he orchestrated their souls being butchered from them. Every Elcarian present started to awkwardly shun their sharp breaths outward in severe discomfort. Caspercartès wailed and fell sidewards to the ground.

"My love!" Fleurcès attempted to reach her writhing husband before her own pain paralysed her and rendered her to the ground.

They all scrambled in agony. Ramalon continued his demonstration of singular dominance. The Elcarians were forever faithful to Melcelore and that was something that, despite their change in allegiance, he could not accept. He could not trust them and decided their existence was more use to him in his hands, quite literally, where their allegiance would not be swayed again. He had plans for The Manced Elcarians, to march toward Landonhome, before turning his attention to the next step to divinity.

The sea of cries in Casparia reached a deafening height. Howls for mercy were heard and Ramalon happily obliged. It was the second time he had performed mass genocide and completed the process. The circular hall of the Elcarian capital was lit up by blinding light continuing his ruthless march.

## Swift Arrivals

It took Ramerick and Zathos several days of continuous galloping, with only a few hours of restoration, to reach the Septalian fortress of Winstanton.

On route, they had confided in one another in the brief moments when they did rest. Ramerick understood that Zathos' place on this world was indeed with him, for that was the best chance he had of seeing his wife again. He regretted every portion of circumstance that led to Wemberlè flying off to The Chopping Sea alone, but he reflected heavily on what Ramerick had lost. No comparison in his mind could relate and he knew that sacrifice would embrace everyone at some point.

As for Ramerick, he was just happy for a companion. He was not a stranger to having company on his journeys. It made him remember the regrettable voyage to Casparia with Pirocès, the trip to Ravenspire with Susmees and now Zathos. Though the prestige of such company wasn't lost on him, it made him wonder briefly why his path had led him to always be the one to chase his endeavours. It seemed no answers for him were just around the corner and he felt mentally tired of always being that one step behind. How he wished for a solution to his many, many problems would come to him for a change, continually mapping out ideas of what he could potentially do to make that happen. They were fruitless attempts.

They had arrived at the open gates of Winstanton at the fourth hour of night. It was deserted. The light from their oil lit torches flickered against the stoney walls, giving off a somewhat eerie gloom, reminiscent of a ghost town. Their mildens trotted over the cobblestones while they tried to see if there was anyone left behind. There was not.

"What do we do?" Ramerick asked.

"I guess we wait," Zathos replied.

"We don't have time for -"

Suddenly, the sound of hooves could be heard from the other side of the gates. They both turned their mildens to view the entrance and saw a small band of ten Knights all carrying torches, trotting into the forecourt. The light bounced off them, making them look even more ferocious. Assassin-like. They approached The Blessèd Mages, removed their helms and bowed their heads.

"You must be Hiyaro," Ramerick said.

"That I am," the leader of The Reinhault replied. "And you must be, The Blessèd Mage of Life."

"Ramerick."

"Honoured to meet you. Zathos," he nodded his head to The Blessèd Mage of Electricity, who nodded back, clearly remembering each other from the battle at The Draughts.

"Thank you for coming."

"Max informed me that you need to get to The Draughts."

"Yes, I need to -" Ramerick interrupted himself as he recognised a familiar face in one of the Knights. "Durgeon Relian!" he exclaimed, unable to keep the joy and surprise from his voice.

"Alexandao!" he replied with a smile, pushing his milden closer to him. "Or should I say, Master of Life?"

Ramerick was taken by surprise upon hearing the name he had grown up with. He had wholly forgotten it with all the events that had happened.

"What are you doing here? Aren't you meant to be marshalling Gallonea?"

"I would have been," Relian explained regretfully. "But I was relieved of my post."

"Why!?"

"It seems King Romany can't handle a bit of embarrassment."

"Understatement," Hiyaro muttered.

"I don't understand," Ramerick quizzed.

"After Cathany signed the document for your release, he blamed me totally for allowing the document to be signed. He relieved me immediately."

"But the Queen said you wouldn't take the fall."

"I think that was unavoidable. We both secretly knew. But I chose to follow my heart Alex. It was only by law that I had to detain you, and do not regret one bit for finding a way to release you. As it happens, I hear you've been on quite an adventure since."

"Quite some yes," he replied solemnly. "I am sorry."

"You do not need to apologise for anything Alex. Only be sorry for our people on Landonhome that Romany has decided to take full Durgeon responsibilities for."

"Blessèd save us!" Hiyaro uttered once more.

"Not even I could save you from that," Zathos ironically jibed, taking a familiar swipe at Romany's incompetence.

"Alas," Relian continued, "it's brought me here to aid you in a far greater purpose. I was conscripted by Hiyaro many years ago. He trained me so that I could offer my protection to this land. Now I am paying it back at a time when it is needed most. But the hour is late. And we have much to discuss."

They convened in one of the nearby huts made of stone and transformed it into a war tent. The room flickered a warm orange, the torches they'd lit bounced off their fine armours. They unrolled a large, scrolled map of Terrasendia onto the table to discuss their next move. Having a geographical picture of movements made their sight clearer.

"Our scouts report tens of thousands of manced souls trudging from Felders Crest in three separate hosts," Hiyaro informed, pointing his finger to relevant destinations on the map. "One to Handenmar, one to Questacère and the other along the main path of The Farrowdawns to Durge Helm. The Farrowdawns are swarmed and the main path to The Draughts are temporarily blocked."

"Therefore," Relian continued, "we need to find another way. One

# Swift Arrivals

which gets us there in time, but not too close to Ramalon's host."

"Our options?" Ramerick asked.

"We have three. One, we take the most direct and quickest route there and risk engaging the host. Two, we wait until his legions have been unleashed onto Terrasendia and have cleared the path."

"Too long," Ramerick insisted. "And the third?"

"There is a lesser-known passageway west of here. A much smaller and quieter route which after heading northwards would take us directly to its entrance."

"The downside?"

Relian looked toward Hiyaro with slight concern. "It would take us almighty close to Drethai Halls."

Ramerick raised his head and pondered in thought. Everyone allowed him the time to contemplate his options. He understood that they were all aware of The Ancient Drethai's involvement and recognised that to be a severe complication. It did not take too much to work out that their intention was to locate Ramerick and surrender him to his brother and so required them to tread very carefully. Even in the presence of two Blessèd Mages, they could inform Ramalon of their whereabouts and put the whole quest at peril.

"These are the only three options?" Zathos asked.

"The only three which gives us a realistic chance of destroying that stone in time. Once we reach The Farrowdawns, we hope that the conflict Terrasendia will have to endure will create the distraction we need to get there much easier. Ultimately, Master of Life, the decision is yours…"

Ramerick stared back at the map, trying to come up with an additional solution, once more wishing the answer to his problem would present itself rather than being chased by him. Alas, the answer did not come, and with every second of hesitation, another life was lost in his mind. He came to the conclusion that there really was only one way under the time constraints.

"We'll take the passageway," he announced.

He knew that it was incredibly risky journeying so close to Drethai Halls but hoped that the essences of his powers would protect him and hopefully shield him from their sight. Stealth would be their crucial weapon, and he chose to embrace that advantage for as long as possible.

"Very well," Hiyaro said. "Athelio, Dexterna, muster the mildens." he commanded two of the Knights.

They wasted no time and prepared immediately.

"What of Landonhome?" Ramerick queried. "How will he attack Gallonea?"

Relian's tone significantly deepened.

"Our scouts also report that another host from Casparia has been deployed and are currently marching for Gallonea."

"The Elcarians have joined Ramalon?"

"In a sense. But not by choice, it seems."

Ramerick gave another confused look which required a little more education.

"They have all been manced, Master of Life," Hiyaro informed.

Ramerick's concern was raised to match theirs.

"All of them?"

"All of them," Relian said.

Ramerick wanted to ask how that was possible, but considering the height of dark achievements his brother had surpassed, nothing surprised him anymore. It gave additional weight to what Max had said about instilling his powers of life onto the land to protect them all from that very fate. Though he still vowed to himself never to use The Protecy again, he regrettably conceded that he may have to soon break that promise to himself to protect more lives.

"How long do we have before they reach their destination?" Ramerick asked.

"Several days, if that. The host is slow moving, but they will not rest. By our calculations, it seems they will all arrive at the same time."

"Makes sense," Ramerick said, putting two and two together, relating the timing to be a deliberate factor in Ramalon's poetic nature.

"Plus, we assume they will have a Dragadelf accompanying each legion."

Ramerick pondered over The Dragadelf and knew their presence tipped the balance of survival heavily against them.

"There are four left. And he has four hosts?"

"Correct."

"Then we must assume one of the hosts will not have the support of a Dragadelf," Ramerick concluded. "He will keep one for himself to get to his destinations much quicker. He knows I am planning to stop him, and he knows he has to achieve his other endeavours before he gets to me."

"Which one do you believe he will leave out?" Hiyaro asked.

Ramerick looked at the map and worked out relatively quickly which realm was safest. He pointed his finger to Lathapràcère.

"There," he confirmed. "It's the coldest realm, and dragons don't do too well in the cold. Even if it is a Dragadelf."

"We must inform them immediately," Hiyaro insisted. "I will send a Bluewing."

"They will still have to prepare for the oncoming manced," Relian warned.

"Yes, but their odds of survival are greater. It will slow them down even more. Every second we can squeeze out will save more lives."

Relian nodded and looked back at the map.

"One to Dwardelfia, one to Durge Helm, and one to Gallonea. Where do you suppose the other will take Ramalon?"

Ramerick looked over to Zathos, whose fallen face indicated that he understood where it would take him next.

"To The Chopping Sea. His next step…"

"Then we must not waste a second more!" Relian said with increased determination.

They all exited the hut and prepared their mildens for departure. Ramerick examined some of the Knights of The Reinhault and had never seen warriors as polished and impressive as them. Their weapons alone struck intimidation, let alone their infamous skill when using them. Their bows were crafted of the finest woods, their arrows topped with the softest feathers, sheathed in their quivers. But the most striking thing about them was their eyes - full of determination and utterly fearless.

Ramerick could sense that Relian wanted to ask him something in the corner of his eye as he was saddling up.

"Is everything okay?" he asked.

"I heard you found him," Relian respectfully leaned in a little closer to Ramerick, out of ear-shot of anyone else. "Your son."

Ramerick looked back with a hint of sorrow. "I did."

"Did it help? Pirocès? Did it help to release you both?"

"Why do you ask?"

"I just want to know if I really did do the right thing."

Ramerick could sense Relian still withheld a little anxiety over his release. Pirocès himself didn't actually help directly, as it turned out. However, his path conflicted with Dancès, who in turn, helped him immensely. If it wasn't for him, he would not have known of his son's whereabouts. The pain that would have caused would have been unimaginable.

"You did the right thing," Ramerick consoled. "Without it, I may have not survived the not-knowing of what happened to him."

"Thank Blessèd!" he replied with relief, drawing in a huge breath. A small tear began to collect in his ducts. "I regret not being able to do more to help you."

"You did what you could."

"No, I didn't. You represent everything that we stand for in this fight! Cathany realised that too and gave me her blessing when I left. You also left a strong impression on her. She asked me if ever I was to see you again, to give you this message."

"Message?"

"*Trust your heart, and use it to inspire those who need your strength.* This world needs you Alex. More than you realise."

Ramerick couldn't help but feel even more poised to believe that even though Cathany's message was metaphorical, he had the capacity to instil the essence of that message literally. The tug of war in his mind raged on further.

"She is too kind. I wish she took the reign of our people. Though I would have felt safer for them if you were there."

"The noblemen know how to fight."

"Without a leader?"

"Perhaps not. But our people still realise who to confide in when they need it most."

"She would save more lives."

"She would. But so will Gallonea. She is strong too."

"I've never seen Gallonea stand-fast before."

"Oh, it is quite a sight!" Relian perfumed. "She has never fallen. And I'd like to say she never will. But this is something else. And I truly fear for our people."

"As do I," Ramerick revealed. "Come. Let's ride!"

They both saddled up and, along with the band, rode swiftly from Winstanton's gates westward to The Farrowdawns. The pitch-black horizon sat underneath the star-lit sky, suggesting that the rocky terrain was not too far ahead. Guided by The Reinhault, they reached an entrance into The Farrowdawns very quickly.

The ever-famous dark curtain of mist blanketing the terrain greeted them suddenly. Somehow, Ramerick got the feeling that The Farrowdawns was expecting them and almost welcomed him into the mystery that awaited him once more.

## The Deep Breath Before the Plunge

"Daddy, can you play with me?" a young Mion cubling asked of her father.

"I have to chop the oak sweetheart, it'll be dark soon," he replied, inhaling his supper.

"Please daddy," she begged. "We won't play long, I promise!"

"Let your father eat darling," her mother requested.

"He's almost finished! Please daddy, I'll help you work tomorrow."

His conscience was no match for her impossibly cute black eyes pleading with him. Despite needing to venture out to chop wood that afternoon and having a four-year-old to help would be more of a hindrance, he decided that there was nothing more important than spending time with his family.

He gave in to her irresistible charm playing on his soft heart, which worked more often than not. He quickly wolfed down his food and played with his daughter and six-year-old son till the first hour of night. Their mother joined in too, playing the family game that they played all too often.

Their furry constitutions typically bore ginger and white. Their physiques were similar to that of a man's skeletal system; only their toasty manes were distinctive of their kind and kept them warm all through the seasons.

Isolated in one of the pockets of the forest of Woodrilne, east of Landonhome, they led a solitary life of peace. A space of open land was where their home of strong wood and sturdy stone sat, which was covered by the surrounding woodland.

When the games were over and the night drew later, the mother and father tucked both their children in, reading them a bedtime story upon their request. Once again, they could not say no to their persistent children playing on their heartstrings and read till they fell asleep. Or so they believed, as they could hear their gentle purr.

The father decided to collect some oak which the mother had asked him to do the next day.

"I need to get a head start," he insisted. "They can help me finish tomorrow."

"Okay," she agreed with a smile. "I'll wait up for you."

She allowed him to go and he quietly snuck out in an attempt to not wake his children. As he walked away from his home into the dark forest that surrounded it, he could see his mischievous children giggling at the window, waving him goodbye.

"Get to bed ya tykes!" he harshly whispered so that the mother could not hear.

He was unable to contain his smile, to which they obliged, scampering back to bed. He walked away with axe in hand and a happy smile on his face, and once out of earshot of his home, began to chop the oaks.

He worked for several hours, the only light coming from the blue of the moon. It was cold, but he did not feel it due to his shaggy mane and his working efforts, occasionally resting for brief periods.

Upon doing so, he realised something uncharacteristically strange in his surroundings. There was no breeze in the air. It was still. It was the first time he had noticed it in all the years he had repeated the same routine each day. He thought nothing of it initially, but usually, he could hear the nightlife of insects cricking or owls hooting. He heard nothing that night. It made him feel a little anxious, causing his fur to

## The Deep Breath Before the Plunge

bristle and stand on end so he decided to cut his work short and make his way back home.

He picked up the pace of his walk, which soon turned into a gentle trot. He had no idea why but had a gut feeling to get back as soon as possible.

Before he arrived at the front door, he suddenly heard a disturbing rumble from afar. He strained his ears to identify what it could be as it grew louder and louder. The deep sound came closer and he heard the unmistakable sound of wood snapping and groaning as the ancient trees gave way to whatever was making the sound.

Suddenly, an unnatural heat and light seared across a portion of the forest, as if the sun had risen and burst though he knew that wasn't possible and daylight was still many hours away. Realising with horror that his home was also in that rapidly incinerating path, he desperately raced back to his house. Much of the forest was now engulfed in roaring flames, the intense heat stinging his eyes and face as he charged onwards to his home.

He arrived at where his house once stood and immediately fell to his knees at the sight. The fire had wholly decimated it. All that was left were the stones of the foundation. All else had perished under the flames, leaving only ashes in its wake. His heartbreaking howl echoed against the dying trees overpowering the merciless crackle of the fires. In a whisker of life, he had lost everything. His cries rendered him paralysed and fell sidewards onto the ground, staring at the devastation of his family home.

His grief was short-lived as somewhere in his consciousness; he could hear the sound of a thousand footsteps gradually getting louder. He rolled over on his back and turned his head to inspect the oncoming bodies. His sight wasn't all too clear, having stared at the bright flames for some time, but he could make out thousands of white orbs that were encroaching toward him.

He reluctantly stumbled to his feet but did not have the desire to move. They got closer to him and their numbers became apparent as they stretched far and wide as the eye could see. Despite being several hours into the night, the flames allowed him to see their constitution more clearly.

The pale complexions told him they were Elcarian. However, their dead faces and desperate pleading eyes confused him somewhat. He did not know what had happened to them. Small white globes nestled into their chest cavities were not a welcome sight.

He panicked and scrambled to his feet, preparing to bolt to safety but as he turned around, the formidable shadow of outstretched black wings engulfed him. His wide eyes connected with a pair of angry glowing orbs which pierced his soul before a bright orange flame erupted from the darkness.

Just east of the mountains that overlooked Mayanhold, an elderly home that hosted some retired dwarves, quickly tried to organise their retreat back to Dwardelfia. The sun had set which made the oncoming balls of light clearer to see. They knew they were in the direct path of Ramalon's host, which was arriving imminently and wasted no time to depart. Only two remained.

"Come, we must move!" ushered the deep voice of Hàquin, the owner of the home. "The Rhinoauros have already departed! They'll be upon us any minute!"

"Leave me, Hàquin," Aldwin frailly replied.

His hair shone white with a tint of lilac. He was very old and had not the strength to survive the rapid journey. Nonetheless, that did not stop Hàquin from doing his best.

"I am not leaving you!"

"You must," Aldwin replied with a tear collecting in his eye. "We both know I cannot make it."

"You can, and you must!"

"Hàquin, Hàquin…" he slowly whispered.

Aldwin gently waved his hands in front of him to instruct him to stop preparing. He looked up from his chair at the dwarf who had taken good care of him for so many years.

"You expect me just to leave you here?"

"Yes…" Aldwin nodded.

"How about stop trying to be a hero and let me save your Blessèd life!"

"I've had a wonderful life," Aldwin explained with a smile. His eyes softened and calmly tailed off to reminisce. "I've done everything a dwarf can. I've seen the world. I've drunk every ale there is. I've lived to an age where I can accept that there is a time to simply move on. And give my place to another, that will shine on this world…"

Hàquin couldn't help but feel sorry for the frail dwarf.

"You wish to end it like this?" he asked, a little choked.

"I wish to end as all dwarves would. In a comfortable chair, an ale in hand, and remembering how lucky I was to live as a dwarf. Would you

## The Deep Breath Before the Plunge

pass me that blanket there, dear boy?" he weakly asked.

Hàquin hesitated but reluctantly heeded his request, realising that to deny an old dwarf what would be understood to be a final request would be disrespectful.

"Thank you for all your stories," Hàquin thanked as he tucked the elderly dwarf in. "And thank you for all you have given me."

"Ahhh," Aldwin relaxed with a smile. "You are still young. And you will survive this. And when you do, make sure you have a drink in my name, will you?"

Hàquin bounced a small laugh.

"That I will," he said, kneeling to him and cupping his hands which remained untucked out of the blanket. He could not help but feel an overwhelming sadness that things would never be the same without his father again.

"Now go!" Aldwin instructed. "Before it's too late!"

A mysterious force stopped Hàquin from moving. He knew it was the love for his father and not wanting to leave him to die alone. Alas, he knew he had no other choice. Tears welled in his eyes, and to save himself the embarrassment of crying in front of his father; he swiftly departed as they trickled down his short tunic.

Aldwin was alone to admire the view from the veranda, which he could see for many miles of rocky terrain. He heard the deep clopping of hooves that belonged to his son's Rhinoauros, which galloped rapidly to Dwardelfia.

He felt accomplished in life, doing everything he could to protect his son. The first duty of any father. It mattered not that thousands of The Manced were just hundreds of metres away from him or the silhouette of a Dragadelf soaring in his direction. He did not fear death and accepted his fate.

He closed his eyes and the last thing he felt in his warm toasty blanket was a more extreme heat, which rapidly scorched through him until there was nothing left but to listen out for his son's toast one day.

"Durgeon!?" barked the voice of Alexa Greyman.

Luanmanu was caught in thought, staring out into the open plain of the darkness from one of Durge Helm's turrets. The stillness in the air created a familiar sense of foreboding, likened to The Battle for Septalia.

"How long do we have?" she asked again.

"What's your proudest moment Alexa?" he asked, in a slight trance.

"Proudest moment?"

"You've achieved so much. Pioneering the bow-throw? Septalia's finest marksman? The only female on the council? What would you say is your finest?"

Alexa reminisced and scanned the long list of her career landmarks which was applauded all over Septalia. Alas, there was only one winner.

"Raising my boy," she proudly answered. "That is my proudest achievement."

Luan happily smiled.

"Nothing greater than that. How old is Luthèn now?"

"He's eight."

"Teaching him well?"

"He's a pain in the bloody arse right now! He's of that age."

Luan couldn't help but laugh. "An age where he finally knows everything, but yet still depends on you?"

"That's the age!"

"I can't remember what it was like to be young," he sadly said. "I wish I found someone. I wish I had the chance to experience what you have with your son."

"There's still time for that," Alexa awkwardly said.

"You believe there will be hope for me?"

"We will survive this, Luan! We will beat back Ramalon's army, and you can have that -"

"- I'm not talking about the war. I'm talking about my bloody age! I'm ancient Alexa. I'll never have what you have… A son. A daughter. It's my biggest regret…"

"You chose to share your heart with this city. With Septalia. You gave yourself for her because some people on this world are always destined for that. You gave your heart to duty. It's a most honourable choice and a most precious sacrifice."

"I hope I've served her well."

"You have. Not a person on this world would think otherwise."

"Thank you," he replied heart-beaten.

"Before Alicèn, you gave us so many years of peace and happiness. And more importantly, your protection gave us all the platform to love. Without you, I may have never had the chance to have a son. To love him, to hold him. To make my purpose seem fulfilling. And for that, you will always carry not just my respects, but also everyone's on this land. You are the father of Septalia, and we will love you in return,

## The Deep Breath Before the Plunge

for all you have given us, till our very end."

Luan was not accustomed to feeling his heart so overwhelmed with emotion. He did not know how to process the happy sadness he felt in what could be their final hours. He responded in the only way he knew how, by burying it deep within.

"They'll be here by sunrise," he swiftly said, exiting before she could look into his tear-filled eyes.

She watched him march along the helm's wall and disappear out of sight before turning her attention out to the dark abyss once more.

Except for the burning torches that peppered the city, Durge Helm was eerily silent, for it was holding its breath for what was to come. Alexa chose to spend what could be her final moments going back to her home to watch her son sleep in peace.

The last of the Questacèreans had filtered into Lathapràcère, looked over by King Thorian Mijkal. He watched his people, both civilians and lancing Knights, hasten the city, which resided high up on a huge mound. So high was it that it occasionally rose above the clouds to uninterrupted sunlight.

The third hour of night transformed the view into the night sky, peppered with stars and faint colours of distant galaxies. It was a chilly, crisp night that the Questacèreans were well used to in their natural climate. An indication that it could help them against the unnatural that would imminently be upon them.

One of Mijkal's advisors had brought him a message from Hiyaro at The Reinhault. It informed him that there was a strong possibility that although a host of some thirty-five thousand manced headed for his city, they did not believe a Dragadelf would accompany that particular host. He could not escape the subtle relief that his city stood a chance in the short term, however should Terrasendia fall, it would not take too long for them to follow soon after.

Some of the civilians on Lathapràcère tended to some of the roses which crunched in the frost. They were known for their expertise in chemicals which helped many things. Erosion to help dig into Rèo's foundations to acquire protecy stones, healing remedies to aid restoration, to gentle preservatives that they gave through glass vials to many of the flowers and trees to provide them with the ability to flourish through the coldest of climates. They would naturally shrink in the night frost, but come sunrise, they would thaw and blossom into a far more beautiful expression than the night before. It happened every night and every day for thousands of years in a cycle of life.

That night, however, was different. The frost shrunk the flowers as usual, but anxiety grew as to whether it would blossom again by the morning. The evil that marched upon them all created such an imbalance of life that it interrupted the natural flow of energies, disturbing nature itself.

Thorian Mijkal retired back to his chambers and, rather than sleeping, focused his efforts on charging up his divine ability in preparation to defend the siege the next day.

The hall of The Hewercraxen, the place where King Thakendrax's throne on Dwardelfia sat, was so wide it could host several thousand dwarves with ease. And it did.

Rows of benches and long tables were lined so that the dwarves of Handenmar that were already there could drink what they believed could indeed be their last drink.

The ceiling went on forever, but hanging from it were banners of all bands of dwarves that had returned to defend their home. It was not a merry gathering like all others, with frolicking and songs of old. It was a sombre moment to reflect on the real prospect that they may not be there come the same hour on the next day.

All bands put aside their small differences and overwhelmingly came together to enjoy an ale from the finest casks Handenmar had to offer.

No one spoke, airing the atmosphere with a melancholy nature that perfumed intensely. They stared down the long lines of their tables, sitting on their plump buttocks, waiting for their King to rise. When he did, every dwarf rose in unison, scraping the benches on the ground of stone as they did.

Thakendrax walked forward from his throne upon a higher platform which made his presence easily seen by everyone. They all stared at him, to which he stared back, taking some time to look upon each and every one of them individually as best as he could.

He had faith in his people to give themselves as much time as they possibly could. Fleeing into The Wintering Sea was within their capability to do, but not in their nature. Thakendrax saw the fear twinkle in their eyes, but it was not as prominent as the fight in them that overshadowed.

He knew that it could frankly be their last night if Ramerick did not find a way. Alas, he did not rely on a factor out of his control for their

## The Deep Breath Before the Plunge

survival. Although the odds of survival plummeted in the knowledge that he would have to deal with a Dragadelf, he took inspiration from his people's tenacity and defiance. It gave him hope.

"Blessèd be with you!" he raised his iron goblet to The Hewercraxen.

"HUW!!!" they sharply chanted back, echoing for some seconds before greedily inhaling their meads till their goblets were empty.

King Romany stood like a statue on the highest level of Gallonea. His figure only seen by the plethoric torches that radiated against him in the night sky.

The circular stronghold had three levels that diminished in circumference the higher up it went. Noblemen were sharpening their swords, gilding their arrow tips and polishing their armours. They were the least equipped realm to deal with such invasion. Gallonea itself was not nestled into rock and stone. Instead, it was isolated out in the open. Despite its positional weakness, she had a few surprises up her sleeve to aid her defence.

Like a bird in the sky, Romany was only a speck in the people's eyesight, unable to see his face against the torches that shone around him. It could not have been more juxtaposed to that of his wife, who was on the busy lower level, ushering civilians in through the gates and helping in whatever way she could.

"You are a blessing, my Queen," an elderly gentleman thanked Cathany on her way through the city.

"Gracelands bless you!" another frail lady said to her.

She was used to the plaudits of gratitude, which she fully deserved, but was seemingly touched further by a flower given to her by a six-year-old girl, who's cheeks glowed red, eyes sparkled blue and was missing a tooth as she warmed her heart with her irresistibly cute smile.

"Please m-m-my Q-Q-Queen!" she stammered. "K-k-keep us s-s-safe!"

Cathany's breath left her with how heartbroken she felt. Not because of her speech impediment, but because the unifying peril affected every corner of the world. And more importantly, she took the little's girls plead very personally as she would represent the future of this world, should they survive. Cathany kneeled to her, cupped her hands and looked warmly into the girl's eyes.

"You will make us all proud one day, my sweetheart."

"Am I going to die?" she quietly asked.

Cathany froze. Just what does one say when a child asked that question? So little in understanding the harsh realities of the world, yet somehow still aware of its dangers. Alas, she was used to dealing with the impossible.

"You're not going to die, lovely!" she answered with a brave smile.

She did her best to cover up the doubt in her conviction and luckily it seemed to convince the girl that she would be safe. The girl smiled and gave her Queen a tight hug before scampering off back to her parents.

Cathany couldn't help but allow her brave tears to drop before quickly wiping them away and ascending the city to join her husband. He did not move from his position, continuing his glance to the stronghold he entrusted himself with defending.

"Romany?" she asked with his back turned. "Is everything okay?"

His motionless response suggested that he was not. She began to walk forward toward him.

"Stop!" he commanded, still not showing his face. "I don't want you to see me like this…"

"Like what?"

Cathany couldn't hear his sobs but could see his body was tense, trying to stabilise his shaking body. He reluctantly turned round to view his wife and couldn't help but feel shameful for his emotions, which he had never demonstrated that strongly before.

"What am I doing Cath!?" he desperately asked. "What am I doing?"

"You are our King!"

"I'm no King!" he wallowed in self-pity. "We're all going to die tomorrow, and there's nothing I can do."

"Romany!" she forcefully said. "You are your people's inspiration! You cannot give up on them now by believing there is no hope!"

"There is no hope Cath!"

"There is if you believe there is! Our people look up to you! If they see someone who has already given up, then no, we will not survive!"

"There's no way we can withstand the evil that is upon us!"

"Stay strong, my love! What would you do if Selbey were here? How strong would you be if our son were still alive?"

The sheer mention of their son, who'd they'd lost, was a risky strategy to try and motivate him, but she knew there was more strength deep down within him. The tears that began to collect more

## The Deep Breath Before the Plunge

prominently in his eyes were beginning to unearth that.

"It changed everything, Cath. I know I'm not the man I once was after him. If he were still here... I... I..."

"Shhhh, it's okay," she soothed, taking his hands. "I know it changed you. You lost a part of yourself, as did I."

"Do you know what it's like? Having the title of being a King and being forced to show strength every second of every day? Knowing that you have none left?"

"You think strength is defined by appearing strong? By being a man and hiding your fears and insecurities? You want to know how I define strength...? Choice. Choice, my love," she whispered, and it inspired him. "How can you make the right choices in life, against what at some point seems impossible? That's what defines strength. That's what inspires courage, courage that your people need from you right now!"

"They should have had you," he sheepishly admitted. "You are our strength. Our people deserve better than a feeble King."

He removed the crown from his head and looked at his wife. She knew precisely what he was going to do and could not deny the temptation he was going to offer.

"Romany," she replied a little regrettably.

"I offer you the crown! Our people love you and you have what it takes to lead us all! Please, take it and show us the way..."

He outstretched his hands to offer the golden headpiece. Cathany thought very hard over the two options she had. She admitted that should she be the focal point of her people, it could inspire everyone to fight that bit harder. On the other hand, sadness took her in that taking up the offer would essentially be giving up on her husband and disbanding her duty as a wife. She heavily weighed up the options and came to her conclusion.

She took the crown from her husband's hands and held it in hers. Once Romany had let go, he finally let out a smile out of relief that he had done the right thing. However, that smile did not last long as she placed the crown back on his head.

His face was full of disbelief as she had rejected his offer.

"Why?" he quivered. "Our people need a strong leader."

"They already have one," she consoled. "You are strong, my love. You always have been."

Her words and undying loyalty seemed to inspire him somewhat and touched him in a way that only she could. At that moment, he was beginning to realise that no matter what, she would never give up on him and would believe in him, to whatever end. It allowed him to find strength in a corner of his heart he did not know existed and took that as a sign of her love, which he'd forgotten was always there.

Together they made their way down the torchlit city, and perhaps for the first time since Romany's reign, he walked among the people as if he was one of them. Gallonea's surprise was undoubtedly in abundance as many civilians and Knights could not quite believe his presence.

He used the hours of night they had left to get to know as many of his people as possible. He spoke to random men and women as he passed through; the power of conversation surprised him. They'd all bowed their heads before and after he had learned their names and what they did. He thanked them sincerely for their roles which shed a little more confidence and courage in the noblemen.

Despite being the quietest it had ever been, Terrasendia could not sleep that night. When the sun rose in the east, they would have to be ready for the fight of their lives.

By that point, the four realms would be as ready as they ever could be. The civilians had retreated to their strongholds; the Knights were well prepared and briefed on just what they were likely to be up against. They knew that to kill a manced lifeform, the orb that powered them must be destroyed. That was common knowledge. As for how to kill, stop, or even slow down a Dragadelf, no one had a formula, only ideas that would be tried at that moment. It was what encapsulated their fears and dampened down spirits of survival most.

Never before were so many people united by such fright and reluctance for the sun to rise. Loved ones were embraced; confinement in people really shone in their darkest hour. Hate and diversity did not exist at that moment, but a universal purpose that they were placed on Rèo as stewards. It was their role to protect it, look after it, and defend it from those that would harm it.

The hearts in every corner of Terrasendia skipped a beat when the first streak of sunlight rose from the horizon.

Their time had come.

Through self-will and incredible determination, they mustered the strength to face their enemy, who they could see was arriving in unimaginable numbers.

Each stronghold began to muster in their own unique, defensive ways as the sea of white balls of light representing The Manced

## The Deep Breath Before the Plunge

trudged toward them. Their purpose was apparent in that they had to bide the one thing that could save them. Time.

On Dwardelfia, King Thakendrax conjured his affinity of gravity to manifest over the hilly plains before their stronghold by the sea. Having that fight against an increase in gravity gave the dwarves that unique physical strength that they used to their advantage.

In addition to that, complicated networks of explosives were riddled underneath the earth that sat between them. He had an idea or two as to what to do should a Dragadelf soar over them.

On Gallonea, a timely revitalised King Romany issued the order to begin the fortress' primary defence from the oncoming manced that circled the stronghold a mile away. They could not see the details of what surrounded them and were unaware that the host was of Elcarian souls, which were immediately given back to their bodies once Ramalon had extracted and tainted it.

A deep grinding of stone was heard as the twenty-foot circular walls began to rotate in a three-sixty motion slowly. Its iconic defence was legendary and, for many years, successfully repelled many invasions and attacks. As the city slowly spun, it was not long before the entire circling began to become uninterrupted with militants of The Manced. There was no turning back but the people took strength in seeing Romany as fearless as they had ever seen in him before.

On Lathapràcère, The Manced trudged up the steep incline toward the capital. Their unnatural empowerment did not process the fatigue it would usually take and therefore had no lactic acid to fill their muscles on their ascent. King Thorian Mijkal waded toward the balcony of his throne room, which was the city's highest point.

The time had come to unleash his powers of ice which he had been charging the whole night, to manifest a freezing blizzard that cut out the suns rays and breath gently over the city and beyond. The Questacèreans, armed with their lances and spears and armoured with typical green and red plated steels, were more than used to the additional freeze. Within minutes, the earth between them and The Manced some mile below had rapidly turned to ice. They would hope that it would prove too much for such unnatural forces to withstand, and at the very least, slow them down.

On Durge Helm, Luan had ordered some days previously for every barrel of oil at their disposal and used them to soak the plain before them. In the same fashion as The Banamie, they saw the plethoric number of manced encroach toward them from the nose of The

Farrowdawns some miles ahead. Drenching miles of square feet was logistically impossible. Therefore, they constructed pathways using barbed blockades and trenches, hoping to bottleneck the advances to a much heavier oil concentration. The archers, led by Alexa Greyman, stood ready with their bows, the ends of their arrow shafts coated in oils to ignite the field at the precise moment.

Meryx Meigar had resumed his customary position with his band of mildens outside the city walls, safe from the fires that would burn. His brother, Max was by his side along with Luan, Lestas Magraw, and other band leaders as they all watched The Manced' march. However, they appeared to halt their advance in the distance.

Max prepared himself to perform the similar enchantment to that which he used during The Draughts. Installing his essences of earth would make their attacks much easier, for they would only need to make contact with their bodies and not physically destroy the orbs.

He made his way to the centre of Septalia's capital, spread his arms underneath his waist, coiled his fingertips and called upon his divine essences and shared it with every weapon on Durge Helm. The men and women on the frontline began to feel a notion of increased strength as a bi-product.

All realms waited for the inevitable as The Manced did not untimely begin their advance. Nor did The Dragadelf reveal themselves. Instead, they waited. It seemed a very deliberate choice to wait until the moment was opportune.

Such a strange contrast omitted, in that the beauty of the sunlight could not outshine the frightening horror of the thousands of white orbs that glared from afar.

Their harrowing stares of souls begging to be freed from their purgatory could not have been more frightening and sad. They all knew who was responsible for the inevitable and asked themselves how one person could conjure such hate upon life? They could not understand. It was those type of natural thoughts that inspired Ramalon further and justified his path.

For many moments nothing happened. Some believed that perhaps Ramalon was having second thoughts about whether to go through with this. At no point did he give off any indication that he wouldn't and was more of hope that there was a glimmer of good in Ramalon's heart. Alas, for those that knew his character, there was no doubt that this was a moment of indulgence.

Ramalon's eyes were closed from afar and could taste the fear in his

## The Deep Breath Before the Plunge

enemies. Such magnitude did give him a sense of euphoria and couldn't help but marvel at his achievements again. The world hinged on him. And he loved every moment of attention before decisively instructing his armies in all four corners of Terrasendia to fulfil his retribution.

Horrors of the worst kind was finally upon them. The distant roars of The Dragadelf were loudly heard on Gallonea, Durge Helm and Dwardelfia. Their presence soared out of the morning skies and flew over their hosts. At that moment, whatever strength on Gallonea that was mustered had taken a heartbreaking hit.

The realisation that a legendary Dragadelf was upon them had not entirely sunk in for many until that moment of seeing their magnificent wings, robust carriages and deafening roars. It depleted their hopes. Understandably, few men cowered to their homes in the city and left their posts, which despite the anger of some braver soldiers, they struggled to stop.

On Durge Helm, the Dragadelf's cry did indeed frighten them but turned that into motivation to survive as per their training, which made their resolve much stronger.

The dwarves on Handenmar, however, completely trusted their King in that a Dragadelf would be upon them and prepared for its presence, to which they only roared back louder, in typical stubbornness.

Alas, it was short-lived as the three Dragadelf had finally been let loose from Ramalon's restrictions and did not wait for their hosts before soaring ferociously toward their targets and began wreaking the unnatural havoc they were reborn for.

It was at that moment when the animated corpses of The Manced unnaturally sprang forward like helpless puppets and advanced on all that was good and green.

The war for Terrasendia had begun.

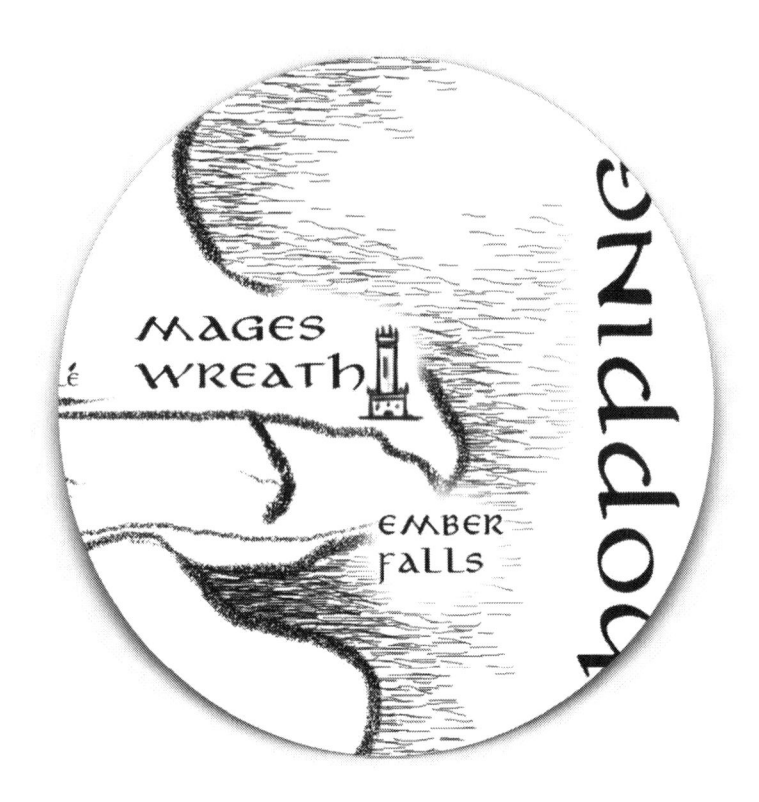

## The Battle for the Oceans

Ramalon stood silently on the edge of Ember Falls. He had soared to Mages Wreath on his remaining Dragadelf, who he had instructed to roam away from his location. He did not need its help to climb his next step.

His eyes closed, processing his thoughts on what he had just done. He felt an overwhelming sense of righteousness in sending forth his legions. The world, in his mind, had turned its back on him. It was his turn to reciprocate.

He could feel in his mind's eye, the people of Terrasendia had begun to realise their mistake, sensing their fear and horror, which only added to his satisfaction. If there was a mythical god of The Understunde, he would have no hesitation to look Sarthanzar dead in his black and red eyes, to challenge even him. That's how powerful he felt. The now familiar surge of invincibility burned through him,

# The Battle for the Oceans

spurring him on to his next endeavour.

His eyes opened to see the vast expanse of The Chopping Sea ahead. From eye to eye lay nothing but chopping swashes as far as the horizon. The rising sun temporarily blinded his vision, but his eyes adapted rather quickly. The waves splashed against the rocks that stooped a mile below him, overlooking the cliff edge.

So many memories came flooding back to him at that moment. He debated with himself as to whether this was where it all began for him. Davinor was the main instigator of the torment and suffering that sent him down his darker path, but he did not for one second think that the people of Mages Wreath would have turned on him as well.

The moment he triumphed and won The Màgjeurs Open, they should have applauded his achievements and admired his efforts and hard work. That recognition never came. When they booed him in his moment of triumph, he could not understand why they hated him for it. Of course, now, he understood completely. They did not accept him, nor did they appreciate the greatness presented before them. They were jealous, angry that they would have to work as hard as him to achieve such accolades. It was a clear insight into their desires that they wanted everything given to them and not earn it as he did.

At that moment it mattered not, for everyone now on Mages Wreath was dead by his hand. Their mangled corpses rotting in The Draughts was a small piece of justice he took for himself. Though a pang of dissatisfaction disturbed him, for Ramacès had freed their souls, stealing his right to serve them life in purgatory. That anger inspired him further.

It was time.

He knew The Blessèd Mage of Water was somewhere in the depths ahead and he was not one for patience. His arrogance told him that he would not have to wait long. It would be only a matter of time before Ramalon would find a way of locating her, and this was her best chance of putting up the best fight she could. He was in her element now and she would utilise every advantage she could get.

The Chopping Sea was indeed usually quiet. It was given its name because it was iconically a hazardous part of the ocean. Unpredictable in its atypical weather patterns and unsafe for any boats wishing to set sail to the unknown east. Ramalon waited, gazing intensely at the waters before becoming increasingly annoyed that nothing was happening.

His instincts again prevailed as a sudden swoosh of wind emerged from behind and flew right above him. It unexpectedly sent him to his knees and he crumpled to the ground before the cliff edge. When he raised his head to inspect the gust, his eyes narrowed and intensified.

He saw The Blessèd Mage of Water, gliding out toward The Chopping Sea, astride her own dragon made entirely of water that she had conjured for herself. She dipped its wing and it flew rapidly across the horizon, gently cutting the surface of the water, before ascending high up into the sky above.

She suspended her dragon some several miles away from the shores, and although they were too far away to see each other's faces, they both knew that the moment had arrived. Both eyes filled with venomous intent to the other, both fighting for opposite outcomes.

Ramalon finally came to a stand, rising slowly and solemnly, preparing himself for the inevitable duel.

Wemberlè had never looked so determined in all her life. Her defiant expression a message to Ramalon that he would not prevail. She totally believed that she would win this fight in her own habitat even though she was alone. Though, she was not naive to the fact of who she was facing. It would be the fight of her life, and she knew it.

They both indulged in the intense stare from afar before it was time for The Blessèd Mage of Water to demonstrate her own definition of divinity.

She propelled her aqua-dragon high up into the skies and along with it, sucked a huge area of the sea with her. The vast swell of water rose several hundreds of metres high before allowing gravity to pull it down and crash back into the ocean. It created a domino effect that raised other portions of the nearby area and caused fierce waves.

Wemberlè flew to other portions of the sea and repeated the process numerous times. The sea slowly bounced up and down with exponential gravitas, which Wemberlè and her dragon navigated effortlessly, embracing her storm.

In just a few short minutes, The Chopping Sea's magnitude collated into one colossal tidal wave. She sent the several-hundred-metre high Tsunami racing toward the shore from some mile out. Like a general commanding her army, Wemberlè soared above it and led the charge.

It was the perfect storm. It needed to be to give her any chance of success. She was throwing everything she had in her at him, and why not? This was her ocean, her world, and she was not going to back down for anyone. However, it mattered not to Ramalon. His very nature clashed poetically with her philosophy.

## The Battle for the Oceans

The oncoming attack took time to build, giving him a little time to witness just what was heading for him. Without a single blink, he gazed slowly from right to left, across the horizon he could no longer see as the unprecedented spectacle covered as far wide as his sight allowed. Not even the sun could pierce through the thick waters that covered its light. A small piece of his consciousness bordered on admiration at the magnificent sight of The Blessèd Mage of Water's strength. To his surprise, a twinge of fear began to stab away at him.

In addition, thousands of Windermares made of water were birthed from the rushing tide and charged alongside their conjurer. Wemberlè knew it would not directly increase the devastation aspect but knew the galloping force would likely intimidate her opponent.

With the skies above him peppered with galloping water-mildens and The Blessèd Mage of Water atop her water-dragon, Ramalon was only moments away from the terrifying prospect of being swallowed by millions of tonnes of water.

He had only one chance to survive and made his choice of action. He intensified his gaze and opened up his protecy before The Blessèd Mage of Water successfully threw The Chopping Sea on top of him.

It hit him with the force of a seismic earthquake, which shuddered and shocked miles into the land of Questacère and Septalia. The ruins of Mages Wreath was engulfed entirely by the devastating wave along with much of the land where Ramalon had been standing.

Wemberlè waited until the sea that consumed her victim had calmed significantly before diving underwater to find out if her attack was successful.

Not many people would have the gall to survive such a devastating blow. Alas, she knew Ramalon was not like many people. He was different. The conventions did not apply to him as they would anyone else.

After a short while of swimming like an elegant mermaid among the ruins, Ramalon's body was nowhere to be seen. She searched the underwater ruins of Mages Wreath, hoping to see his floating corpse, for which she could not. Each growing moment made her anxiety spike.

The waters itself began to slip back into the ocean, for which she retreated back to, to confirm Ramalon's death. She found herself in a lonely spot of the ocean bed which, by comparison, was relatively shallow. The suns rays only just being able to pierce her location.

At that moment, she felt the weight of horror from within. She saw the roof on the ocean begin to slowly crust over with an earthy substance which she knew was not natural. She understood Ramalon had the ability to use earth magic, and that was precisely what she was witnessing.

The land above her spread as far as she could see, drowning out any light that came from the surface. Despite being in her natural habitat, she became fearful that the advantage of her battlefield was being wiped out. She needed the scales tipped in her favour, her survival depended on it.

She swam to an area where she hoped to escape what seemed to be an enclosure of stone above her and began to swim faster, thinning her fins to stream much more rapidly. However, it was in vain for the ocean bed rose ahead of her, right up to the water's roof. She realised she was trapped. The last remaining streaks of sunlight disappeared. It rendered her blind in the pitch black of her watery tomb.

Her heart started to race and bounce heavily against the water, rippling it gently from her chest. Luckily for her, her skill underwater was so masterful that she did not need actual sight to see. She tuned her senses so sensitively that she could hear the slightest ripple, the slightest vibration for many miles.

Despite her growing fear, she knew she had to remain as calm as possible for her senses to work. She closed her eyes amid the total darkness and scanned for her enemy. He did not appear.

She had to prepare for the eventuality of facing him directly and so designed a plan. She knew that Ramalon was somewhere inside.

The water was calm, no longer affected by the tide's natural currents, which despite her incarceration, she could still control.

Suddenly, she sensed a gentle tremor. Or more-so, she picked up the notion that something was moving from behind her.

She turned around and against the black abyss, a stoney figure in the shape of Ramalon came to her senses. His body had morphed into the typical golem, entombing himself in the elements of rock, which he must have done moments before The Chopping Sea crashed into him. He did not attack immediately, wanting to stand before her in admiration for how much power she had demonstrated... Before he took it for himself.

Even though they could not see each other directly, she knew he could sense her fear, which she desperately tried to mask with sheer determination. Her teeth gritted together and her stance poised, as she charged up her protecy in the only plan she had left.

# The Battle for the Oceans

The only advantage that Wemberlè had was that even though Ramalon had the ability to conjure multiple affinities, he was fortunately stuck with the channel of earth magic to sustain being underwater. Were he to open another channel, the protective rock entombing his body would dissolve and leave him vulnerable.

They stood off among one another and it was Wemberlè who struck first, gathering a portion of the water and unleashing a powerful jet onto Ramalon. He defended with a stoney fist, which upon continuous contact, only built a shield of stone similar to that of Melcelore's defence, which grew the more the water struck. Wemberlè recognised her attack was making things worse and quickly stopped, only for that fragment of stone to be hurtled back towards her. A small vortex trailed the rock, but Wemberlè smoothly evaded the attack which she felt smash against the wall behind her.

He remained rooted centre-stage while she swam around the enclosure, trying to use her speed and agility to overcome the slower movements of Ramalon, always looking to strike him while his guard was down.

Ramalon became a little frustrated dancing back and forth, trying to keep up with The Blessèd Mages movements, always trying to face her. Losing patience, he impulsively ripped off parts of the enclosure and cast them in her direction. Even that proved no match for her stealthy movements, gracefully ducking and spinning around the missiles.

However, Wemberlè knew she could not sustain this strategy. She had to unleash her ultimate plan, which she had been conjuring for some time. It was now or never.

Missile upon missile continued to rain upon her. Ramalon even had the idea to bring the whole lot down in the hope she would not survive. However, if he did that, she may escape his death trap, making his goal that much more difficult.

His patience seemed for a moment to pay off as Wemberlè faltered. Appearing exhausted from her efforts, she collapsed some twenty-metres away from him. He briefly wondered why she had allowed herself to be fatigued so quickly but had little time to doubt her further as she suddenly snapped out of her feigned exhaustion and released another flume of water straight at him. He responded in the same way as before, building the shield of stone in front of him.

However, this time, Wemberlè continued the attack. She knew that by doing so, the shield was growing bigger and stronger - all part of the plan. Luckily, Ramalon had not spotted what was happening.

Parts of the rocky enclosure began to destabilise and fracture. Her plan was risky as the shield grew so big that she would not escape its thrust if she relaxed her jet-stream. It really was do or die for The Blessèd Mage, as she gritted her teeth, willing her plan to life before it was too late. Ramalon was sensing victory, albeit utterly distracted from what was happening.

Finally, upon the very last drop of water Wemberlè could muster, the enclosure obliterated from behind Ramalon. The whirlpool that she had been conjuring sucked his body from the duel and pulled him into the expansive vortex that swirled into the ocean bed. It took him by complete surprise and he realised how ferocious the undercurrents were to generate such an attack, albeit all too late.

He clambered as best as he could to avoid the swirling currents dragging him into what felt like the gates of The Understunde. Down he scrambled into the depths of the ocean bed and out of sight.

Wemberlè closed up the hole and the ocean was at last calm once more. A huge sigh of relief warmed her body as she crumbled to the ocean bed, sifting up clouds of sand that gently floated back down. Water flooded through her expanding gills, restoring her depleted energy. She was consumed by the euphoria that she had done it.

Ramalon was no more, buried under thousands of tonnes of the natural element; she was convinced she had won The Battle for the Oceans. She showed Ramalon that the power of The Blessèd Order would always outshine the darkness he followed.

She looked up to the surface of the sea and took the sun's rays as a hopeful sign of light and positivity for Terrasendia.

Meanwhile, the Dragadelf wreaked havoc on the land's defences. Despite the hosts of Ramalon's manced not yet reaching their destinations because of the stronghold's ability to slow them down, their aerial presence made efforts to contain the oncoming armies much more difficult.

On Durge Helm, the only form of defence from the Dragadelf's fires came from the archers, who were instructed to aim for its glaring eyes,. That did prove relatively successful, as it was unable to land any of it's typical fires to maximum devastation.

The Manced trudged their ways through the oil-soaked plains as Meryx Meigar waited until a good number were already on the fields before them. He then instructed the torches to ignite the relevant paths, which rapidly scorched and lit up the area before them, causing utter

# The Battle for the Oceans

devastation. The affected militants were instantly dismantled, smashing their magical globes and freeing their souls. Only a small number had been hit by comparison.

They began to filter into parts of the field which was not ignited, forcing them into the bottleneck as planned, which made attacking them from range much more manageable.

On Gallonea, Romany inspired his troops to prioritise halting the Dragadelf too. They had built giant crossbows, capable of slicing through its wings with ease and should their arrows land on their armoured scales, they could prove devastating. The wooden weapons were also on a platform that could rotate, making it much easier to manoeuvre.

However, the land before them was not defended by any real physical barrier which allowed The Manced to manically race toward the circular fortress. It was time for Gallonea to show her stubborn signature.

Cathany instructed the workmen of the city who deployed the walls to spin in a complete circle. The sound of heavy stone ground as it successfully rotated, making any attempt to scale the walls much more difficult. Alas, The Manced still tried, slipping in their grips and retrying with unnatural energy.

Archers and spears attempted to fend off any bodies getting relatively close to the top. On a few occasions, however, a few militants did manage to successfully scale its walls, which were met by swordsmen swiping directly into the white orbs, instantly smashing them to escape to The Gracelands.

King Thakendrax, who now assumed the position of an almighty god, increasing the gravity all around Dwardelfia, had managed successfully to slow The Manced down. The gravity was so much that their unnatural efforts began to wain. Large portions of the swarm crumpled to the ground a mile away from the dwarven capital.

As for the Dragadelf which soared above them, the cleverness in a dragon's nature knew that Thakendrax was halting their advance considerably well and it tried to cut the head off the snake. As it came for their King, the dwarves let fly a network of explosive fireworks, which mounted a stout defence of their King. The counter-attack forced the beast to frustratingly fly away and try again.

In the freezing blizzard caused by King Thorian Mijkal, Lathapràcère, too was proving a formidable defence. In addition to the slope that the elven capital sat atop, the freeze began to numb The

Manced. Despite their unnatural sources of energy, they struggled to clamber effectively.

The news that a Dragadelf would not directly confront them was, of course, welcome and did make their lands easier to defend. However, this was all still a delaying tactic. There was no way the icy temperatures would outlast such barbarity and they prepared for the inevitable fight.

Each corner of Terrasendia was so far proving it could hold it's own. Alas, they all knew the loom of evil would be ever more challenging to keep at bay.

The water flowed naturally in Wemberlè's gills again. She had recuperated after many hours and some measure of strength floated back to her again.

Time seemed to pass so quickly for it was already dusk. The light was fading and with it came a strange contradiction of relief against the horrors of the dark.

She had images in her mind of how Terrasendia would be in disbelief as to what had happened. Picturing all of The Manced suddenly dissemble and crumple before them all, leaving just the Dragadelf to deal with for The Dragastone remained. That in itself would still leave them in a world of uncertainty.

However, something did feel strange in the waters. She sensed with her ultra fine-tuned detection that there was an alarming presence stirring in the depths. Her anxiety spiked back up again when she realised with heart-stopping terror her gravest mistake. She stared blankly at the open waters ahead, almost in apology for failing the oceans she was entrusted to protect.

All of a sudden, the ocean bed rapidly crumbled beneath her feet to create a vast sinkhole that, despite still being underwater, dragged her down to the depths mirroring what she did to Ramalon hours ago. She tried to propel herself out of danger, but the force was too strong, even for her.

She was in an unstoppable dive until she crashed into Ramalon's fist made of stone, emerging from the sea floor in his embodied form of rock. The impact instantly split her skull, causing her to lose consciousness. The Blessèd Mage of Water floated helplessly before her enemy.

His face was full of anger; having experienced just a moment where he was outwitted by someone he felt was inferior to him. Although

# The Battle for the Oceans

that was only telling half of the story. The real frustration was that the blow he just delivered was an unacceptable way to end it all. It wasn't poetic enough for him. Such a simple blow was so unsavoury and unfulfilling. He felt a substantial similarity at that moment to his duel with Davinor, hoping she was still alive to give her a more fitting end that exercised his poetic signature.

Luckily for him, he noticed the gills of Wemberlè contract and relax, suggesting she was alive. He approached her stunned body and felt righteous once more. Her eyes slowly opened, and judging by her lack of response, she was unaware of what had happened and indeed, what was about to take place. Ramalon slowly waded forward to claim his prize.

"Another step..." he declared, raising his hand to force conjured stone into her gills.

It blocked any path for water to filter through, water that she depended on to function in her natural habitat. Her despairing awareness of what was happening grew the more the suffocation took over. She was essentially suffocating, the perfect justice for Ramalon, who found irony in The Blessèd Mage of Water drowning in her own element.

She scrambled in utter peril trying to escape, but Ramalon felt only obliged to make matters worse and increase the stone filtering through her body which she could do nothing about. Soon, her veins cemented and her eyes turned to stone before he injected one final burst, causing her whole body to explode.

The elements of earth mixed with the infusions of her blood formed like red clouds before him. The Blessèd Mage of Water, was no more.

He wasted no time in finalising the event. The concrete ruins sank to the ocean bed, leaving her Blessèd blood free for the taking.

He outstretched his hand and the red mist began to absorb into his palm, dissolving in his grasp as it filtered into his body. The mist diminished until every last drop had been absorbed into his possession. He had claimed the affinity of water.

He felt the element run purely through his veins. That sense of cleanliness the water provided, streaming through him as if he were breathing it in through gills.

His growing power was almost complete. He took a moment to indulge once more in his latest achievement, realising that he had won The Battle of the Oceans.

"Two more steps..." he whispered.

## A Matter of Time

Terrasendia's defences held firm. Alas, it could only last so long.

The battles that had raged upon the land felt like they had been at war for many weeks. It had barely been a day, fending off the relentless Dragadelf who continued to battle against their prey. Successfully each corner held its own against the flying infernos. That success also came from the ground, halting the advance of the oncoming manced. They all had a defensive strategy, to protect the weaponry that deflected the aerial attacks. Were they to crumble, it would not be long until dragonbreath consumed the cities.

However, Ramalon began to twist the knife from afar, giving his militants additional empowerment that fuelled them with unnatural energy to advance more quickly.

It already was for the noblemen on Gallonea. As the legendary fortress continued to spin causing The Manced to slip off the walls,

## A Matter of Time

they continued their efforts with merciless intent. They did not stop. Something had to be done and quickly before the walls were overcome with animated corpses. If that should come to pass and the fortress was overrun, the crossbows warding off the Dragadelf would collapse, and with nothing warding them off, the incineration of the city would be sure and swift.

To that fear, after several hours of trying, the Dragadelf managed on several occasions to safely pick off numerous crossbows, piercing holes in their defences and allowing it to move more freely.

In addition, the bodies began to pile up outside the rotating walls, like an infestation of maggots, squirming to reach the top. Romany continued to bark orders below, which were instantly followed. The spearmen and swordsmen were called into action more prominently as more militants began to slip through the net and infect the city.

As they got closer, they understood that the form of manced souls were indeed of Elcarian descent. Their gaunt, pale expressions symbolised the horrific nature even more. They needed help badly.

"I'm going down there!" Romany impulsively decided.

"You can't!" Cathany cried, stepping after him as he tried to make his way through. "Now is not the time to be a hero! We need our King safe!"

He turned on the spot to confront her.

"I'm not trying to be heroic. Fewer people will die if they know their King is fighting with them! Down there, ready to sacrifice himself for others! Take the reins, my love. You'll do a better job than I ever could."

Cathany did not know precisely what to say, but Romany's heroic sacrifice left her no alternative other than to heed his wish. He marched off with a handful of his trusted Knights, down to the walls and front line. Cathany returned to the balcony where she would take up command.

Several hours on Gallonea passed and the infestation began to spread more vigorously in every portion of the city's circumference. She spotted her husband down below, occasionally engaging in melees which reminded her of how he used to be before their son's death. Mighty, strong and fearless.

However, her fond memories were interrupted by a black speck in the sky. It rapidly approached her with frightening velocity. It became clear the Dragadelf was on a direct charge at the Queen of Landonhome. Her heart stopped at the prospect of its wrath. One spit of fire and she knew she would not survive. All her blockades of strength were beginning to crumble against such mythology, unearthing the true weight of her fear.

"Draw..." she whimpered, petrified. "Draw! DRAW!"

Her desperate command did not fall on deaf ears, but it seemed that the Dragadelf had found a particular angle where the aerial defences could not reach.

"FLY!" she instructed, but it was more out of panic than tactical timing and issued for the crossbows to fire too early.

Their sharp missiles were instantly evaded by the winged beast, who had time to efficiently see the attacks and perform an evasive manoeuvre. The men in charge of reloading the giant shafts hurried as quickly as they could to click the arrows back into place, but their fright got the better out of them too, knowing how close the Dragadelf was to their Queen.

Up to that point, Gallonea had successfully held off the flying inferno. The last of the crossbows let fly into its path and missed their target by a mere metre, as it had a clear view of its goal. It's jaw unhinged delightfully upon Cathany and erupted its molten belly.

Its fiery breath ripped the air with a searing pace, but it was met by an equal force of fire that came from the skies behind. The connection exploded, sending a wave of heat radiating over the fortress. Sweat pores instantly opened and began to profuse amongst the battling men down below. It was felt among the civilians on the higher levels too.

The oncoming Dragadelf fluttered its wings and bounced in front of her, but its gaze was drawn above. Cathany cried a sigh of relief and quickly inspected her saviour. She was equally mortified to see a Drogadera crunching its claws on one of the buildings behind her. However, the feminine dragon did not gaze upon her for its next meal but back toward the Dragadelf to ward off its evil malice.

Sat atop the beautiful Drogadera lined with unique pyrovines, was the equally impressive Màgjeur Ethelba. Her timely arrival brought euphoric relief to Cathany. The cavalry had arrived.

The Blessèd Mage of Fire's timing could not have been more opportune. Behind her was her own band of Rolgan Knights, descending down from their Windermares who, like their masters, were lined with the orange glow of pyrovines too.

Like a vast flock of birds, they parachuted inside the capital walls to provide a much-needed boost of defence and morale, albeit just a small number of some three hundred Knights. Though every one of them was more skilled in battle than the whole of Gallonea. They wasted no time demonstrating their ruthless skill, fending off multiple manced and aiding the noblemen with spears, swords and fiery magic.

The standoff between the two beasts took centre-stage above the circular stronghold. A Dragadelf would surely be too strong for Ethelba's Drogadera, given that its fusion held a third of it's DNA. However, the additional destruction of The Blessèd Mage of Fire certainly brought some form of parity to the contest. Admittedly, the odds still tipped heavily in the Dragadelf's favour in terms of power, though that did not stop her facing her opponent head on.

"Jòsièra," she whispered to her fiery steed she had ridden for many years. Her language was not that of the common voice, but of foreign decent. Her eyes narrowed to a frightening glare, signalling her intent. "Ignalèas!" she commanded through gritted teeth, the translation of which meant *ignite*.

The battle-cry from the Drogadera was elegantly terrifying, whilst the Dragadelf's own roar appeared to be that little bit louder, harsher and uglier.

They flew straight into each other and brawled viciously, spitting fires and physical attacks in a dogged fight, which they soon took to the skies.

The need for reinforcements was indeed dire, and even with the skill and prowess of the famous Knights of Rolgan below, they were still hugely outnumbered and suppression still remained the unifying strategy. They could not entirely beat back such overwhelming numbers with the strength they had, but it did give them the one thing that Terrasendia so desperately needed. Time.

In addition to Thakendrax's increased gravity, the rain began to plummet down onto Dwardelfia, splashing harshly like a monsoon of hailstones.

The plains soaked, making the advance of The Manced even more challenging, bogging them down. On some occasions, the saturated ground became so sludgy that it consumed the entirety of some militants. The white orbs buried in mud could be seen diffusing out of the foundations before floating high up into the sky. More of a symbol that the world had naturally reclaimed that life.

The network of fireworks they deployed to the skies above also proved a success in warding off the beast. Its cover did not allow it to get too close and when its fires did spit, it was far enough away to prevent inflicting any real damage. The explosions sparkled in the now grey sky that formed above, crystallising the debris. They had enough explosives down in the stores of The Hewercraxen to last them months. On occasions, they used some of the more piercing fireworks in an attempt to counter-attack.

Although suppression was the focal task, the stubbornness and impatience of Thakendrax began to wear thin. He was in a war against himself, deciding whether to take the Rhinoauros by the horns and ride out to meet them head-on or simply wait and bide time for Ramerick's coveted plan, which he didn't know was even in motion, to work. It was not in their nature to wait for the enemy to come to them.

The walls that protected Dwardelfia were long and wide. Their catapults contained specific gunpowder to maximise the explosive effect. The Manced were not yet in range, but suddenly, they began to advance much quicker than anticipated. Their injection of energy from Ramalon animated them enough to plough through the mud much more effectively as the storm of souls filtered forward en masse.

Thakendrax ordered for the trebuchets to let fly their explosives. Fireballs hurtled into the field, landing to devastating effect, instantly dismantling the effected militants. However, some did not reach their targets and were destroyed mid-flight by the Dragadelf's flames. It provided good cover for The Manced to finally get to the walls that protected the dwarven capital.

The corpses began to pile and stack up, making it much easier for the remaining squirming manced to scale on top of each other to the tip. Glass vials of liquids, which were being thrown from heights of the city, landed on the collecting bodies and exploded effectively to halt their climb. Bodies spewed away from the walls, collapsing their corpse-made ladders. However, due to the sheer number of manced, they just rebuilt it in the same fashion and continued climbing.

The dwarves were prepared for the invasion, arming themselves with double-sided axes, shields and war-hammers that they used to beat them back. It wasn't long before portions of the walls were beginning to be exposed and numerous manced began to spill into the city, like a cup that was overfilling. The dwarves quickly took care of the ones that slipped through the net as there weren't too many at that point.

Thakendrax sensed that time was not on their hands and was gravely concerned as he spotted several parts of his walls being overrun. He had to do something, but in the process, knew it was risky.

He increased the level of gravity which drained a large portion of his powers. The process squeezed the piles of bodies that built outside the walls into the ground, crushing on top of one another and dismantling thousands of souls in the process. The white orbs floated away from the battlefield, into the rainy clouds and out of sight.

He only wished he had the power to apply that devastation to the whole battlefield, for which he did not have the strength. He had to find a moment to rest and relaxed his protecy temporarily to recover.

The concern became more dramatic in the sense that despite destroying a portion of the enemy, it was only a slither compared to how many remained, who once again gave no reprieve in attempting the same process once more.

It did give the dwarves time to recover, but they noticed that the walls they sat atop had begun to fracture. They learned that their King's magic was risky and that it was one of the downsides. To make matters worse, The Manced showed surprising nouse in battle and rather than stacking among one another like before, they positioned themselves so that it gave them a little space before the frontline and the walls. The dwarves wondered what on Rèo they were doing.

Suddenly a wave of manced manically ran headfirst into the walls. Their craniums instantly cracked against the thick rock before unnaturally picking themselves up and retreating back into the ranks before the next wave repeated the same bludgeoning process again and again. It became gravely apparent what was happening.

"Gracelands save us!" a dwarf uttered on one of the turrets as he could see the fractures in the walls begin to slowly crack further amid the suicidal launches.

Thakendrax was well aware of what was happening and instructed his armies to retreat back and move to plan B. There was nothing he could do with his remaining strength to stop the walls from eventually crumbling.

"Protect our aerial defences at all costs!" he commanded to his dwarven generals.

The forecourts and walls scaled back with impressive speed and military efficiency to temporarily make Dwardelfia seem deserted. Vials were still being tossed from the city's great heights to slow them down as much as possible.

However, it only took several hours for the cracks to take significant damage until at last, the whole wall completely collapsed from one end of the city to the other in a total demolition of their defence.

Dwardelfia was now totally exposed and The Manced wasted no time infiltrating the city, spreading its filth and evil like a disease at will. However, among the depths of The Hewercraxen, Thakendrax had rallied his troops.

The Manced made their way to attempt to kill the ones responsible for their aerial defences before they heard the heavy clopping of hooves vibrating into the ground.

Thakendrax rode out first, followed by several thousand other dwarves riding their cantankerous Rhinoauros's in an epic charge toward the infestation that spread into the city.

The horned cavalry pierced with ease through the unorganised and undefended manced, trampling them to their instant destruction.

They'd suppressed the present advance, but at a cost. They battled among the forecourts with vigour and typical stubbornness, knowing they were outnumbered still ten-to-one.

The crunch of frozen grass began to thaw on the slope leading to Lathapràcère. The effect of the icy temperatures became less apparent the more they climbed. Mijkal watched from his high tower to see the specks of light bleed brighter through the blizzard he had conjured. It was not enough to stop them and prepared the Questacèreans for their tactical moves.

Some of the Màgjeurs who specialised in water began to conjure vast flumes, which gushed onto the slopes and slid down the hill. Twinned with the icy temperatures, the waters instantly froze, trapping the manced on their ascent. Those who trampled over the trapped militants had to ascend on ice, often sliding down into the ascending host.

However, The Manced managed to find a way to progress steadily, launching themselves from sturdier ground to smash their fists into thinner pockets of ice. It gave them holds to grab into and continue their attack.

Mijkal was undoubtedly thankful that a Dragadelf was not present but kept his wits about him just in case the rumours it would not come were false. It could melt the ice with one breath and leave them dangerously exposed. Alas, it was time for the Questacèrean King to deploy proactivity rather than reactivity.

He ordered his Questacèrean chiefs to instruct the first line of physical defence. A wave of some several hundred toboggans made their way to the edge of the level part of the city, ready for their dives.

## A Matter of Time

The carts were typically made of streamlined wood and shaped aerodynamically to increase speed. The nose was as sharp as a needle, the sides forked out with blades that would instantly slice through flesh, and each craft held a brave pilot that would lie on their backs, steering it to maximise devastation.

There was little time to waste and Mijkal ordered the first wave to go. Like a slide, the toboggans shot down the steep hill with hair-rippling velocity, slicing into The Manced ranks like a hot knife through butter and they did not stop until they reached the bottom.

For the brave pilots that kamikazed through the thick fog of uncertainty, the attack when on forever. The hope was that when they reached the bottom, the army would all be upon the slope, which lasted for several miles. However, as the ground started to level off, the militants did not seem to become less concentrated. They had not anticipated that thirty-five thousand corpses could have filled the entirety of the slope above. However, they quickly worked out that their calculations were well off.

The plummeting Questacèreans became fearful for their lives as the toboggans had nearly come to a halt. They drew their mortal weapons, stabbing and slicing any militants that attempted to jump inside the carriage. However, it seemed luck was not on their side, as when their crafts stopped at the bottom, none would survive the swarming horror they had not anticipated.

Mijkal had to make a judgement call at that moment. Should he wait and allow the evil to fester among him, or should he play out another advantage to his disposal? He weighed up the options and mustered his Questacèrean generals to arm their lancing bands.

Some two-thousand speared lancers sat atop of their mildens and prepared to charge down into the filth. The idea was that there was still enough room for them to do so with enough speed to pierce the lines effectively. Mijkal held back many Questacèrean Màgjeurs in what would appear to be the last line of defence.

The Blessèd Mage of Ice could only watch his gallant galloping Knights race out of Lathapràcère and into the abyss of the clouds below. It took some time for every one of his lancers to empty from his city, but as he saw the last of them disappear out of sight, they noticed that they could not see a single ball of light in the mist, suggesting they had wiped out a significant number of the frontlines. A stillness was then born once more, for many hours.

They used that time, filled with harrowing anxiety, to muster what defence they had left, as they did not know if the band of lancers was successful or not. However, it did give them the additional time they needed.

A scout from one of the watchtowers noticed a ball of light appear through the thick cloud below…

One soon became hundreds, which soon became thousands ascending back to the capital in the same squirming fashion. The alarm was raised and Mijkal had to muster every bit of strength and defensive capabilities at his disposal to fend off the invasion.

The Manced had finally reached the top.

Although they defended with magical attacks of all kinds of affinities, their trampling advance was much quicker due to more corpses that littered the ground.

The civilians of Questacère volunteered themselves into action as a last line of defence. Anyone who had the skill to use The Protecy or any form of protection was called to the frontlines.

Portions of Durge Helm were aflame from the Dragadelf's fires. The smog from the burning city clouded out any sunlight that tried to seep through. Soldiers coughed and spluttered out the toxicity that congealed in their lungs, some falling to their knees; it was that bad. Stung, watery eyes streamed, trying to hold their positions and keep a lookout for the winged beast.

Luckily, the city's high walls and turrets were not so badly damaged and could maintain some of its defences, orchestrated by Alexa Greyman.

Operations to douse the fires with buckets of water were underway to reduce the smoke that poisoned the city.

Even though the scaled armour could not be pierced by the marksmen's arrows, the Dragadelf's huge sails were vulnerable to attack and could easily be ripped to shreds through a cloud of well aimed arrow shafts. Alas, upon many such attacks, the beast spun with impressive agility like an ugly spider descending from its web to evade the plethoric arrows that hurtled toward it. It would successfully unleash its dragonbreath to terrible effect before dipping back out to the safety of the skies.

Greyman was reluctant to spare any of her archers but ordered some who were already on the lower levels to make their way to the outer wall to aid the ground forces that would repel the assault that was moments away. The bottlenecked militants began to filter through en masse.

Because of Meigar's earth magic, all it took was for the arrow tips to make contact with the manced soul for them to be dismantled, making it easier for them to be felled. She ordered waves of the feathered knives to soar into the lines to good effect. They had enough arrows to last them for days, but the real concern was just how much manpower was available to use them.

The Dragadelf stayed tactical and showed surprising levels of intelligence by circling Aries Hollow. It unleashed its dragonbreath on what appeared to be plain rock and stone behind them. It was some distance away from any archers range. No one thought that that area needed to be covered as the civilians were deep beneath the ground.

Then it dawned on Lestas Magraw what it was doing. It hastened his attention.

"Durgeon!" Magraw alerted. "We have a problem."

"Master of the Mind, we have many problems," Luan replied.

"If we don't stop the beast, it'll bring the whole hollow down onto us! We'll be buried under millions of tonnes of rock!"

Luan turned to see what the Dragadelf was doing in the mountain that overshadowed the capital. A small avalanche of stone began to crumble down onto the city. Its attention was now the immediate focus.

"What do you suggest?" Luan asked.

"Are there any depressions within the mountain? An area where we can trap it?"

"Yes!" Farooq Manwa informed. "There's one just south of where it is now! A deep one at that."

"Good! I'll try to lure the beast as best as I can to it," Magraw suggested. "How quickly can you assemble the explosives, Farooq?"

"With a few good men, not longer than an hour. How will we know when to detonate?"

"You make that call when we're deep enough. All my efforts will be concentrated on restraining it."

Farooq hurried away with several soldiers, understanding the task at hand before quickly turning back around.

"Forgive me, Master of the Mind, but how will you get away in time?"

Magraw did not respond and Farooq seemingly waited for an answer which did not come.

"We're wasting time," Magraw pointed out.

Farooq looked upon his Durgeon for confirmation to go ahead.

"Do it," Luan ordered.

The band leader bowed his head and reluctantly gathered his men to construct the demolition. Magraw's suggestion of heroic sacrifice did not seem to impress Luan.

"I hope you know what you're doing," Luan warned. "Our experience of trapping Dragadelf has not gone all too well in the past."

"So I've heard."

"How sure can you be that this will work?" Luan asked, a little unconvinced.

"I don't," Magraw admitted before marching off to the sliver of mountain behind.

Placed in the heart of the city, Meigar, whose tense hands were by his waist with fingers curled, calling on the Blessèd powers that divined within, spotted Magraw heading off. They shared a very disapproving look toward one another as if to say that The Blessèd Mage of Mind had lost his mind to confront such lethal mythology by himself. Alas, there was nothing Max could do but look on in despair, a little gutted that he was going alone.

Meanwhile, The Manced were flocking forward a lot faster now. Meryx Meigar and his band of Knights prepared to ride their mildens out to meet them head-on. They wanted to time their advance correctly while they still had some long-ranged support from the city.

"STAND WITH HONOUR!" Meryx bellowed, which was met by the symbolic declaration of his band of Knights behind.

The Manced advanced on the plains before them and Meryx issued the charge, hurtling their galloping mildens clean through the ranks, dissembling their constitutions, hazing the battlefields with a white haze from their escaping souls as they battled fiercely against the odds.

Meanwhile, Magraw took to the mountain entirely into the realm of the unknown. He did not know if he had the divine skill to make his plan work, but he stuck to his vows as a Blessèd Mage to try and to protect this world using every means available.

He found the area where the Dragadelf was raining its dragonbreath, turning the fissured ground into molten lava. He didn't anticipate how quickly the beast was accomplishing its task as much of the area was melting away. As he hid behind a corner, he could see where the flatter part descended into a much more enclosed area where Farooq's men were waiting.

He tried to time his approach to catch the beast woefully off guard,

## A Matter of Time

closing his eyes to channel his powers to maximum effect. The Dragadelf's back was turned, showing it's squirming tail wriggling as it's fires erupted. That was perhaps his best chance, and he slowly emerged to expose his position.

He held out his right hand while placing the fingertips of his left hand on his temple to connect more precisely. In a sudden moment, the beast's volatile movements began to simmer down, apparently feeling the essence of calm infiltrate its body. The flames ceased and slowly, it seemed to almost fall asleep in its crouching position. It's snores deeply rumbled, crackling on exhalation.

Magraw's powers to manipulate its mind had worked. However, the real test of his skill came when he knew that sending it to sleep was not the plan. He had to gently ease off the hypnotherapy to lure it into a more obedient state. The depression was less than a hundred metres away but still positioned himself behind the beast.

Magraw maintained a strong connection and slowly weaned off the sedation. It gradually took effect as it began to mobilise a little more fluently. It was then when The Blessèd Mage of the Mind started to instruct it to slowly and carefully crawl forward. It obliged.

The muscular legs and arms attached to the wings squirmed forward under Magraw's instruction. The power he felt controlling something as mythical and destructive as a Dragadelf got to him. He could not help but indulge in a wry, gloating smile at the elation of taming such a creature, but had to keep the same distance to sustain that control. He walked forward, still at all times remaining behind the beast. Perhaps he would survive this after all, he thought to himself.

They were metres away from the decline when the Dragadelf unexpectedly stopped before the drop. Not what Magraw had instructed - his brows creased together and sweat beaded on his temples as he pushed his Protecy to the limit. The Dragadelf remained motionless. It's back turned. Magraw realised all too late why it had halted.

The Dragadelf snaked its marvellous head round to view Lestas Magraw, alone, scared and truly vulnerable. Its unrelenting snare pierced into his soul. Its expression was that of pure triumph and hunger.

Magraw understood at that moment, he had massively underestimated the intelligence of a Dragadelf; a terrible miscalculation. At no point was it ever under his control and it appeared that the beast only feigned obedience to lure him out into the open. The Blessèd Mage of the Mind had been outwitted.

The Dragadelf was now facing him directly, rearing up with wings spread at full span. It roared triumphantly into the sky as Magraw braced for the end. And a great triumph it was, for Magraw had no more tricks up his sleeves and surrendered completely to its wrath.

Rather than offloading its fiery attack, hunger got the better of it and decided to try and eat him whole. A succulent, juicy meal to satisfy the bloodlust - it was the ultimate predator after all and let instinct take over. Its jaw unhinged to a reveal rows of razor sharp teeth, a sharp tongue rolling in between. It drooled its acidic saliva, eroding the ground as it splashed.

Suddenly, a war cry echoed from a nearby elevation on the mountainside, signalling aid. A morphed form of stone in the shape of Max Meigar jumped from a height and slammed his fist of hard rock into the beasts' skull.

It cruddered and bamboozled the Dragadelf momentarily, causing it to become angrier. While its discombobulation temporarily disabled it, Meigar ordered Magraw to run for cover to which he did, but only to a place he could helplessly watch on. By coming to his aid, Meigar's earth magic upon the weaponry on Durge Helm had temporality ceased. Alas, he was about to embark on his gravest challenge yet.

The beast wormed around, angrily thrashing and ripping up boulders to intimidate The Blessèd Mage of Earth before confronting him head-on. He took the opportunity to slam his fist into the ground, quaking and breaking the stoney earth which cracked rapidly into the beast's direction. A fragment of stone propelled itself from the ground and crashed into its carriage. It proved successful as it retreated slightly, and Magraw sensed a weakness in the beast's defence and once more exposed himself to try and control its mind.

"NO!" Meigar furiously exclaimed.

The Dragadelf took that momentary lapse to fuel its belly and unleash a continuous flame from its mouth onto Magraw. Meigar heroically outspread his arms to increase the area shielding his frailer counterpart behind him, who was also now trapped by the excess of flames that scorched past.

The Blessèd Mage of Earth yelled in barbaric pain as the flames burned so hot, it melted away portions of his embodiment of stone and into the vulnerable skin underneath. He fell to his knees still trying to protect Magraw behind, but he was moments away from being unable to sustain the defence any longer as their fates loomed.

Luckily for them, an arrow whistled from below and struck the beast directly into a gum, which caused enough pain for it to stop its dragonbreath. Alexa Greyman and several other archers began to formulate quickly in strategical positions among the rocks, to let fly their arrows onto the Dragadelf's head, hoping to strike an eye or two.

It painfully roared and was smart enough to concede temporary defeat as arrows bounced off its armoured scales and ruptured portions of its wings. It had no choice but to scramble away and fly to safety.

Smoke hazed from The Blessèd Mage of Earth who remained rooted on his knees, breathing heavily. His strength had wained giving everything he had to protect Magraw. He quickly came to inspect the devastation that Max had experienced and was traumatised to see that his body was half stone, half flesh, which was now burnt and blistered seemingly beyond healing. Max stared openly into the distance, utterly spent at his efforts.

"Max!" Magraw quickly consoled. He was afraid to touch him, fearful that it would make the pain worse. "Talk to me... Max?... Max?"

And just like that, he realised that even though Max remained stupefied in his kneeling position, his eyes along with his body had frozen open and he had stopped breathing.

His final pose was that of half-man and half essences of the divine affinity he was heralded for. Lestas embraced that notion as a symbolic way to end a life that had been so crucial to Terrasendia's fight.

Magraw's eyes squeezed shut as his emotions threatened to overwhelm him, unable to detain the single tear that escaped from them. Despite the differences they had on occasions, it by no means outweighed the value they placed on each other, which was demonstrated in Max's final moments of astounding bravery.

"Master of the Mind! We cannot stay here!" Alexa urged. "We must return to high ground!"

She understood what had happened but managed to stay focussed on survival, burying her shock and grief and channelling it into her efforts to stay alive. She remained regimented, willing Magraw to follow, which he reluctantly did, leaving his kneeling friend behind but knowing he had his blessings to send his soul to The Gracelands in peace.

His plan had failed and to make matters worse, Max's ritual to the weaponry on Durge Helm was no longer in effect. In addition to that, several of Greyman's archers had to be pulled away from the aerial defence to which the Dragadelf took complete advantage, unleashing more dragonbreath onto the Septalian capital.

Meryx Meigar, who was unaware of his brother's death, pulled his band back from outside the walls to gain what little protection it could offer. However, the assault had managed to breach the perimeter and the fortress would soon be overrun with ferocious corpses. Though they continued to fend them off in the forecourts, halting their advances in smaller and confined spaces. They wondered why their weapons were not as effective, often slicing through limbs to which The Manced carried on their suicidal thrusts and not being dismantled.

At that moment, Meryx understood his brother's fate and that weakening sense of hope and belief ripped through every man and woman fighting on the frontline. That waining strength echoed into every portion of Terrasendia that fought for everything good and green.

## The Garden of Ramacès

Ramerick, Zathos and the small band from The Reinhault, including Relian, secretly made their way through The Farrowdawns. Led by Hiyaro, they rode their mildens through a quiet passage in the rocky terrain, occasionally venturing through underground chasms and less hostile pockets of the region.

"Getting to The Draughts is relatively straight forward in terms of how quickly we could arrive," informed Hiyaro. "We know these paths well."

Despite their stealth, nothing was concrete in terms of their safety. At any moment, the hostility of The Farrowdawns could erupt and they could be encountered by bands of Rawblers or other hostiles, putting the whole quest in jeopardy. Luckily their presence remained unidentified.

In a situation with so many moving parts, Ramerick kept reminding himself that it all came down to one thing - taking his brother's sword and using it to destroy The Dragastone. It filled him with a heavier burden, knowing everyone's life on Terrasendia came down to the defining moments ahead. The land was dying and they were running out of time.

He often wondered what Ramacès looked like before remembering that he had once seen him in a premonition. They were both at Monarchy Hall, looking at one another before being incinerated by the flame. He understood that moment to have been more symbolic than he first thought, working out that it was at the hand of Ramalon that his brother perished. A fate he only wished would not also meet.

Though he pondered what precisely Ramacès' role was in stopping Ramalon. Was it just to provide a means to destroy The Dragastone, or was there a more fulfilling purpose?

"You knew my brother?" he asked of Hiyaro.

"I did," he replied with a hint of reverence. "I fought alongside him when he gave his life."

"How did you meet?"

"… We detained him."

"What did he do wrong?"

"Nothing," he replied, a little assertive.

"So why was he detained?"

"Our laws are our laws. We have conscripted men, women and even children given the circumstance to train them. The minimum term is two years, though we released your brother long before that."

"Why?"

"Because he was one of a kind," Hiyaro praised, staring off into the distance.

"A phenomenal man," Zathos praised. "Just like your father. Fierce. And mighty!"

"You were with him too? At the end?"

Zathos nodded. "I was tasked with stopping Ramalon from getting to him that day. Max asked for our help but kept our arrival secret."

Ramerick was reluctant to ask anything that would trigger an emotional response regarding Wemberlè's involvement that day and left it at that. He knew Zathos on the outside appeared strong, but being a master of disguises himself he knew that his insides were eating away at the thought of never seeing her again. They did not

## The Garden of Ramacès

know his wife's fate, though were they to see Ramalon from now on in, it would all but confirm her death and indeed Aristuto's, for Ramerick would be last.

"We have defended this world in more ways than in the books you have read," Hiyaro reminisced. "But this? This is our defining moment. And we are with you, son of Felder! Every step of the way…"

They'd journeyed for several days through The Farrowdawns, completely uninterrupted - much to their relief.

Hiyaro informed them all the news that came as a little more favourable to Ramerick, in that they had passed Drethai Halls and were heading away from there. Such relief for him that they had passed seemingly unnoticed, as that place haunted him with unwanted memories. Most specifically of Orbow, landing both her marks on Joric and Jàque. He tried to close his eyes to break off his nightmarish thoughts, alas it only made them worse.

He distracted himself by bringing him back to his task at hand. He knew how dangerous these parts of the world were and couldn't help but believe how calm the journey had been.

"Are The Farrowdawns usually this quiet?"

"No. They are not," Hiyaro informed. "It is irregular."

"Anything to be concerned about?"

"Not with two Blessèd Mages behind me," he smirked.

"One of which has vowed never to use The Protecy again."

"That still leaves -" Hiyaro interrupted himself, bringing the band to a halt.

Ahead of them, surrounded by rocky terrain, was a path laid full of greenery, reminiscent of a forest deep in The Farrowdawns.

"Talking of leaves," Zathos joked.

"Good Gracelands," Relian gasped. He appeared stunned by how beautiful the terrain had become. It was evident that this was completely unexpected.

"Is this a problem?" Ramerick asked.

"Oh, no. It is far from a problem," Hiyaro informed.

"What is it?"

"The Garden of Ramacès," Zathos proudly proclaimed.

"A garden?" Ramerick queried. "How is it named after my brother?"

"Because he is the one that created it."

"It was the most beautiful moment any of us had ever seen," Hiyaro praised. "When he died, his blood fell onto the land that consumed him. His blood birthed this amazing event. A symbol that his soul was good and green and how we should be forever grateful at knowing such a man."

"Could that be why our journey thus far has remained unscathed?" Relian inquired.

"Without a shadow of a doubt. Life has been rebalanced, forcing the evil that once resided here to be banished."

"So we're close?" Ramerick asked.

Hiyaro turned his head back toward him. "We are here."

They made their way through the beautiful trees and untouched grass that carpeted their arrival. At various points, they had to hack through the overgrown jungle with machetes and swords to get through. Though it was not a typical jungle with ugly vines and contaminated soil, it was as if a groundsman had been looking after it, curing it with care and keeping its beauty in order. Though they were all on edge, they could not help but give in to temptation and enjoy the wonder they walked through.

It wasn't too long before they reached the main entrance to The Draughts. It was clear the vast hole of the entrance led down into what was once the most feared place on Terrasendia. The garden's beauty had transformed even that. Flowers flourished, plants entwined, and everything was slow and tranquil - a complete juxtaposition to the ugly terrain that had consumed their journey thus far.

They dismounted their mildens upon Hiyaro's instruction and left them at the entrance. They would make their way down on foot, though Zathos was the only one who guided his Windermare down with them.

"He's been here before," Zathos told him, relating to his winged milden. "The ghost remains, but he does not fear what once was."

They descended the long tunnel, having no time to waste and climbed down the barks and fine grass. Upon their clamber down, Ramerick placed his foot on the ground to a sudden crunch. He stopped and looked down to inspect what he'd trodden on and immediately raised his head before closing his eyes.

He was shocked to realised that his foot had landed through the ribcage of a corpse. Upon giving it his entire weight, it made the chest cavity of that host concave, snapping the connecting ribs like branches from a tree. So grotesque was the sound, that he imagined the same sickening pain in his own chest.

Not that he was directly looking at the ground on their descent, but the charcoaled body consumed by the grass and soil that grew from underneath it, weaving its green blades up and through the burnt limbs. It was as if the land reclaimed the body that had been unjustly taken from it, accepting them back into the foundations of the world again.

He was cautious not to tread on another corpse out of respect. However, it grew more challenging when they reached the bottom as there were many more to avoid. They were all identically mutilated with gaping holes in their chests where the artificial soul once resided.

When they arrived beneath the roof of the entrance, they viewed The Draughts in its entirety. They were no longer looking down but in every direction ahead at the sheer wonder that had been transformed. The whole of the chasm, spanning as far wide and so high they could hardly make out the ceiling, had turned into an exponential growth of forestry.

It birthed larger than life fine timbers and barks that uprooted from the ground. Attached to their seismic branches grew enormous flowers that continued to blossom. Bushes and thickets multiplied beautifully, and life was rife. Birds chirped in their nests; butterflies fluttered amongst the crickets. It was like its own eco-system that was sustained by one form of energy at the heart of this glorious garden.

A singular light some distance away, suspended half a mile above, was the source and foundation for all life that resided in the enclosure. It shone like a star in the sky; only this star illuminated brighter than the blue of the moon. The glare beamed vertically into the ground and lit up much of the enclosure.

They advanced deeper into The Garden of Ramacès, noticing just how much life blossomed over such a short amount of time. It was also sad to know this was also a mass graveyard. Ramerick scanned for any signs of his brother's sword, but Hiyaro brought the band to a halt, not too far away from the beaming light.

"Is it here?" he whispered. "My brother's sword?"

"Up there," Zathos advised to look more closely at the source of light.

Upon inspection, Ramerick's pupils narrowed and were able to see the form around the light a little clearer. As it was some half a mile above, he still could not work out precisely what it was.

"What is it?" he queried.

"Your brother's sword!" Zathos informed.

His jaw came ajar, realising what he was looking at. The answer to

Terrasendia's safety, in direct eyesight, and how close he was. He could just about make out the stoney figure of his brother suspended in mid-air. The Meigarthian sword's silhouette now came into fruition the longer he stared and understood that's where the source of light originated from. He was not told the precise details of how he died, only obituaries of how heroic his sacrifice was. Though, the sword's location did cause a logistical problem.

"How do we get up there?" he asked, still looking at his brother above.

When he turned his head back, he saw Zathos with a smile on his face, patting the muscular neck of his white Windermare to suggest that is precisely how he was going to get up there.

Ramerick wasted no time and eagerly mounted Zathos' Windermare. The marvellous sensation cushioned his buttocks as he nestled comfortably astride its bare back. He was not afraid of falling off, remembering the stories he had once told his son about the beautiful creatures and how it was impossible to do so unless done deliberately.

He looked back up toward the sword and realised to get up there; he would need some space to ascend on the right path. He would have to circle round his destination several times before correctly aligning.

The runway was clear and he kicked the sides of his feet into the milden's sides and sped into a gallop. The speed was phenomenal; his hair rippled, the moisture squeezed from his eyes before its wings spread, dipped and launched them into the air.

He circled The Draughts a few times, taking in the inherent beauty created by his brother, flying high with the birds in the ultimate form of freedom.

He was so close to grabbing the sword and ending this nightmare, but it did not feel like an end. His suspicions of this all being too easy could not be ignored. Alas, the milden aligned itself from afar; the path was clear to grab that sword and save Terrasendia.

He got so close to his brother's statue that he could make out the extraordinary detail of his wonderful armour just moments before he outstretched his hand.

His suspicions rang true as a sudden force of black cloud rapidly thumped into his chest, gassed straight through him and out through to the other side. It knocked him clean off his Windermare and into a free-fall to the ground.

As The Blessèd Mage of Life, his preservative powers would likely

## The Garden of Ramacès

grant him immunity to death, but the experience of splattering to the ground was not something that he wanted.

Luckily for him, the Windermare regathered its strength very quickly and dived down alongside him. Just seconds away from the ground, he grabbed on to its white mane as tightly as he could and straddled his leg over its back. The winged milden curved the fall, cushioning his weight to squeeze into his back safely, scraping his hooves through the grass, unearthing chunks of soil and leaving long skid-marks before ascending once more.

He circled The Draughts, briefly wondering what on Rèo that was, before correctly working it out. He realised going for the sword again wouldn't be possible just yet as he came around and saw the perpetrators. Thirteen black ghosts morphed into a physical form that positioned themselves in front of the band below.

The Ancient Drethai had finally made an appearance.

Ramerick's anger got the better of him. His teeth gritted, exposing his spite for the ones who caused Jàqueson's death and couldn't shy away from revenge. He brought his milden to land and positioned himself in front of Hiyaro's band. He forcefully unsheathed Sythero. It's pyrovines burned hot in the presence of evil. He heroically confronted them, leading from the front. He did not fear the shadow spirits.

The Drethai, spearheaded by Dreanor, formulated in a V-shape position behind him. All were bearing their full constitutions, each diversifying in their crafts. Some leant more toward darker magics, others were built more gregariously for physical combat, while others more toned and slender for speed and precision. Dreanor, however, remained balanced and almost had a little bit of everything. His ten-foot-tall stature helped his tool of intimidation. The Shadow King wickedly sneered, laughing deeply with his lips closed.

"Ramerick," he announced in his deep voice, elongating his name as slowly as possible. "We've missed you."

Ramerick had no time to play games. He did not hide his anger at them.

"I am so glad you're here!" he whispered so intensely, the collected saliva spat from his lips.

"Now, now," Dreanor soothed, "your veiled vulnerability will get the better of you. Just like before."

Ramerick's eyes strained full of intent, the look of a man who was willing to go to dark places to ascertain revenge. And what made matters worse was seeing the youthful dark complexion of Orbow among the ranks. She could not help but hide her playful smile.

"Remember me?" she toyed happily. "How's Jàquey?"

The simple mention of his name by her lips irked him, filling him with poisonous rage that he found impossible to contain. He merely stared upon the shadow spirits.

"Ramerick?" Zathos reasoned, "do not let yourself be antagonised. It is not why we are here."

"In good company, I see," Dreanor praised.

Zathos stood in front of Ramerick to seize command. "Leave this place. Now. Or we will have no choice but to expel you by force," he threatened.

"Oh, please, Master of Sparks! You know us better than that. Our deity wants him alive," Dreanor insisted to Ramerick. "And you will come with us -"

"- I have a message for my brother," he harshly interrupted. "If he wants me, he can come and claim me *himself*!"

Dreanor laughed in the same manner again. "Oh Master of Life, how you've grown from when we saw you last. You must have gone to the bottom of your heart to achieve such divinity. A place we know all too well."

Dreanor was astute enough to realise that to become The Blessèd Mage of Life, he would have had to have taken it from Eveleve, which they understood was his mother. They took great pride in prising every notion of torment to him, bending his mind, convincing and manipulating him that he was deep down, inherently evil just like them.

"This is your last chance," Ramerick warned, "deliver that message, or I will destroy *this*…"

He revealed The Dragastone from his tunic and boasted it in front of their faces. It's glimmer radiated, and The Drethai felt its power. They struggled to contain their awe and mesmerisation for such an artefact. Dreanor took him a little more seriously then.

"You cannot fool us. We know you can't destroy it."

"… Is that so?" Ramerick challenged.

For the first time, he sensed a truth behind Dreanor's masked eyes. A hint of fear.

"Give it to us. And we'll let you live…"

Ramerick arrogantly kept his eyes on him and ruffled The Dragastone back into his tunic.

# The Garden of Ramacès

"I wish you luck when my brother finds out that you've failed him again," he forewarned with menace.

Dreanor didn't even conclude with a final declaration. Instead just turned his face into something more malicious and threatening, bearing a murky evil shadow, mirrored by the rest of the order, like poltergeists preparing their haunting. They were ready to take them by force.

Zathos prepared his protecy of volts, Hiyaro and his band members prepared their weapons of war-hammers, swords, spears and bows.

Though Zathos was a marvel and supposedly the most powerful Màgjeur in The Draughts, it was unclear how much stronger The Drethai had become after their reincarnation. They seemed more powerful and whole than their encounter with Ethelba that day. Of course, on that occasion, they waited for the deliberate reason of distracting them from Orbow's arrow. They no longer had reason to wait, and the shackles of what they were capable of were now unchained. The balance of strength was far from clear.

"Well, isn't this an interesting gathering..." came a familiar voice to all in The Draughts. The Ancient Drethai turned on their spots to confront the man they knew all too well, arriving from the entrance. "I hope I'm not interrupting?" Susmees rhetorically asked, accompanied by twenty or so Wandlers, armed with wands and staffs to conjure their magic. Such an old-fashioned platform seldom existed but this was Susmees' band that he had known all his life. They had come to defend what was good and green.

Ramerick could not help but feel alleviated to see him arrive when they most needed them. By bringing his wizard friends with him, dressed in typical dangling robes, The Drethai felt the heat.

"The wizard and his wand!" Orbow taunted.

"The betrayer!" Dreanor spat.

"Hello, friends," the once Questacèrean prince ironically greeted. "Though I must say, you're looking well."

"Coward!" Dreathitus spat.

They all had just as much reason to hate him as he was once of them and defied their greed to Melcelore's trap.

"KILL HIM!" Dreanor impulsively ordered several members of The Drethai.

They engaged with Susmees and his band of Wandlers, who cast intricate magics from their wands and more powerful forces from their staffs. Susmees himself confidently flicked his wrist to initiate elaborate magic from his wand, both to defend and attack.

"I'll deal with him," Dreanor retorted toward Ramerick.

However, he was now behind Zathos, whose eyes had turned to electrifying volts that sparkled his eyes. He unleashed his divinity directly onto Dreanor, who repelled it with equally impressive nouse, creating a cloud of volts to squib down the attack. He counter-attacked by sending zapping currents back to The Blessèd Mage, who deflected with chains of lightning. Hiyaro's men flanked from the lighting storm to engage on some of the more robust members of The Drethai.

The destructive fray consumed The Draughts. Magical brawls between some of the dark Màgjeurs and Wandlers clashed, with several fatalities for Susmees' band and none for the shadow spirits. Hiyaro's men worked well together, using teamwork as much as possible, but the ten Knights of The Reinhault couldn't seem to land any of their standard blows. The Drethai were too strong and cunning.

"RAMERICK!" Zathos yelled, "YOU MUST GO! ARRRGGHH!" he wailed, struggling in his duel against a reinvigorated Dreanor.

Judging by the amount of power the Shadow King demonstrated, it was clear they all had become more dangerous than before. Whether that was a natural strengthening or whether Dreanor had downplayed his strength against Ethelba was unclear, but it was certain that they were in trouble.

Ramerick hurriedly turned his Windermare and galloped away from the melee, hoping not to be pursued. He needed to get to that sword by any means necessary. If they would fall at the hands of The Drethai, then their duty was at least to destroy The Dragastone and save Terrasendia.

Luckily for him, his gallop toward take-off was clear, as The Drethai were all engaged within their encounters... All but one.

The Windermare gusted its wings and ascended into the air once more. They'd barely made it thirty metres into the air when Orbow, who stood frighteningly still and quiet at the heart of the battlefield, imposed her mark. Her eyes closed, her head bowed as she conjured her black and dark green bow along with her cruel arrow that she elegantly pulled back on the bowstring. Zathos noticed all too late.

"STOP HER!" he bellowed to anyone available to heed the command.

The only one close enough to do something about was Relian, who luckily overcame his duel with Malumpire - the sword swishing Drethai, reminiscent of a ninja. He swiped his blade through his

# The Garden of Ramacès

opponent's midriff, turning it into gas at the fatal blow as his opponent dissolved away into nothing. He became free to advance on Orbow, which he did from behind, spinning and twisting through the melee to get to her in time.

She took aim at the Windermare flying high, not looking at her target but instead using her dark-senses to feel where it was. Relian was clear to engage, lifting his sword he lunged, sending his steel hurtling down towards her back, but as his body left the ground, Orbow quickly turned and released the feathered knife into Relian's neck.

His body cruelly crumpled to the ground before her. The arrow jarred in the carotid artery below his head, blood squelched and shot from his neck. He froze very quickly upon his landing, for he was dead.

"RELIAN!!!" screamed Hiyaro, fighting with more vigour and determination to avenge his companion. Alas, Orbow felt no remorse and very quickly returned to her initial target.

At that point, no one else could get to her and looked to hope that her legend would outlast her. Her head bowed, her eyes closed once more, and she released the dark green arrow high into the air once more, whistling as it soared. There was not a thing anyone could do to stop it from landing directly into Ramerick's Windermare.

It pierced the muscular neck with ease. The high pitched neigh confirmed the blow was fatal. Alas, it died just moments later in mid-flight. Its death was symbolic of how it lived its life, taking to the skies in the ultimate form of freedom. Its final call of duty was to at the very least protect its rider for as long as it possibly could and tried to flatten out the sharp descent. However, it's magnificent body gave up, dived and crash-landed into a patch of moss and grass, cushioning the landing somewhat.

They still landed with a heavy thud, flinging Ramerick from its back to a continuous roll that would have killed him were it not for his powers of life preservation. It rendered him paralysed temporarily, his muscles suspended while he tried to recuperate, the air forced out of him, he was in a large amount of pain.

Zathos wailed in grief as he watched his milden dramatically fall. He used it to spur his anger further onto Dreanor but suddenly was forced out of the duel by Dreathitus, who attempted to cleave his skull in with his huge battle-axe. He evaded the blow and immediately defended another chain of volts from another member of The Ancient

Drethai, pinning him down and allowing Dreanor a clear path to Ramerick.

Together, the ancient order formulated themselves, creating a barrier between the advancing Dreanor and what was left of Susmees' Wandlers and Hiyaro's Knights. Zathos too, tried his best to break the lines, but The Drethai collectively worked together to stop them from coming to Ramerick's aid.

As he came around, he gasped for air that had been expelled from his lungs. Sythero luckily landed close by and he squirmed to pick up his legendary sword. He was tremendously wounded but managed to reclaim it in time.

He was mortified to learn that The Dragastone was no longer in his possession. He rummaged through his tunic and realised it must have slipped out as he rolled moments earlier.

He began to retrace his landing, hoping to spot its gleam quickly, but in his dazed, distracted state, he was unaware of Dreanor advancing toward him. He quickly found the stone nestled in a patch of grass and hurried towards it.

Out of nowhere, the ten-foot Shadow King lunged down in front of him, swiping his thick, sharp sword toward him. He defended with an upward guard which Sythero hissed as the mortal weapons clashed. They briefly duelled, with Ramerick finding unnatural strength to fight and pulling off some signature evasive moves, but he was no match for Dreanor.

He overexposed himself, and the Shadow King landed a tremendous backhand into Ramerick's face, splattering blood from his mouth and sending him to the ground. Dreanor triumphantly stared at his prey, knowing he had the upper hand before turning his attention to The Dragastone.

Hope began to fade. If Dreanor took the stone and escaped with it, Terrasendia would not survive the little time it had left. He had to find something and even though his strength wained, he managed to conjure from the deepest darkest corners some dwindling stamina. He hurled himself back up and fought with his heart once more, lunging at Dreanor's back. However, he was too cunning and had already prepared his next move. He rapidly swiped his sword across Sythero, sending it spinning away leaving Ramerick exposed.

Dreanor did not hesitate to take full advantage.

He punched his evil steel directly through Ramerick's belly and out of his back. His eyes widened in shock at the unbelievable amount of pain he felt. His diaphragm was paralysed; he could not breathe, completely stupefied that Dreanor had landed the fatal blow. Cries of grief were heard as the scene could be seen through The Drethai's defences.

With the blade still inserted through his gut, Ramerick gently fell to his knees. Dreanor lightly laughed and leaned in closer to Ramerick, bringing their eyes level. He conjured a triumphant sneer.

"Survive that," he whispered.

Ramerick's body had had enough. He wondered what would happen now, being The Blessèd Mage of Life. Surely he couldn't die, he thought? Alas, nothing happened apart from experiencing the poisonous toxin of death taking hold of him.

Dreanor slowly eased the steel from his chest, enjoying and indulging in every second of its withdrawal, before allowing Ramerick to ungracefully flump to the ground. The triumphant Shadow King rose and marched toward The Dragastone, which was now his for the taking.

Ramerick lay motionless, staring at the light above. He had failed. There was no way he could get the stone back with the strength he had. His band could not breach the line of defence The Drethai had successfully assembled and he spared a considerable thought for all the lives he had let down. He was so close. Moments away from grabbing his brother's sword, he had given everything.

He had enough strength to turn his head to view his victor humble in the presence of such power. Dreanor hesitated before reaching down and finally placed his hands onto The Dragastone. Its influence surged through him magnificently. He indulged in its glory and had the temptation to take it for himself before realising that he had an oath to fulfil to his deity. He lifted the stone in the air, claiming victory, which shone brightly against the malice of his black face.

Soon after, he relaxed the claim and turned back to Ramerick. It seemed he would not be leaving without him.

"Time to go, friend of the shadows," Dreanor said and began to march back to the helpless Blessèd Mage of Life to take him back to Ramalon.

A sudden state of nirvana appeared to consume Ramerick. Time seemed to slow and everything around him began to drown out like he was underwater. It was the strangest sensation he had ever felt and, therefore couldn't pinpoint precisely what was happening. Was it the powers of life preservation finally taking over, he thought? Or maybe he was dying?

One thing that did come into his reality was a voice, distant and faint, calling out to him... It was too quiet to make out any words, but it happened again a little louder, echoing in his mind. It became clear whatever it was, was attempting to communicate with him, encouraging him somewhat. He wondered who the voice belonged to. He had never heard it before but somehow recognised it. A sense that he should know who it was.

Dreanor meanwhile, was still marching toward him when the voice became clear enough to be audible.

"*Rise, Ramerick...*" he heard the echo of a strong, male voice in the distance. "*Rise with every ounce of strength you have left...*"

He had no idea how he heard the voice but felt obliged to listen. He did not know where it came from, but he somehow mustered the natural essences from within to hoist himself to his knees. He strained gravely in his attempts, blood gushing from his mortal wound.

Dreanor was peeved that Ramerick's powers had appeared to defy his kill, although he was somewhat relieved as he needed to take him back alive and wasn't completely sure his retribution would not kill him. He could not help his own temptation to kill him, despite risking Ramalon's wrath.

Ramerick managed to turn his head up to the roof of The Draughts and realised something very coincidental... Or not, so he pondered. He was directly underneath his brother of stone, suspended some half a mile above him. He stared up at the light again, which beamed back down upon him as if The Gracelands were welcoming his soul, but realised something even more marvellous was happening.

The light shone ever brighter as he saw the silhouette of the Meigarthian sword in Ramacès' hand had magically released itself from his stoney grasp and was diving directly down on top of him. The blade gently spun on its plight.

All eyes and attention turned to the falling blade. Hearts stopped upon recognising the slither of hope it presented. That same foreign strength began to stabilise Ramerick's body, keeping him upright for the pivotal moment.

Dreanor recognised what was happening, although he didn't fully understand the hidden meaning behind it. It mattered not, as he clocked it too late. The sword was already moments away from its destination.

The Blessèd Mage of Life could not quite believe what was

happening and surprised him further by allowing that same foreign impulse to motor his right hand toward the falling sword, which at last fell perfectly into his palm.

As he instinctively caught Ramacès' sword, stretching as high as he possibly could, the sword flashed the brightest light he had ever seen, illuminating every corner of The Draughts to blinding white.

It brought a stop to time itself.

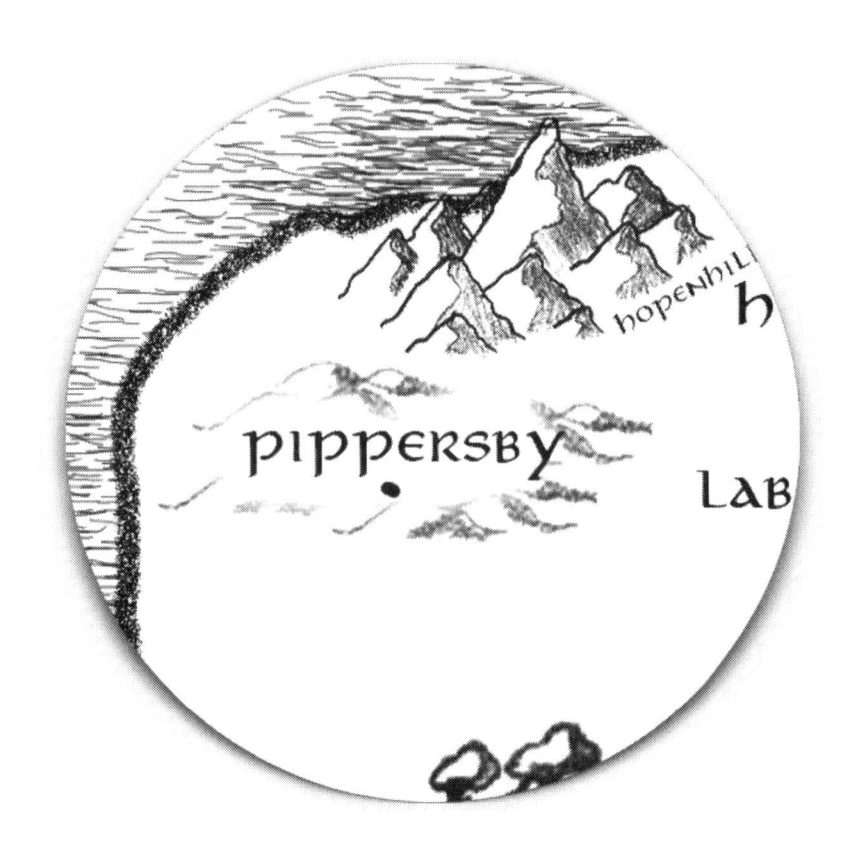

## One Lasting Time

    The blinding light shone through Ramerick's eyelids. He felt strange and totally spaced out, like being knocked unconscious and waking up from that drowning sensation.

    What on Rèo had just happened, he asked himself? How did the sword so perfectly reach his hands at such a precise moment? What gave his body that foreign strength, as if a puppeteer had pulled on his strings?

    He gathered he could survive Dreanor's fatal strike because of his inherited powers but the rest was entirely unexplainable.

    Without him realising, the brightness had gone and he became aware of the cold cobblestones on his back, staring up at the blue sky above. Was this The Gracelands, he wondered?

# One Lasting Time

He connected to his breath once more, realising that he was, at least in some form, still alive. He was still dressed in the same tunic, the wound around his gut now merely a grizzly scar, as if it had happened decades ago. He gradually rose to a sitting position and examined the beautiful village that surrounded him. He recognised it instantly, bringing with it a strong feeling of nostalgia.

"Home..." he gently whispered, full of sentiment.

He was back on Pippersby but it wasn't exactly as he remembered. It appeared wholly deserted. There was no movement on the main street, the smoke from his workplace of Garrison Vardy's Smithwins did not plume, there were no smells of sweetbreads from the bakeries or fishes from the markets. It was quiet, and almost unrecognisable.

He stumbled to his feet with a sense that there was no real urgency to do anything. He was not accustomed to the intricacies of time, but he felt wherever it was he had found himself in, time had stopped entirely. It was a similar sensation to when he picked up The Time Stone so long ago, like it had deposited in part, the ability to sense it. No stressful notions that Terrasendia had no time left to defend itself, no worries nor fears of anything anymore. Though he couldn't be sure any of this was real, he couldn't escape the comfort he was experiencing. A stark contrast to his life for so long.

Why was he back home, he wondered again? And how? One moment he was staring into the dead eyes of Dreanor; the next he was back on Pippersby, it didn't make sense. It was too strong a reality to be a dream, yet too strange and quiet for it to be real.

Unsure of what he was supposed to do, he began to amble through the village, looking upon the empty sparring yard of the barracks belonging to The Durge. He passed their local pub - *The Spuddy Nugget*, recalling some fond memories of Branmir and Brody. His betrayal and redemption felt like it happened in a different lifetime. He couldn't imagine how much more painful his life could be. Time only proved that wrong.

He looked toward the town hall where professor Gregrick would teach his students and remembered where Jàque had once studied. Upon the memory, he made his way back to his home, anxious about what he might see. He felt his heart beat a little harder now that he just might see them again.

Still, there was no sign of movement from the quaint village as he arrived at the sight of his family home. He remained on the street, looking at the house he had built for his family. The door was closed, so too were the windows. A thin curtain veiled the transparency to see within. He was a little scared to go and turn the circular doorknob of his house, not knowing what was happening. Alas, his curiosity got the better of him and he began to encroach on his home.

"*Ramerick,*" came a deep, strong voice from behind him. It was the same voice that had encouraged him just moments ago at The Draughts.

He froze on the street. The voice was so familiar to him. He knew he had heard it before and suddenly remembered where. He cast his memory back to that magical moment when he stared upon his father in that parallel dimension and how the mention of his name was in the same way before being consumed by The Dragadelf's fires. The same tone, the same voice. He recognised the voice belonged to him - to his father.

"Father…" He turned around for visual confirmation.

Alas, the great figure of the man in front of him was not the man he'd expected to see. Instead, the likeliness and similarities between his father and the man standing before him like a King, made apparent who it was.

"Hello brother," Ramacès greeted with a warm smile.

His appearance was almost a complete mirror of their father. The robust frame, the fine beard right down to the Royal cloak that draped behind him connected by his leathered armour. The brother he'd never met.

"Ramacès," Ramerick declared, astonished.

"It's a relief to meet you at last," Ramacès said happily. "I daresay I'd have liked to have done so under better circumstances."

"I thought you were… Huh! You sound just like him. Like our father."

"Do I? Huh! Isn't that odd?" he replied with a smile. "And you look just like him."

"Fierce and mighty? Somehow I don't think so."

Ramacès bounced a subtle laugh. "A nobleman through and through. Too modest."

"What is this?" Ramerick asked more broadly.

"This? It's the boundary."

"The boundary?" he repeated back, a little perplexed.

"Yes. Like a purgatory, but much more pleasant."

"I'll say."

"It's the suspension, bridging the gap between life and what comes after. Very few know such a place exists. They simply pass to the other side. But as The Blessèd Mage of Life, you have a right that others don't. The right of choice."

"I don't understand. Am I dead?"

"Dead? No, you are not dead. It's a little complicated."

"You're telling me."

"There is no time at the boundary - it does not exist."

"And what's beyond?"

"… Our hearts desire."

Ramerick knew precisely what that was. It's what he had wanted since that life-changing day when Pippersby burned. That pang of anxiety struck him again, sensing such a long-awaited moment was being mooted.

"And how does one get there? How does one cross that line?"

"It's my understanding you can only cross that line when your purpose on this side is fulfilled," he gestured with his left hand.

"And what of you? Have you not fulfilled your purpose?"

"Not yet."

"Gracelands Ramacès, you died! What you did - the sacrifice you made to save Terrasendia, it has become legend! Everyone knows your name and what you died for. What more could you possible give?"

"Save it? No, I did not save Terrasendia. I only gave it the time it needed."

"And somehow that doesn't qualify? I don't understand."

"Giving my life to save others wasn't the only thing our father fore-planned for me, no. I came to understand in life," he lectured with his left hand again and indicted with a small nod to one direction of the street they were on, "that Ramalon was the only one strong enough to defeat the evil which was Melcelore. And the only one that can defeat Ramalon, is *you*. And so my purpose has come down to this very moment, before I cross that line to the other side," he gestured with his right hand and looked to the opposite side of the street, "I must give everything I have to the only one who can truly save Terrasendia. Only *you* can restore peace. That was our father's plan all along."

It did not come as a shock to Ramerick. In fact, it brought an overwhelming relief to understand he was right all along. Though at the same time, he felt used again, knowing that their father saw his three sons' fate all along.

"Did it get to you too?" Ramerick asked more solemnly. "To know we were all just part of some plan?"

Ramacès tried to deny the truthful sadness on his face and his eyes. Alas, he fought it with a struggling smile.

"There are some people who just weren't made for the world, brother," he mourned. "We were the sacrifice Terrasendia needed, so that thousands of others could live. Freely. Happily. In peace."

Despite the brutal acceptance, he found it comforting that he had his brother there to confide in. Finally, someone that he could relate to. He was perhaps talking to the only person who could understand just what he was going through, as he had gone through the same acceptance himself.

"… We never stood a chance, did we?" he rhetorically asked, accepting his role.

Ramacès slowly shook his head. "No. No, we didn't… But it was not our fault. And we must understand that."

"I'm glad I finally met you," Ramerick revealed as a tear tried to fall from his eye. "I wish I'd known you sooner."

"And I you, brother. And I you," he consoled.

They shared a pause filled with sadness between them. Ramerick did not feel bad that he was consuming too much time, as it did not exist at that moment, and he used it to regather some emotional strength.

The meeting had brought some seldom moments of happiness and somewhat peace for them both. They couldn't remember a time in their lives when life was so still. They indulged in the tranquillity of peace and restoration they'd both desired for so long.

"I still don't understand entirely why I'm here?"

"Because fate has consumed us both. Ramalon has grown too powerful for you or anyone to stop. It's unclear whether our father saw just how strong he would become."

"You think he missed something?"

"I always found it difficult to believe he would have foreseen just how the world would hinge on a knifes edge as it is now. I sensed Ramalon's war would be inevitable and so preserved my soul in my sword so that there would be a way to defeat him when the time came. And by way of destroying The Dragastone. Together!"

"Through the sword? Please tell me Max was right. You're telling me it can do it?…"

"Yes, Ramerick. It can… And it will!" he proclaimed.

A shy sense of relief came upon confirmation. He knew deep down it was right to trust Meigar, and it had paid off knowing the sword can destroy it and restore peace.

"Since I cannot terminate it due to my physical form, and you cannot due to the hex, there is only one way to do it," Ramacès continued to explain. "All three of our protecy's must open at the same time. I foresaw The Dragastone would soon become more fragile than anyone would realise, including Ramalon it would seem. And I can only activate mine when the sword makes contact with the stone."

"Strike the stone with the sword, and it's finished?"

"Yes! It will not withstand all three of our connections open at the same time."

This was information that Ramerick had already learned from Clethance at the summoning but hearing it from the ethereal soul of his brother made it more than just a theory. Hearing it directly from Ramacès was more reassuring as it was concrete confirmation.

"What happens if the sword touches and his protecy isn't opened?"

"The hex is only active when his protecy is open. If by chance, he has any ideas to be clever and not use it, you can terminate it yourself. Hex free!" he boasted with a smile. "Either way, should you make contact, it will be destroyed!"

A sense of duty enthralled Ramerick once more. He felt determined to see out his task through to the very end.

"However," Ramacès warned, "there is something you should see…"

Behind Ramacès was an area where they could see moving images of the fight Terrasendia was engaging in. Like a birds-eye view, it dipped in and out of various scenes to maximise the truthful horror more clearly. Ramerick walked over to his brother and side by side, they watched on, witnessing every corner of the land going through their desperate struggle to contain and fight back Ramalon's forces and the Dragadelf. Despite time being frozen at that current moment for them, it was unclear if what they were viewing was past, present or future, but it seemed at the very least an inevitability one way or another.

"As you can see, Terrasendia is running out of time…" Ramacès cautioned.

Indeed, the infestation on Gallonea was beginning to mount, Ethelba and Jòsièra were being overwhelmed against the Dragadelf soaring the skies, blistering and bursting the clouds wide open. The dwarves of Handenmar were being pushed back to The Hewercraxen on their Rhinoauros. The Questacèreans were holding the fort well but the civilians were not as trained in battle and it was unclear how long they could prevail. Lastly, the scene flicked to their friend Max Meigar's body, half entombed by stone on Aries Hollow as Durge Helm organised the civilians deep in the catacombs to flee into Aries Hollow and beyond.

"Max!" Ramerick gasped.

"Were it not for him, we would not be having this conversation right now," he sadly informed.

Durge Helm had been breached and The Manced ran riot, ripping through the capital.

Ramalon's purge was relentless and if they did not destroy the stone immediately when time resumed, Terrasendia would surely fall, that much was clear.

"They're being slaughtered…" Ramerick frightfully whispered.

"They need more time," Ramacès suggested.

"How?" Ramerick worryingly asked, genuinely concerned at how dire the land was in.

"There is a way. And I hate to ask this of you, understanding what you've already gone through. But I think you need to embrace your fears once more."

Ramerick turned his head away from his brother, learning very quickly what he was getting at.

"You mean use The Protecy?" Ramerick responded unimpressed.

"Yes!"

"In case you hadn't figured it out by now, the last time I connected to The Dragastone, I nearly died."

"I'm well aware," Ramacès admitted.

"Then you'll know why I won't ever use it again."

"Even if it could provide the difference between life and death?"

"It's a poison brother! I'm sure you would have felt that too. I won't use it again."

Ramacès conceded to his brother's stubbornness, but only to allow the moving images in front of them to send the message more clearly than he ever could. He was in no rush to shove the images down his throat, and the longer they played out, the more they pricked Ramerick's sense of guilt.

"I know what you're doing," Ramerick accused.

"What I'm doing?"

"Showing me this. Guilt-tripping me into using it. A subtle way of saying this is all my fault this is happening."

"I don't control the stipulations of the barrier brother. This is all happening. My question to you is, how can you ignore this when you have the power to help?"

"How?" Ramerick huffed. "How on Rèo could I help this!? The only way I see that can save them all is to destroy that stone!"

"It's not enough."

"What do you mean it's not enough?"

"When you go back, you may not retrieve the stone from Dreanor's grasp. If that happens, Terrasendia will imminently fall. You won't have the time to retrieve it and save them."

"So what do you suggest?"

"Delay! As much as is physically possible! Preserve as much life as can be preserved to give you time to destroy it."

"And how *precisely* can I do that?"

The pause that instilled between them birthed an uncomfortable tension for the first time.

"They're losing hope," Ramacès explained, "they are losing heart! And in the face of such an adversary who can blame them? They need to be reminded of what they are fighting for!"

"They already know."

"No, they don't! They've lost the will to fight with everything they have, both outside and within. They've lost faith that their fight will mean something. You are The Blessèd Mage of Life," he inspired. "And together with the power of The Dragastone, you have the immeasurable power to remind them of that endeavour, to every core and corner of the land. To every heart that beats for what's good and green! They need your strength brother! Your courage! Remind them that their hearts beat strong, and maybe, just maybe, it will provide them with enough fight to give you as much time as possible, for you to save Terrasendia... It is your destiny!"

Ramerick was not easily swayed; however, his brother's motivation and complete faith in his abilities was exceptional. No wonder he rose to such an aspired figure. It landed flush on his heart in a way that he could not ignore his compelling message, even with all his fears.

"And what if I did that and Ramalon initiates the hex?" Ramerick queried.

"Is that what you fear?" he asked a little more disbelieving. "Or is it the poison the stone presents?"

Ramerick narrowed his eyes in confusion, unable to land on the answer to that particular conundrum.

"I... I don't know anymore," he replied plainly.

"I don't think you understand the true measure of power you have."

"I'm well aware of The Dragastone's power -"

"- I'm not talking about the bloody Dragastone! I'm talking about how much fear Ramalon is harbouring right now!..."

"What? What does he have to fear in this moment?"

"Ramalon fears *you*, brother!" Ramacès emboldened. "In so many more ways than you realise."

Ramerick was a little surprised to hear that. So far, every sign indicated that Ramalon was in perfect control of everything that had happened. Even through his deception to destroy The Dragasphere, he gave no indication that he was truthfully fearful of Ramerick.

"In what way?" he asked.

"Ramalon is fully aware that the stone is fractured and vulnerable. If you use the stone's power simultaneously, he knows that it could break and destroy him and everything he has built. The hex he planted is only there as a last resort. He is too smart to play-god and risk its destruction! But that's not all..." He approached Ramerick a little closer, whose attention was now fully grasped. "If you do not die by his hand, he will see that as a total failure. He would not be able to live with it! As you know, he sees things in a very particular way. If something tips him off course, he becomes mentally unstable, vulnerable, but at the cost of risking him at his most dangerous. Use it. Change the narrative..." he urged with a hint of mystery attached.

Ramerick did not need to clarify what he meant. He understood what he was implying, as he had come to the same conclusion. It gave him confidence that there may be another way to effect Ramalon, should he fail to retrieve The Dragastone from Dreanor. His fears were somewhat quelling from his brother's inspiration.

"How do we know this for certain?"

"I'm asking you to trust me. The brother you've never known."

"That's reassuring," he jested. "And what if you're wrong? What if I fail? Fail everything?"

"You won't," Ramacès encouraged.

"Please! Give me the honest answer; I don't care how brutal it is. If I fall, Ramalon would own my soul, forever. Wouldn't he?"

Ramacès breathed heavily through his nose. He was reluctant to demoralise his hopes by being honest, but he knew he could not cover the harsh truth to save bravery. He nodded to confirm the uncertainty, which rose the stakes even higher.

## One Lasting Time

Ramerick turned away to contemplate his decision. He reluctantly reminisced over the pockets of annihilation Terrasendia was going through again, weighing up the balance of risk and reward. His fears were still rife but asked if he could live with himself if he allowed it to fall, knowing there was something he could have done. His eyes closed, deliberating his options, before landing decisively on his decision.

"Okay..." Ramerick resigned to his brother's plea. "I'll do it..."

An overwhelmed Ramacès could not hide his contained relief.

"You mean it?" he asked enthusiastically.

"Yes."

Ramacès' demeanour relaxed with total reprieve. "You really are our father's son," he worshipped. "Blessèd be with you brother!"

"Have you seen him?... Our father?"

Ramacès pondered his answer. "He is in our hearts. So too is our mother. And we must never forget them for everything they have done too. We all are important pieces of the puzzle of fate - our sacrifices written in the stars."

Despite his mysterious reply not giving him a direct answer, it didn't distract Ramerick from sparing a thought for their mother, who also played a vital part in this fight. Suddenly the weight of expectation came crashing down on his shoulders once more, understanding just how much faith and responsibility was placed on him. It rendered him sorrowful but defiant.

"Quite ironic don't you think?"

"Hmm?"

"How we need *time* to save Terrasendia. The thing that our father was known for."

Ramacès pondered ironically, delighting at the thought. "Yes. Yes, I suppose it is. Maybe it's a sign, telling you that it's the right thing to do..."

Ramerick sighed. "How do I do this?"

Ramacès unveiled within his Kingly cape his Meigarthian sword. He held it in his palms and presented it toward Ramerick.

"Take it. It was the doorway to me, and is the doorway back..."

Before Ramerick decided to take it and pass back onto The Draughts, he took the luxury of suspended time to ask something that had been on his mind since entering the boundary.

"I have to ask... Are they here?"

He clocked a subtle notion of fear and reluctance within Ramacès' eye before giving his answer as if he was a little afraid he would ask the question. He swallowed a rapid build-up of saliva that collected in his throat. He did not want to disrespect his brother's intelligence by asking who he was referring to.

"If it is your heart's desire…" he replied a little reservedly.

Ramerick's heart skipped a sudden beat and looked back toward his family home once more, and in particular, the window to their lounge. He could not see the inside clearly, due to the thin curtains that draped across. However, the warm colours of oranges and yellows began to glow from within, flickering shadows from the fireplace.

His breath suspended as someone had just lit that fire from the hearth, only to recognise the revealing silhouette of Amba coming to stand from setting it off. Moments later, she was joined by Jàque, who had run into the lounge to give his mother a huge cuddle. She lifted him up and they hugged tightly, squeezing the love out of each other.

Ramerick could not help the moisture collect in his eyes, struggling to breathe fluently against his trembling heart. In his reality, time appeared to slow down. It felt like an age to him as he watched them play. Watched them laugh. Watched them live…

Suddenly, that impulsive sense of duty subsided somewhat, much to Ramacès' fear. The weight of responsibly measured against the desire of his heart was the ultimate form of conflict. At that moment, he forgot entirely about his purpose, seeing his family on the other side, hearing his sons giggle and Amba's chuckle. It all became too much.

"Ramerick…" Ramacès' demeanour took a sudden shift of significant urgency. He felt frightful at what was happening. "Ramerick, please listen to me…"

There was no response.

His attempts to connect with his brother were becoming increasingly difficult as it appeared his mind raced towards temptation, transfixed in the oasis of his heart's desire ahead of him. Ramacès elevated his concern.

"Ramerick?" he asked more strenuous. "Come back to me…"

"I knew it… Just because they're dead, doesn't mean they're gone," he claimed, entirely deluded.

The happiness in Ramerick's heart became stronger; the more the reality of seeing his family again became a possibility. He felt he was right all along to trust his heart. He wasn't mad at all, despite what others may have thought. He knew he would see them again and nothing was going to take the imminent moment away from him. It was so powerful, it completely overcame what remained of the reality around him.

"You can't go to them," Ramacès harshly reprimanded. "Not yet..."

Gormless and like a man possessed, he stared into his brother's eyes with a tone of anger that he was being denied of his wish. He felt utterly betrayed. Not the plan Ramacès had hoped for.

"What are you doing?" Ramerick menacingly whispered, igniting his seething anger, trying to establish what's real and what's not. "Why show this to me? Why antagonise me?"

"Brother, it is not me!" he honestly replied, full of concern. "I cannot control the conditions of the boundary, you must believe me! I would never do such a thing!"

"You said earlier that I have the choice," Ramerick examined.

His eyes became transfixed on his family home, mellowing out and becoming despondent, understanding just how close he was to end the pain. He seemed inconsolable - impossible to persuade.

Ramacès became genuinely fearful that everything he had built in life could be destroyed in a singular moment of self indulgence on his brother's behalf. How demoralising it would seem if the reason for that came from someone merely following their heart. If Ramerick entered his home, in effect, he would have crossed the line to the other side, for there would be no return when that happened.

"Ramerick, please listen to me," Ramacès urged. "You must fight this! I know it would seem unnatural for you not to do this, and it is! It's totally unnatural for you to defy your heart's desire, especially when nothing is stopping you from reaching it... But please, brother," he pleaded like never before. "Resist! You must!"

Ramerick's eyes remained transfixed on his family's silhouettes behind the curtain and had seemingly made up his mind. Without recognising anything else, he walked forward across the street, trancelike and did not stop until he reached the door to his home.

The impulse to end all the hurt hooked and hoisted him in, like a painful addiction that he wanted to surrender to. At that moment, he wanted it to be over so badly. He'd had enough and had no desire for anything else.

"Ramerick!" Ramacès pleaded more desperately. "Once you open that door, there is no going back. Ramalon will kill all that is good and green."

He arrived at the door, stopped, and examined what it meant should he open it.

"Why would I want to go back when everything I want is right behind this door?" his voice monotonous and emotionless.

"Your destiny and purpose have not yet been filled…"

The urge to open the front door was the strongest force he had ever experienced in his short life. The pain, the suffering and the satisfying notion of an endless existence with his family was the only thought he could process. Nothing could stop him. It was his choice.

He placed his hand on the circular doorknob and turned it so that the catch released. Ramacès held his breath, for all it needed was one small push and he would pass onto the other side…

Ramerick would be greeted by his son jumping into his arms and the warm embrace that would entail from Amba would make him whole again. The pieces of the puzzle scrambling his mind would formulate back into their perfect position and all he'd know for the rest of his existence would be happiness till the end of his days… Alas, a mysterious force unknown to him stopped him from delivering that push. It was a confusing sensation that he could not entirely process.

"*Why can't I do this?*" he thought to himself, bringing him back to some form of truthful reality. And then it hit him with the force of a thousand Dragastone's. "Should I open this door, how many other families would not see their loved ones again?" he quietly asked.

The selflessness in his heart took over once more and he realised why he could not give in to selfishness just yet. The fondness in Ramacès grew. He smiled sadly at him as he fully understood what his brother was walking away from at that moment.

"You really are our father's son… I couldn't be more proud to have you as my brother," he praised. "Yes, Ramerick. Thousands more families would not see their loved ones again should you open that door. You are their only hope. The choice is yours, but Terrasendia will fall should you choose to walk away from them now."

Though that sounded like a painful weight on Ramerick's heart, it did not come as a heartbreaking sacrifice he would have to make. The good in his heart overwhelmed him and instinctively made him realise how selfish he would be to give the door that gentle, desiring push, which he still held unturned. It wasn't him and he knew his destiny still needed to be fulfilled. However, he realised one grave notion that rendered him fearful.

"And what if I do fail?" he gravely asked. "Ramalon could own my soul. I would never see them again…"

Ramacès' eyes shared the same concerning thought.

## One Lasting Time

"Yes. That could happen," he quietly admitted.

Ramerick couldn't help the internal war that began to rage once again between his mind and heart. His heart was telling him to push that door while he still had the chance, against his mind that argued that he could never have eternal peace should he turn his back on the thousands of other fathers, mothers, sons and daughters that needed and depended on him so desperately. It became compelling which side had to win.

He gently relaxed the doorknob, which flicked the catch back into its closed position and very gently laid his fingertips on the wooden door, resting his forehead onto it. He closed his eyes, realising just how close he was to all his pain being remedied and forgotten…

"Just a little longer," Ramerick whispered to the door, hoping his two loved ones on the other side could hear. "I promise. Just a little longer…"

He took as long as he needed to indulge in the touching moment. Tears dropped from his closed eyes and bowed head which splashed onto the porch that led into his front door. He imagined the many other families he would not wish that upon, a choice between life and death. It gave him the strength to do what was placed upon him to do all along, sacrificing the moment he had wished upon for so long.

"You would have made a fine King," Ramacès consoled in awe, witnessing the most admirable sacrifice he had ever seen. Pride didn't do it justice. "The cost of sacrifice is what pains great men. I can't help but feel sad that I never knew you. I'd have been stronger, that's for sure."

Ramerick peeled away from the door, looking at it as if he was looking at them.

"I'll see you soon," he whispered.

He took one last look at the door before he slowly walked backwards from it, coming into view the window that still played the silhouette of his family playing inside. He took one last glance at them to inspire every ounce of strength before turning around to his brother, determined to see it through.

"I'm ready."

Ramacès delicately approached him, admiring every fibre of his brother.

"I'll be with you. Every step of the way!" Ramacès lifted his Meigarthian sword and held it in both palms, presenting it to his brother again. "Now take my sword and defend Terrasendia with everything you have left…"

His words galvanised an already-inspired Ramerick who reached out to take it. As his hand drew closer to the tacky leather handle, blinding light rose brighter until his mitts connected to it and blinded everything in sight once more.

## The Eleventh Hour

Adrenaline scorched through Ramerick's veins as he initiated The Protecy of life. The galvanisation of such magnificent power uplifted his physical and mental resistance more than was possibly imaginable. Never before had he felt so fierce and mighty, just like his father. He felt invincible.

Ramacès was proved right. Despite not having The Dragastone in his hands, Ramerick was fearful he would somehow be hexed, however no such torture ensued and his protecy of life was in full flow.

He passed back onto The Draughts, where time had seemingly stopped for the entire duration he was at the boundary, only to resume the exact moment he caught the falling sword.

Sourcing the unique powers of life like a star's nucleus, magnificent swirls of white light radiated out of the Meigarthian sword he held in the skyward position.

It repeatedly rippled out of the blade like solar flares and continued to echo its pulses in every direction of The Draughts. Ramacès' Garden was consumed by the essences of life, blossoming the greenery instantly and causing it to gregariously grow to breathtaking beauty once more.

The Ancient Drethai were forced to immediately scramble their constitutions to black gas once more in an attempt to escape the tremendous essences of power that blistered their skins. They hissed and screeched their deathly tones, signalling their pain. However, the stone was still in Dreanor's grasp as he dissolved and swam away with only half of what he came for. Alas, there was no chance he could get close to Ramerick now, for his divinity was shining bright.

As the rippling light set aflame to their trailing gases, The Wandlers and Zathos tried to recapture the fleeing shadow spirits with intricate magics that slowed them down and made it very tricky for them to escape, evading and manoeuvring efficiently. It was unclear how they could all be stopped and gathered they only needed Dreanor.

However, they could not tell which one of the thirteen balls of gas was his and could not concentrate their restraint on one individual.

In the process of trapping The Ancient Drethai, the essences of life boomed out of The Draughts, cracking the earth like a clap of distant thunder. Its power rapidly spread through the foundations and headed for every corner of the land.

The fight in the four corners raged heavily. It was hardly a fight any longer, but more an extermination as The Manced and The Dragadelf applied the pressure to Terrasendia's neck.

The dwarves were forced back to the frigates and crusades on The Wintering Sea to save as many lives as they could. The noblemen on Gallonea had to ascend from the bottom levels to ward off the infiltration, which was now complete on the bottom. The rampage was relentless and did not stop nor even slow with the waining strength of their opponent. They showed no mercy. Durge Helm was now wholly flushed out and what remained of the defences were to blockade The Manced from gaining on the retreating civilians that spread into the mountains of Aries Hollow. The Questacèreans had lost ground too, utterly surrounded now by the trampling militants that had reached the peak. Mijkal did his best to rally what was left of the city but knew their time was near its end.

Unknown to him, a dishevelled singular scarlet rose that entwined

## The Eleventh Hour

from a stoney bannister in the gardens began to thaw and strengthen its claret colours. It continued to grow and birthed other roses from the vines it rooted. It was clocked by one of the retreating Questacèreans, who took the moment of reprieve to view its blossoming. A symbol of hope and of things to come.

A looming force mysteriously began uplifting the Questacèrean and the others around, who were receiving the same peculiar empowerment. The essence of Ramerick's power had reached them, and every corner of Terrasendia...

All who fought for what's good and green did not know why, nor how, but a surge of electrifying adrenaline stimulated their bodies. It was not a malicious sensation, but more a rapid emboldening that fuelled them. Their hearts beat much stronger than before, making them more animated to endure. It was a reinvigoration of life that lifted the feeling of utmost despair and supercharged their spirits. It could not have been more welcomed at such a dire moment.

In every corner of the land, the people rallied with everything they could muster and began one last throw of the dice. A final push at the eleventh hour, to whatever end.

With the endowment of natural strength, they forced back The Manced in every corner, battle-crying ferociously into their enemies.

On Gallonea, the scaling militants attempting to siege the higher levels were met with man's heroism, fending them off the walls as they reached the top. Ethelba and Jòsièra mounted an impressive fightback in the skies, which forced The Dragadelf to retreat out of sight.

On Durge Helm, the blockades of men thrusted forward their guards together to push The Manced back, stabbing and slicing the white orbs in the process. The retreating civilians had more time to flee, as the might of the Septalians held firm.

Upon feeling the endowment of Ramerick's strength, Thakendrax changed his mind and assembled his Rhinoauros to charge, in kamikaze-like fashion through the ranks of filth that bled into Dwardelfia. They pierced through the lines, trampling over corpses in a relentless stampede. They did not stop until they rode out of the city's broken walls and out through the last remaining rank of The Manced beyond the plain ahead. Thakendrax was the first to experience the emptiness ahead of him and kept going to allow space for them to about-turn and repeat the process back into the city once more.

Lathapràcère was reminiscent of a moat, surrounded not by water but by The Manced that enclosed their final moments. Suddenly, among the misty depths of the slope, came thousands of rallying lancers who descended earlier out of sight, only to return and aid the capital. Their mildens galloped with speed that just was not possible on the ascent. The essences of life gave them all that increased desire to fight.

Terrasendia had heard Ramerick's call.

Despite his emboldening of life across the land to provide the time that was so desperately needed, it was only temporary. What would ensue with the time they had borrowed would define Terrasendia's fate.

## The Darkest Revenge

The Garden of Ramacès was reinvigorated. Every corner received the magical elixir of life, which made a stark contrast to the dark and perilous times they found themselves in.

With the sword still posed in the skyward position, the radiating swirls of life began to simmer and come to a complete stop. The experience of feeling that power again took Ramerick's breath away. A sense of liberation ran rife but still felt guilty for using it. It was entirely against his nature and using such power, knowing it came from a poisonous source, placed a dirty stain on his conscience. He told himself that he did it in the name of all that's good and green and hoped it would provide the time he needed to save Terrasendia.

He looked up toward The Draughts entrance, which was some distance away, to see a very challenging situation develop. The Ancient Drethai were squirming and twisting their black gasses, evading the more effective spells from The Wandlers and Zathos that attempted to capture them. The diffusion of colours that clashed sparked magnificent colours that flared off upon connection. The network of magics covering the entrance created a wall they struggled to get past, often diving into it to force their way through.

Ramerick sprinted as fast as he could toward the entrance, picking up Sythero that luckily was on his route, and did not stop. They were so close now. All that was needed was for him to strike the stone with the Meigarthian sword and Terrasendia would be saved. However, the chances of such wish diminished by every second The Drethai were not in their custody.

They could not hold the blockade forever as it was consuming much of their magical stamina, and to their frustration, one of them slipped the net and escaped into Terrasendia and beyond their reach. They did not know which one it was but hoped it was not Dreanor.

Suddenly another swirl of black gas pierced through the lines. And then another, and then two more, followed by another few. It was clear their escape was inevitable, and so were left with only one choice that Susmees orchestrated.

They relaxed their magics, temporarily disbanding the magical blockade and allowed them all to escape. The purpose was to charge up a more substantial form of energy that they could only hope would work. Wands were raised, so too were the staffs that could land more devastation than intricacies.

The remaining Drethai instantly swam out of the main chamber of The Draughts and travelled up the vast tunnel that was the entrance.

There, The Wandlers used that to their advantage, deploying powerful beams of gravity from their staffs to slow them down, while others cast energies of lightning bolts that jolted out of their wands to paralyse all they could.

Unfortunately for them, most of The Drethai were seemingly too far away to be affected by their attempts. All but two. They squeezed every portion of energy they could muster to pull the two gasses that were not so lucky, back toward them, before sealing off the entrance once more with a more concentrated fusion of magic to which they had the time to deploy.

The two black gasses attempted to break free from their magical chains but were in vain, for The Wandlers had successfully constricted their movements and successfully incarcerated them.

Ramerick held his breath, still racing through the invigorated

## The Darkest Revenge

greenery, leaving a trail of wind rushing through the long grass behind him. He kept wishing for at least one of them to be Dreanor, for he could not see which members they had captured. The war could not end there and then if Dreanor had not been apprehended.

When he arrived at the surrounding Wandlers and Knights of The Reinhault, the two gasses morphed back into their physical form to reveal their identities. They were immediately bound on their knees. The pathway cleared for Ramerick to approach, only to deal a bitter blow to their hopes.

Neither of them was Dreanor. He had gotten away and The Dragastone was now beyond their reach...

"NO!!!" he lashed out, closing his eyes and turning away in disgust.

He panted heavily in frustration. That drowning feeling of resignation loomed large among the entire band, as they all understood what this meant. They had failed. Terrasendia would continue to bleed, and the alarming realisation came to the fore. Just how long did it have left?

All eyes were on The Blessèd Mage of Life, who struggled to hide his dismay, staring out to Ramacès' Garden.

"We were so close," he whispered to himself.

How quickly things had turned. Moments ago, that spirit of echoing hope was rife, only to be snatched away in a single swipe, leaving them substantially discouraged.

When the shock began to set in, he turned back to the band and only just clocked the identity of one of the Drethai that had been captured. Despite the harrowing recognition of their failure, there was the smallest chance of some reprieve. Ramerick's mind began to zone out and brought the deep rumbling emotions to the surface as he stared upon the face of Orbow, who looked utterly petrified when glancing back into his vengeful eyes.

He could not hide his angering satisfaction at seeing her face, sensing his chance of revenge. Flashes of that unforgettable moment he ripped her arrow from his son's heart came flooding back. He began to shake uncontrollably, trying to keep the lid on his seething rage. His lips closed, his teeth gritted, flaring his nostrils like a steaming dragon. It masked the dooming imminence of Terrasendia's fate, which brought a sense of dark comfort.

"Ramerick... *Ramerick!*" came the mellowed voice of Zathos. It was clear he had been trying to get his attention for some moments before he resurfaced from his trancelike state.

"It's her," Ramerick vengefully whispered.

"Ramerick, what do we do? Dreanor is not here. We cannot destroy the stone," he fearfully informed.

That internal war raged beneath his skull again. Conflicted between the allure of revenge and the very imminent reality of Terrasendia's doom, he struggled to fathom precisely what to do. Alas, he managed to find some form of normality to think clearly. He looked upon the other member of The Drethai who remained rooted at the knees and did not know which one it was.

"Who is that?" he interrogated.

"That is Dreadath."

Perhaps the more human-looking of the shadow order, Dreadath was likened to that of a typical mercenary. Chiselled in physique, like a Knight who'd trained three hours a day to enhance physical strength. Assassin-like, bearing the conventional charcoaled complexion that stained his skin - a reminder of Melcelore's curse that he was once under. It would seem purely from the cold, determined look in his eye that a torturous approach to ascertain information would simply not work. It spoke a thousand truths that he would not answer nor bend to that type of interrogation, willing to die for his order's cause.

"What would you have us do?" Hiyaro asked. "We need that stone. It is the only way to end the war!"

"The stone is gone," Zathos argued.

"We need to retrieve it!"

"We cannot possibly search the skies and hope."

"Then we need to find where he is heading with it. We need to find Ramalon!"

Zathos nodded in agreement, knowing that wherever that was, it was the most dangerous place on Rèo now. However, they had run out of choices.

"Ramerick. Where would your brother be right now?" Zathos asked.

Ramerick's attention was elsewhere, distracted upon seeing Susmees behind Orbow with his wand raised, pointing toward her kneeling body, presumably ready to execute her. The concern was also shared among the rest of them. It dawned on Ramerick just how strongly Susmees hated Orbow as well, recalling the information that he had shared about Orbow killing his mother, Miala.

"Susmees?" Ramerick asked calmly. His response was muted, to say the least. His eyes were full of fulfilment, understanding he was one spell away from ascertaining his long-lasting revenge. Ramerick could not care for Orbow's life, but he felt conflicted as he wanted to be the one to give her a fitting end. On the other hand, he knew the amount of pain that she had caused Susmees as well and could not help the kindness in his heart take over.

Orbow quickly fathomed what was happening and feebly sobbed for her shadowed life. Her pathetic pleas could not have been more opposite than the stoney defiance of Dreadath beside her, who remained chillingly calm.

Susmees looked into her eye as she swivelled around. It was the moment he had been waiting for, for so long, and could not contain his delight. It seemed Ramerick had conceded that it was just as much Susmees' right as his to be the one to extract that satisfaction and gave him the all-clear with a reassuring nod.

However, before he could cast any such spell, he lowered his wand and stared into her cowering eyes to conclude his triumph.

"I see you. As clear as day. And it was all I needed to see..." Susmees slowly confessed before glancing back toward Ramerick, inviting him to be the one to do it.

Ramerick understood that Susmees felt right to allow him to be the one to take such an opportunity and restore some balance that life stole. He fathomed he had more reason to do it after losing his son, for which there was no greater loss.

Ramerick fondly looked at Susmees, and without saying it, was forever thankful to him for gifting the vengeance to him. He gently nodded his head in appreciation. Orbow meanwhile, shook her head, pleading with her captors to let her go, profusely apologising for all that she had done.

"Ramerick?" Zathos advised. "With the greatest respect, we do not have time for this."

"I agree," Hiyaro said. "Vengeance must wait,"

"No," Ramerick declared sinisterly.

"They will stall! And every second we spend doing nothing is a second we lose to -"

"- I ask you to trust me," he interrupted more confidently. He concluded that the opportunity to patch up the scar that stained his heart with grief for so long could no longer wait. "Let me have this."

They didn't have a choice. They had no answer to how to retrieve The Dragastone, which now was surely beyond their reach. They placed their trust in him once more, paving the way for his revenge. Ramerick approached Orbow, exposing Sythero in her sight, and stopped within arms reach.

"Release her binds," he instructed.

Susmees cocked his head, confused at the order but obliged with a flick of the wand, releasing the constraints from her wrists. She did not attempt to flee, for she would only be brought back down by The Wandlers again. She remained stupefied on her knees, continuing her pleas.

This was unchartered territory for Ramerick. Killing somebody who could not defend themselves could be construed as evil itself. However, this was entirely different. There was no question that keeping her alive would make the world a safer place, it justified her defenceless execution in his mind. The Ancient Drethai, as via his own experience with them, were inherently evil. Ramerick would defend his actions by saying that sometimes to eradicate evil, it must be fought with the same intent.

It was a dark place… Luckily for Ramerick, he had been there before and the causes for such venture was right in front of him. How ironic, he thought?

Finally, he lifted the lid on his impulses, dedicated what he was about to do to his son, and thumped the sole of his boot into her chest, flinging her body backwards to land in an ugly way. It bent her trapped leg beneath her and cruelly snapped, causing her to wail in agony.

Dreadath to one side, remained eerily despondent, hearing Orbow's cries for help. He knew precisely what would happen to them both and still carried his order's belief to the utmost end.

Ramerick slowly and menacingly approached her, getting to a position where he found himself standing directly over her, armed with Sythero. She continued to whimper like a childish brat between his legs, adding more sugar to the bittersweet revenge. He knew he could not hold this moment forever but wanted to extract every portion of satisfaction he could, staring at her pitiful black eyes. Alas, the time was right.

He swivelled Sythero round to reverse his grip on the sword and with both hands, raised it above his head, aiming with one pressing motion to stab her black heart.

However, in the blink of an eye and with one last seeming attempt to save her own life, Ramerick was no longer looking at Orbow beneath him but instead the terrified face of the love of his life.

"Amba…" he whispered, utterly mortified.

He suspended the sword above his head, looking at her frightful face, full of life.

"Alex..." Amba frantically panted in equal horror, not quite believing he would do such a thing to her.

Time seemingly stopped. It was as if they were in their own bubble with each other, and after a few short moments to contemplate how she was there, he began to break down at her resurrection. He remained stooped over her before she raised her hand, encouraging him to hold hers, calming him in the process.

His heart coerced his desire to believe it was her so dearly that he would do anything to take her hand.

"It's me," she cried and smiled. "You wouldn't hurt me, would you?"

Ramerick didn't know what to do, looking at the magical smile that reminded him of how happy he once felt. The temptation became too much and he lowered his sword, stumbling down to his knees on top of her. Her hand found its way to his cheek and cupped it delicately, staring fondly into each other's eyes.

"Shhhh," she soothed in the same way as she had done for many years. "You can't do it, can you? I'm so proud of you." Ramerick remained hypnotised at her charm. "Close them... Close your eyes," she advised.

He heeded her request and saw not only her but also Jàque as well. His heart's desire. He indulged luxuriously in the moment while, unknown to him, Amba conjured a small blade, in her hidden hand. The colours of black and dark green completed the blade's formulation.

"Together forever..." she declared before she took advantage of his closed eyes and rapidly thrust the blade toward his heart in the hope his powers would not withstand such a fatal blow.

However, the blade never reached the intended target, for Ramerick had fathomed her deceptive illusion and encouraged her to make such a move.

With his eyes closed, he caught the thrusting arm dead in its tracks. He opened his eyes to see through the revealing fright in hers before he pulled the arm toward him, jolting her body up and punched the glowing steel of Sythero through her cold heart.

Amba's eyes widened in painful shock. She looked furious at him, like a betrayal she could never forgive. She grimaced as if she was trying to resist death taking over. However, Ramerick quietly stared through her eyes and into her soul, understanding it was Orbow trying to sustain the image of Amba, playing on the darker portions of his heart for as long as she could.

It wasn't too long before the under-layer of Amba's skin began to melt away into the black foundations for which it was. Until it was no longer a recognisable figure of Amba, but the still, lifeless face of Orbow that laid dead on the ground.

He had gone there. He had gone to the deepest darkest place in his heart to finally gain revenge. A poetic justification in his own right to demonstrate his own manipulation. It was a testament to him, whether better or for worse, just how far he had grown and how unrecognisable he was from the nobleman he left behind on Pippersby that day.

Time seemed to resume and everyone that watched wondered what had happened. Ramerick slid his sword out of Orbow's chest, withdrawing sludges of black blood that drenched the blade, and came to stand.

He felt righteous. It was not the life that he took but that which would take lives, and he felt every bit more confident that he did the right thing.

Zathos and Hiyaro nodded in recognition for what he just did, giving him the impression that they agreed with what he'd done. However, Zathos wasted no time pressing on with the more urgent matter.

"Ramerick, what now? What do we do?"

"… Change the narrative," he declared, more determined than before.

"How?"

"I'm tired of chasing," he confessed. "I'm tired of playing into his hands. It's time he came to me."

"But he will have no need to do that. It's only a matter of time before Dreanor delivers The Dragastone," Zathos informed more openly.

"I have something he wants even more than that," he said mysteriously.

He unclipped the necklace that contained his protecy stone of life and held it in his hands. He walked over to the defiant Dreadath, who remained motionless and found the perfect way to turn the tide.

"You will survive this," he told him with unwavering confidence, "but only to give your master this message. If he does not show himself, here with The Dragastone by sunrise, I will destroy my protecy stone…"

Everyone froze, realising the incredible risk that he was taking. The threat he issued was simple. If Ramerick destroyed his protecy stone of life, he would die, making Ramalon's last step impossible.

Dreadath's eyes grew colder and angrier. It seemed his resolve and defiance was being tested in that Ramerick had found a way to use him. It was in Dreadath's interest to deliver that message as it was a direct threat to his deity, the one who he'd sworn to serve. And by not providing the information, it could be construed as a betrayal to his god - something that definitely was not in his interest. With no words, Ramerick could tell just how much Dreadath despised him for threatening such a motion.

"Ramerick," Zathos cautioned; alas, his concern was ignored.

"Release his binds!" Ramerick ordered to Susmees, who also was very reluctant to do so. "Now!" he implied more forcefully, to which his order was finally carried out.

The magical bracelets on Dreadath's wrists dissolved and he was free to leave. Though, his reluctance to do so gave Ramerick all the confidence he needed to confirm this was the right move. Ramalon would not have wanted that and threatened him in the most fearful way possible.

"Deliver that message. Now..." Ramerick ordered.

The black gas consumed Dreadath once more, returning the filthiest of looks before it dissolved and swam out of The Draughts beyond their sight.

"Ramerick, what are you doing?" Hiyaro demanded. "If you die, Terrasendia will not survive!"

"Terrasendia will fall regardless," Ramerick painfully replied.

"How sure are you that he will even come?" Zathos queried. "He will know all he has to do is wait!"

"He won't. I'm sure of it," he reassured. "It's all about destiny. It has to be perfect for him. My death is his final step, and it means more to him than every death on Terrasendia he is responsible for. In his eyes, if I do not die by his hand, he fails. And that is something he will never be able to live with..."

Zathos however, no longer took a defensive stance, understanding precisely what he was doing.

"Playing on his fears," Zathos praised.

Ramerick nodded. "He fears being denied his right to divinity more than anything! If he kills me then so be it, but if he doesn't come, everything is lost anyway. Neither one of us wants my stone destroyed, but making him believe that I would do it gives us that chance in a million. He will come!" he encouraged.

Hiyaro began to understand just how much bargaining right he had bought and joined Zathos in their togetherness. It was the only way.

"There is one problem," Hiyaro warned on the contrary.

"I calculate a few more than that," Zathos joked.

"You're asking Terrasendia to hold on. What if they do not survive the night? What if they fall before Ramalon arrives?"

"They won't!" Ramerick stated.

"How can you be sure?"

"Because our hearts now beat as one! And we will fight far beyond the boundaries and capabilities they thought were possible."

Despite Hiyaro's change in direction, he remained unconvinced.

"I do not see any other way," Zathos admitted. "We will protect you as long as we can when he comes."

"I'm sorry, but I can't allow you to be here when he does," Ramerick gravely instructed, much to their disheartenment. "It has to be me. And me alone. If you're here, he will use you against me. I could not be responsible nor save you if it came to that…"

Despite their hearts telling them all to be heroes and stand with The Blessèd Mage of Life, they reluctantly agreed. Their hearts told them that they would rather die trying to defend what's good and green, but their heads told them it would damage the chances of success were they to remain.

"What would you have us do?" Zathos quietly asked.

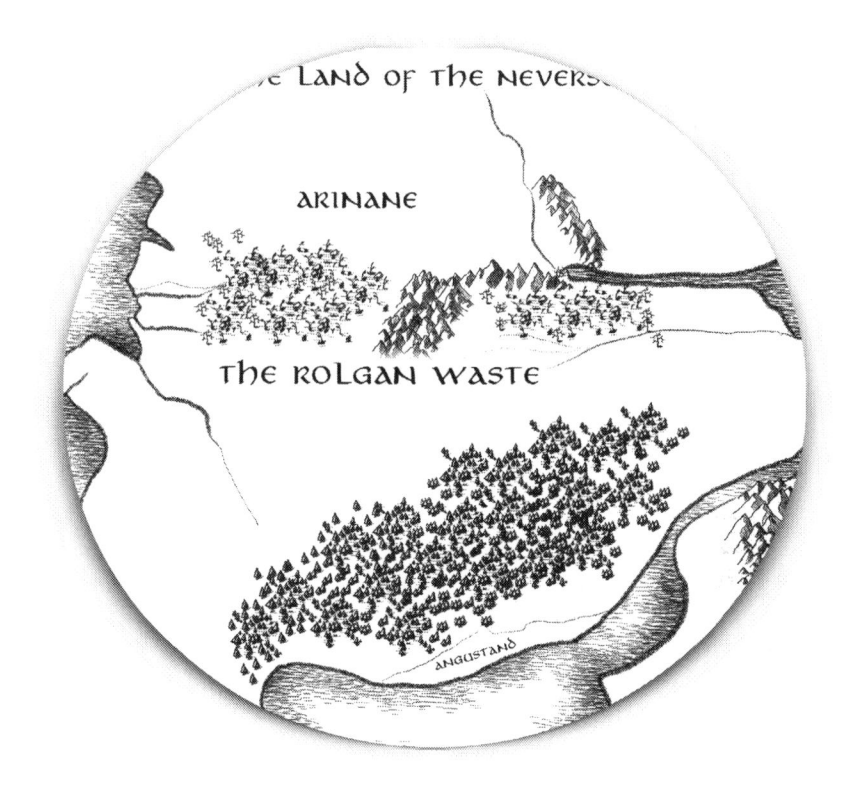

# Rolganfire

The razor-thin glow on the horizon, reminiscent of a crescent moon, provided the only source of light on The Rolgan Waste. It was the ninth hour of night and the early stages of sunrise were beginning to dissolve into the starlit sky.

Ramalon had flown through the night on his Dragadelf from Mages Wreath immediately after his victory over Wemberlè. He could feel the cool, calming element of water running through his veins and knew that he could call upon its affinity at any time. Combined with the other four that he had acquired, the concept of invincibility grew stronger. He had one more left to attain before he reached the last step on his Staircase to Divinity.

He expected a more hostile environment when he arrived at The Rolgan Waste. It was notoriously consumed by the hurricane that never stopped. However upon his arrival, no such storm was present.

All was quiet. The warm air of the northern climate was still and eerie under the starlit sky. A clue that gifted Ramalon the whereabouts of his next kill.

No life could survive the destructive force that decimated the breadth of Rolgan; hence it's name. Not even rocks and rubble were able to withstand its winds over time. Not a grain of sand was permitted to land for long on the levelled, flat rock that stretched as far as the eye could see.

It was rumoured that very few had ever crossed The Rolgan Waste into the aridness of Arinane and The Lands of the Neverseen.

Arinane, Ramalon thought as he took centre stage in the barren wasteland. He grew warm with the fond memory of the Charzeryx he had shared his soul with many moons ago. The sentiment rose within, remembering what kind of person he was back then and what an evolution he had experienced to now. Though a large part of him determined that he had not changed at all, he accepted the lessons he had learned along the way had shaped him into what he was always destined to become and with each lesson, another key unlocked another door to the powers he had within.

However, as he stood silently next to his simmering Dragadelf, a portion of apprehension bubbled to the surface of his thoughts. He closed his eyes. Charging up his powers, increasing the flow of his protecy to expel more destructively when it was needed.

It was perhaps the first time he had to concede to doubting his philosophical notion of merely trusting the powers he possessed. He anticipated his next opponent would possibly be a more significant challenge than anything he had faced before, even Melcelore, to some extent. This was Aristuto, who was exceptionally powerful, perhaps the most powerful and destructive of all The Blessèd Order. He conceded for the first time, he may actually require the help of his Dragadelf when the time came.

Alas, that time had arrived.

The distant screeches of what sounded like a small band of dragons pierced the sharp silence. It had no foundations to echo from, which was peculiar. It was too dark to make out the specifics of what was ahead. However, judging by his Dragadelf's reaction, it was clear he sensed his kind were approaching. Its anger scalded the oxygen nearby, creating a wave of heat that made Ramalon sweat.

He did not know precisely what to expect, although he was prepared for anything. Images of their last encounter remained so strong in his mind. When fire meets air, it is not a match up for the faint-hearted, as one fuels the other in a cycle of devastating combustion. Ramalon knew he would have to get creative if he was to emerge victorious.

The one thing that he did admit was a disadvantage was the lack of sight, as the sun's rising rays were nowhere near strong enough to light the battlefield. His Dragadelf's senses were strong enough to fight in practically no light at all, but his own sight was very poor indeed and was left with one option.

He knelt down and placed his hand onto the warm foundations beneath him and suddenly the stone began to glow a scarlet red. The heat that he produced began to spread out in front of him, illuminating the area from right to left. The hotter it got, the more it turned into oranges and yellows, reminiscent of a molten river that lit the large expanse of nothingness. Symbolically, Ramalon used it to welcome The Blessèd Mage of Air to the fight.

That welcome was delightfully received with the gesture being returned by igniting the glowing lava like oil being set aflame.

The burning line of fire created a barrier in front of him, reminiscent of a forest blaze that would not be doused. There was no question about it, there was now plenty of light through the blazing fires and through the air rippling heatwave, Ramalon finally identified his opponent.

The Blessèd Mage of Air stared calmly and confidently back at him. It was clear he used his divine elements to fuel the flames between them; whether that helped or hindered was unclear.

Accompanied by three dragons, a Dralen, a Drogadera and a Charzeryx that he'd acquired from Dragonsnout, Aristuto had brought his own beasts to the fight. The Dragadelf that heeded to Ramalon contained the DNA of all three cousins.

From behind their masters, they roared their mights toward each other in their own unique ways, with the Dragadelf much larger and louder than all three combined.

After the dragons stopped their songs which seemed to last an eternity, their masters opened the ceremony.

"We meet again," Aristuto greeted through the flames. His voice a little raised to carry through the sound of melting stone and stirring dragons. "You've changed, boy!" The term *boy* irked Ramalon, likening him to a child for which he was not. Though he did not rise to the antagonism, he tried instead to cover it up inside, but it leaked through his eyes. "I must say, it's quite a rise! You must be very proud of yourself," Aristuto patronised with thinly veiled sarcasm. "Though it ends here, Ramalon. I give you this one chance, take your Dragadelf and your armies north, to The Lands of the Neverseen and never come back!"

Ramalon had no intention of doing so and disrespectfully cast a flume of water that doused the fires temporarily in front of them. The parting created a clear view between them both, hissing steam from the scalding rocks, though the light was still bright from the fiery wall that extended across their line of sight.

With that, Aristuto understood the fate of Wemberlè and took it as a sign that Ramalon was prepared to go all the way.

"Have you ever heard of *Rolganfire* boy?" The Blessèd Mage of Air smugly asked. Ramalon's eyes narrowed. His head slowly shook. "Allow me to show you..."

Though Ramalon was fully prepared for any eventuality, he did not imagine the level of immense force that ensued. He sensed the wind gradually tickling his face and began to blow the flames toward him faster by the second. It did not take much to work out that Aristuto was releasing the binds on the natural phenomena for one simple reason.

Suddenly, the hurricane that had been held back was unleashed from the shadows much quicker than anticipated, bringing its full destructive force from behind The Blessèd Mage of Air, who used his divine powers to increase the hurricane's energy. That twinned perfectly with the three dragons, who reared their heads toward the night sky and unleashed their fiery dragonbreath into the rushing winds. Instead of blowing out the fires, the increased oxygen concentration from Aristuto rapidly ignited the hurricane and set fire to the searing skies. The combination of such an attack was known as Rolganfire, Aristuto's signature, and the colossal inferno blazed toward Ramalon and his Dragadelf.

Only once before had he ever seen such sheer power of that scale. He cast his mind back to the grid of fire that was used to kill Arinane, to the firewall he used against Peter Palgan to win The Màgjeurs Open, and to Wemberlè hurling The Chopping Sea on top of him. None of them compared to this unique magnitude. Only his casting of The Protecy to destroy The Dragasphere was questionably stronger. Alas, this was different. Personal. It was positively magical and spellbinding to him, and he had but one response.

## Rolganfire

"Perfection," he whispered in admiration as his pupils squeezed shut to block out the blinding light that sped toward him.

His defence came by way of conjuring a vast bubble of water with his right hand, shielding both him and his Dragadelf.

Fire met water in an epic storm that hissed and steamed ferociously upon connection. The fire boiled Ramalon's defence, scalding his face and he very quickly understood that this attack was simply not going to stop. Ramalon was on the back foot. He had to act and fast.

He attempted to relax and allow his protecy to flow more purely, but even that struggled to match the supernatural force of Rolganfire which forced the wall of water ever closer toward him.

Aristuto understood that Ramalon was bound to one protecy at a time. Were he to release his defence of water which was proving moderately effective, the Rolganfire would consume him and his Dragadelf, though uncertainty ensued whether the beast would die under the extreme heat. After all, it was born from flames and how much immunity it had to its element was unclear.

Both Ramalon and the Dragadelf were being pushed back. It's head looking from right to left, trying to identify an opening it could fly through, but they were both trapped within Ramalon's bubble. He was struggling with ideas but came up with a plan to counter-attack.

Using a large portion of his magical stamina, he increased the water flow to expand upwards, which created more room and protection for his winged inferno to escape. Upon instruction, the Dragadelf activated its wings, soared into the fiery skies and disappeared. It seemed unafraid to be surrounded by the immense heat which brought concern to Aristuto, for he did not know where it had gone and could not spare an ounce of concentration to search for it. At the same time, his three dragons needed to keep fuelling the Rolganfire to keep the devastating attack alive.

Unfortunately for Ramalon, he could not sustain his defence any longer and with the remaining space he had left of his protective bubble, he used that time to quickly change the line of affinity. Typically, he morphed into his trusted defence of stone, embodying its element which had previously saved him on so many occasions.

The full force of Aristuto's attack scorched into Ramalon's body, causing immense pain. Ramalon wailed, feeling the burn through the stone, not expecting his defence to be so ineffective against the legendary attack. It was like standing at the heart of The Understunde, feeling Sarthanzar's rage head-on. He could not accept that his power was, at that point, inferior. It spurred on his rage and resolve to a place, not even he had ever gone to.

Consumed by nothing but turbulent inferno, he heavily braced against it, attempting to get closer to Aristuto. Alas, his embodiment was beginning to wain and portions of stone on various parts of Ramalon's body began to melt away, exposing his skin and torching it immediately, spattering his blood. He'd never felt pain like it before, crumbling to his knees in total agony. He had to call upon every masterful nuance of The Protecy to ensure the stoney constitution quickly morphed over the portions of exposure before it became fatal.

Ramalon sensed he was in trouble and did not feel confident he could last much longer. He was in a fight against a combination of the natural and the supernatural, which he needed a portion of luck to survive.

Fortunately for him, the blessings of Sarthanzar were with him, for his Dragadelf swooped in from the side in a pincer movement and cruelly crunched it's razor claws into the Dralen's midriff. It ceased it's breath immediately, roaring out brutally for the attack was fatal. The Dragadelf flexed its wings in a gust and cruelly hoisted the Dralen's dead carcass up into the air in such an ugly and distasteful way. It's boiling blood disappeared into the Rolganfire and beyond.

The Drogadera and the Charzeryx ceased their dragonbreath and instead wailed their grief toward the escaping Dragadelf. They could not abandon their cousin to such barbarity and so together, they flew after them, ascending into the dark rushing skies.

The tide had suddenly turned. Although the natural hurricane still raged furiously, it was no longer fuelled by Rolganfire giving Ramalon a moment of respite. Aristuto didn't need to concentrate his energies on fuelling the air any longer and could use it for another resource.

Ramalon felt relieved to no longer be under the immensity of Aristuto's attack and began to place his foot into the duel. As the dragon's cry was heard through the ferocious winds above, Ramalon continued his slow advance against the gale toward his target.

However, Aristuto was too cunning to face him off directly and so lifted his body up into the air, relaxed and allowed the natural force behind him to sail his body across the plains of The Rolgan Waste. He was fleeing the duel which made Ramalon fearful that he was escaping his fate, something that was entirely unacceptable to him.

Suddenly, an enormous thud crashed into the earth as the Dralen's body was unceremoniously dumped onto the battleground from above. That was quickly followed by another thud, this time from the Charzeryx' mangled carcass that landed on the stone. Not even the two of them combined were a match for the Dragadelf that would surely overcome the remaining Drogadera.

Ramalon had to find a way to catch up with Aristuto, who had fled the scene and so used his unnatural strength from the elements of earth to hurl himself high up into the air before morphing back into the flesh and like a parachute, allowed the hurricane to take his body with it in similar fashion.

In mid-air he spiralled out of control. To make matters worse, it was still pitch black on The Rolgan Waste so he tried to channel the affinity of fire to expel in specific directions to stabilise his uncontrollable glide and keep his flight sustained. It also provided a tiny portion of light, which helped him see a little clearer.

He managed to maintain a more controlled position as he rode the wave of wind, randomly casting lines of fire to try and spot The Blessèd Mage of Air, for which he could not.

He became distracted by a distant cry from above, which surely confirmed the Drogadera's demise, as he would have felt it if his Dragadelf had fallen. No such feeling came to the fore and his confidence increased by the second.

Suddenly, one of his flares that he'd conjured directly out in front appeared to be caught in the dark and as his body sped toward it, it exploded in front of him. He passed directly through the intense heat, melting his skin and setting his robes aflame which was instantly extinguished by the rushing winds.

He landed with a grotesque roll on the unyielding rock, causing bone-crudding pain and all of the air to momentarily shoot from his lungs. His diaphragm was paralysed, gasping for breath. His face was red from the radiation and his shoulder, exposed from the singed robes, blistered and bloodied. To make matters worse, he had no time to recover as he knew Aristuto was imposing himself from the dark.

How could he have let his guard down so easily, he thought? It angered him at how naive he had been during the fight. What hurt his pride and ego more was that he was experiencing mortality - the complete opposite of his ambition.

With what little he could conjure, he used his anger to impulsively throw balls of fire in the direction he thought Aristuto was ahead. The wind pelted in his face, causing the moisture in his eyes to squeeze away, although his attacks could still pierce through the oncoming force.

His anger subsided temporality to learn that Aristuto was not in the direction he thought but rather cleverly had sneaked behind him to land an attack. Ramalon caught the manoeuvre just in time and landed his flame directly in the darkness behind him, only to meet a very familiar defence that had occurred at the top of Dawnmorth's tower.

His flame consumed a spherical defence from The Blessèd Mage of Air, who'd conjured a bubble of air to encompass his safety. However, they both were now totally exposed to one another.

Ramalon's skin remained gravely burned and the longer the heat was maintained, the more pain he experienced. He was not at full strength, which Aristuto was fully aware of too. Their eyes met through the heat waves, intensely expelling their might to one another before Aristuto attempted to trap Ramalon's protecy precisely as he did on Dawnmorth. Ramalon anticipated such a move and preempted his response.

He squibbed down his own intensity, but just enough to maintain effectiveness to his fire, which made it seemingly more difficult for The Blessèd Mage of Air to trap. He called upon his own divinity, increasing the volume of air. It caused flares to often erupt from the line of Ramalon's fire, which made both of them struggle to control the volatile combustion.

If it wasn't for Ramalon's depleted strength, he probably would have enough to overpower his opponent, but as he wasn't, he had to be crafty.

The ferocious winds still battered behind him and directly into Aristuto who, in the process of trying to trap his counterpart, became trapped himself under Ramalon's mastery of The Protecy. He had one play to try and restore parity. The stench of glory perfumed against The Blessèd Mage of Air.

He directed his focus on funnelling a large portion of the hurricane directly into his defensive ball of air, which generated an erratic and unstable reaction, spewing atoms of fire all over the place, but with the intention to implode it to maximum effect. His idea was that if he was going to fall, he would take them both with him in a heroic display of sacrifice. Ramalon however, had sussed out what he was doing and in secret, carefully installed his response.

Emerging through the shadows came the vast silhouette of the Dragadelf, grounding itself behind its master. Aristuto was only moments away from completing his suicidal air-bomb but understood it would not be ready to detonate before Ramalon acted first. His eyes were that of a man who understood his fate and could not have been more opposite to the intense, satisfied eyes of his competitor.

In pure poetic fashion, he instructed his Dragadelf to raise its head toward the early morning sky and in precisely the same manner as the three dragons previously, it released it's dragonbreath into the hurricane, setting it aflame once more. It was a carbon-copy of Rolganfire and used The Blessèd Mage of Air's signature move against him. Ramalon himself quickly morphed back into the embodiment of stone to survive the apocalyptic force that he sent mercilessly into his victim.

"NOOOOOOOOOOOO!!!" Aristuto helplessly wailed as he felt his powers wither and dissolve, thwarting the self-detonating air-bomb he'd attempted to construct.

His defensive bubble corroded against the immense radiation and was totally exposed to the brutal heat that incinerated his body. He spread his arms wide, yelling with all his might, before his flesh began to peel from the bone, spattering his divine blood onto the ground behind what remained of his defiant skeleton. Until finally, the marrow had utterly disintegrated into thin air. The perfect way to bring an end to The Blessèd Mage of Air, Ramalon thought.

Upon his death, the consuming pyro-storm surprisingly began to simmer down and cease to a complete stillness…

Ramalon morphed back into flesh and immediately crumpled into the ground in utter exhaustion. That was perhaps the most challenging and draining fight he had to date. Consumed by euphoria, he stared up toward the fading stars, experiencing the oasis of relief and joy that was his reward.

His Dragadelf crouched down to inspect the damage done to his master with some concern. Never before had he felt so spent and utterly depleted. He was weak and living entirely off of fumes.

Alas, his glory and the thought of what he would become by finishing the job motivated him to carry out his task. He stumbled to his feet and gingerly walked over to the blood that was splattered on the ground. The faint light from the rising sun, still some way below the horizon, allowed him to identify where the blood dropped.

His movements were painful, chafing his exposed, bloody skin against his clothing. Alas, nothing would now stop him from claiming his last affinity.

He stooped over the blood that stained the rocks below and

painfully knelt on the ground. He placed his hand in the pool of The Blessèd Mage of Air's blood and began the process of absorbing its power and affinity for himself. Like gravity, every drop of claret filtered along the ground and directly into his palm. He lifted his hand ever so gently so that he could appreciate more the powers of air he fletched.

The smooth sensations swam up his arm and circulated throughout his body. He closed his eyes to indulge once more in how divine he felt. Every time he performed such a callous and evil practice, he was aware of getting ever more closer to immortality.

At last, the process was complete and Ramalon had finally claimed all six destructive affinities. It restored some level of his waining stamina and came to stand triumphantly in the dark. His Dragadelf crunched its claws into the ground, which crumbled like sand and roared it's might to acknowledge his master's powers.

As he listened to the ear-splitting cry which crackled for miles, he knew that he had only one more step to climb on his Staircase to Divinity…

The ceremonious triumph was interrupted by balls of black gas which circled and morphed into their constitutions before their master. The Ancient Drethai had arrived.

Ramalon did not react to their arrival, maintaining his focus. He was still embellishing the mesmerisation of defeating Aristuto. The shadow spirits stood before him, camouflaged in the dark background. Dreanor as usual spearheaded the ones that had arrived.

"Master," he respectfully announced, bowing his crowned head, exposing a fissure on his dark skull from the wound suffered by Ramacès many moons ago.

Ramalon slowly opened his eyes. "And what do you bring me?" he quietly asked as if the epic battle that had just taken place was nothing to him.

"We found it, Master! And we retrieved it."

"It?"

"The Dragastone!"

Dreanor revealed the relic from his hands. It illuminated the charcoaled complexions of The Drethai and shone marvellously. He looked up toward Ramalon to see that his unimpressed expression remained.

"Master?" Dreanor asked, unsure. "Does this not satisfy you?"

"And where did you obtain this?"

"The Draughts. That is where we found your brother -"

"- And where is he?" Ramalon wearily asked, looking among the ranks of the shadow order, veiling his threatening menace. "Where is my brother? The one you were tasked with bringing to me…"

The knife of anxiety was beginning to turn in Dreanor's throat. He knew his task was to bring both The Dragastone *and* Ramerick before him and had only achieved half of his duty. He swallowed the build of saliva that collected and learned very quickly that his failure was not going to be forgiven this time.

"… Master," Dreanor whimpered, slumping himself to the ground on both knees. "We were overpowered by something I had never seen before!"

Ramalon's expression remained underwhelmed, except for the intensity in his eyes, which soon shifted substantially to a more harrowing and unforgiving stare.

"You failed me," Ramalon explained, dangerously enunciating every syllable. "You understand that by not bringing him before me, you have left me exposed!"

"Master, I believe it had something to do with the sword!"

"What sword?"

"Your brother's sword!"

"Ramerick's blade is nothing but a Rolganic heirloom!"

"Not Ramerick's Master, it is the sword of Ramacès of which I speak!"

Ramalon blinked. His eyebrows furrowed and looked confused.

"Ramacès' sword?" he queried, looking downwards in deep thought.

"One moment, I had him under my control ready to bring him before you, and the next, the blade erupted a power far greater than anything we've ever experienced. Even our sworn nemesis, Master!"

Hearing that irked Ramalon immensely. Dreanor had not realised how much he offended his deity by admitting that whatever it was they had experienced was a power far greater than he himself. Something Ramalon took as an unforgivable betrayal.

His anger became impossible to contain; his body fumed and shook as not only was he insulted, but he had worked out how grave a miscalculation he had made.

It pained him to discover the truth behind what Ramacès really did that day when he sacrificed himself. He understood Ramerick had learned before him that Ramacès had preserved his soul in his sword, with the purpose to one day help destroy The Dragastone via his share in its ownership. It would mean Ramerick could sidestep the hex he planted and initiate its termination. There was no other explanation for Ramerick going to The Draughts.

How could he have missed something so vital, he asked himself? His embarrassment blew his barriers of stability wide open and rendered him exposed, vulnerable and more dangerous than ever before.

Luckily for him however, The Drethai did retrieve The Dragastone, which he did take as advantageous.

He marched over and swiped The Dragastone from Dreanor's offering hands and turned his back to them all. His eyes closed, worshipping the prized possession in his hands once more. He held it with the same delicacy as holding a new-born child, feeling spellbound that it was back in his grasp again.

"Things have now changed..." Ramalon warned. "From this moment forth, the value and protection of The Dragastone is of paramount importance. You will give your lives to defend it..."

Dreanor, still on his knees, did not know whether that was a merciful pardon or merely another chance to serve him. Ramalon was weak from his battle and that was their only saving grace.

"As always Master, we serve at your pleasure," Dreanor reminded him, utterly relieved.

"As long as the stone remains in my possession, they will never survive," Ramalon uncharacteristically spat. His furious impulses exposed his weakened stature.

The Ancient Drethai bowed their heads in unison. However, they were suddenly distracted by the arrival of another ball of black gas that morphed into form.

"Dreadath!" Dreanor exclaimed. "Where is Orb -"

Ramalon quickly extended his hand toward Dreanor to issue instant silence. He stared upon Dreadath, whose cold eyes never faltered... Alas, this was the first time such fear could be seen behind his notorious stare.

"Master," Dreadath solemnly greeted.

"I was wondering where a few of you had got to."

Dreanor realised very quickly that the fact that Dreadath had been released was not good news. He would not have escaped death, were it not for Ramerick's gain.

"I survived because your brother wanted me to deliver a message,"

Dreadath informed.

"Doing the enemies bidding now, I see?" Ramalon fumed. "And what did my brother hath to say?"

"He wants The Dragastone back."

"Of course he does."

"He said if you do not confront him at The Draughts, by sunrise… He will destroy his protecy stone of life."

Ramalon froze - petrified to hear of the ransom. Both Ramerick and Ramacès were proved right. They had unveiled and exposed, Ramalon's greatest fear and he could not believe how transparent his flaws had became.

Destroying the protecy stone of life would ultimately mean denying him his final kill and his last step to divinity. Everything he had built, both in enterprise and sentimentality, would all be for nothing. He had no choice but to accept his brother's demand.

The trapped feeling was likened to a caged dragon, distressed and panic-stricken. The notion of something forcing his hand banished all sense of reason and control.

Caught in a world where one half was achieving his poetic vengeance, while the other exposed the flaw in his philosophy perfectly. The balance of what was more important to him tipped heavily to one side and turned his world upside down.

In the process, it flicked the switch in Ramalon's mind…

"Master?" Dreanor tested quietly.

"AHHHHHHHHHHHHHHH!!!" Ramalon screamed like never before, unable to determine what was real or not anymore.

He lashed out his frustration onto The Ancient Drethai, releasing his fury entirely. He demonstrated his divine powers by wildly unleashing multiple affinities onto every member of The Ancient Drethai. Though they tried to defend themselves with dark magics, they was no match against the wrath of their deity who had spoken.

He wasn't sure he had ever felt that passionate about anything before, as he murdered every member in blind anger. Their deaths were confirmed upon seeing their black blood stain the ground beneath them and their bodies lifeless and still.

The Ancient Drethai were no more.

Ramalon could not care. Killing the ghosts of Terrasendia that had haunted the land for so many years did not make him feel any more powerful or satisfied.

He had lost control and that was mirrored by the squirming and thrashing of his Dragadelf behind him, feeling the same frustration.

Wasting no time with remorse or regret, he buried The Dragastone into his robes and climbed on top of his winged beast, who'd temporarily simmered down to allow easy boarding. It received instructions from its master to soar as fast as it could to The Draughts, for the rising rays of the sun beneath the horizon would soon warm his face.

## *The Trust in Heart*

The final stand consumed Terrasendia.

The elixir of motivation that powered the heart began to wain against such adversity. It had proved somewhat effective as for several hours they had beaten the enemy back, or at the very least held on with everything they could. However, the hope in Ramerick began to fade, wondering if the plan he was entrusted to fulfil was even close to being achieved.

Such a dooming realisation drowned their spirits and forced their hand to save as many lives as they could, for the sustainability of motivation could be held no longer.

The plains of Dwardelfia still swarmed with manced and as Thakendrax repeated the charge of his Rhinoauros back and forth between the city and open plains, his dwarves were being picked off each time. To make matters worse, the aerial defences which were barely holding, could not reach the outer distances away from the city. And there, the Dragadelf took full advantage.

Out of the morning skies, it glided from one end of the plain to the other, unleashing its dragonbreath onto the dwarves. Its attack was utterly devastating, instantly cremating portions of Thakendrax's army. One more round of charges would certainly all but end them. The Blessèd Mage of Gravitas had no options.

Still, on the open plains he directed one last charge into the city and made their way to the frigates and boats in an attempt to escape. Before they could successfully do that, they had to clear The Hewercraxen of Manced, for that was the only way to the dockyard.

They charged back through the city, cleaving off heads and dispelling white orbs before they reached the famous hall where they began to gut out the filth.

However, their hearts sank upon realising that the Dragadelf had wiped out a large portion of their fleet already. The sails were aflame and the wooden decks burned or destroyed. There was no way out for all of them. They were trapped within the vast hall of The Hewercraxen.

Thakendrax solemnly conceded that this would be their final stand. But if they were going to perish, they would do so in true dwarven-might, taking as much filth with them as they could. In particular, Thakendrax only had eyes for one thing to make his sacrifice worth doing.

He dismounted his Rhinoauros and organised his people to form a circle around his throne. That was where he would lure the Dragadelf in and bring down The Hewercraxen on top of it and everyone inside.

The dwarves understood what they had been asked to do and used every portion of fight left in them to give their King as much of a chance to pull off the sacrifice as they could.

The dwarves brawled inside The Hewercraxen. Thakendrax made his way to his throne and called upon the divine powers of gravity, deliberately crumbling the roof and destabilising the strong pillars that supported the famous hall. The Manced attempted to distract his efforts, but the fight in the dwarves contained their threats.

Until the moment had come to them at last. Staring beyond The Hewercraxen's entrance came the Dragadelf's eyes emerging through the dusty ruins of the city. It's constitution came into full view, sensing The Blessèd Mage of Gravitas' power and being drawn to him, as was the plan.

It's claws and wings entered the vast hall where the melee still ran rife. It's eyes only on the dwarven King who fearlessly stared back.

"Now there's a good boy!" Thakendrax lured.

The Questacèreans, now surrounded by the swarm of manced that lit up the inner city's circumference, were staring at their end. Being enclosed from the outside in, they too were trapped and could only squeeze out every second of survival they possibly could by calling upon the essences of life that they had received, for they had not the natural strength left to endure. Hope was all they had.

Mijkal positioned himself on the front line, casting breezes of freezing clouds that slowed their advance, but not even he had enough divinity to stop them all. They were being overpowered by the sheer number that just did not stop.

Not that he had any time to spare, but he noticed the tower that his chambers laid atop had grown its flowers and greenery again. Not even the frosting temperatures and surrounding evil could stop the thriving life. Mijkal took that as a sign to keep going and grind out every essence of hope against the blackening curtain that was drawing closer.

The trust he placed in Ramerick was absolute, for that was all he could do in the hope he would prevail.

"FALL BACK!!! FALL BACK!!!" issued the command of Luan, who galvanised the motion of retreat among the Septalians. The idea was that they would fortify their positions within the catacombs where the civilians previously resided, for they could hold them for much longer in a confined space.

It was an unsavoury move, as for the last few hours, the fightback was proving successful and in some cases, pushed The Manced back entirely. However, the enemy's numbers were too great and twinned with the Dragadelf, whose actions scorched The Blessèd Mage of Earth was crushing; he had no choice.

Meryx Meigar issued his mildens to pull back too, along with Farooq Manwa's bands and the other Durgeons of Septalia, to solidify the defence within the catacombs.

Alexa Greyman was forced to pull back her archers as well, understanding that holding her band's position on the high turrets would in fact trap them when The Manced completed their invasion of the city. However, her heart did not waver. Despite her orders, she defied them, knowing that the escaping civilians streaming into Aries Hollow would be given those extra seconds to retreat should she stay.

The moment of her insubordination was mixed with the moving memories of her son who she knew she would never see again. It was unlikely they would retreat in time anyway and only hoped her sacrifice would prove the difference between him making it and not. That devotion was also shared by the last remaining members of her band, who followed the sentiment and gave their all.

After barking the orders several times, Luan reluctantly accepted their decision and gave his heartfelt thanks before marshalling what was assuringly their final defence in the catacombs.

Nearly all Septalian Knights had entered the caves and formulated blockades that would provide their last act of buying time. The Manced scaled the mountains that encompassed the catacombs below in an attempt to pursue the fleeing civilians. They began to run riot onto a city that was on its last legs.

"Lestas!" cried Meryx as he spotted him on their retreat. "Where is my brother?"

A breathless Magraw looked solemnly into his eyes, and without using words, Meryx understood the fate of his brother.

"I am sorry," Magraw apologised sincerely. "I am so sorry…"

Meryx removed his helmet, closed his eyes and looked mournfully down toward the ground, suppressing his grief. He clutched Magraw's shoulder for help, but there was no time for heartache.

The substantial sound of smashing stone came from above as The Manced crashed through the roof of the catacombs.

In a surprising manoeuvre, a plethora of militants spilt into the caves from above, instantly animating their bodies upon splattering to the ground. Their already difficult plan became nearly impractical with their position suddenly impossible to defend, splitting their efforts to contain that as well as the main entrance. Alas, they expelled their Septalian wrath onto The Manced, fighting with everything they had left.

What was left of their courageous hearts was shattered upon seeing the silhouette of the Dragadelf entering the chasm. It gazed greedily into Septalia's last defence…

The ferocious roars of crying dragons deafened Gallonea below. Ethelba's rejuvenation was only temporary, as she and Jòsièra began to feel the weight of greatness cranking up the pressure.

## The Trust in Heart

By then, the nobleman and Rolgan Knights were forced onto the very top level, for their time was running out. The Manced swarmed most of Gallonea and continued their plaguing scourge. The hearts of men were flailing. Even the civilians took it upon them to arm themselves and fight with every last bit of drive they had.

Ethelba could not devote a second of time to slow them down, for a momentary lapse in defence would certainly prove costly against the Dragadelf.

However, that fear seemed inevitable, for the Dragadelf landed a sufficient swipe of its sharp tail across Jòsièra's belly, which caused it to burst wide open, spilling her molten blood. She painfully screamed to the top of her lungs and like a falling spider, her wings cramped up and flexed, struggling to maintain control of their spiralling plunge. They dived directly into the plains below, just outside Gallonea's walls. Luckily, Jòsièra fluttered her elegant wings just before their crash landing to give some absorption.

The Drogadera was fatally injured. She was losing a lot of blood, and her strength was waning by the second. Ethelba dismounted her dragon and struggled to see what she could do to help. She attempted to seal the wound by melting portions of her dragon-scales to congeal and stop the bleed. Jòsièra wailed in agony at her master's attempts, trying to escape the pain but they had no time to lick their wounds.

The Blessèd Mage of Fire was soon surrounded by oncoming militants, frenzying toward her with unnatural speed. Much of her energy remained depleted from the fire battle in the sky but she had enough to hurl a whirling ring of fire around her and her wounded Drogadera and successfully repel the advance.

The unlucky militants that ran through the fire instantly dismantled, followed by the white mist to wisp into The Gracelands.

However, that momentary protection was soon in jeopardy once more. Ethelba did not see the Dragadelf emerging from above, exposing it's sharp claws and aiming for the petite Blessèd Mage. Were it not for the heroic sacrifice of Jòsièra who, with one last surge of life, propelled herself directly at the oncoming Dragadelf to take the blow, Ethelba would not have seen it in time.

Her sacrifice ensued with another fatal cry, confirming the cruel mangling that would take her life. Ethelba had to keep the ring of fire going, otherwise she would be overrun with manced. She could only watch on in utter despair, viewing the desperate suffering of her faithful Drogadera.

With no respect for the suffering creature at it's feet, the Dragadelf stomped Jòsièra's broken body into the ground and, swooping in for a final blow, it exposed it's cruel razor-sharp claws and pierced them directly into the Drogadera's eyes. Though the dying Drogadera did not have the energy to fight back, she did have the strength to express her agony and squirm distastefully.

The Dragadelf continued its torment and did not release the claws now embedded firmly inside her skull. After some feeble wriggling and decrepit fluttering of Jòsièra's wings, the Dragadelf began to pull at the Drogadera's crown, like a vulture tearing apart a piece of meat. After a few attempts, her cranium began to fissure and crack against the immense strength, making Ethelba weep uncontrollably.

The skull eventually cracked at the temples and yet the Dragadelf carried on its merciless mutilation, ripping down her spine and detaching one vertebra at a time. The horrible sound of deep cracking bone echoed sickeningly.

Jòsièra understood her fate and with one last grunt of effort, she expelled the last of her fires from her core which shot out through her mouth and exposed spine, burning the Dragadelf's eyes. Alas, it was nowhere near enough to make any difference. In fact, in only spurred it's hate on further.

As the dragonbreath erupted through her cracked spine, the Dragadelf waited until it stopped, only to then dive its wing through her exposed spine, broken ribs and mythical organs to find what it was looking for. With no mercy, it pierced its claws through her weak, pulsing heart and with one enormous pull, it ripped Jòsièra's heart from the connecting vessels and straight out of her back. Blood spurted everywhere, followed by a complete stillness to Jòsièra's disfigured body and her lifeless eyes, which all but confirmed her death.

The Dragadelf roared to the skies to celebrate its gruesome triumph and total domination of its opponent. The disgusting display was nothing more than a platform to demonstrate its phenomenal strength and bravado.

Ethelba was completely numb. She could not have envisaged a worse end for something so beautiful and so full of good. It inspired her rage, which she allowed to flow through her protecy.

All of a sudden, her ring of fire extended out, blazing much of the area around her, obliterating the lower walls of Gallonea. The flare radiated toward the Dragadelf as well, who felt the burn and returned its dragonbreath onto her. She concentrated all her energy on meeting it with her own fires again, ferociously scorching the ground ablaze, taking the beast head-on, alone.

Despite her anger fuelling what appeared to be an equal measure of strength, she no longer had the defensive ring around her to withstand The Manced that manically charged in her direction. She was trapped and did not know how to escape what appeared to be her fate.

During their epic pyro-storm, she noticed a singular streak of sunlight from the corner of her eye that rose from the horizon.

The borrowed time that Terrasendia had bought was up.

## The Band of Brothers

Under the lonely statue of Ramacès some half a mile above, Ramerick waited. The haunting stillness hummed an air of anxiety as he knelt by his Meigarthian sword and Sythero, stabbed firmly into the soil. His palms and pits greased, tightly clutching his necklace, which gleamed a fluorescent white. He remained fully committed to going through with its termination should Ramalon not arrive.

He knew deep down that he would come, having understood that Ramalon's final step to divinity was more important to him than all the rest combined. Just how much of an advantage could he possibly squeeze to give him that one desperate chance to destroy The

Dragastone?

Though the fear of failure and the possibility of eternal purgatory frightened him to the marrow, he only hoped that Ramalon would be too naive and blinded by vanity and power to understand what he was truly capable of. Especially considering how close he was to his heart's desire.

One thing that did surprise him somewhat was that he no longer feared using The Protecy. He actually indulged in the prospect of harnessing its power in his own symbolic rhetoric, should it come to that. As The Dragastone had fractured, it would only render Ramalon more fearful the more active it was. The chances were that it would still hold both their protecy's at the same time but he was fairly confident that if he did strike it with the Meigarthian sword, it's destruction would be complete.

The dying embers of the previous conflict omitted a warm glowing orange, but Ramacès' Garden remained invigorated and full of life. The mixture of offensive smokey aromas, infused with the natural greenery's calming scent captured the glooming reality perfectly.

He instructed Hiyaro, Zathos and Susmees to take their bands as far away from The Draughts as possible, for he had to be alone. This one last desperate attempt to lure Ramalon in was vital and he could not take the chance of their presence ruining that. One way or another, the end was in sight, but for whom was entirely uncertain.

He glanced up toward the stoney figure of his brother above, looking to him for inspiration and hope. That wish became short-lived, for the warming presence of the rising sun warmed The Draughts' entrance.

Time had expired and Ramalon was nowhere to be seen. Many moments of nothingness passed...

Ramerick's mouth slowly came agape, his eyes bemused as to why his brother had not come. He felt so assured he would. What if he was wrong and Ramalon really did not come? Would he really cut off his nose to spite his face? He began to doubt if he really understood his brother and exactly how important it was for him to climb that last step - how could he have misjudged it so massively?

The passing of the seconds felt like an eternity as the sun rose higher, but he trusted his instincts to wait just a few moments longer. However, after realising that Ramalon was not coming, his heart regrettably sank. It was their only play left and the cold heart of his brother seemed to prove him wrong. They both were to lose... Alas, for

Ramerick and Terrasendia, the sheer gravity of loss would ultimately weigh heavier on their shoulders.

The shaking of his hand vibrated against his protecy stone as he was left with no choice but to call Ramalon's bluff. He spared one last thought for those on Terrasendia who had depended on him and gave his deepest apologies to all that he'd failed. The trust in his heart wasn't enough to save them. Though he thought to himself that if they had done anything differently, the outcome would likely have been the same and that did not comfort him in his last moments.

With nothing left to hope for and no back-up plan to save Terrasendia in time, he allowed the opportunity of stillness and peace in Ramacès' Garden to remember what he fought for. He looked among the beauty life had to offer and conceded that although he would destroy his stone, it would provide a small portion of pride that Ramalon would never again be able to touch.

He rose from his kneeling position, ripped the necklace from his neck and held the white, gleaming elixir in front of his eyes. He closed them one final time and, using the magical senses of The Protecy, he latched on to the crux of the connection, ready to terminate its essence.

Amid the slow decay of time, he felt a substantial presence looming at the entrance. His heart stopped, pleading to any supernatural there ever was, for it to be him… That prayer was answered.

A sudden fireball scorched across The Draughts and completely obliterated the statue of Ramacès above. The rocky fragments and debris of his brother rained over him like a brief monsoon.

Despite the obliteration of his brother's remains, Ramerick could not help but feel encouraged and inspired that Ramalon had come, quickly relaxing the termination of his stone. He uplifted his Meigarthian sword and held it firmly in his grasp. Ramerick's ransom had worked. Hope had been re-kindled.

Gliding into the underground chasm, the Dragadelf circled the entirety of The Draughts and set aflame to Ramacès' Garden. The timbers of woods and greenery ignited with ease, destroying the ecosystem and soon turned it into what looked like the chamber of an erupting volcano.

Heat seared, fire roared and the smoggy toxins stung sharply at the back of their throats, coughing deeply to break up the mucus. Ramalon, who straddled the mythical beast, had caught sight of his brother, who remained in the centre of The Draughts seemingly unafraid.

## The Band of Brothers

Destroying what remained of Ramacès' body and burning his garden had to be a small win for Ramalon, Ramerick thought. A clear acknowledgement of his frustration that he had missed his brother's long term plan. Still keeping some distance, he brought his Dragadelf to land in front of Ramerick, sweeping fiery embers in his direction.

Fuelled by the fright of what they could do to the other, their eyes absorbed into one another. A sense of paralysis consumed them both. There was nothing left to hide.

Ramalon felt cheated, like a fish being hooked by the lip. He argued in his mind that because he achieved so much more than his brothers ever could, it should by definition, give him the right to dictate terms. Alas, he conceded that Ramerick's thundering blackmail was critical. The simple notion that he had come was proof enough of how desperate and vulnerable his brother made him.

For Ramerick, he could not hide his everlasting hatred for the brother he'd barely known. Not only thoughts about the war that raged in his name, but images of his son came to the fore as well. It birthed a niggling temptation to destroy his protecy stone out of spite and impulsion, which grew more potent by the second. It became more personal.

The standoff buckled their diaphragms, causing their breaths to stammer out. Ramalon cautiously dismounted his mythical inferno, gingerly footing the ground as if he was walking on thin ice, afraid it may crack with one weighty step. He could not withdraw his gaze from his deceitful brother in fear that it would somehow result in immediate termination if he did.

He felt weaker than ever, not yet recovered from his efforts with Aristuto and Wemberlè, he had no time to recharge. However, his arrogance and determination powered him through the barriers of fatigue, biting off more than he could admittedly chew. Despite his trust in The Dragastone, the notion that it was damaged and could be used by Ramerick only played down his heralded advantage. He anxiously approached his brother and stopped with some distance still between them.

It seemed that fate had summoned them both to their last endeavours. Alas, it was Ramalon who blinked first.

"So here we are..." he nervously announced. "Tell me, brother. What right do you have to challenge me?" he asked with a lick of hatred.

"I have the same right as every man, woman and child you take the life of Ramalon," he responded firmly.

Rarely did he find anything humorous, but Ramalon could not help but scoff a reserved laugh. His eyes drew toward the Meigarthian blade in his brother's hands.

"It's a shame about our dear older brother. If he can hear me in there," he goaded toward the sword. "I'll admit. You came close. Very, close. But I now understand the truth behind what he did that day... You know, when I planned your death, I did not foresee you would actually present me with eternal life. How perfect things have turned out. But I wonder. What would hurt you most? Death? No, no, that would not be enough," he mused, trying to establish the core of Ramerick's worst fear. "Life? You've endured so much pain it would not surprise me that simply living would be torment enough. Or maybe there's something else..." Ramalon's eyes wandered as he tapped his long fingers on his chin, then tailed back into his brother's face, landing convincingly on a theorem. "You want to see him again, don't you? You seek the means to see your son again..." he slowly revealed with something that resembled a wicked smile. "Your heart's desire..."

A painful pang gutted in Ramerick's stomach, for his worst fear had been prized open with the knife of truth. He swallowed the collecting saliva, his body becoming frailer as his heart thudded more intensely. Though he endeavoured to show strength, resisting the urge to give Ramalon the reactions he craved.

"If you take my soul, you'll never achieve divinity," Ramerick lectured.

"Wrong! When I take your soul, who on this world could ever challenge me? That by definition is divinity! And only you stand between me and immortality that awaits. But I offer you a choice..." he aired suspiciously. "Give me your protecy stone, and I will allow your soul to pass wherever it please. I will allow you eternity with your son. Deny me, and you will receive no such mercy..."

Having his worst fear of being soul manced laid bare onto the table, it was only right to respond in the same reprimanding manner.

"You seem to forget that you have more to lose," Ramerick lied.

"Is that so?"

"In this..." Ramerick revealed his necklace in his hand and teased it toward his brother. His reaction was far from subtle, sensing how close he was to it and how anxious it was that Ramerick could terminate it in a flash. "Show me The Dragastone. Or I *will* destroy it!" he threatened.

Ramalon took offence to his offer being rejected but reluctantly obliged his brother's demand. "As you wish," he whispered. That familiar irking riled Ramalon ragged, reaching inside his robes and presenting The Dragastone in all its flawless glory.

An ethereal haze of bright lights gleamed on both sides. The stones shone marvellously, lighting up each other's faces in awe. Jealousy ran through Ramalon to know that its power was shared by the man standing before him.

Ramerick remained defiant that all he needed to do was touch his sword with The Dragastone and it would be over. On the flip side, should his necklace be out of his possession for even a moment, he would have no bargaining chip left and he would be at his brother's mercy. It seemed that both would have to make the ultimate concession to untie the impasse. Time was very much of the essence, for every second that went by, a life was lost on Terrasendia.

"Let's finish this the only way we can," Ramerick proposed. "Lay down the stone and I will do the same…"

Ramerick knew there was no way Ramalon would give up The Dragastone just like that and had no choice but to expose both of their fears to present him with that slight chance he so desperately needed.

Ramalon considered the proposal and despite leaving The Dragastone exposed, he entrusted the confidence he always placed upon it to prevail. There was no doubt about it; he was immensely more powerful than Ramerick, even in his weakened state and so cautiously accepted. After all, since discovering his true powers, he had yet to fail any challenge, boosting his confidence in his abilities further.

Despite his brother being The Blessèd Mage of Life and, ironically him being the closest thing to an immortal, the level of immunity Ramalon could endure surely had a breaking point. The attraction of surpassing yet another impossible feat and killing that which could not be killed, brought his pathological poetic justice to the surface once more, tempting him further to achieve what no one else could.

It seemed both of them were relieved at the mutual resignation of their stones as they placed them down ceremoniously on the ground before them. What was clear was that whoever would lose this battle would lose everything.

With the stones out of both their grasps, it would seem any attempt to reclaim them would be futile, as the other could unleash an attack and thwart their attempts before they could reach them. There was no going back now.

Amid the tense standoff between them, Ramalon understood what he was sure that his brother didn't.

"You are a fool, brother. How blind you really are!"

Before Ramerick could respond, he sensed the looming presence of the Dragadelf emerge behind Ramalon. It's deathly growl simmered as it bore its unrelenting gaze onto him. It seemed that Ramalon had given the mythical dragon instructions to inflict harm onto his brother at the right moment.

Nothing could have been a more poetic end for Ramalon than to use the Dragadelf, the symbol and flagship of The Dragastone's existence, to pave the way for his final step to divinity.

Ramerick genuinely did not know what to make of this. The concept of his association with the beasts ended when he tried to terminate The Dragastone… Or so he thought.

All of a sudden, Ramerick experienced vivid sensations that became so strong that he began to feel the Dragadelf's presence within him. It's warm, windy breath flowed as he breathed it himself, it's molten blood boiled and it's heartbeat pulsed so strong it nearly cracked a rib. He felt the power that made him come to the defining conclusion that he still had a share in The Dragadelf's ownership. A concept that surprised him and yet he was infinitely encouraged by. Unaware of this connection, Ramalon entertained his looming victory.

"Your soul it is," Ramalon declared, moments before inciting his Dragadelf to rain fire onto his brother.

Despite the sentimentality, he knew Ramalon never used the Dragadelf to fight his battles for him. He began to understand that his brother was not convinced he could kill him by himself, and even though he gave off that aura of supreme confidence, he spotted behind Ramalon's eyes true fear. That was precisely the reason why he was choosing to use the Dragadelf instead of attempting it himself. He was sacrificing his ego and self-righteous pride in order to certify victory in his mind. That sense of desperation reminded Ramerick of one vital concept. Ramalon was mortal.

The beast's neck wriggled in preparation, it's claws grounded firmly and it's hungry growl rumbled… But it did not obey its master's instruction right away.

Ramalon blinked. He could not quite understand why the Dragadelf was not breathing its dragonbreath onto his brother as commanded. He slowly turned around to see it's magnificent head looking back and forth among both of the brothers. It appeared a little distressed and unsure of Ramalon's command.

"Kill him! NOW!" Ramalon barked. Still, the Dragadelf did not heed the command. "NOW!!!!" he ordered once more, which tipped the distressed beast over the edge.

It seemed it was trapped in two minds, one half wanting to fulfil its command, while the other argued that doing so would be a harmful betrayal. Unable to come to a decision, it roared its deafening might to no one in particular and began to thrash it's wings and tail unpredictably.

Ramalon had to dive for cover as the Dragadelf had seemingly lost control. Somehow, amid the chaos, it's swishing tail swiped The Dragastone in one direction down the stretch of The Draughts while sending the necklace down the other. Sythero was sent spiralling into the distance, though Ramerick did not clock which direction it headed.

Both brothers quickly saw where both stones went, but it was too risky to make any sudden movements. They did not know the state of mind the Dragadelf was in, nor who it would really answer to. Ramalon took centre stage of its connection and attempted to reason with it. Eventually, his words successfully soothed the beast, which brought it down to some form of calmness.

Ramalon looked jealously toward his brother, completely dumfounded. Rarely was he surprised and he could not understand why Ramerick still had control over his Dragadelf. Something which was a surprise to them both.

"This cannot be..." he whispered in genuine disbelief. "You violated their loyalty!"

"Apparently not."

"The Dragadelf are MINE!!!" he venomously spat.

"No," Ramerick could not help but slap a justified smile on his face, working it out on the spot. "You stopped that from happening the moment you hexed that stone!"

Ramalon shook his head defiantly. "They answer to power! They will only obey me!"

The Dragadelf seemed to acknowledge that statement with a hesitant wriggle of the neck and grumbling purr. It did not feel like a convincing reaction, only to then ease away from them both, like a whimpering dog sensing danger. It darted it's head back and forth between them and could no longer withstand the stress. It gusted its wings and flew directly toward the entrance, soaring out of sight.

It was the first time Ramalon's command was not obeyed and he took his retreat as a heartbreaking betrayal. Memories of Arinane came flooding back to the surface and how similar it all felt to not have something so perfect belong to him anymore. He was scared to experience that sense of loss again, which caused his walls of stability to crumble.

"For as long as I live, you will never be immortal!" Ramerick declared, utterly defiant and charged.

His brother looked entirely despondent, watching the beast abandon him, like a child who would never get to see their loving parent again. Accepting the loss, he turned his head back toward Ramerick, his gormless face reminiscent of stone. His eyes fixed onto his brother's, deadpan and vacant of emotion. A dangerous pause was born…

"Well, we'll have to change that then, won't we?" he replied bluntly.

With both brothers poised and charged, Ramalon yelled to the top of his lungs and conjured a colossal wave of black heat from his palm that mercilessly ripped across the space between them.

Ramerick responded by gripping the Meigarthian sword in one hand and with the other unleashing his own protecy of trademark white fire. Once more, their phenomenal fires combusted into a violent fireball, spitting out licks of flames.

The Dragastone down the stretch of The Draughts lit up like a star, recognising both active protecy's. And thus, Terrasendia held its breath, for its fate laid in the hands of The Band of Brothers.

Any life that was in Ramacès' Garden was now destroyed. The sheer heat omitted from their flames seared so intensely that it rivalled the sun's surface.

As Ramalon hurled his epic fires onto Ramerick, he unchained every magical restraint of The Protecy he could. He had never felt so exposed in his life and could not survive the torturous jealously.

Ramerick, on the other hand, was under no illusion. Their duel in Monarchy Hall was all part of Ramalon's broader plan to destroy The Dragasphere and curtailed a portion of his strength. There was nothing to hide anymore. No deceitful plans, no cunning moves to gain an advantage. It was merely an unshackled demonstration of his truthful power. However, Ramalon was not as strong as he had envisaged. His strength had not yet recovered from his earlier battles and that gave Ramerick hope that he could place his own foot in the duel.

With that said, Ramalon's overwhelming mastery did push the ball of black fire ever closer to Ramerick's position. The radiation began to melt his skin, causing him to wail in agony. It regenerated and healed over due to his divine powers with incredible speed but he felt that his limits of life preservation were not infinite, as his divinity would seem. Just how much he could mortally take was entirely unknown.

Ramerick had to do something before he was consumed and knew that he needed to somehow get to The Dragastone. He concentrated on relaxing his protecy to increase the flow. It moved the fire's concentration back to the middle, but only temporarily, for Ramalon did the same and encroached the flames back onto him again.

Something had changed in Ramalon's mind as he seemed more unstable, unhinged even, as he gritted his teeth in desperation. He had lost all composure at the abandonment by his Dragadelf and the possibility of failing at his last hurdle. His sudden uncertainty and fear pushed him further to the edge of his sanity. Ramerick on the other hand, maintained his steely, hopeful determination that he was on level footing with his brother, which urged him to dig deeper than he ever thought he was capable of.

Both brothers were exerting a tremendous amount of effort in their powers, fuelling each others protecy against the other, to the point where suddenly, they both felt a substantial jolt in their attacks. An escaping feeling likened to that of blowing up a balloon that had already been pierced. It caused them to work harder to achieve the same level of energy.

It wasn't too long before they understood why as they caught sight of The Dragastone expelling fire from itself. Both brothers understood what this meant in that The Dragastone was weakening. Its fracture could not contain the entirety of both protecy's opened simultaneously and forced the stone's casing to break. The theory of the stone's vulnerability was proving to be spot on.

Ramalon's anxiety rose and he decided to act fast. He needed to ease the pressure somehow and turned his affinity into water, hissing steam as Ramerick's fires continued. He swirled impressive jet-streams in his brother's direction, which he combated away with fires as usual.

For Ramerick, it was in his interest to conjure as much of The Protecy as he possibly could, as it would only damage The Dragastone further. Still, he needed to get to it, for that was the only way for certain to end the war. His own protecy stone was no longer essential for either of them. He tried to edge his way closer to where The Dragastone was, but Ramalon was wise to his plan.

With the knowledge of how fragile The Dragastone had become,

Ramalon could not simmer his temper with the balance of how much energy to conjure. In a desperate attempt to reclaim the advantage, he showcased his maleficent evil and impulsively barraged his brother with attacks from all affinities. And it worked. Shocks of lightning, spikes of ice, and rock fragments were all conjured and fired rapidly, using the force of air to land his blows more substantially.

Ramerick had no choice but to take cover behind several of the structural pillars that remained. Their foundations shattered when hit by Ramalon's hurling missiles and continued to jump to the nearest one, counter-attacking with his own flames. Alas, they were infective against the various affinities. He was being forced away from where The Dragastone laid and was then seemingly further away from it than his brother.

He decided that because Ramalon was more cautious about using his protecy, he unleashed a devastating white fireball onto him, hoping to take advantage of his paranoia. It may have worked were it not for his brother omitting a lightning strike first, which landed flush into his chest. The force sent him spiralling some fifty metres back, landing in a pile of ashes behind.

Searing aftershocks began to electrify his body and he became temporarily paralysed. The essences of restoration began to flow through his body, repairing the damage. He tried to stabilise and bring himself to look at how close Ramalon was to reclaiming the stone... In the blink of an eye, he arrived at where it was and had already reclaimed it into his hands.

Staring from afar, he could sense the happiness and euphoria that it was back in his possession. And yet, he had no bargaining chip left, in that he no longer knew where his protecy stone had got to.

Ramalon studied the stone carefully in his hands to identify that The Dragastone was indeed damaged beyond repair. However, it remained strong and robust enough to complete his mission, which gave him confidence.

With his task seeming now impossible to overcome, Ramerick noticed the handle of Sythero buried in a nearby pile of ash. He came up with an idea to get closer to the stone, though he was not entirely convinced it would work.

With his fears somewhat quelled, Ramalon indulged in the brief lull. He took inspiration and strength from having the stone in his hands. Staring down the main stretch of The Draughts, he delivered his final piece.

# The Band of Brothers

"So... Brother... How would you like your soul ripped from you?" he perfumed his arrogance, panting heavily. His voice was raised to carry through the vast expanse of crackling rubble.

Ramerick stumbled to his feet, using the Meigarthian sword to hoist himself up. Struggling for clean air against the toxic fumes that choked him, he responded from the heart.

"You can't do that..." he shook his head, raising his voice in the same manner.

"And why not?"

"Because I'd like to die, just how I lived my life... And I lived happily... And so, you cannot grant me that... For you do not know what it is like... To be truly happy..."

Ramalon's eyes intensified once more. He understood that to be true and replaced it with continuing hatred once more.

"I didn't say anything about dying!" he vehemently replied through gritted teeth.

Anticipating another attack, Ramerick quickly dived for Sythero and channelled his protecy to ignite his legendary sword.

The move instantly charged and cooked The Dragastone in Ramalon's hands, causing him to drop it immediately and be hit by a resulting flame that erupted from its casing. The force sent Ramalon spiralling back, which gave Ramerick a chance to get closer to it.

The Dragastone was equidistant from both of them at that point and Ramalon grew angrier and more impulsive than ever before. His grip on everything he has built was slipping through his fingers.

Ramalon aggressively sent a plethora of various attacks once more to slow him down but Ramerick wielded both swords and positioned them in an "X" position to ward off the attacks. Both Sythero and the powers running through the Meigarthian blade successfully absorbed every missile, causing Ramalon's desperation to overload him.

Realising his ineffectual attempts, he'd had enough and allowed his impulses to run riot. Hoping that The Dragastone would withstand the intensity, he unleashed an apocalyptic hurricane of fire similar to Rolganfire which entirely consumed his brother. He blessed it with every portion of frustration and anger he could muster, hoping to end his brother in the same way as their father. An end that in his eyes would be fitting and poetic enough.

The magic in Sythero lit up substantially and deflected most of the passing inferno. The immense radiation however, caused immeasurable pain onto The Blessèd Mage of Life. He could feel his flesh scorch and peel away, only for his essence of life to rapidly regenerate the damage, and repeat the torture.

The up-side for him was that both protecy's of fire were being conjured at the same time which caused The Dragastone to once more fracture and spew flames from its casing. The down-side was that the threshold of his powers was being put to the sword.

It became a race between the fragility of the stone and how much Ramerick's body could possibly endure. He'd never felt pain like that in all his life.

To his frightening surprise, he began to sense the unique smell of melting steel that he familiarised all too well. Amid the intense heat, Sythero; his magical relic that was forged from fire itself, could not withstand the unprecedented flames and began to melt in his hand.

"AHHHHHHHHH!!!" Ramerick cried against the raging inferno.

The additional protection Sythero gave finally disintegrated away, exposing Ramerick's body to the full blast, entirely unprotected. Although the Meigarthian sword did not melt, it could not protect him from the devastation that ravaged him.

His skin was being torched alive, feeling his muscles peel from his bones when the flesh was gone. The divine powers of eternal life began to fade under the intense threshold he could endure. Alas, the essences failed to repair his body in time, resulting in Ramerick finally surrendering to the colossal pressure.

His body flew back and he flummoxed to the ground, cremating everything in the nearby radius. Luckily, The Dragastone became so volatile in its fracturing that Ramalon was forced to cease his attack the moment he could.

Its resistance hung by a thread, as well as Ramalon himself, who desperately inhaled what air was left, crumpling to his knees. He too, was spent of energy and wondered whether he had done enough to kill his brother. No such feelings of divinity or immortality crowned him.

Utterly spent of fight and willpower, Ramerick lay motionless - scorched on the blackened earth beneath him. His mind detached from his body and though he was still alive, the notion that he had defied death so stunningly paralysed him. The powers of his protecy stone, somewhere in The Draughts, nearly spent. He had nothing left anymore to give and resigned all hope.

It was a step too far. Even processing the concept that he had lost didn't bother him anymore. Not even the imagined voices of his

## The Band of Brothers

family, whispering in his mind to get up and fight, could inspire him to persist and fight any longer. Complete despondence consumed him. He was done.

To make matters worse for The Blessèd Mage of Life, and to that extent Terrasendia, Ramalon struggled to his feet. Fate loomed as he regained his magical stamina and made his way toward his fallen brother.

Time decayed and slowed down. Ramerick would allow it to happen, knowing there was nothing he could do. He couldn't feel his broken body any longer... Except for a strange sensation that began to manifest from his hand, still wrapped around the Meigarthian sword.

To his utter surprise, he felt his arm motor to life without his conscious instruction, as if possessed with a surge of adrenaline. That same empowerment began to spread to his heart and then around his entire body. It was the exact strength he received when he caught the sword in front of Dreanor and thus, he knew precisely what was happening.

Once more, Ramacès was giving his shoulder to lean on. And more...

Connected to his brother's soul via the sword, it magically instilled into Ramerick, his brother's strength. It brought him to stumble to his feet at that magical moment with the purpose to help him finish this once and for all.

Ramalon stopped in his tracks, with the stone once again an equal distance between them. Completely bewildered at how his brother was still alive, let alone seemingly strong enough to re-challenge him, tipped his frustration over the edge. He could not work out why his powers of life did not fail and defy him accomplishing the impossible.

With his body being powered by Ramacès' strength, he inspired the dying embers in Ramerick to give everything he had left. Sourced by sheer hatred, he stared full of intent and determination toward his evil brother, one last time.

Ramalon understood just where he got his revival of strength from. He sensed via their eye contact that he was not only looking at Ramerick but Ramacès too, connecting The Band of Brothers once more.

He pieced the puzzle together and the penny dropped with the same force as a thousand crashing Dragastone's. That precise moment, he understood, was foreseen by their father. And more poignantly, he had seen the outcome of what was to happen, which allowed Felder to let every event over the last thirty years to happen. A revelation that he understood both Ramerick and Ramacès had also foreseen. It rendered Ramalon utterly afraid for his life, knowing he was up against the mere existence of his father's sons.

His eyes mellowed, his mouth gaped, understanding that everything he had built was never going to last…

Ironically he felt as though his soul had left him and in one last attempt to defy destiny, he unleashed the same mythical hurricane of fire, yelling at the top of his lungs.

The fires ripped through Ramerick's body once more, entombing him like their father. However this time, instead of defending himself, Ramerick allowed the inferno to torch his body, concentrating everything he had left on the powers of preserving life.

With the Meigarthian sword in the hand powered by Ramacès' strength, Ramerick trudged into the phenomenal heat, like ploughing through thick snow. The deathly pain resumed once more, but luckily the elixir of life held together at that moment, re-piecing his melting skin faster than ever before.

After several minutes of enduring the biblical inferno, Ramacès got his brother to within several metres of The Dragastone, animating ever closer.

Both their faces grimaced with pain and unrelenting fury onto one another. There was nothing Ramalon could do then but hope the powers of life would not outlast him.

Ramerick finally arrived within arms reach of The Dragastone that had consumed all of their lives. It's roaring flames continued to erratically erupt from the fissures in its casing. Ramerick contorted his burning muscles to raise the Meigarthian sword in both hands, which was so heavy it felt like lifting a thousand swords.

Ramalon sensed his time was up and once more yelled with as much primal instinct as was humanly possible, which sounded more like a desperate plea to not go through with it.

Ramerick denied that request and opened his protecy onto his Meigarthian sword. White fire set aflame to the entirety of the blade in the pyro-storm, leaving just one more protecy to open…

And with that, he too yelled to the top of his lungs, echoing his destiny inside his fiery tomb and swung the blade with incredible might, down onto The Dragastone.

The force connected with the same devastation as when it crashed into Monarchy Hall thirty years ago. Unable to withstand the sheer velocity of all three protecy's opened at the same time, it overcharged and self-destructed, resulting in a titanic explosion that consumed both brothers and beyond.

Every structural pillar in The Draughts instantly vaporised in the detonation. The blast continued upward, forcing through millions of tonnes of rock above and obliterated the chasms roof wide open. Reminiscent of a super-volcano, rock and stone were erupted so high, it disappeared from the atmosphere of Rèo. Everything within many miles of The Draughts was utterly decimated as The Dragastone's destruction echoed into every corner of Terrasendia.

The Dragadelf were the first to feel its existence was no more, ceasing their fiery breaths in their various locations and contorting their colossal bodies into themselves. The mere presence of The Dragastone that had sustained them and allowed them to survive was gone. Their constitutions began to struggle with the absence of the energy that fed them for thirty years, spreading their wings as wide as they could, roaring to the skies, before imploding with incredible force.

Everything nearby was blown back at their destruction. The sound of a thousand thunders echoed throughout the land. Molten blood spattered the halls of The Hewercraxen, in the catacombs on Durge Helm, and in front of Ethelba on Gallonea. The lonely Dragadelf that escaped the Draughts exploded as well, leaving a magnificent cloud of debris against the morning sky.

Adding to The Dragadelf's demise, The Manced also shared that same depletion of ownership. Giving off ear-splitting deathly cries, every white orb that powered a host began to pull away from their exposed chests before eventually popping out and causing every globe to smash. Their tortured bodies instantly crumbled to the ground, the life in their eyes ceased to exist, while their souls cried into eternity, finally escaping their purgatory. They were free at last.

Ramalon's armies ceased to exist all over the land, staving off the threat with only seconds left to spare. Euphoria consumed every corner, but it was a muted sense of joy, for no one could believe that Terrasendia was truly saved...

The ghostly remnants of battle haunted all those that survived. They could not process just how lucky they were to be alive - that the war was really over. They honoured their survival with a stillness that calmed.

A white haze began to distil over Terrasendia, reminiscent of a mourning fog. The hundreds of thousands of souls that had been freed were also cause for joyful sadness, in that they were free to pass to The Gracelands at last.

Everything was quiet. Still. It was a gentle peace that resided in everything good and green, for they had won and were finally safe.

After many moments of tranquillity, many knew precisely how they overcame such grave odds. Some would have fathomed the details; others would have simply believed that there was a god after all and that he had saved them. Alas, for those that knew him, they honoured The Blessèd Mage of Life.

It began on Durge Helm, with Luan understanding that Ramerick had managed to destroy The Dragastone. He closed his fist and gently beat his chest in a two-beat rhythm, symbolic of a heartbeat. It brought back memories of doing the same for Ramacès when they chose to place their faith in him. It felt right to honour Ramerick in the same way.

The beating sentiment was also followed immediately by the remaining band members and Knights that had survived on Durge Helm, hailing their saviour. The sound of beating hearts bounced off the chasm walls and did not stop there.

The sombreness magically echoed throughout the land and appeared everyone could hear it and caused them all to respond in the same way.

The Dwarves on Dwardelfia, the nobleman on Gallonea, and that too of the Questacèreans on Lathapràcère, all began to look up to the skies, hoping that somehow The Blessèd Mage of Life could see them. Their closed fists symbolically began to beat their chests in the same two-beat rhythm, thanking and saluting him for their hearts still continued because of him.

It was a sign that Terrasendia was whole once more. It could not have been a more fitting tribute to what Ramerick had given them all, for the hearts of what was good and green would pulse into everlasting peace.

Felder's everlasting wish for the land…

# *An Eternal Light*

Ramerick's eyes slowly opened. The calming colour of baby blue painted the sky. The white softness of the passing clouds floated across. The sense a thousand years had passed in a heartbeat.

The need to understand what had happened was of no importance anymore. The sensations of touch tingled his fingers again; the flow of breath softly filled his lungs. The essences of life pieced his broken body together, for he began to remember entirely what had happened.

For the first time in recent memory, he felt at one with himself. He smiled at the sky, feeling safe. Feeling whole. All that he set out to achieve he had done. His last endeavour was, at last, complete. What was left for him, he asked himself? The answer was simple to him. Nothing. Nothing but to answer the call to his heart's desire...

Regaining control of his muscles which had never felt so heavy before, he pulled himself up to sit and admire the view of nothingness all around him.

What remained of The Draughts resembled nothing more than a giant crater of the moon. The whole area had been entirely levelled from the monumental blast, leaving nothing but a barren wilderness.

A sense of loneliness instilled. At last, a peace he found for himself. He knew that Terrasendia was saved, which filled what was left of his beating heart with all the sense of duty that he needed to pass.

He caught a glimpse from the corner of his eye of something that did appear to survive. A mound, which he stumbled to his feet to go and investigate. As he walked heavily across the clean stone, he noticed that Ramalon's body had also miraculously survived the vaporisation.

A sudden fear struck his heart that he could still somehow be alive. He stared upon the lifeless form that his brother took, wondering when his eyes would flicker open and animate his evil once more... After staring for many minutes, no such thing happened.

Confirmation of his death came when he noticed his skin begin to crust over with a substance that was of striking resemblance to him. The essences of stone began to spread from the foundations he laid upon and dissolve into his flesh. Even his clothes were consumed by the magical infusion, which continued to spread.

That was no typical ploy on Ramalon's part. It was the world's way of reclaiming his body back to the material world. The very last part of him that morphed into stone was his head and closed eyes. It took a little longer to complete and it was difficult to tell when it had to the naked eye. Alas, it finally did and Ramalon's eyes would never open again.

Staring upon his brother's statue, he closed his own eyes with relief, understanding that it was all over. Terrasendia was saved at last. He took those moments to indulge in fulfilling destiny, feeling no remorse for his brother. The world was a safer place without him, despite his forgotten role in their father's plan.

Alas, after thirty years, Felder's plan had worked. After so long and with so many moving parts, it all stemmed down to the fate of his three sons, all playing the lead role to acquire that peace. Ramalon for being the only one to destroy Melcelore, against the combined efforts of Ramacès and himself to be the only ones to stop Ramalon.

Though he did spare a sombre thought for Ramacès, without whom he would not have prevailed. In a way, he was glad that it was him that truly saved Terrasendia, though his modesty did not hide the fact that he gave up everything too. It felt strange to take just a little credit for himself, reminding himself that a nobleman's heart was to give, not to receive. Somehow, it appeared that Ramacès somewhere had heard his thoughts and replied in the only way he could.

His garden that had been totally wiped out began to regrow from the statue of Ramalon. Vines and grass began to seep through the stone, which gently cracked open, symbolising that he too, had fulfilled his destiny. It appeared that he heard his voice once more…

"You too brother," he solemnly whispered in reply. "You too."

As well as a gentle smile from the heart, a tear began to trickle down his cheek again. It glistened a streak of light that he assumed was just the natural moisture that collected in his eye. However, after it's persistent sparkling, it brought his attention to inspect it with a little more detail.

In the distance, a singular streak of white light shone. His eyebrows furrowed in bemusement and began to weightily plod toward it. As he got close, he understood what it was.

In the aftermath of the blast, his necklace containing his protecy stone of life had survived. Its gleaming light was more dimming than a shine, for the life it had held together was seemingly dwindling.

He crouched down, wincing like an elderly man, to collect his necklace and held it firmly in his hand. His breath flowed purer than

## An Eternal Light

before, his heart began to thump against his ribcage.

There was nothing left for him to do anymore. No quests. Nothing to owe to life, for it was Terrasendia's turn to give him something in return. His time had come.

Holding the protecy stone in his hands, he closed his eyes and established its mythical connection. He made his peace with Terrasendia and in return, it echoed its eternal gratitude. And that was all that was left, before terminating the crux of the connection and thus destroying his protecy stone of life...

A universe of white light shone in every direction and he could no longer feel the crisp breath running through him nor the beating heart that thumped inside. Every sensation vanished as paradise took him, to his heart's desire.

The blinding white began to fade. In the same way as when the puzzled-pieces fell in life, they pieced themselves together in death, formulating where he was. Though he was not in The Draughts anymore. He was standing on a familiar cobblestone street, with smoke puffing from the chimneys of homes and the blacksmith's hut. Hearth-lit fires glowed, for the sun had just set, giving the sky a beautiful orange warmth. He knew he was in the boundary once more, but more importantly to him, he was home.

He stood on the cobblestone street, in the precise spot where he spoke to Ramacès. The main difference was that life on Pippersby had seemingly resumed.

He wondered whether this was all just an illusion before choosing to believe that it was not. Every part of it was real and nothing could convince him otherwise.

He caught sight of his home directly in front of him and to his heart's joy which he didn't even try to contain, he saw the hearth light through the veiled curtain like before. And what filled him with more happiness was that he knew that Amba had lit it.

He saw her silhouette rise and immediately being flummoxed with a massive hug from Jàqueson, who had come charging in. A tear streamed down Alex's eye, as he merely admired the sight of his loving family again for a moment. He really was home. His heart wrenched with sadness and utter joy at seeing them again. He'd never been so happy in all his life to know that nothing was going to stop him from opening that door. It reminded him of his promise to them both that he would see them again. And a nobleman would always keep their promise.

And so, he wasted no more time that didn't exist anymore and walked up toward the door. Every step he took made him grow more anxious, nervous, doubting whether his heart's desire indeed laid moments ahead.

Feeling detached from any reality, he arrived at the door, feeling compelled not to rush. He could sense them both on the other side waiting for him, just like every day he returned from work. If he was breathing right now, he wasn't sure he'd be able to continue against the sheer bliss.

The moment felt right. He placed his hand on the circular doorknob and waited. He was afraid to turn the handle and release the catch, somehow scared that if he did, it would wake him up from the dream that he didn't want to believe he was in.

Tears flooded his eyes again, trying to blink profusely to swat them away before anyone saw. He imagined just what their reaction would be when they saw him. The cheeky smile of Jàqueson that would beam as wide as a half moon, the warm smile of Amba that he missed so dearly. In his moment of peace, it reminded him that he was yet to ask for her hand in marriage. Even to that moment, he felt he would be so lucky should she say yes.

All of a sudden, he felt the catch of the door unlock in his hand. His body froze and his ghost left him floating lighter than a feather, for it was not him that initiated it's unlocking.

Having never wanted something so badly in his memory, he relaxed his grip on the door which slowly opened from the inside.

A bright beam of light was born in the vacating space of the opening door for which he struggled to see through. The further it opened, the brighter the light became until it finally widened fully.

His eyes softened, his heart mellowed, smiling into the glancing light. And from that moment, all Alex knew was beautiful white and everlasting happiness, till the end of days.